"You caught me by surprise."

She dropped her hand to rest it against his chest, and pin-pricks of electricity zipped along his ribs. "One second you were my weird, dorky best friend Graham, being annoying and inscrutable."

"Um…"

"And the next…" Her gaze flickered down to his mouth and then back up. "The next you were kissing me."

He remembered.

Oh, wow, did he remember. It rushed back to him now. The heat of her lips and the way her body seemed to fit so perfectly against his. The shock of it all. The pleasure— and the hopelessness.

"I'm sorry, E, I should have asked—"

"Shh."

He clamped his mouth shut so hard it hurt his jaw.

"You took me by surprise. But this whole time I've been wandering around the festival, trying to figure out what just happened, I—" She paused to lick her lips, and what was she doing to him? "I couldn't stop thinking about it."

"You couldn't?" His voice *squeaked*—this was pathetic.

She shook her head. "You took me by surprise, and I—I was wondering." She paused again, because she was actually trying to kill him. "Could we try it again?"

THE HOUSE ON
MULBERRY STREET

THE HOUSE ON MULBERRY STREET

JEANNIE CHIN

FOREVER

New York Boston

Copyright © 2023 by Jeannie Chin

Cover art by Tom Hallman.
Cover design by Daniela Medina.
Cover copyright © 2023 by Hachette Book Group, Inc.

Forever
Hachette Book Group
1290 Avenue of the Americas, New York, NY 10104
read-forever.com
twitter.com/readforeverpub

First Edition: March 2023

Forever is an imprint of Grand Central Publishing. The Forever name and logo are trademarks of Hachette Book Group, Inc.

The publisher is not responsible for websites (or their content) that are not owned by the publisher.

The Hachette Speakers Bureau provides a wide range of authors for speaking events. To find out more, go to www.hachettespeakersbureau.com or call (866) 376-6591.

ISBNs: 978-1-5387-5366-8 (mass market); 978-1-5387-5365-1 (ebook)

Printed in the United States of America

OPM

10 9 8 7 6 5 4 3 2 1

*To everyone working on plan B, C, D, E,
or even F in life. Keep going. You never
know when your dream might be just
around the corner.*

ACKNOWLEDGMENTS

Bringing this book into the world felt about as laborious as Elizabeth's journey toward creating her festival. Writing optimistic stories about love in a pandemic is hard, y'all. That said, getting to tell this anti-model-minority-stereotype, best-friends-to-more story has been a dream come true. It would not have been possible without my wonderful, insightful editor, Madeleine Colavita, and my incredibly supportive agent, Emily Sylvan-Kim. You and everyone at Forever and Prospect Agency have my eternal gratitude.

Thank you to my Knit Net Night friends and the NMG book club as well as whatever is left of the groups formerly known as Bad Girlz Write and Capital Region Romance Writers of America for their laughter and cheer.

Thank you as always to my wonderful little family. S. and M., you are the bedrock and the joy of my life.

And finally, thank you to you, the reader, for giving this book the gift of your time. You make this whole adventure worthwhile.

THE HOUSE ON
MULBERRY STREET

CHAPTER ONE

* * * * * * * * * * * * * *

One *crisis at a time.* How many times had Elizabeth Wu's stepdad Ned told her that back when she was in high school?

He'd always said it so calmly, too. She hadn't understood how he could take everything in stride like that—be it a lost reservation at their family's inn or her failing chemistry *again* or that one time she and her best friend, Graham, maybe kind of accidentally got arrested.

Long story.

Ten years on, she still struggled to remain on an even keel, no matter how hard she tried to channel her inner Ned.

"Where is it?" she muttered, clicking through her inbox on the clunky old computer behind the front desk at the Sweetbriar Inn.

"You tried, 'Wherever you put it'?" her mother suggested, her tone dry as the Sahara. She had a thick Chinese accent and a tiny bit of a speech impediment—a lingering aftereffect of the stroke she'd had the previous year—but neither got in the way of her giving her youngest daughter a hard time. She was currently on the other side of the lobby, taking pictures of her cat for her legions of loyal social media followers. Because that was totally normal.

Somehow, Elizabeth managed to contain her eye roll, but she couldn't hold back the deadpan retort of "Why no, Mother, it never occurred to me. What on earth would I ever do without you?"

Her mom mumbled something less than flattering in Mandarin. As the baby, raised mostly here in the sheltered small town of Blue Cedar Falls, North Carolina, Elizabeth wasn't as fluent as either her mother or her older sisters, June and May, but she knew enough. She looked up from the computer screen with narrowed eyes.

Her mother just waved her off. "Never mind. You clearly don't need my help."

Right. A fact Elizabeth had demonstrated when she'd moved out at age eighteen. Her chest gave a little squeeze.

A fact that both her mother and Ned had been reminding her of ever since.

"What is it Elizabeth doesn't need help with today?" Elizabeth's oldest sister, June, breezed through the front door of the inn. A year ago, Elizabeth would have read all kinds of condescension into a comment like that.

Then again, a year ago June wouldn't have been *breezing* in, period, and she definitely wouldn't have been breezing in with sex hair and a hickey on her neck, wearing the same clothes she'd headed off in the day before.

Elizabeth had zero room to judge, of course. June was in a committed relationship with the owner and proprietor of the bar across the street, Clay Hawthorne—and even if she weren't, good for her. Heaven knew Elizabeth had made more dramatic entrances after less well-considered nights.

With the coast mercifully clear for a minute, she went back to scouring her inbox. Desperate, she clicked on the folder full of stuff her students from the community center had sent her, and voilà! There it was.

Confirmation from Mayor Horton's office about her appointment for...

Crap. Four days from now.

That wasn't good—both that she'd misfiled it so clumsily and that it was coming up so soon. Mentally, she bumped it up her list of crises.

For the better part of a year now, Elizabeth had been working hard, trying to get serious about her career as an artist. Between staffing half a dozen shifts a week here at the inn, teaching art classes to kids and seniors at the community center, and leading paint and sips for everyone in between at Ella's Wine Bar down the street, she'd been putting her real dream on the back burner for much too long.

Things had gotten off to a rocky start—like that was anything new. She'd applied to dozens of artist's residencies around the country, then sat there as the rejections flowed in. One night of *way* too much alcohol and a few months of soul-searching later, she made her peace with it. The savings she'd earmarked for the residencies had gone into renting a vacant in-law apartment on a friend's property and converting it into a studio. She'd been on a roll, creatively speaking, ever since, but breaking into the professional art world was proving a tough nut to crack.

She bristled, remembering the look on snooty Patty Boyd's face the last time she'd visited her gallery with the latest pieces from her portfolio.

Well, she'd show Patty—and everybody else, for that

matter. If no one wanted to display Elizabeth's work, she'd create her own venue.

Better yet, she'd build off her sisters' success. She'd make something this town could be proud of.

The First Annual Blue Cedar Falls Clothesline Arts Festival would give her a showcase for her paintings, but it would also boost the entire local arts scene. She'd cast a wide net, calling for submissions from artists nation-wide, but she'd put a spotlight on independent creatives living and working right here in the western Carolinas. It would be a great networking opportunity for everyone involved, not to mention another chance to pull in visitors to bolster local businesses like the inn. All she had to do was convince the mayor's office to give her a tiny bit of funding and a permit to use Pine Hollow Park for the weekend, and she'd be off and running.

Or at least that was what she told herself every time she tried to gather her thoughts for the speech she was going to give to the mayor.

The truth of the matter was that she had her work cut out for her. She had four days to both nail down that speech and try to turn it into some sort of coherent presentation. She was also well aware that she didn't have much experience organizing events. Or in any area, really. Her sisters' good reputations would only get her so far.

Fortunately, she had an ace in the hole.

And she was off to see him—just as soon as she finished covering this shift, taught her watercolor class to the men and women of the Blue Cedar Falls Silver Club, ran a half dozen errands, and picked up a gallon of milk.

One crisis at a time, indeed.

Finally, at a quarter past five, she set the milk jug down on the floor of her certified pre-owned rust bucket of a twelve-year-old Prius. She was tired down to her bones, but a lightness buoyed her up, too, as she set her sights on home.

She started the car and pointed it north, turning off Main Street and onto Magnolia Way, before finally arriving at the old Hemlock House.

She shook her head as she pulled into one of the parking spots out back. With a name like that, it was no wonder the place hadn't survived as a bed-and-breakfast—though according to Ned's family lore, it had given the Sweetbriar Inn a run for its money back in the seventies. Main Street had won the battle for the soul of Blue Cedar Falls' tourism eventually, and the big old building on the other end of town had been sold and turned into apartments. The current owners had tried to rename it, but Hemlock House had stuck. Elizabeth wouldn't have had it any other way.

Grabbing the milk, her purse, and the giant wheeled crate of supplies she hauled around to all her teaching jobs, she headed in. The lock on the front door of the building was as broken as ever, the log cabin facing half-overrun with vines—which probably wasn't good for the place, structurally, but it sure was pretty. She strode down the faded carpet of the hallway toward door number three, and with every step, a little of the tension she'd been holding in her shoulders faded away.

Only to dissolve completely the instant she walked in the door. She sucked in a deep breath. The place smelled like oil paint and lemon Pledge and lingering hints of the terrible curry her roommate, Graham, had tried to cook the night before.

Parking her crate by the door and tossing her keys somewhere in the direction of the bowl where they were supposed to go, she glanced around. Graham's shiny brown work shoes were lined up neatly on the rug. Smiling, she kicked off her own boots. "Honey, I'm home!"

She headed past the big, comfy old couch they'd scored at the ReStore last fall, which looked extra snazzy with the new red, white, and black afghan she'd crocheted to go over the back of it. She deposited the milk in the fridge and took a second to rearrange the magnetic word poetry from the freaking Emerson quotation Graham had put there that morning into a Taylor Swift lyric, just to see his eye twitch later when he found it.

Then her gaze caught on the calendar.

Crap. Right. She pulled a marker out of the messy bun she'd put her hair in while she'd been teaching and scribbled, "Meeting with Mayor!!!" on the square for Tuesday—exactly like she should have the minute she got the confirmation from his secretary. She rolled her eyes at herself.

Because the thing was that Graham wasn't just her roommate. He also wasn't just her dorky best friend from high school or her dorky best friend to this day.

He ran the front office of the town hall, handling complaints from indignant citizens, spear-heading initiatives—whatever that meant—and reporting directly to Mayor Horton himself. Heck—chances were, *he'd* known about her meeting with the mayor before she had.

Which was probably for the best. He wouldn't be blindsided by what she was about to shout at him next.

"When you're done putting your khakis away, can I talk to you? I need your help with something."

Heavy footfalls from behind her had her turning, a smile spreading across her face. He was going to be so annoyed about this. He liked to leave work at work and keep home at home, but what could she do? She needed to rock this presentation to Mayor Horton.

And Graham was her ace in the hole.

"So, funny story," she started, preparing to launch into her explanation about how she'd maybe sort of accidentally misfiled this email and possibly kind of forgotten to do any prep work for her presentation, and could he maybe help her look at it together over dinner tonight?

But before she could get any further, she frowned.

Because there Graham stood, looking like his usual post-work self, his khakis and muted button-down traded in for loose-fit jeans and a dark gray T-shirt with a logo for a band from the nineties. All ready for their usual Friday night routine of takeout on their couch, followed by a night out at the bar with their friends.

But his honey-brown hair was mussed. The weird beard he'd started growing out of nowhere the week before masked his mouth in a way she was never going to get used to, no matter how it transformed his face—in a good way.

While his eyes...

She missed his glasses, which he'd recently stopped wearing as often, choosing contacts most days. But that wasn't the heart of the issue. Instead of holding flickers of warmth in their umber depths, his eyes were blank.

Stone.

"Hey," he said, quiet but firm. "We need to talk."

CHAPTER TWO

❀ ❀ ❀ ❀ ❀ ❀ ❀ ❀ ❀ ❀ ❀ ❀ ❀

This was it. No more putting it off.

Graham Lewis stood there, a careful distance away, taking in every detail as Elizabeth's smile slowly faded.

Heaven help him, she was beautiful. Her long black hair hung to the middle of her back, the purple streaks he'd helped her dye in it gleaming in the sun. Her sleeveless black dress showed off the colorful bands of ink tattooed around her upper arms, while a purple-and-gold shawl she'd knitted hung around her long neck.

He swallowed hard.

He'd always thought she was beautiful, was the thing. That first day she arrived at Blue Cedar Falls Elementary, she'd looked like something out of a cartoon. Seven years old and dressed in rainbows, her hair braided into pigtails with sparkly ribbons at the ends, she was the brightest creature he'd ever seen. He didn't have the words for it then, but as he'd gawked at her from the other side of the classroom, something inside of him had shifted.

Twenty years on, nothing had changed about the way he saw her—even if everything else in their lives had. They'd journeyed from strangers to classmates to randomly assigned middle school science fair partners. Equally inept when it came to test tubes and data collection, they'd muddled through, only to come out the other side as friends. One season as members of the backstage tech crew for the high school musical, bonding over broken sets and finnicky stage lights and late-night milkshakes after rehearsals, and they'd somehow morphed into best friends—as improbable as that had seemed. He'd never been cool enough for her, but that was part of what *made* her cool. She honestly, sincerely didn't care.

They'd made it through her tumultuous senior year and a month of her secretly living in his parents' tree house, through high school graduation and his four years away at college all the way in Charlotte.

Through his half dozen perfectly pleasant but ultimately tepid relationships with women who at least saw him as an option.

And through he didn't even know how many romantic partners for her. They came in all stripes and flavors—mostly men, but a couple of women, too—from that stoner she met in detention to the captain of the girls' volleyball team to some business mogul from New York who had spent a summer here a couple of years back.

He and Elizabeth had been through everything together, it seemed, and it all had landed them here. Platonic best friends and roommates, sharing an apartment and living out of each other's pockets, hanging out most every night, and it was great. He helped her balance her checking account, and she got him to hang out with people other than his work colleagues and his board gaming crew. It worked. Everything between them worked.

Except that it didn't.

Which was what had led him here.

Her throat bobbed, and she released her hand from the fridge to tuck a stray lock of hair behind her ear.

"What's up?" she asked, voice too bright.

And he could lie. He could do the same thing he'd been doing for the past three months and pretend that nothing was going on.

"Come on." He nodded toward the living room. "Let's sit."

"Dude. You're freaking me out. Did someone die or something? Oh God, please tell me nobody died, or I'm going to feel like such a jerk for saying that."

A rough huff of a laugh escaped him as he took his spot on the recliner. "Nobody died."

"Phew." She still wasn't any more relaxed as she moved to perch on the edge of the couch. She usually sprawled out with abandon, comfortable here in their home, and he hated that things were changing already, but wasn't that what he'd wanted?

A change?

Ever since Elizabeth started applying to residencies all over the country that spring, the inevitability of it all had struck him. She was going to move on from him. Maybe not today—but that was only because the art dealers of the world couldn't see what was so obvious to him. She was extraordinary, and someday, somebody else would realize it.

In the meantime, he'd been sitting here for years, quietly in love with her.

He'd been happy with their friendship, of course. He'd never pushed for or expected anything more. But he'd allowed himself to build his life around her while she was making other plans. Their current situation—living out of each other's pockets like this—it couldn't last. It wouldn't.

It was time to move on. Literally.

"Elizabeth." His voice caught. "I think it's time for me to move out."

His heart pounded against his ribs. He braced himself.

But somehow, he wasn't braced for her to *laugh*. "Oh, good grief, Graham, you had me so scared."

"I mean it."

"Sure, sure." She stood up. "So what do you want for dinner? I was thinking Jade Garden?"

He rose, too. "I bought a house, E."

That made her stop. She turned to him, confusion in her eyes. "Wait."

"I can't wait anymore." He shook his head.

The thing was that he was a simple guy. All he'd ever wanted was a nice house in his hometown. A white picket fence, two point five kids. A wife who loved him and a decent job where he felt like he was doing some good.

"You're serious." But disbelief still dripped from her tone.

"I told you I was thinking about it."

She threw her hands up. "You also told me you were going to buy an air fryer. I told you that was a terrible idea, too."

"I'm waiting for a decent sale."

"But a house? *Why*?"

Because he'd been in love with her for twenty years. Being best friends with her was great, but if he kept living with her he was never going to get over her and start looking for what he wanted in life.

Not that he could tell her that.

"It was time for a change," he said instead, because at least that was true. "I'm almost thirty, E."

"So am I. So what? You turn thirty and suddenly you're legally obligated to become boring and responsible?"

"Not legally, but..."

She narrowed her eyes. "Is this about your brother?"

"No." Ugh, why hadn't he said yes? "I mean—maybe."

His big brother, Pete, had just made junior partner at his law firm up in DC. Their father was over the moon about it, and yes, okay, that might have had something to do with Graham's decision.

He went to adjust his nonexistent glasses, then dragged his palm down his face. The scruff on his jaw still surprised him sometimes, but he seized on the changes he'd made to his appearance. "I just—I've been in a rut this year. It was time to shake things up." He pointed at his chin and then his eyes. "Like with the beard and the contacts."

"Great! A beard and contacts are a completely normal way to 'shake things up.'" She crossed the distance toward him and reached up to put her hands on his shoulders, and he hated how it still gave him feelings when she touched him so casually. But then she gave him a little shake. "Graham. Buying a house is *not* a normal way to shake things up."

He put his hands over hers. With what little self-preservation he had, he gently but firmly pushed them away.

He hated that he hated that, too.

"It's not just how I look," he told her. "I'm going after all my goals." He swallowed hard. "I'm getting back on dating sites."

In theory. In practice, he still hadn't had the heart. But he would. Soon.

Huffing, she brushed a bit of hair back from her face.

"Dating—also a normal, not ridiculous way to break out of a rut."

This was missing the point.

"It's a great house, E." Like that would convince her. It really was, though. "On Mulberry—just a few blocks off Main Street. I can walk to work—or to the historical society." Both his job-job and his volunteer job. Whereas from this place, they were a fifteen-minute drive.

Really, the only mystery was that he'd stayed here as long as he had.

"Great, so you're abandoning me to save on gas?" She took a step back, and was—was that hurt creeping into her voice?

"I'm not abandoning you." It felt like he was, when she put it that way, though. "Our lease isn't up for six months, and you know I'll keep paying my fair share."

"Like I would let you do that," she huffed. "But seriously—our lease isn't up for six months. That's all the more reason it makes no sense for you to move."

Six months or six years. He always would have kept coming up with a reason to stay.

"You know how the housing market is," he said instead. "It'll take a while for everything to go through. And I'll want some time to do a bit of work on the place." He forced a smile, trying to focus on the house as opposed to her reaction.

He'd known she wouldn't be happy. They had it good here at Poison Place—as he liked to call it. Things were comfortable. Easy. There was a reason he'd talked about his interest in buying a home in only veiled hypotheticals and throwaway remarks.

But he was taken aback by how personally hurt she seemed to be. He was doing everything in his power to make it clear that this wasn't about her. Of course, it sort of was, but not in a way that mattered. This was about him and how he felt about her and how he had to stop feeling it before it crushed him. He might not want his brother's fancy job. He might be boring right down to his toes. But he deserved to be happy.

And he had to believe that this new house would help him get there.

Or at least it would help him stop getting his heart stomped on over and over again.

"It's got these amazing skylights," he told her. "And a bonus room in the back and this great kitchen."

"But you don't cook."

"I try to cook."

"But you *shouldn't* cook," she said, her voice shaky.

No. Last night's terrible curry proved that. "But I try. I'm going to learn."

She turned those deep brown eyes on him, and his resolve—both to move and to keep his real reasons to himself—almost wavered. "You really want this, huh?"

No. Not at all.

"I do," he promised.

"Wow." She turned away and rubbed her wrist over her face. "Well, all right, then."

"E…"

"It's fine." She scrubbed her eyes again, and his heart squeezed. "Just super dusty in here."

He'd stress-cleaned the entire time he'd been waiting for her to get home. "Look…"

"No, seriously, it's cool. I just." She gestured at the door. "I think I'm gonna go get some fresh air. On account of the dust and all."

"You don't have to—"

"I do," she said. She twisted back to glance at him, and her eyes were clear. "I'll probably grab dinner, too."

"You want me to come with?" They always had dinner on Friday nights before heading out with their friends.

"Nah. I'll, uh—" She stopped to grab her purse. She dropped her keys then stooped to pick them up. "I changed my mind about the Jade Garden. We were just there last week. I'll swing by that new place over on Birch Street. The one you didn't like—I could really use a salad."

He pulled up short.

"You hate salads." They both did. The only reason she would say that was if she didn't want him to follow her.

Her gaze darted up to his again, and it lanced through him. "Yeah, well. We all have to put up with things we hate sometimes, right?"

She tugged open the door.

She was out the other side of it before he could figure out what to say. She shot him a sad smile. It flickered at the corners, and she looked away.

The door slammed shut behind her.

Into the silence, staring at it, he echoed, "Right."

CHAPTER THREE

✳ ✳ ✳ ✳ ✳ ✳ ✳ ✳ ✳ ✳ ✳ ✳ ✳ ✳ ✳ ✳

May: *Grabbed our usual table in the back. Want me to order you anything?*

Elizabeth sighed, thumb hovering over the reply button on her phone.

She'd just parked in the back lot behind the Junebug, Main Street's newest—not to mention only—bar. She was about ten minutes late to meet up with her friends for their usual hangout. That wasn't exactly atypical; she did her best, but she and punctuality had had a tumultuous relationship for nearly her entire life. The reasons for her tardiness were different this time.

Terrible salad acquired—the new place on Birch Street, Bowled Over, had continued to, well, not exactly bowl her over—she'd headed over to Pine Hollow Park. She'd eaten her pile of microgreens and quinoa out of sheer spite, perched on a park bench and messing around on her phone.

The entire time, she'd been stewing about Graham.

Freaking Graham. And his freaking *house*.

What was he thinking?

On one hand, it made total sense. Even back in high

school, when they were first starting their odd couple routine, Graham was this steady guy. All he purported to want in life was to follow his mom into a life of quiet civil servitude and domestic bliss, no matter what his father wanted for him or what his brother set out to achieve. The public service life had been easy enough to come by, and for a while there, the domestic bliss had looked like it would fall into place for him, too. Sure, they'd ended up getting an apartment together while he was looking for Mrs. Right and she was bumbling her way through life, but he'd dated all these nice, responsible girls. It had always felt like a matter of time before one of them realized what a catch he was and they were off to the races with a little bungalow a couple of blocks off Main Street and a set of handsome, obedient, above average children.

Only...none of that had ever happened. All of his relationships had fizzled before they could get too serious. There was no spark, or she liked the Yankees, or some other incompatibility would emerge. Eventually, the two of them had gotten the place at Hemlock House, and he'd kind of stopped dating. Sure, she'd had her little flirtation with leaving town, but she'd gotten over it. She was here to stay, and she'd told him as much with aplomb. He'd seemed thrilled with the decision, helping her move the majority of her art stuff into the new studio space she'd rented and picking out a cozy recliner to take advantage of all the space they suddenly had without her easel cluttering up half their living room. They slipped back into their normal routine, and everything had been so comfortable and easy that she hadn't looked at it too closely.

Maybe she should have.

She'd been taking him for granted—okay, fine, she got that. He was a great roommate and an even better friend, and as his friend, she should have been looking out for what he wanted. A weird apartment in an old building named after a famous poison wasn't in his life plan.

But suddenly it was like she just didn't know what was going on with him. Wasn't he happy with their arrangement? Why wouldn't he tell her he'd started seriously looking for a place of his own?

How could she not have *known*? Because she'd been too wrapped up in her own drama? Between her mom's health and her sisters' relationship soap operas and the family's business and her new studio and the Clothesline Arts Festival, she'd been a little involved, it was true. But there was more to it than that.

This little itch in the back of her mind kept tugging at her. Graham hadn't told her, and he hadn't told her on purpose. She didn't want to read too much into things, but it wasn't a stretch to say he'd outright hidden it from her.

She just didn't know why.

Her phone buzzed again in her hand. She glanced down to see another text from her sister May—this one was just a question mark, which meant it had been too long since she'd replied. She rolled her eyes. May might be chiller now than she used to be, back when she was living her pressure cooker corporate life in New York, but she could still be high strung. What if Elizabeth had been driving?

That said, it was time to make a decision. As she peered out the windshield again, her gaze caught on Graham's sensible four-door sedan parked on the other side of the lot. She'd run out of the apartment like such a coward earlier. The idea of facing him now and having to act like everything was normal when he'd blown up her entire life made her stomach go all squirmy inside. She needed more time to get her head on straight. But the idea of running away again was even worse. Things would really be weird then.

Okay, so she had to go in. She could do this. She could handle him and act like she was fine. Who knew? Once they'd had a drink or two, maybe she could even figure out how to shake some answers out of him. Or convince him that his plan was stupid.

Resolved, she blanked the screen of her phone and tossed it in her purse. No need to tell her sister she was here when she was literally about to walk in the door.

Inside, the Junebug was just the right amount of crowded. Some eighties headbanger played on the juke-box, loud enough to make it feel like a bar but not so loud that you couldn't hear the people around you.

She cast her gaze around. Quickly, she spotted her crew at their usual table. There was Chloe, with her short pink hair and a funky vintage jacket Elizabeth was still annoyed that she'd seen first at the secondhand store in Lincoln. Beside her sat her long-term boyfriend, Tom, who somehow managed to wear a manbun and not look like a jerk. Archer and his husband, Stefano. Dahlia. May, who had somehow blended into Elizabeth's gang of weirdos upon her return to town, despite generally having her life together.

Graham.

As if he could sense her stare, he chose that moment to look up, and Elizabeth immediately pivoted. She strode toward the bar, cursing the way her face flashed hot.

Nice job not making it weird.

The owner, Clay, was tending bar tonight, and he met her there, a twinkle in his green eyes and a towel slung over his broad shoulder. She sighed internally. Not only was the guy off the market, but he was off the market because he was attached at the hip to her big sister June. With his tattoos, his rugged physique, and that hint of reddish scruff on his jaw that always rode the tender edge of becoming a beard, he was more Elizabeth's type, honestly, but the world was a funny place sometimes.

"You're running later than usual."

"Well, you know me," she joked, but it didn't feel funny. "The only thing I've ever been early to was my own birth."

Two months early, in fact. Apparently, she'd been so premature, it had scared everybody half to death; sometimes she joked that she'd made it her mission in life to never repeat the mistake, as a way of explaining her chronic tardiness.

Clay softened his smirk and changed the subject. "So what can I get you tonight?"

She scanned the taps. "Pint of the amber?" Her stomach growled. "And a basket of cheese fries."

"Coming right up." Clay's gaze shifted to a spot just over her shoulder.

A warm, familiar presence behind Elizabeth made her stiffen. In the mirror behind the bar, she spotted Graham, and her insides gave a little squirm, which was stupid.

"Another pitcher of IPA for the table," Graham requested.

Clay nodded and got to work. As Graham sidled his way into the space beside her, Elizabeth did her best to keep her cool. Her anger and disbelief and betrayal didn't want to be squashed, though, and she didn't know how to look at him without blowing up. Even his beard— which she reluctantly had to admit was just as attractive as Clay's—was tainted, now that he'd told her it went hand in hand with the house-buying crap. Tension hung in the air between them, and it sucked.

"So," he said, his voice steady, but she could hear the hint of nerves in it. "Cheese fries?"

She rolled her eyes and tipped her head toward the back table. "Like there aren't three baskets of them over there already."

"Just saying. After that big dinner salad you had..."

The teasing lilt to his tone melted her—just a smidge. "My big dinner salad was amazing and very filling, I'll have you know."

"Thus the obvious need for an order of cheese fries all to yourself."

"I was going to share." She definitely was not. She was starving, her big dinner salad had been a giant pile of terrible spite leaves, and she was going to scarf down the entire order of fries the instant it came out of the kitchen.

"Zoe'll bring the fries out in a few," Clay told them as he set down her pint and Graham's pitcher.

"Thanks." Elizabeth reached for her beer at the same time Graham reached for both the pint glass and the pitcher, and their hands brushed. A weird tingle sped up her arm.

"Sorry." He pulled away as if he had felt it too, and seriously, what was up with all of this new tension between them?

"I got it," she insisted.

"Sure, sure."

Drink firmly in hand, she turned and headed for their table. Of course, being the last one there, she didn't have much choice about where to sit. Everybody had left her the chair next to Graham, same as usual. She dropped into it, trying to ignore her unnatural awareness of her best friend sitting beside her, which normally wouldn't have been any big deal at all.

At least she had Chloe on her other side. "Nice jacket," she said, poking at the soft faux suede.

"Thanks." Chloe gave her a half-hearted smile.

Elizabeth scrunched up her brow. That was an unusually reserved response. Chloe never missed a chance to rub her shopping victory in Elizabeth's face.

Wasn't *anyone* going to act like themselves today?

"So what did I miss?" she asked, turning her attention to the rest of the table.

"Not much." Archer gestured toward the other end of the group. "May is complaining about getting sent to Rio next spring *for free.*"

"I'm complaining about them sending me there during Carnival," May clarified with a shudder. "So many people."

"So many people *in Rio,*" Archer reminded her.

Elizabeth chuckled. Her gang of oddballs had accepted May with open arms, but they were never going to get over her job as a freelance travel writer, or its perks.

"Think you can talk Han into going with you on this one?" Elizabeth asked. May's boyfriend wasn't a big traveler, but he was a big fan of May.

May rolled her eyes. "Working on it, but you know how he is. He leaves the restaurant alone for five minutes and apparently it's going to go under."

"Keep us posted," Stefano insisted, "because if he does leave, I want it on the record that I'm giving up Chinese takeout for Lent next year."

"Such a sacrifice." Archer patted his hand. "Giving up your favorite food when your favorite chef is gone."

"I can tell you what I'm giving up, and I'm not waiting for Lent," Dahlia said, scowling. "Submitting work to Patty Boyd's gallery."

"Lent?" Elizabeth's brows shot up. "I keep telling you, you need to give that up for good."

"I'm starting to believe you." Sighing, Dahlia took a swig of her beer before wordlessly passing it over to Graham to refill from the pitcher.

Like Elizabeth, Dahlia was an aspiring artist. Her sculptures were incredible, but much like Elizabeth, she'd had no luck finding an outlet for them. It didn't help that Patty owned the only gallery in town, and that she seemed to have a personal vendetta against the two of them. The last time Elizabeth had bothered trying to show the woman any of her new pieces, she'd turned her nose up with a sneer, scarcely deigning to look. It was so wildly unprofessional that Elizabeth had resolved never to put herself through the indignity again. She'd rather be a literal starving artist than deal with someone so hellbent on making artists feel like crap about themselves.

"What did the witch do now?" Tom asked.

Dahlia accepted her newly filled glass. "Acquire a new artist from freaking Charlotte who does practically the same stuff I do."

Elizabeth winced. "Seriously?"

"Seriously. I mean, the guy is good, and I guess his stuff is more commercial."

"Still." Elizabeth shot Dahlia a sympathetic look. "That sucks."

"We have *got* to get your indie art festival off the ground," Archer said.

Crap. Right. The indie art festival she was supposed to

be working on her proposal for this weekend—hopefully with Graham's help.

Since she had yet to actually manage to bring it up to Graham—or, you know, look him in the eye—she wasn't holding out so much hope for that.

She raised her beer in Archer's direction anyway. "Fingers crossed." Time to change the subject. She looked around. "Anything else new?"

And then she remembered exactly what *was* new.

She cast a sideways glance at Graham. Had he dropped his bombshell on the entire crew yet? Her stomach tightened. Did everybody already know that he was abandoning her?

Or was he going to make her relive hearing the news all over again?

Which was worse?

He met her gaze and opened his mouth.

Okay, so yeah, it was option B.

"Actually," he started. "I have some news."

She looked away and took a big gulp of her beer. She hadn't been able to observe her own little mental breakdown when he told her, but she supposed the one upshot of option B was getting to watch everybody else react.

"You know how I've been talking forever about getting my own place?"

"You mean since middle school?" Tom asked.

"Yeah." Graham chuckled, but his smile betrayed his nerves—and his pride. Ugh, he really was excited about this. "Well, I put in an offer on the old Carroway Place. The one on Mulberry Street."

Dahlia held up a hand. "Whoa—wait—"

"The purple one?" Archer asked.

"That's the one," Graham agreed. Of course it would

be purple. He wasn't just abandoning her for a house; it also had to be her favorite flavor.

"And?" Stefano asked.

"And..." Graham drew out the word before breaking out in a broader smile. "I got the word today that the Carroways accepted the offer."

The whole table erupted. Stefano and Tom offered unreserved congratulations. Chloe barely reacted at all, which seriously, what was up with her? May shot Elizabeth exactly the concerned look Elizabeth had been waiting for, with Archer and Dahlia splitting the difference, somehow managing to both salute Graham and sneak pity glances Elizabeth's way.

Great, just great. She took a sip of her beer, but even though it wasn't their stupid IPA, it tasted bitter.

"How long until you close?" Archer asked.

"Six weeks is what they're guessing, but you know how it goes."

"Not at all." Dahlia, who had also always lived in an apartment, raised a glass. "But good luck to you."

"Hear, hear," Elizabeth said, raising her glass, too.

Everybody followed suit and toasted, but as soon as they were done, May fixed Elizabeth with another knowing look. Putting on a neutral tone, she asked, "And how are you feeling about all of this?"

"How do you think?" Elizabeth wasn't going to let on how betrayed she felt, but she couldn't seem to keep the sour note from her voice. "I have six weeks to find a new roommate."

Graham shook his head, turning to look at her, and this time, she couldn't avoid his gaze. "I told you I'm not going to move in right away."

"You say that now..."

"I mean it," he said, too earnestly, and why was it lighting this fire inside her?

"Sure, sure." The words came out so dismissive, but that was probably better than the resentment she was keeping in.

"Don't be like that."

"Like what?" An immature child? She'd heard that enough times.

The worst part was that if he said it, she wasn't even sure that he'd be wrong.

"Like this. You ran away earlier—"

"I was hungry. And it was dusty."

Crap, it was threatening to get dusty in here now.

She glanced away, only to find their other friends trying to act like they weren't paying attention while hanging on their every word. Her sister in particular had that concerned expression firing on all cylinders, and Elizabeth didn't need any of this.

"I just want to live in a house where I don't have to share any walls with anybody," Graham insisted. "A place of my own."

Either the dust problem was spreading, or he was getting emotional, too.

Fighting to keep her voice constrained, she hissed, "Well, you could have told me that."

"You would have tried to talk me out of it."

"Of course I would have!" She threw her hands up. "Our life is awesome. Why does it have to change?" There was that stupid dust again. "Why does anything have to change?"

Then out of nowhere, Chloe blurted, "We're pregnant."

Elizabeth just about got whiplash, she jerked her neck around so hard.

Tom's eyebrows hit his hairline, but it took him only a second to recover. "Babe..." He pulled her into his arms, and she leaned into him, and something in Elizabeth's chest pulled.

The thing was that she'd never particularly cared about getting married or having kids. She'd dated a bunch, but the people she was attracted to usually ended up being losers or jerks. Even if she ever had found someone she had insane sexual chemistry with *and* actually liked to talk to, what then? She could barely commit to a hair color, much less a human being.

And kids. She liked the ones that ended up in the classes she taught at the community center, but how could she be responsible for another human being? She wasn't dead set against it or anything, but she couldn't imagine being a mom. Laying down rules, setting expectations. None of it had ever felt like it was for her.

Tom and Chloe had been together forever. Clearly they were the real deal, and Elizabeth had always been happy for the both of them.

But she'd always thought Chloe was like her. A *free spirit*, to put it kindly.

The terrified yet exhilarated grin on Chloe's face said maybe she wasn't that far off the mark.

"I'm sorry," Chloe said, laughing, as she leaned in to Tom. "I just couldn't keep it in a second longer."

"We found out today," Tom explained. "She made it twelve hours."

Elizabeth reached out a hand, and Chloe took it. "True restraint," she offered.

"I know, right?" Chloe swabbed at her eyes.

Quieter, Elizabeth asked, "Are you okay?"

"I have absolutely no idea." Chloe laughed again, and

it was verging on the hysterical. But at least she was still laughing—right?

"Well, I think it's awesome." Graham leaned in, extending his arm across the table to offer a high five to Tom. Of course he would be excited.

Who knew? With his whole making a change and buying a house thing, maybe that wife and kids he'd always wanted would be next.

Chloe and Tom were having a baby. May and June were in committed relationships. Graham was becoming a property tax–paying member of society.

And meanwhile, Elizabeth was right here. Exactly where she'd always been.

So much for not wanting anything to change.

CHAPTER FOUR

S o, wow," Graham said, joining Tom over by the dart-board later that evening.

Tom shook his head and stepped up to the line, his gaze on the target as he adjusted his grip on his first dart. "Right?"

On paper, Tom wasn't the kind of guy Graham would have imagined himself becoming close friends with. He had a man bun, and all his jeans had holes in them. He was an aspiring science fiction author–slash–waiter.

But he was with Chloe, and Chloe was one of Elizabeth's best friends, and any friend of Elizabeth's was a friend of...well, everybody else Elizabeth was friends with. It was part of the magic of who she was, and yet one more reason he was grateful to have her in his life.

In the end, he and Tom had fallen in together. The guy was easy to talk to, and he always had an interesting perspective to share. He was calm, cool, collected.

Even now, with everything going on.

Graham cast a glance toward the corner of the room, where Elizabeth and Dahlia continued to confer with Chloe, who still seemed shaken up. Her announcement had taken everybody aback—herself included, apparently. Elizabeth had seemed particularly shocked, though she'd pulled it together quickly and now was acting as a rock for her friend.

Graham didn't know if he could do the same for Tom. Or heck—if Tom even needed a supportive ear at all. But when May's boyfriend, Han, had shown up and the two of them had challenged Archer and Stefano to a game of pool, it had seemed like a natural time to split up a bit. Graham had caught Tom's eye and nodded over in this direction, and here they were.

After a moment's consideration, Tom lined up his shot and let the dart fly. It ended up in the outer ring, just outside the bull's-eye.

"You seem to be taking everything in stride," Graham commented.

A soft grin curled Tom's mouth. "I'm over the moon."

"Yeah?" A happy glow warmed Graham's chest—and if it was tinged by just a touch of envy, well, he could swallow that for now. "I didn't even know you guys were trying."

"We weren't, which was part of what makes it so awesome." Tom's second dart went farther afield, and he sighed before lining up his third.

"Yeah?"

"I mean, we'd talked about it, of course, and we'd both agreed we wanted kids eventually. But the timing never seemed right. She wanted to finish this project or reach this income."

Chloe was a graphic designer—one of the more financially successful creative types in the group, but freelancing was tough, uncertain work.

Tom took his last shot and landed a perfect bull's-eye.

"Nice." Graham high-fived him and gathered his own darts.

Tom collected his and updated his score on the board before returning to the space behind the line. "Anyway, the way things were going, I wasn't sure if we would ever pull the trigger." He shrugged. "I wish we could have planned it out perfectly, but life doesn't really go according to plan, you know?"

Graham glanced in the direction of the girls again. "You think she's going to be okay with it all?"

"Absolutely," he said, full of confidence. "I know she's kind of freaking out at the moment, but you should have seen her the minute that little red plus showed up. She fell in love with that baby instantaneously." He shook his head, a soft glow in his eyes. "She's worried about how she's going to handle being a parent and working and having a life, but I have no doubt. If anyone can pull it off, it's her."

"Definitely."

"Now I just need to convince her of that." He shook his head. "She's so much more than she thinks she is."

And there was that tug of envy in Graham's chest again. He felt the exact same way about Elizabeth.

Swallowing, he shifted his focus to the board. He threw his first dart and scored a whopping eight points. His second and third shots were better, but without any bull's-eyes, he was already running awfully far behind.

"Sorry we stole your thunder, though," Tom said as he went to take his next turn. "Congrats again on the house, man."

"Yeah, I'm excited." Not as excited as he would be if he were about to have a kid with the love of his life, but it was a start.

Tom followed his gaze as he glanced in the girls' direction again. "Not everybody is, though."

He raised his brows, and Graham's heart sank, his stomach turning over.

Elizabeth's reaction to his decision to buy the place on Mulberry Street was a double-edged sword. On the one hand, he supposed he should be flattered that she cared. It would have been a way worse blow if she'd just said "cool" and wished him well.

Did she have to be so resentful, though? Or keep acting like he was excited to be rid of her?

When the truth was that he was anything but?

Tearing his gaze away from her, he reached for his beer and took a long pull.

"You guys going to be okay?" Tom asked carefully.

"Yeah. I think."

"You ever think about telling her?" Tom punctuated the question by tossing a dart directly into the middle of the bull's-eye.

Graham's heart got stuck in his throat. "Absolutely not."

He knew that Tom knew how he felt, but he was pretty sure that nobody else did. Not even Chloe.

Tom blew out a breath and let his next dart fly. "Your funeral."

"I just don't want to lose her as a friend," Graham said, and wow, that sounded pathetic, even to him.

Tom's last dart landed in the triple score ring on the twenty. He shot a meaningful look Graham's way before tipping his head toward the girls. "Not to be a broken record, but maybe you should tell her that."

To be fair, Graham had been trying to tell her that all evening, only she kept yelling at him or running away.

Maybe what he really needed to do was show it to her.

The thought rolled around in his mind as he continued to have his rear end handed to him at darts. He and Tom shifted gears to talk about lighter fare, from the project Graham was working on in his volunteer job with the local historical society, to the novel Tom had been banging away at for five years but which he was "really starting to turn the corner on," to a goofy podcast they both liked to listen to. All the while, he tried to ignore the tug in his chest telling him to go over to Elizabeth and try again to fix this.

As it so happened, he had a lot of experience ignoring his impulses around Elizabeth, so at least that part wasn't hard.

Finally, the evening started to wind down. Stefano waved them all good night and guided a slightly-more-than-tipsy Archer to their car. May and Han headed out with them, and when Chloe started to yawn, Tom decided they should call it a night, too. Dahlia grabbed her coat and looked to Elizabeth, still seated at the table, and then at Graham, standing nearby. Usually he and Elizabeth drove together, but after she'd decided she'd rather eat a salad than talk to him about his decision, they'd made their own ways here tonight.

"I really should…" Dahlia made a motion toward the door.

Elizabeth looked down at the brownie she'd just ordered with a sigh. "It's fine. I have chocolate to keep me company."

And this was Graham's chance. "I'll stay."

Dahlia cast Elizabeth a questioning gaze, but Elizabeth smiled and waved her off.

The instant Dahlia was out the door, Elizabeth's smile faded. Dropping her gaze, she picked up her fork and stabbed at a corner of the brownie. "You don't have to stay, you know."

Phew boy, talk about a minefield. "I know."

"Like, I can just meet you at home." She grimaced. "Or—I mean. At our place. You know. The apartment."

Never mind, "minefield" was clearly too subtle a description.

"It's home," he told her, voice firm and probably betraying way too much.

It was the truth, though. Their apartment at Poison Place was his home in the truest sense of the word. Buying a house was about trying to move on with his life, but he was well aware that getting what he wanted meant giving up some of the best parts of what he already had.

No way he was going to let them all slip through his fingers without a fight.

He couldn't keep pining for her for the rest of his life, but he refused to lose Elizabeth through some sort of a misunderstanding, or a failure to try hard enough on his part. He was going to keep her as a friend by *being* her friend—no matter how hard she was trying to push him away right now.

He approached the table and pulled out the chair kitty-corner from hers. He paused for a second, giving her a chance to tell him to get lost, but she just shrugged and kept eating her brownie.

He sat down. Normally, he'd steal her fork and grab a bite for himself, but nothing was entirely normal right now.

"Good?" he asked instead.

"Awesome." Her mouth pulled to the side even as she was paying the compliment, though, and he remembered that it had been her sister June's idea for Clay to start offering leftovers from the bakery across the street as dessert here at the bar.

It was yet one more thing Elizabeth and Graham had in common: overachieving older siblings whose shadows they could never quite seem to escape from. Graham hadn't wanted Peter's success, but he'd never been allowed to forget it, either. Elizabeth didn't want to run an inn, but she still chose to work at it—which meant she would always be working side by side with June.

The two of them had repaired their relationship some over the past year or so. But they were just so different. Graham wished Elizabeth could stop comparing herself to her sister. She had her own amazing talents.

But it was like Tom had said about Chloe—Elizabeth was so much more than she would ever believe.

They sat there for a few minutes. Clay had turned down the jukebox, and somebody had queued up what seemed like a bunch of eighties power ballads, setting quite the ambiance when you paired them with the low, yellow-tinged lighting and the clinking of the empty glasses and pitchers a busboy was starting to collect.

Eventually, Elizabeth addressed him, tipping her head toward the dartboard. "Looked like you got owned pretty bad by Tom over there."

"Royally."

She shot him a brief glance. "He holding up okay?"

"Yeah. Great, actually. Chloe?"

"She's going to be okay, I think. Pretty shaken by it all, though."

"I'm sure."

The weight of the silence between them weighed on him. Usually, they could talk about anything, or if they didn't want to talk, they were great at just sitting together, people watching and eating brownies or whatever.

He wanted to ask her if she was okay. Wanted to try yet again to convince her that nothing was going to change and that his decision to move had nothing to do with her—at least not in the way she thought it did. But it was late. What good would it do them to go round and round about it all again?

Then he remembered...

"Hey, so earlier. When you first got home this afternoon, before..." Well, he didn't need to specify, did he? "You started saying something about needing a favor of some sort."

"Oh." She stuck her fork into the remaining section of her brownie with a little too much force, and it made a harsh sound against the plate. "Yeah. Kind of slipped my mind with, you know. Everything."

Right.

He took a deep breath. "Well. I'm all ears now."

She searched his gaze. It felt like the first time she'd really looked at him all night, and the stone that had been sitting on his chest finally started to feel a little less heavy.

"Sooo, you know that clothesline arts festival I'm trying to get off the ground?"

Ah, he knew she'd seemed squirrelly earlier when Dahlia had brought it up.

He smirked. "You mean the one you have a ten thirty meeting with Mayor Horton about on Tuesday?"

She swatted at him playfully, and okay, yeah, that stone on his chest got even lighter. "Ugh, how do you know more about my schedule than I do?"

"Just one of my many talents." Before he could stop

himself, he curled his hand around hers. His breath caught, the same way it always did, but for once hers did, too. He was probably imagining things, but the casual touch felt charged in a way that was new. He let go, and she pulled her hand back.

She did it a little more slowly than she normally would, though. Avoiding his gaze, she tucked a strand of hair behind her ear. It was hard to tell in the dim bar light, but was that a hint of a flush to her cheek?

No. He rolled his eyes at himself in his head. He'd finally taken the first step to put some space between them. He wasn't going to set himself back now, imagining she was catching feelings after all this time.

"Anyway," she said, clearing her throat.

Ignoring any weirdness he'd concocted in his brain, he continued on. "Let me guess. You want to work on your pitch together?"

Relief smoothed her brow. "Would you mind?"

"Of course not." His ribs squeezed. This was how he would show her that he was still her friend. Talking to her head-on. Helping her when she needed it.

Who knew? Maybe they could make it through this big change unscathed after all. Maybe he could salvage the friendship that had always meant so much to him.

But then she took her soft bottom lip between her teeth. "You're really sure you don't mind?"

Projecting confidence, he reached out his hand again. He closed it over hers and squeezed. A completely platonic, supportive gesture, even if it still meant more to him than it did to her. He swallowed and waited until she looked at him again.

"You're still my best friend, E," he promised her. "No matter where I live, nothing about that is ever going to change." No matter how much, deep down, he might wish it would. His friendship with her was worth more than any hopeless crush. "You know that, right?"

"I guess so," she allowed. She turned her hand over, and they clasped palms for a second.

Their gazes held a beat too long.

Then she pulled away and picked up her fork again. "Tomorrow afternoon work for you?"

"Yeah." He dropped his hand below the table, flexing his fingers where she'd held them. He smiled, relieved to have some normalcy returning, even if things still felt unsettled.

Voice too perky, she grinned in return. "Awesome." She waved her fork around. "I'll steal a pie from the inn. Put some terrible documentary on in the background."

The corner of his mouth tilted higher. "I love the terrible documentaries you pick."

"You say that now…" she warned, laughing.

It wasn't even a lie, though. Left to his own devices, he'd watch the same old sitcoms and police procedurals over and over again. Elizabeth chose some clunkers sometimes, sure, but she always chose thoughtfully. Her off-the-wall suggestions were the spice of life in his otherwise boring and contained little world.

A pang fired off behind his ribs. Her terrible documentaries were among the things he'd probably miss the most after he moved out.

And there they went, sustaining eye contact way too long again.

Needing to do something to cut the tension, he stopped holding himself back and nabbed her fork out of her hand.

"Hey," she squawked as he stole a big chunk of the little bit of brownie she had left.

"Payment for my help," he told her with his mouth full.

"Ew." She shoved a napkin in his direction.

Taking it, he closed his mouth and chewed.

"So it's a date then?" she asked. "Tomorrow?"

He swallowed to hide his reaction to the word. She didn't mean it like that.

He raised a brow. "A local-government grant-pitching, pie-eating, documentary-watching date?"

She shrugged and took her fork back. "Let no one say I don't know how to have a good time."

She skewered the last bite of brownie and popped it into her mouth.

"They wouldn't dare," he told her.

No one in the world was more fun than her.

Which was why it was going to hurt so much to leave her.

CHAPTER FIVE

✳ ✳ ✳ ✳ ✳ ✳ ✳ ✳ ✳ ✳ ✳ ✳ ✳ ✳

O kay," Graham said, plunking down in his recliner on the other side of the room. "I'll admit it. You've really outdone yourself this time."

Elizabeth looked up from her laptop and raised a brow. "With my amazing pitch that's totally going to win over the mayor?"

"No." Graham was wearing his glasses today for once, and he adjusted them pointedly. "With how terrible this documentary is."

She rolled her eyes and returned to the document where she was editing her notes. They'd been hard at work all afternoon, demolishing half the blueberry pie she'd dutifully stolen from the inn and pinning down what she was going to say to Mayor Horton about her art festival. They were both dressed comfortably in sweats and pajamas, and the documentary playing on the TV in the background had been good ambiance.

"You just don't appreciate art."

"You're really calling this art?"

He gestured at the screen, and she glanced up again in time to catch a slow-motion, grainy black-and-white shot of a white woman with a single tear sliding down her cheek, and okay, fine. Art was a stretch.

She'd actually kind of had her doubts about this movie, truth be told. The art house film blog she followed had recommended it, but "with reservations." Turned out that when an art house film blog declares a movie to be "a little slow paced," they mean business.

Had they ever.

But she'd liked the director's last project, and she'd figured, why not give it a try? What was the worst that could happen? Graham would hate it and, what? Leave?

Subconsciously, maybe that was *exactly* why she'd picked it—not to mention why she'd kicked her shoes off and left them in the middle of the entryway the night before. And snagged the last of the coffee without starting another pot this morning. And left the dirty breakfast dishes in the sink instead of doing them, even though it was her turn.

And yes, that was all petty, petty, petty. Graham was sitting with her here, working on a beautiful Saturday afternoon. She should be grateful—and she was.

She just didn't feel a whole lot of incentive to be a great roommate today was all.

They hadn't talked about the pink elephant in the room since the night before. She'd stewed about it plenty while she worked her shift at the inn that morning, of course, and this afternoon as they'd moved around each other in their usual, well-practiced dance. Just like last night, nothing had been "usual" about it, though. She'd been aware of him in a way that was just plain weird, and as a result, she'd been a bumbling klutz. They'd bumped into each other a half dozen times. Each collision had carried that strange charge to it, and she was sick of everything being off between them.

Over in the recliner, Graham laughed, and she followed his gaze back to the screen. The crying white lady was covered in paint now, and Elizabeth had to stifle a snicker herself.

"See what you'll be missing after you move out?" she blurted.

Honestly, ignoring a pink elephant in a room this small was *exhausting*.

He flinched and jerked his gaze to hers, only to look away again immediately.

When he spoke, his tone was breezy, though, and he waved a hand dismissively. "Please. The house has a finished basement I'm going to turn into a media room. You can come over and we can watch terrible documentaries with surround sound."

She huffed out a laugh. He'd tried to get a decent sound system installed here half a dozen times but had never found anything to his liking.

Just one way his life would be so great once he was gone.

She pouted, trying to cover up the twinge of hurt in her chest. "Yeah, but I won't be able to wear my sexy PJs."

She extended a leg dramatically, showing off her baggy fleece X-Men pajama pants.

Graham's throat bobbed before he looked away, and seriously, why was he acting so weird? "You and your sexy, fifteen-year-old PJs are welcome anytime."

And there was something about the way he said it. It shouldn't have rankled her, but it did, touching on a nerve.

"But that's the thing." Shutting her laptop, she shoved

it aside and crossed her arms. "At the new place—you're going to have to welcome me."

He scrunched up his brow. "How is that a problem?"

"It just ... *is*."

It was a problem because for the last however many years, she'd just *been* welcome. This had been home to both of them, everything shared equally. They could have a fight—rare, but it happened—and it wouldn't affect whether or not she could poke him about it the next morning.

Finally, she settled on "Welcomes can be worn out."

She knew that better than anyone.

At age eighteen, after a huge fight with her mom about something utterly *stupid*, Elizabeth had left. It had been the culmination of so many things. From day one, at birth, compared to her sisters, May and June, Elizabeth had always been the odd one out. More often than not, she'd felt like the black sheep. She still didn't understand why her mom had bucked the naming trend with her, but it had presaged the rest of her life. Her sisters were both perfect overachievers while she was ... herself. Being herself was awesome, for the most part, but all the awesomeness came part and parcel with a flexible interpretation of arrival times, a messy room, mediocre grades, friends her mom and Ned didn't approve of—life plans her mom and Ned didn't approve of.

Being someone her mom and Ned didn't approve of.

After she walked out of her house, she was always "welcome."

But nothing was ever, ever the same. It wasn't home anymore. Her family never came to her place, and she was a guest at theirs. A guest her mom felt free to nag and judge, but still.

And none of that was happening here with Graham. They didn't have the same kind of baggage, and nobody was leaving in a justified rage.

She couldn't help feeling like it was the same kind of end, though.

Flexing her jaw, she sat back into the cushions of the couch. "I just don't see why you want to go."

"I told you..." Graham started, and ugh, why had she had to bring this up?

"I know, I know. You're a responsible adult who loves paying property taxes."

He rolled his eyes. "I don't *love* paying property taxes. I just like good schools and nice roads."

"Tomato, tom-ah-to." She scowled in a vain effort to keep her mouth shut and not make this any worse. But she couldn't help herself, could she? She cast him a pointed look. A tinge of the hurt she was trying so hard not to feel leaked into her tone. "There's something chasing you away. I just don't know what it is." Her voice broke. God, this was pathetic. "So I can't help but assume it's me."

"E..."

Ugh, they were going around in circles, having the same argument she'd been so desperate to avoid yesterday that she'd decided to have a salad to get out of it. She waved a hand dismissively and blinked yet more dust from her eyes. "Never mind."

"It's not what you're thinking," he said carefully.

And okay. That was the most true thing he'd said to her since he announced his big decision.

"Then tell me what to think."

But whatever brief glimpse of unfettered honestly he'd given her, it was gone just as quickly. "That I really want to live in a house?"

She shook her head. "Not buying it."

"There's nothing else I can tell you," he said earnestly.

But that was a whole other kind of problem—a bigger problem than the house or his sudden desire to move on with his life.

Time was, he would have been able to tell her anything.

Ten o'clock Tuesday morning, Graham sat in his office at the town hall working on a report, watching the clock, and fielding a flurry of texts from his mother, who was apparently having a slow day down at the clerk's office.

Mom: *What do you think about this for the living room?*

Graham chuckled as he tapped on the latest design inspiration photo his mother had sent him. It wasn't terrible—he liked the blue walls and the off-white accents and dark wood furniture.

When he'd decided to start house hunting in earnest a month or two ago, his mom had been the first one he'd told. She'd encouraged him without reservation, which he'd needed, truth be told. His dad wasn't as excited; he still thought Graham should have gone off to law school and ended up at a big firm, climbing his way up the ladder like Peter was. His job running the front office of the town hall? It had been acceptable, but only because his father assumed he'd use it as a stepping-stone to a bigger, better government job somewhere else. Setting down roots here was the opposite of his father's plans for him.

Graham's mom alone understood that Graham preferred the simple life. A job where he could do some good, a house of his own in his own hometown. A nice life with a nice girl who could help remind him to have some fun from time to time, but who didn't mind that he was boring by nature.

That last part was going to take some time, but he was confident that getting out on his own was the right first step toward it. And if his mom had seemed a little sad on his behalf when he'd made it clear that he was planning to live alone in the new house... Well. He was a little sad about it, too, but it was for the best.

In the handful of days since his offer had been accepted, she'd shaken off that bit of disappointment faster than he had and started channeling all of her energy into helping him plan how he was going to redecorate.

Another picture came in before he could even reply to the first. It was in the same vein, but with more built-in shelving, which would be awesome for his ever-growing collection of history books and board games and local memorabilia.

Still, as he looked at both pictures side by side, a twinge of regret tugged at the inside of his chest. The design ideas were great. He liked them. It would be amazing to be able to do whatever he wanted with his own space.

None of them had any personal touches, though. He could fix that, in time, of course. His books and personal effects would lend plenty of character.

Not the same kind of character that permeated his and Elizabeth's apartment, though. She had such a flair for design, tossing together elements that shouldn't work but always did. From her constantly rotating gallery of art pieces, featuring her own work as well as that of their friends, to her creative paint choices on the walls to random rugs and vintage pieces to afghans she made herself... their home was colorful and cozy and... *home*.

No interior design magazine screenshot could encapsulate how he felt. So instead he just replied with a thumbs-up, a thanks, and a promise to chat about this more next time he came over.

He tried to dig back into the report he was writing, but with one eye on the clock, he struggled to focus. He smirked to himself when ten thirty arrived and passed. At ten forty-three, he started counting silently in his head.

He didn't make it far before Mindy, the admin who worked reception in the front office, knocked on his door. She raised a brow. "I believe you were expecting..."

"Holy crap, Graham." Elizabeth swept into his office in a flurry. "I am so sorry, I swear I was going to be on time, but a kid in my preschool class threw up on my shoes. I brought extra *everything*, because you know the gremlins always manage to get paint on my clothes, and I wanted to look professional—"

"It's fine," Graham assured her, rising from his desk. He nodded at Mindy, who shook her head fondly and left them to it.

But Elizabeth was on a tear. "But the only other shoes I had were sneakers, so I had to go home and get some nice ones." She pulled up the hem of her long black skirt to show off a pair of black boots that looked exactly like all her other pairs of black boots. "And then I hit every light between Hemlock House and here, and—"

"It's fine," he repeated.

"—I don't know which room the meeting is in, so I came here, and—"

"E." He stepped out from behind his desk and put his hands on her shoulders. She jerked her gaze up, and he could have fallen into those soft brown eyes. He gave her shoulders a gentle rub. "It's fine."

"But I was supposed to meet the mayor at ten thirty."

He shook his head. "You were supposed to be *here* at

ten thirty, because your actual meeting with the mayor is at eleven."

"But you told me—" Realization dawned in her eyes, and she narrowed them. "Wait."

"Let's just say that you're consistent and leave it at that, shall we?" He let go of her and stepped back.

"Rude."

"I prefer to call it effective."

Deflating, she dropped into the chair on the other side of his desk. She looked to the clock on the wall and threw up her hands. "Well, now what am I going to do with fifteen minutes to kill?"

"Be grateful you're not fifteen minutes late?"

"Yeah, yeah. Oh!" She held up a finger before leaning over to root through her bag. "Since I am here early, I don't want to forget this." She came up with a small potted plant. It was one of those types that wasn't a cactus but kind of looked like one. "It's a succulent," she told him. "Super easy, barely needs any water or light. Figured even you couldn't kill it."

"I love your faith in me."

To be fair, he had managed to kill an awful lot of plants.

He accepted the succulent and looked it over. It had short, thick, stalk-like leaves in a cheery pale green, and the terracotta pot bore an intricate, colorful, swirly design painted in Elizabeth's distinctive brushstrokes.

"Pretty," he remarked.

"I had some free time between classes," she told him, playing it down, but she always did that. "I don't know if you'll want to keep it here, or maybe bring it with. You know." She let out a breath like a sigh. "To the house."

His chest warmed. They hadn't spoken much about his

impending move since she'd accused him again, rightfully, of hiding something about his motivations from her.

He could accept a peace offering when he saw it. "I love it." He set it down on his desk for now, but no way he wasn't going to relocate it to his new place as soon as he got the keys in his hand. "Thank you."

"You're welcome," she said, and she even seemed to maybe mean it.

They gazed at each other for a moment that seemed to stretch until it had no choice except to break.

Clearing his throat, he looked away. Early as she may be, there was no reason to squander the found time.

"Shall I show you to the conference room?"

She stood up with a groan. "Sure—why not?"

She gathered up her bag again, and he took her down the hall. Elizabeth was his best friend, and she met him at his desk to go to lunch now and then when they both happened to have a few spare moments, but she rarely ventured any deeper into the building.

Even now, she gave a little shudder. "This feels like being taken to the principal's office."

It was a place she'd visited often enough to know. Unlike Graham. Outside of the handful of times he'd gotten caught up in her schemes—and of course that one instance when Officer Dwight had had to get involved— he'd kept his nose clean in high school.

"I promise, Mayor Horton can't give you detention."

"I suppose there's that."

They turned the corner, only to find the door to the conference room closed. He pulled up short. "Huh."

"What?" Elizabeth asked, almost walking right into him.

Ignoring how close she was, he frowned. "I thought this was going to be open for you to get set up."

He reached for his phone to look up the room reservation schedule, but before he could grab it, voices approached. He barely had time to move out of the way—and back even farther into Elizabeth's space—before the door swung open.

Bringing him face-to-face with none other than the local gallery owner, Main Street Business Association president, and most prolific utilizer of the town hall comment card system in history...Patty Boyd.

Elizabeth muttered a curse behind him, but Graham spoke over her. "Patty. Fancy running into you here."

"Good morning, Graham." Patty was in her late forties, blond, and immaculately and unironically dressed in a blazer and jeans with a silk scarf tied around her neck. She had an amazing talent for sounding both warm and condescending at the same time. The mix shifted as she moved her gaze to the spot behind him. "Elizabeth."

"Elizabeth Wu?" Mayor Horton's booming voice rang out. "Well, I'll be, is that girl running early?"

Elizabeth took a deep breath and straightened her posture. "For once in my life." She slipped past both Graham and Patty to stride into the conference room. She cast a backward glance at Graham. "With a little help."

"That's our Graham," the mayor agreed, "keeps the whole place running sometimes, I swear." As Patty moved aside, he came into view. Mayor Horton was a larger, older white man with short white hair and a perpetually red face. He made a beckoning motion. "Come in, come in."

Graham had hoped to sit in for Elizabeth's pitch and help if he could, so he didn't argue. Patty shifted further out of the way to let him past, but she wasn't done yet.

"You won't forget what we discussed, John," Patty said.

"You can count on me," Mayor Horton agreed.

Graham and Elizabeth shared a questioning glance, but Graham shrugged. He had no idea what they were talking about, which was disconcerting.

More disconcerting was the timing. He had a bad feeling that whatever they'd discussed, he was going to find out all about it soon.

With a tight smile that practically screamed *bless your hearts*, Patty swept out of the room. Mayor Horton gestured for Graham to close the door. The second it was shut, the mayor relaxed into his chair. "That woman is a force of nature."

"That she is," Graham agreed. A year prior, Patty had teamed up with her rival, eighty-something-year-old Dottie Gallagher, to oppose the opening of the Junebug, and it had been a headache and a half.

"Sit down," the mayor invited them both. Elizabeth took a tentative seat at the other end of the table, while Graham pulled out one in the middle. To Graham, Mayor Horton said, "I've been meaning to chase you down, Lewis."

Graham really didn't want to pull focus from Elizabeth's pitch, but small-town politics meant a certain amount of buddying around. "Is that so, sir?"

"I hear you're buying the old Carroway place?"

Great, exactly what he wanted to talk about right now.

With a quick glance in Elizabeth's direction, he nodded, trying to project the excitement he felt about the house and none of the trepidation he felt about Elizabeth still being mad at him about it. "Sure am."

"Good." Mayor Horton gave the table an enthusiastic thump. "That's what I like to see—young people putting down roots here." He considered for a second. "Though I do like to see them flying high, too. Your father tells me Pete's doing pretty well for himself."

Graham's father was a county judge, and he and the mayor had a regular tee time. Graham shouldn't be surprised by any of this, and yet the smooth transition to his second least favorite topic of conversation still caught him off guard.

"That he is. Just made junior partner, in fact."

"That's right." Mayor Horton stroked his chin thoughtfully. "Where is he now, DC?"

Graham nodded.

"Well, your old man's pleased as punch."

Graham dug the nail of his thumb into the pad of his index finger. "He sure is."

"Think Pete'll come down for Judge Lewis's sixtieth?"

Their father's big birthday was still a ways away yet, but it was the social event of the season, at least among Blue Cedar Falls's government officials.

"It's on his calendar."

On his other side, Elizabeth started to fidget with her bracelets. Graham turned to her, more than ready to get down to business.

The mayor took his cue. "And Ms. Wu, lovely to see you at town hall—and not because Officer Dwight brought you in."

She laughed nervously. "One time," she joked.

"Really? Was it just the once?" Mayor Horton's eyes twinkled, showing this was all just for fun, but Elizabeth was sensitive about the trouble she'd gotten into in the past.

"Pretty sure..."

"Well, never mind. How's your mother doing?"

Wow, the mayor was in a chatty mood today. Elizabeth

did valiantly, catching him up on everything going on in the Wu-Miller household and at the Sweetbriar Inn. She was as funny and charming as ever, outwardly. It wouldn't have been obvious to anybody else, but the way she kept fiddling with her bracelets betrayed her nerves.

Finally, Mayor Horton shifted forward in his seat. "Now, tell me, young lady, what brings you here today."

She breathed out a rough exhalation and squared her shoulders. "Well, sir." She opened up her bag and pulled out a copy of the pitch they'd worked on over the weekend, and which she'd practiced for Graham the night before. "As you know, Blue Cedar Falls has been experiencing a tourism boom over the past year."

"Thanks in no small part to your sisters," Mayor Horton agreed, taking the printout and skimming it over.

Elizabeth didn't miss a beat, even at the praise for June and May. "I think there's a huge opportunity to continue to build on it. We have festivals that bring in foodies, leaf peepers, you name it. But tons of tourists come to the western Carolinas for folk art. Pottery."

Mayor Horton frowned slightly. "Most of that business is out in Seagrove."

"But it extends out into Asheville, too." Elizabeth's voice rose in pitch. "And I think we can bring them here, with the First Annual Blue Cedar Falls Clothesline Arts Festival."

With that, she launched into the nitty-gritty of her idea: a weekend-long event showcasing indie artists. Graham knew for a fact that the entire thing had started as a pipe dream between her and Dahlia after a night out at the Junebug bemoaning the gatekeepers who continued to deny them entry into the fine art gallery scene. Pride filled his chest, though, as she explained how the vision for the entire thing had grown. She wanted to shine a light on small artists' workshops from around the area, while also creating opportunities for local Main Street hospitality businesses.

"We keep it all informal," Elizabeth encouraged. "Thus the 'Clothesline' part of the 'Clothesline Festival.' The two-dimensional work we literally hang on clotheslines all over town, with sculptural pieces interspersed, displayed on crates, even."

Mayor Horton nodded. "Folksy. Accessible. I like it."

"Really?"

"Definitely." The mayor set the paper aside. "But I can't fund it."

Elizabeth visibly flinched. "Wait—"

"What exactly do you think Patty Boyd cornered me to talk about, coincidentally not half an hour before I was scheduled to meet with you, young lady?"

It was Graham's turn to frown. "How did she even know—"

Mayor Horton waved a hand in the air. "That woman works in mysterious ways. And you know how the gossip mill is."

Graham and Elizabeth sat back in their chairs as one. That they most certainly did.

"Look." Mayor Horton darted a glance at the door and cupped a hand over his mouth. "I'm on your side. But I can't give you approval for this unilaterally or I will never hear the end of it. Boyd doesn't want anything pulling customers away from her gallery."

"But what about serving different kinds of customers? Creating a venue for different kinds of artists?"

"Like I said, you've got my vote. Now you just need to get a half dozen others." The mayor nodded. "I'm going to put a good word in for you with the town council and get you on their agenda for next month. You can present your case there."

"Town council?" Elizabeth repeated.

If she'd been nervous here, she'd be even more rattled there—especially with Patty in the room. But Graham could see the strategy in it. Putting this in their corner took the heat off the mayor and distributed it around a bit.

"I can help you," Graham offered. "We could put together some slides."

"Slides?" Elizabeth didn't crawl under the table or anything, but she looked like she wanted to.

"It'll be like high school speech class."

"I hated high school speech class."

That she had. Graham had, too, but that was another story.

"I have full faith in you." Mayor Horton stood. "Lewis, you can get her all the details?"

"Absolutely, sir."

"I look forward to your presentation, Ms. Wu."

"Me, too," Elizabeth said weakly.

She waited until the mayor had stridden out of the room and halfway down the hall before slumping and letting her forehead thunk against the table. "Graham..."

"I know." His hand itched to reach out and grab hers, but he kept it tightly in his lap. He just wanted to fix this, was all. "You got this. You heard what he said. He's on your side. He's even going to put in a good word for you."

"They're going to eat me alive," she said into the table. "Patty Boyd is going to pick her perfectly straight teeth with my bones."

"That's...disturbingly graphic."

She lifted her head and fixed him with a despairing gaze. "What am I supposed to do?"

He lost the war against himself. Rolling his chair closer, he put his hand out, and she placed hers in his palm. He gave her fingers a gentle squeeze. They touched reassuringly all the time, so this was no big deal. So why did it feel different now?

"We'll handle it," he assured her. "I'll talk to my folks."

They were both involved in local government and had strong networks that included the movers and shakers around town.

Pouting, she sat up straighter and pulled her hand away to push her hair out of her face. "Ugh, no."

"What? It's for a good cause. They'll both be happy to help."

"Your mom will be happy to help."

Graham swallowed. "My dad, too."

"Your dad hates me."

"He does not."

To be fair, he wasn't Elizabeth's biggest fan. He pretended he didn't, but he'd held a grudge against her ever since senior year—like he still blamed her for the handful of times Graham had gotten in trouble for actually having some fun for once.

Elizabeth knew it, too. "He absolutely does."

Graham shook his head. "That's not the point. The point is that we have options and resources. I work in town hall. I see town council members every day. A couple of them are even members of the historical society."

"I appreciate the help, but you're not going to lobby every person in Blue Cedar Falls on my behalf."

He would, if he thought it would help.

But he saw where she was going here, and it wasn't

anywhere good. "This is your baby," he reassured her. "And you bring a lot to the table. You know every independent artist in the western half of the state."

"Most of the eastern half, too."

"So use that." He sucked in a deep breath and raised his brows meaningfully. "And you have other connections, too."

She narrowed her eyes. "I do not need to drag my sisters into this."

"June has single-handedly launched half a dozen festivals in the past year. She knows what she's doing."

"She's never had the mayor turn her down flat."

"Because Patty Boyd's never taken a personal interest in thwarting her before."

"That's true…"

A light sparked in Elizabeth's eyes, and it lit a flame behind Graham's ribs. There was the fighter he'd been rooting for for years. "You can do this, E."

"Well, I'm certainly not going to let Patty Boyd take one measly meeting and walk all over me."

Graham grinned. "That's the spirit."

The spirit he loved in this woman—the spirit he loved in this town.

Blue Cedar Falls had been undergoing a sea change recently, and it was one that had been a long time coming. It wasn't being led by the Patty Boyds of this world.

It was being led by the June, May, and—yes—Elizabeth Wus.

He had complete faith in them.

And he couldn't wait to see what they did next.

CHAPTER SIX

❖ ❖ ❖ ❖ ❖ ❖ ❖ ❖ ❖ ❖ ❖ ❖ ❖ ❖

The next evening, after a meal of her mother's home-cooked Chinese mushrooms and short ribs, Elizabeth retired to the living room with her sisters. Their mom had wandered off to play mahjong on the computer behind the front desk, while Ned did dishes in the kitchen. June and May settled themselves on opposite ends of the couch.

Feeling like a cartoon villain, Elizabeth remained standing, though. She steepled her fingers in front of her chest. "Now, I'm sure you're all wondering why I've gathered you here today."

"Uh." May scrunched up her face and held up the giant popcorn bowl in one hand and the remote control in the other. "Trash TV night at the Wu house? Like we do basically every Wednesday?"

"I'm wondering," Ned called from the kitchen.

"Aren't you supposed to be at Tim's for poker night by now?" June shot back in reply.

"Your mother's short ribs have their own clause in our marriage. They will not be rushed, and I will clean every dish."

Elizabeth was never going to understand her mom and stepdad's marriage—or Ned's dedication to her short ribs, for all that they were awesome—but who was she to judge? People probably looked at all the weird idiosyncrasies of her and Graham's cohabitation with the same level of confusion.

Not that they were married or anything. Or even going to be living together for much longer.

But none of that was the point.

Assuming Ned knew his own business, she cleared her throat pointedly. "Can we get back to me and my evil scheme?"

"Wait." June tilted her head to the side. "An evil scheme that goes beyond getting me to watch people from the nineteenth century ripping their bodices off?"

May grinned and shoved a handful of popcorn in her mouth. "That's not evil. That's awesome."

Even before May had moved back home that spring, she and Elizabeth had had a standing arrangement to watch guilty-pleasure shows together. They used to text each other about them, but now that May was local, they got to indulge in person. Elizabeth had been skeptical about roping June into joining them at first; her older sister had a tiiiiiny bit of a judgmental streak. But getting to watch once prim and proper June be scandalized by a Mr. Darcy type taking off his shirt had only made these evenings better.

True to form, June shook her head. "I will never understand either of you."

"What's to understand?" May countered, and okay, they were getting seriously off track again.

Enough of this dramatic exposition nonsense.

Fast and loud, Elizabeth spoke over them, "I'm

launching a clothesline arts festival and my only option is to do it over Patty Boyd's dead body."

That got her sisters' attention. They both shut up and whipped their heads around, blinking owlishly, the family resemblance never more clear.

May was the one to recover first. "Dude. That sounds awesome."

Not far behind, June leaned forward to sit literally on the edge of her seat. "Who gets to murder Patty?" She held up a hand. "Please tell me we're not just expecting her to die of natural causes in this scenario."

It was Elizabeth's turn to pause for a few dramatic blinks. "Not sure how I feel about you jumping to the practicalities of homicide so quickly, but I do appreciate the enthusiasm."

May set the popcorn aside and fluttered a hand in June's direction. "Don't mind her. She's just had it out for Patty ever since she decided to be the last holdout against the Junebug opening up shop."

"Fat lot of good it did her," June scoffed.

May rolled her eyes and kept the focus on Elizabeth. "Tell us everything."

A warm feeling gathered in her chest. She hadn't told her family about her nascent plans to start a new festival in town, and she'd had her reasons. Most of them had to do with her history—and her sisters' completely different one. They started wildly successful cultural events. She bumbled around, babbling about art and showing up late to work shifts they could have paid somebody minimum wage to cover.

None of what she was doing with this festival was in character for her. Even stepping into the same ring her sisters operated in invited unflattering comparisons.

But if they could do it, so could she. Or at least that's what she'd told herself as she'd settled in to start getting serious about her career as an artist this fall.

Her doubts had lingered, though. She'd assumed her sisters' doubts about her abilities would, too. When Graham had encouraged her to bring them on board, she'd balked at first, despairing over the idea of trying to convince them that she was really capable of pulling off this kind of event—and maybe chafing a bit at asking them for help. But even she'd known he was right. It would be shooting herself in the foot to leave them out of this. Now here they were, staring at her expectantly, no questions asked.

Well, no questions that weren't about hypothetical murder, in any case. "Okay." She jumped right into her spiel, which she had to admit was getting more and more coherent every time she told it. Stupid Graham, being right about how practice made perfect. She hadn't practiced her oboe back in high school, and she'd done okay, but maybe with public speaking it was a different story.

As she laid out her vision for the arts festival, with informal displays of carefully curated works by local, unsigned artists spread out all across town, her sisters nodded along. They asked a couple of clarifying questions here and there but mostly let her do her thing.

Right until she got to the part about Patty Boyd showing up before her pitch to the mayor and ruining everything.

"I bet it was Mindy." June narrowed her eyes. "She means well—bless her heart—but she does love to gossip."

May shook her head. "It doesn't matter. Cat's out of the bag now."

As if she had a weird feline version of Google set up to send her alerts, their mom's cat, Sunny, chose that exact moment to hop up onto the back of the couch and flick her tail in May's ear.

With a long-suffering sigh, May shooed the beast down and took her into her lap, where Sunny deigned to be petted for a moment.

"May's right," June conceded. "Whoever, ahem, spread the news"—she looked to Sunny—"no cats are stuck in bags of any kind. What matters at this point is what we do to get the town council to give you the okay." With that, she reached over to the side table and picked up a clipboard, complete with yellow legal pad and a clicky ballpoint pen.

The warmth in Elizabeth's chest somehow managed to both brighten and turn sour. June had her business face on, and that always made Elizabeth nervous.

Deflecting, she asked, "Is it some kind of organized person magic that you can just make those things materialize out of thin air?"

"Pretty much," May muttered.

June threw her hands up. "Who doesn't keep something to write on handy in their own home?"

Elizabeth and May both held their hands up at once.

Ignoring them, June clicked the pen and started to make a list. "Okay, so the obvious first prong of the plan is to start lobbying town council members."

"Graham is already on that."

Elizabeth had come to her sisters for practical advice on getting her festival through the town council, but she didn't like the way June was making it sound like she was starting from square one.

"Good," June acknowledged, "but I have some ins that he might not." Lifting her chin, she called, "Ned?"

"Yes, dear?"

"Can you casually slip into conversation with Tim that I've been meaning to grab coffee with his niece sometime soon?"

"Yes, dear."

Tim was the owner and operator of Tim's Hardware, a Blue Cedar Falls institution, and his niece Brynn was one of the newer members of the town council.

"Ooh." June made another note on her pad, addressing them again. "And I can talk to Lou Ellen at the *Chronicle*. If it's going up before the town council, she might be interested in a story about the behind-the-scenes planning."

Something turned over in Elizabeth's gut. Okay, she'd understood that trying to launch a new event would put her under a spotlight. Going under a microscope was another matter.

"A story in the paper?"

"It'll be good practice. You'll have to do all kinds of media when it comes time to promote the event itself."

Foolish, naïve Elizabeth, getting nervous about speaking in front of the town council. Opening herself up to that kind of public scrutiny, given her reputation, wasn't going to be easy. Little had she suspected that that would be the kiddie pool.

She looked to May, but she was nodding along with June. "I can talk to Tori, too. Getting the travel bureau behind you would be a big boost, I bet."

"Right. Um, great."

"Excellent." June nodded confidently and drew a line down the middle of the page, separating it in half. "Prong two is dealing with Patty herself."

"Is that prong really necessary?" It was a funny word,

"prong." "This could be less of a fork situation and more of a sword, you know?" Swords were cooler.

"Everything gets easier if you can remove the objections standing in your way." June tapped the clicky end of her pen against her chin. "Murder is still a good option, but I'd like to have a few other ideas on the table."

Elizabeth put up both her hands. "Okay, just for the record, I feel like I need to be very specific here in stating that I don't *actually* want to murder anybody."

"Duly noted." June's mouth pulled toward the side. "She's a tough cookie to crack, though. When she was trying to hold up the Junebug from opening, she wouldn't even let Clay in the door."

"What?" Elizabeth said dryly. "Clay? That big teddy bear?"

June rolled her eyes. They all knew full well that for all his soft, squishy insides, Clay looked like a grizzly on the outside.

"I suppose actually making her part of the festival is out of the question," May mused.

"Um, it's an anti-gallery event." That was the entire point.

"May's not wrong. Could the festival be indie focused but still have a gallery presence?"

"Anti. Gallery."

"I hear you," May countered, "but—"

"But nothing." And Elizabeth could hear herself getting wound up here. But it was one thing for her sisters to get out their clipboards and start organizing her efforts for her. It was another for them to try telling her she should change her whole vision.

This wasn't going to turn into some corporate gallery-sponsored event, showing the same dozen artists Patty had been doting on for years. This was a chance for her and her friends and other, struggling artists like them to break through and find an audience for their work.

Her face flashed warm as she remembered all the times Patty had flat out rejected her work. Her entire life, that woman had been discouraging her. Even back in high school, when Patty had been a judge at the senior art show. She'd barely looked at Elizabeth's mixed media piece. It had been unsophisticated, sure. Elizabeth had been eighteen and living in Graham's parents' tree house. But she'd spent weeks on it, pouring her anger at her family and herself onto the canvas.

And Patty had just walked right by it, her nose in the air, muttering something about "delinquents" to the other judges. No wonder first prize had gone to some insipid landscape. It was the same kind of art Patty always backed, without emotion or any real point of view.

"I just think if you expanded—" June tried.

"This is my idea, you guys." Elizabeth resisted stamping her foot like the literal child her family so often treated her as, and she hated that she was getting so worked up about this.

June and May exchanged a look that only made it worse. Stupid perfect sisters with their stupid matching names and matching brains.

"Of course it's your idea," May allowed.

"Then respect it." Elizabeth's face glowed hot. She couldn't think when she got embarrassed and angry like this. "Respect that I have the, like, vision or whatever. I'm going to see it through."

"First time for everything, I suppose."

They all whipped around as one to find their mother

wandering out of the office that connected their living room to the inn's lobby.

June let out an exasperated sigh. "Be nice," she warned.

That angry, embarrassed flush eclipsing Elizabeth's face grew hotter. She refused to get emotional about these ridiculous, snide comments her mom always threw her way, but her eyes still stung, and her throat threatened to close.

She fought past it. "Thanks, Mom. Really appreciate the vote of confidence."

In the kitchen, the water shut off. Ned emerged, drying his hands on a towel. He came over to her side, and she half expected him to sling an arm around her shoulder, the way he would have done when she was a kid and he was still trying to win her over.

Those gestures had come to an end the night she'd left, though. All over again, she wished she could go back in time and give her former self a good slap upside the head. She'd said such awful things. Some of them had been true.

Others had been hurtful and mean. She'd felt rejected, so she'd rejected everyone around her.

And things had never been quite the same ever since.

While he kept a careful distance, Ned confided quietly, "You know she doesn't mean it."

She shot him a look of thanks, but if she otherwise acknowledged it, she was going to lose her cool.

"Don't mind me." Their mother fluttered a hand in the direction of the kitchen. "Just making tea."

"There's hot water in the lobby, Li," Ned reminded her.

She made a look of pure disdain, and Ned sighed affectionately. The lobby coffee and tea station was perfectly serviceable; it even had the fancy coffee creamers that the Wu sisters preferred but that their mom would never buy for the private residence. But heaven forbid anyone suggest she make her evening tea with anything less than freshly boiled filtered water.

She gave Ned's arm a loving pat on her way past him. Over her shoulder, she chided him, "You're late for poker night."

"Believe me." He glanced at June. "I know."

The casual banter gave Elizabeth a minute to cool her jets. Hot shame and annoyance still simmered inside her, but she could put it aside.

One crisis at a time.

And almost thirty years of her mother acting like she was a giant disappointment was the furthest thing from a crisis.

"All right." She clapped her hands together and tried to pull her sisters' focus back to her. "Operation No-Murders Art Festival is a go."

"Are we tied to that name?" June asked.

"Are you going to stop asking if we can murder people?"

June pretended to consider it. "Probably not."

"Then we're sticking with the name for now." She tipped her head toward the clipboard. "And our first steps are..."

June lifted the clipboard and read from her notes. "Lobby the members of the town council."

"And put together a presentation for the actual meeting." Elizabeth pre-empted her sisters before they could jump on that. "Which I have well in hand."

June pursed her lips, but whatever advice she was going to give, she held on to it for now. She moved on to the next bullet points. "Talk to the media and the travel bureau." She nodded toward May for that second part. "And last but not least, find a non-murderous way to get Patty to back down without stepping on Elizabeth's"— she made air quotes—" 'like, vision' for the festival."

Frowning, May peeked over June's shoulder. "That's a big list."

Enormous. But Elizabeth was all the more determined to see it through now. She put her hands on her hips. "Nothing I can't handle."

So why did she suddenly feel like she'd taken the wheel of a runaway train?

CHAPTER SEVEN

❄ ❄ ❄ ❄ ❄ ❄ ❄ ❄ ❄ ❄ ❄ ❄ ❄

All right, folks, last order of business." Duke Moore was both president of the Blue Cedar Falls Historical Society and a longtime member of the town council. He was a middle-aged white man with a bushy mustache and a twinkle in his eye that only grew when he was about to ask for something.

"Here we go," Graham's father muttered beside him. Apparently, he recognized Duke's tells too.

They were currently gathered in the meeting room at the town hall for the historical society's monthly business meeting. Graham was a longtime, enthusiastic member, while his father was a longtime, reluctant one. A couple dozen people had shown up tonight, which was a decent turnout. Graham and his father sat in the second row. In front of them sat Tracey Moore, Duke's wife, and Bobbi, their daughter, who happened to be one of Elizabeth's sister June's best friends.

Clearly having overheard Graham's dad, Bobbi turned in her chair and gave both Lewis men a knowing wink.

Up at the front of the room, Duke barreled on. "Our

spring fundraiser is about to kick off. We've got the steering committee all set, but our usual volunteer coordinator has stepped down on account of needing some new hip joints."

Said former volunteer coordinator, Dottie Gallagher, raised her cane into the air. "If anybody wants to coordinate volunteers to help fundraise *that*, find me after the meeting."

Graham chuckled along with most everybody else, Duke included.

"So who here'd like to try to fill Dottie's size-six sensible shoes?" Duke's gaze darted around, his brows raised expectantly.

In the deafening silence that followed, something struck Graham—he usually stuck to the small stuff, volunteering for a shift here or helping out there. But he'd been trying to branch out more of late. Growing a beard, getting some new contacts, buying a house, joining that pick-up game at the board game café on Main Street. A role like this would be a good opportunity to try something new.

Plus, it couldn't hurt to score a little extra face time with a town council member. Who knew? Maybe he could throw in a good word for Elizabeth's festival proposal.

He lifted his hand. "I can help out."

"Graham, that's my boy." Duke smiled.

Bobbi turned around in her chair again to give him a silent little bit of applause, and he grinned. His grin didn't last long, though, as he caught his father's expression shifting into a scowl.

Oh, brother.

Duke wound up the last bit of the meeting. Once they'd

adjourned, folks rose from their seats. Duke made his way on over, coming to stand beside Tracey and Bobbi. He extended a hand to Graham. "Let's set up a meeting for sometime this week."

"Sounds good, sir."

"Judge Lewis." Duke tipped an imaginary hat at Graham's father.

They stood around, exchanging pleasantries for a few minutes, but Duke inevitably got called away. Graham's dad motioned toward the door.

Graham fell into step beside him. His dad waited until they made it to the parking lot before catching his eye. "Volunteer coordinator?"

He clearly wasn't impressed.

"Somebody's got to do it," Graham said by way of explanation. As they approached his car, he hit the button to unlock it.

His parents lived only a few blocks away, so his father had walked over for the meeting tonight, and it was an unspoken expectation that Graham would give him a lift back and stay for supper.

As his father got in beside him, he scoffed. "Somebody, sure, but I keep telling you: you want to rise in this town, you've got to sign up for the big-picture stuff. Steering committees, planning committees. Volunteer coordinator is a cog."

"Look at me go," Graham said beneath his breath, moving his finger around in a circle like a spinning gear.

"I'm serious."

Graham didn't doubt that. His father went to these meetings to network, and that was about it. In public, the Honorable Judge Lewis was the face of selfless community participation. In private, though, he rarely minced words about the historical society being a waste of time. Uninterested in having this conversation yet again, Graham turned on the radio, automatically switching the dial to a country station neither of them minded. Fortunately, his dad took the hint and dropped it, too.

At his family's house, he parked behind his mom's station wagon. They headed inside.

The family house was a classic two-story home with white clapboard on the outside, dark blue shutters, and precisely the sort of picture-perfect picket fence Elizabeth made fun of him for loving. Inside, it was all warm yellows and tans, and even the scent of the place set him instantly at ease.

The fact that that usual homey, clean-laundry and apple-pie-candle scent was layered with that of his mom's pot roast? Well, that was just gravy.

"Honey, we're home," his father called.

"Just in time to set the table," his mother replied from the other room.

They found her in the kitchen, taking the lid off the pressure cooker he'd gotten her for Christmas a couple years past. She'd become a master of the thing, inspiring him to grab one for his and Elizabeth's place, too. That had...not turned out as well. Probably because he'd been the one operating it.

His parents shared a chaste peck on the cheek. Graham slid past them to grab utensils out of the drawer, but his mom pushed his father away and reached an arm out. Graham gave her a tight hug, trying to avoid the steam coming out of the pot as he did.

"How was the meeting?" she asked, letting him go.

"The usual," Graham's father replied. He rolled his

eyes. "Duke bloviated, your son signed up for a thankless job."

His mom's eyes lit up. "Ooh, which one?"

There was the enthusiasm he'd been looking for. "Volunteer coordinator for the spring fundraiser."

"Good for you!" She held out a hand, and he pretended to be embarrassed, but he returned the high five happily.

His father sat down at the head of the table, and Graham laid out the napkins, knives, and forks while his mother served up. Before long, they were all seated. His father led a quick grace, and they tucked in. Graham hummed his approval at his first bite.

"You like it?" his mom asked.

"Awesome," he said with his mouth full.

"It's so easy," she went on. "I keep telling you, I can show you how to make it."

"We already made our donation to the fire department," his father agreed.

Graham rolled his eyes. "One time." At both parents' skeptical look, he corrected himself. "Okay, fine, maybe three."

"Maybe it's best the boy find a partner who can cook," his father said.

"Elizabeth can cook." He shrugged, realizing too late how that sounded. Elizabeth wasn't his partner. She was his roommate—and she wouldn't even be that for long now.

His father's knife made a harsh sound against his plate. Graham refused to look over and meet his eyes, but he did glance up toward his mom, who shot him a soft smile.

"I'm sure she can." Her smile brightened, and she

visibly shifted gears. "So the funniest thing happened today..."

She launched into a story about her friend Fran's grandson coming in with his father that afternoon and trying to get a pet license for a pet unicorn. Graham's father perked up a bit, now that conversation had been deftly redirected away from both his unambitious volunteer position and his unambitious choice in roommates. Graham did his best to keep the focus off his own life for the rest of the meal, and between the quirky visitors to the clerk's office, drama at his father's job at the county courthouse, and the terrible season the Panthers were off to so far, it was easy enough to do.

"That wide receiver," his dad groaned, and he and his mom laughed.

And for a minute, it was all just so... great.

He loved family dinner after historical society meetings. He loved this house and his mom's laugh and the family's inability to pick a professional sports team to root for that could actually win a game.

The sore spot in the pit of his stomach gave a little twinge. Someday, this was going to be *his* family. He'd be older and grayer, with a partner who would probably be getting old and gray, too. His adult children would be seated beside them—if they chose to stay close to home. Which would be their choice. Not his. They'd have meals like this, right in the house he was buying up the street, and it'd be great.

Someday.

He was still lost somewhere between the actual conversation and the one he was imagining in his head when dinner wrapped up.

His father stood. "Thanks, Lucille. If you'll excuse me—couple of big cases on the docket tomorrow."

"Of course." Graham's mom smiled indulgently.

"He always comes up with something, huh?" Graham asked as he pitched in to clear the table.

"Thirty-five years and counting," she acknowledged, but she didn't seem to mind.

Graham would never quite understand their partnership, but their division of labor seemed to work well enough for them. Dividing up the work was definitely something he'd do differently when it was his family someday. He might be useless when it came to cooking, but the least he could do was help clean up afterward.

He and his mother worked together in parallel, chatting idly. The comfortable, familiar rhythm set him at ease, even if his mom kept redirecting conversation back to her ideas for how he should decorate his house.

"Let me get in the place first, would you?" He said it jokingly, but he meant it. He was excited about the new house, and he couldn't wait to move in. But was there really any need to rush things on the paint colors?

She held out a hand, and he passed her a dishwasher detergent pod. "I just want you to be able to hit the ground running." She put the pod in, closed up the door, and pressed the button to start the machine. "You know how you can be."

He frowned. "How's that?"

"Oh, sweetheart, nothing bad." She patted his arm. "You just take your time about some things to the point where I wonder if they're going to happen at all."

"That's not true."

Was it?

She raised her brows as if to say *Yes, it definitely is. Are you seriously trying to pretend otherwise?* Out loud, she said, "Oh, I can think of a few areas." Instead of elaborating, she tipped her head toward the hall. "Do you need to get home, or do you have time to go poke through the attic with me for a bit?"

He tugged out his phone, even though his watch was right there on his wrist, to check both the time and his messages. He'd texted Elizabeth before the historical society meeting to see if she wanted to catch up tonight on the anime they were binge-watching together. Her reply had been a *Not sure, I'll let you know*. And then he hadn't heard anything since.

A twinge of unease curled through him, but he pushed it down. Things between them would get back to normal soon enough. He just needed to be patient—and if his mother's offhand comment was on the mark, apparently he had plenty of practice with taking his time.

He tucked his phone back into his pocket and nodded. "Sure, why not?"

For as long as Graham could remember, the attic had served as a special kind of hoarder purgatory for the Lewis family. Downstairs, everything was as neat as a pin, but that was partly because any old furniture or items that weren't regularly in use got chucked up here. Supposedly it was a holding station—just a place to keep things to make sure nobody changed their mind. But getting stuff back down was a pain, so detritus was basically left here to die.

At the top of the stairs, Graham pulled the cord to turn on the bare overhead bulb. It flickered to life, and he immediately sneezed. "Good grief, Mom—"

"Oh, it's not as bad as it looks." She bustled past him.

It was worse. Boxes and shelves and dust-cloth covered furniture stretched as far as the eye could see.

"So I guess you and Dad aren't thinking about down-sizing anytime soon," he remarked dryly as he followed her off into the trenches.

She looked back at him, brows scrunched up. "Now why on earth would we do that?"

"Just saying."

"Ah, here we go." They'd arrived at the furniture-graveyard section of the disaster. She tugged up the corner of a drop cloth, and a billow of dust rose into the air. Nodding, she lifted the rest of it off to reveal the old family room couch. "This is in pretty good shape, really—just needs some new slipcovers."

"Okay." He ran his hand along the upholstery and sneezed again.

"Have you talked to Elizabeth about what you're taking with you and what she's keeping?"

Graham swallowed and dropped his hand.

Ha.

"Not yet," he said, voice tighter than he would have liked.

She shot him another sharp, too-knowing look. "Y'all will have to get that sorted out, you know."

"I know."

"There's plenty here that you can take, of course, but if you need to order anything new, these things take time."

He rubbed at his nose, but the growing headache gathering at his temples had nothing to do with his dust allergy and everything to do with his allergy to finalizing the logistics of his move. Just telling Elizabeth about the house had felt like ripping off a Band-Aid—and taking half a shin's worth of leg hair with it. She needed some time to process before he started trying to nail down how they'd divvy up their stuff. Heck, he probably did, too.

"I know," he said, deflecting. "We're both pretty busy right now, though." He cast about for a way to change the subject. "Mayor Lewis is making her take her festival idea to the town council."

That got his mom's attention. She let go of the drop cloth she'd been peeking under and turned to him. "Well, that doesn't bode particularly well."

His stomach sank. He'd told his mom about Elizabeth's idea before, and she'd been nothing but encouraging. Unlike his dad, she actually enjoyed being involved in town events, and she usually had her ear to the ground about this kind of thing. Her tone was different now. "No?"

"Committees and councils are where good ideas go to die." She shook her head. "If John's referred you there, you really need an airtight proposal."

"I know."

She spoke over him. "I'm talking numbers. Projected revenue, attendance, marketing, and promotion."

He'd known all of that. And yet. *Yikes.* "Okay—"

"Comps." She looked over at him. "Do you have comps? You know, other festivals of the sort that you can hold up for comparison?"

Hmm. "We can get all the data we need for Pumpkin Festival and Taste of Blue Cedar Falls."

"That's a good start. You probably need an arts festival, too, though. Preferably one in a similar area. A successful one, obviously."

He frowned. He had some ideas for where to start with that; he had colleagues in a lot of other small towns whom he'd met at various local-government networking events.

Elizabeth was the one who knew the arts community, though.

"I'll talk it over with Elizabeth."

"Good luck," his mother offered cheerfully, moving on to the next pile. Under her breath, she murmured, "You're going to need it."

CHAPTER EIGHT

❖ ❖ ❖ ❖ ❖ ❖ ❖ ❖ ❖ ❖ ❖

So." That Friday night, Elizabeth slipped into her usual spot at her friends' table, right between Graham and Chloe. As she sat, her elbow accidentally brushed Graham's, and she jerked it away, still boggled by the weird frisson of awareness that danced up her arm at the contact. Her response to being close to him was new—and considering they were still trying to find their footing again in their friendship, not entirely welcome. When it already felt like she was losing him, the last thing she needed was to go ahead and catch feelings for him. Fighting not to let her reaction show, she addressed the group. "What'd I miss?"

"You mean besides dinner?" Graham asked, desert dry.

Ouch. She glanced up at him and immediately had to look away. The guy was so nice, he didn't even have the decency to be sullen or passive-aggressive or anything. Unguarded hurt colored his eyes, and this was so unfair.

"Sorry." She took a sip of her beer. "Got held up with turning over a few rooms across the street." She chanced another look at him. "I texted you."

Later than she should have. She'd fully meant to meet him at the apartment and do dinner like they always did, but June had mentioned that she could use the help, and Elizabeth had jumped on the opportunity—both to earn some bonus points with her sister and to avoid Graham.

Which sucked. She loved Friday night takeout before heading to the bar.

At the moment, though, changing linens and scrubbing toilets felt easier than having an extended, one-on-one conversation with her best friend.

She'd done a pretty okay job at being nice to him this week. Not prodding him for answers he clearly didn't want to provide. She'd even given him that sweet succulent as a peace offering.

The offering had been hollow, though.

His decision to move out—and more importantly, his refusal to explain his real reason for doing so—was still eating her up inside. She was probably being childish, but she didn't trust herself to keep her feelings bottled up if they spent any significant amount of time alone together. She didn't want to rehash the same old argument anymore. She didn't want to keep poking at him like a loose tooth.

So. Avoidance. Just until she could get her head on straight.

She'd hoped a salad would do the trick last week, but it hadn't. Menial labor tonight hadn't either, and she was starting to fear that nothing would. Except maybe time.

Stupid time.

"Weird." May frowned over on the other end of the table. "June didn't tell me she needed help."

Crap.

"I was there already." She waved a hand, deflecting. "She probably didn't want to bother you, anyway. We all know that you're on deadline."

"This deadline is *killing* me." Needing no further segue, May started regaling them with the story of the demanding editor who was apparently working her into an early grave.

Elizabeth gratefully tuned out for a minute. She cared, of course, but she'd heard this tune before. She took a sip of her beer and snuck a glimpse at Graham, who seemed content enough to let May hijack all of the attention. Thank goodness.

As she relaxed and tried to get her heartbeat back down to a normal rate, her gaze caught on Chloe, who was playing with her tiny little straw as if she wasn't really listening, either.

Elizabeth smirked. "Is that a Shirley Temple?"

"Shut up." Chloe kicked her under the table, but a genuine smile broke across her face. "Shirley Temples are awesome. Zoe even hooked me up with extra cherries."

Holding her hands up in submission, Elizabeth grinned. "No argument here."

Chole's expression dimmed. "And it's not like I can have anything else."

"That must suck." Around them, conversation continued to flow. Elizabeth leaned in a little closer. Outside of a couple of texts, the two of them hadn't had much chance to catch up this week. "How are you holding up?"

"Okay?" Well, that was the least convincing assurance Elizabeth had ever heard. Chloe grimaced. "I mean, no booze and barely any caffeine is terrible, and I'm nauseated, like, half the day. Oh, and I'm drowning in the general existential dread of wondering if I'm going to be a horrible mother who leaves my unborn child scarred for life."

Elizabeth's brows rose and rose as Chloe rattled through the list. "Is that all?"

Chloe pursed her lips. "I'm also supposed to microwave lunch meat? It's complicated."

"Clearly." Elizabeth had no clue how she would handle it if she had been so unceremoniously thrust into this kind of predicament.

"Yeah. So. Terrible? But outside of all of that, I think I'm doing pretty great."

"Thanks, Mrs. Lincoln." Elizabeth was joking, but she kept her expression open, trying to be clear that she was here to listen. Or even help, if there was any way she could.

Chloe rolled her eyes and fiddled with her stir stick again. "I just wish I knew what was coming, you know?"

"Yeah?"

Lowering her voice, Chloe confided, "Tom acts like it'll all be fantastic and nothing will go wrong and we can totally handle everything. I want to believe it, but everything feels really..." She gestured vaguely with her hands. "...topsy turvy? Like imminent disaster could strike at any moment?"

"To be fair, that's how our lives feel pretty much all the time."

"I know. But there's this new element of feeling like I have no control over anything. It's unsettling."

"Sounds it." Elizabeth took a sip of her drink, but Chloe didn't volunteer anything else.

What was she supposed to say? The two of them had always been scatterbrains together, and now they were both trying to be responsible, albeit for very different reasons. If Elizabeth had any good advice, she would have told it to herself by now.

"I have nothing to offer except stupid platitudes," she admitted. "You're going to do great? It'll all work out for the best?"

Chloe scrunched up her brow. "Thanks. I think."

This all felt so inadequate. She took another gulp of her beer before setting down her glass and reaching for Chloe's hand. "Well, one stupid platitude I can recite to you is true."

"What's that?"

"Whatever happens, you've got us." She gave Chloe's hand a gentle squeeze.

A suspicious gleam appeared in Chloe's eyes. With a choked laugh, she pulled her hand away to scrub at them. "Ugh, hormones."

"They're the worst."

Chloe sniffed and then smiled brightly, clearly ready to move on. "So how's stuff with you? Festival plans progressing at all?"

Elizabeth resisted the urge to thunk her forehead against the table. Barely.

Instead, she shrugged dramatically. "My sisters have a battle plan, but every time I try to remind them that I'm the general, they look at me like I'm one of those useless baby kings."

"Actually," Graham interrupted—too smoothly. He must have been listening the entire time. "I talked to my mom yesterday."

"Yeah?" She looked over at him as neutrally as she could manage. Their gazes connected, and for a second, it was like looking into the sun.

"Uh." He blinked and glanced away. "Yeah. She had

a few ideas. The biggest one was that we should get some comps." When Elizabeth raised her brows at him, he explained, "Similar events in similar towns. The more specific the better."

"Ooh," Dahlia piped up. "There's the Four Winds Festival out near Wilmington next weekend."

Chloe nodded, her expression brightening. "That one's really great."

"I was there five years ago or so," May said. "It's a cute town. Half Moon Cove, I think it's called."

"Oh!" It was like a lightbulb went on over Elizabeth's head. "Isn't Kat involved with that one?" She and Dahlia had met Kat Jones at a workshop they'd gone to in Asheville ages ago and become fast—if long-distance—friends.

"Yeah! You should ask her about it."

Graham stroked his beard thoughtfully. "Half Moon Cove. I think I met a guy from there at a local-government conference. Wonder if he could dig up any numbers for us that we could include in the presentation."

"Do you mind messaging him?" Elizabeth asked, making eye contact again, but it was less intense this time.

"Of course."

"Or you guys could just, you know." Dahlia made a shooing motion with her hands. "Go."

Elizabeth and Graham whipped their heads toward her as one. "What?"

Like she was talking to a couple of idiots, she said, slowly, "You should go. To the festival. Next weekend. It's not that far away."

"It kind of is," Elizabeth countered. North Carolina was a really wide state. It took half the day to get to the beach from here.

Dahlia waved off her concern. "I'm just saying. You can spend all the time in the world messaging Kat and your"—she gestured vaguely at Graham—"town government nerd friend."

"He's not a nerd," Graham protested.

Elizabeth pulled a face. "Are you sure?"

Graham sighed. "He's kind of a nerd."

"You can try to track them down all you want from here," Dahlia plowed on. "Or you can actually head on over there and check it out in person."

"It's not a terrible idea..." Elizabeth mused. It was a great one, honestly. So great she wished she'd come up with it herself. She'd have to get someone to cover her class at the community center, and probably a shift or two at the inn, but all of that was doable. She loved impromptu road trips and art festivals and time with her friends. Getting to do something tangible that would help make her dream a reality was the icing on the cake.

"I mean," Graham started, glancing at her, "I'd be up for it."

"I'd offer to go," Dahlia said, "but I'm teaching a class at the Folk Arts Center that weekend."

"Same, but..." Chloe put a hand on her belly and wrinkled her nose. "I wasn't kidding about the morning sickness thing."

"Of course." Elizabeth's throat tightened, and she looked to Graham, whose expression was open and...did she daresay even a little hopeful?

"So I guess it'd just be you and me," Graham said carefully.

Just like that, her excitement faded, replaced by a ripple of anxiety.

She'd spent the past week barely able to look at her

best friend, nursing this hurt she had no right to feel, avoiding him because it was easier than trying to explain how she didn't want him to leave her. And now, what? They were just going to jump in a car together and drive across the state for a weekend away?

She sucked in a deep breath and pushed her discomfort aside. Damn right, that was what they were going to do. This festival was her baby, and if she wanted to prove that she could handle the work of getting it approved, she needed to take the reins of this thing. She was also a big enough person to admit she needed Graham's eyes and ears and his ability to focus on the details of government administration.

So she'd have to spend a dozen hours in a car with him; his car was big enough to squeeze the luggage in around the pink elephant that would be sitting in the back seat. She could focus on the work and ignore the new tension between them.

Who knew? Maybe they could even find a way past it and get back to being *them* again.

As best she could, she forced a smile. "What are we waiting for? Let's get packing."

CHAPTER NINE

Okay, three crises. Handling three crises at a time was acceptable, right?

Dropping to sit in the desk chair behind the counter at the inn, Elizabeth rolled her eyes at herself. She couldn't help imagining Ned's unimpressed expression in her head, but she didn't have time to give herself one of her stepfather's trademark lectures right now.

She hovered her thumbs over the keyboard on her phone, Graham's most recent message staring back at her on the screen. *Still planning to leave at ten?*

Absolutely, she typed back, glancing at the time on the front desk computer and suppressing a groan when it read eight forty-five. They were leaving for Half Moon Cove's art festival in an hour and fifteen minutes, and after several days of psyching herself up for it, she was almost, vaguely sort of ready. Emotionally speaking, that was. Logistically, she was a mess.

Graham texted back a thumbs-up emoji, followed by *Cool, see you at eleven.*

She stuck her tongue out at her phone, but she didn't have time to insist that no, really, she was going to finish up here at the inn on time. Traffic around Charlotte got ugly by noon. She was determined to beat it, even if it meant leaving for the festival with nothing but the clothes on her back.

That was one crisis... well, probably not handled, but at least back-burnered for now. Nodding to herself, she turned her phone facedown so she couldn't get distracted by it and returned to crises number two and three, namely rejiggering the room turnover schedule so the Hernandezes in room five could get a late check-out that afternoon and confirming a meeting with Deandre Harris from the town council to discuss her proposal for the festival next week. She focused on the turnover schedule first, wincing, because it was going to be tight, getting all the rooms ready for incoming guests. The Hernandezes were return visitors, though. They came back every year, and it was worth going the extra mile to keep their business.

With that settled, she returned to her email, where she typed out the most professional reply she could manage—even if she was interrupted by a guest needing extra towels, a phone call looking for a booking for next week, and her mom's cat deciding to sit on the flipping keyboard.

"Shoo," she muttered at the furball. Sunny flicked her tail, fixed her with a dirty look, then licked herself in an unmentionable place before finally deigning to go find someplace else to sit.

"Oh, good, I was hoping I'd catch you."

Elizabeth held up a single finger as she finished reviewing her message and hit send.

Undeterred, June pulled up the other chair and plopped her trusty clipboard down on the desk. "I just had coffee with Brynn. Tim's niece."

"Oh?" Elizabeth signed out of her email. Take that, crisis three. Now well and truly prepared for crisis four, she turned to face her sister. "What did she think of the festival proposal?"

True to her word, June had gone to bat for Elizabeth, helping talk up her plans to everyone she knew around town with any kind of influence. Which was basically everybody.

And if that still chafed sometimes, Elizabeth was trying her best not to look a gift horse in the mouth. June's help was invaluable. It wasn't her fault that every time she offered to coordinate another meeting or make another introduction, Elizabeth reverted back to her ten-year-old self and all she could see was her perfect, goody-two-shoes sixteen-year-old sister telling her she was doing everything in her life wrong.

Which, to be fair, she usually was.

Not now, though. She was doing this right. Making up for her past mistakes as a wayward, irresponsible youth who could never hold on to the second glove in a pair for more than two days, and showing everyone that she had something to contribute to this town.

"She's tentatively interested." June's mouth pulled to the side. "Though from the sound of it, Patty's got her ear, too. We're going to have to put some more work in there, trying to get her on your side."

"Duly noted." Elizabeth spun her chair around and snagged the sketchbook she'd started keeping all of her notes in. She flipped it to the green Post-it Note marking her place for festival planning stuff and scribbled "talk to Brynn" as yet another item on her never-ending to-do list. "I'll try and see if I can sit down with her after me and Graham get back."

"Don't forget to follow up with Deandre, either."

Elizabeth fought not to bristle. "Just confirmed it, literally while you were sitting here."

"And the interview with Lou Ellen from the *Chronicle*—"

"Two p.m. next Wednesday." She pointed at the line for it in her journal, neatly written in purple pen. She'd even given herself a smiley-face sticker she'd swiped from her teaching supplies for getting it set up.

"Okay, good." June flashed her a smile as she stood. "Just don't want anything slipping through the cracks."

Elizabeth could have thrown her hands up in the air, but she seriously did not have time for a fight right now. June meant well, and someday, if Elizabeth managed to not screw anything up for a few years in a row, maybe she'd start treating her like a grown-up instead of a delinquent baby sister.

She closed her journal and stuffed it in the bag at her feet, along with her phone and the ten pens she'd somehow managed to strew around the computer area. "I've got it all covered, promise." Hefting her bag over her shoulder, she glanced around. "You good?"

"Yup."

Elizabeth sucked in a deep breath. "Thanks for letting me switch around my shifts this weekend. This trip out to Half Moon Cove—"

"—is important." June nodded. "I get it."

She really did, which helped assuage Elizabeth's guilt at least a little bit. "I know, I just hate flaking on you at the last minute."

Back in high school, she screwed up her schedule all the time. It hadn't seemed like a big deal. Her mom and Ned ran the inn, for the most part, and after she moved out, it wasn't like she could disappoint them any more. She'd left the family, in their eyes; there was no sin worse than that. In her book, she'd done no such thing. She'd just needed some space. A chance to live without her mom and June breathing down her neck every freaking second of the day.

Not that they would ever see it that way.

In any case, she'd dug a pretty big hole for herself back then. The past few years, she'd been trying to make amends and work her way back into the family's good graces. She showed up for every shift, and she was the first one to volunteer to cover for one of her sisters when they had something come up. She was well within her rights to ask for them to do the same this one time when she had something important to do out of town.

So why did it still feel like her being a deadbeat, like she used to be?

June shook her head. "It's not flaking." One corner of her mouth lifted. "It's research. And you know how much I love research."

"You cannot come with me."

"I'm really good at taking notes," June said, her eyes going wide. She wasn't being serious, but she was putting on a decent show.

Elizabeth cast her gaze to the ceiling. "I'm taking Graham with me."

June held her hands in front of her chest. "Say no more. I would trust this mission to no one less worthy."

Forget that "this mission" wasn't June's to entrust to anyone. Or that Graham was "worthy" in a way that clearly Elizabeth was not.

Shaking her head, Elizabeth rose to her feet and pushed in the chair. She gave a little salute. "Well then, I'm off."

"Weren't you supposed to be off twenty minutes ago?"

Was it really nine twenty already? Crap. "Shh."

"Have fun," June called after her as she scurried for the exit. "Bring back pictures and brochures."

"Yes, Mom," she groaned.

Mark that four crises handled—if June's general checking up on whether or not she was capable of doing her job counted as a crisis, which it basically did.

Now she just had to hope she didn't run into four more on her way out the door…

"Ugh, I'm sorry."

Graham scrunched up his brows as he put on his blinker to try to merge left. "Why?"

Elizabeth waved a hand expansively at the sea of cars surrounding them. "If we'd left when you wanted to, we wouldn't have hit all this traffic."

"There's always traffic around Charlotte." It was one of the reasons he never went there unless he had to.

"But there would have been less of it an hour ago."

"Maybe." He shrugged. It wasn't as if he'd really expected her to be ready to go on time. He'd been driving her around for over a decade now. Heck, back when they were teenagers, he half wondered if her main reason for hanging out with him was that he had a license and the keys to his dad's ancient Accord.

"I just got caught by June at the inn, and then I had this parent call me in a tizzy while I was packing because their kid broke the ceramic horse she made."

Some patient minivan driver let him into the next lane, and he lifted a hand in thanks as he slid over. He chanced a glance in Elizabeth's direction to find her scowling. Why was this bothering her so much?

"Seriously, it's fine." He gestured around a bit. "So we go ten miles an hour for a little while. It's a bright, sunny day, not too hot, not too cold." He lifted the half-empty bag of Funyuns from his lap. "We have snacks. It's all good."

There wasn't much else he could do to show her he meant it, so he reached over and gave her knee a quick pat.

She jumped at the contact, and he pulled his hand back to his side of the car.

She'd been doing that a lot lately. Something hot and unpleasant squirmed around in his gut. They'd never been wildly affectionate—they were just friends, after all. But time was they could share a quick hug or a knee squeeze without her flinching.

Ever since he'd told her about having his offer accepted on the new house, flinching had been the name of the game, though. She hadn't brought it up again since they'd had it out while working on her presentation for Mayor Horton. But his decision hung in the air between them.

Kind of like the Funyuns did.

He closed up the bag and wordlessly handed it to her. She grabbed one out before sealing the top with a binder clip and tossing it into the back seat. She rattled the tin of breath mints she always kept in her purse, and he held out his palm for her to drop one into.

As he popped the mint into his mouth, he repeated in his head his hope that whatever animus she felt toward him right now would clear up just as easily as his onion breath. That the disruption to the status quo would be worth it—in the end. Their friendship was strong. It could survive him trying to snuff out the torch he'd always carried for her.

Right?

The silence between them wasn't easy or comfortable, though. As he navigated them along the most obnoxious stretch of I-485, he tried to focus on driving, but it was tough. Elizabeth's choice of music for the day wasn't exactly helping, either. Her tastes had always run toward the angsty end of the indie rock spectrum, but the number of angry anthems about women being done wrong was starting to weigh on him.

Finally, he broke, reaching over to turn the stereo down. "You want to play the alphabet game?"

"Again? And in a traffic jam?"

Okay, fine, it was less fun to try to spot letters on highway signs and license plates when you weren't going anywhere.

"I spy with my little eye?"

"Are we seven?" she asked.

He tried not to let his exasperation show. All he wanted was a fun, normal road trip, just like all the other fun, normal road trips they had taken in the past.

"Do you have any better suggestions?"

She shifted in her seat. "Not really."

Great.

At long last, they reached their exit. The local highway they got onto was almost as much of a mess as the interstate had been, but at least they were moving again. He rolled down the window a smidge, letting the last of the Funyun air out, and she did likewise.

A cool breeze rushed in, welcome and making him realize exactly how stagnant it had started to feel.

Maybe it did the same for her.

She turned toward him. "So how's Operation New and Improved Graham going?"

"Excuse you?" What was he more surprised by? What she'd said or the lack of sarcasm in her tone?

"You know. Like you said—the whole turning-over-a-new-leaf thing. New house." If she flinched saying that this time, it was hard to tell with his eyes on the road. "New beard. New contacts. How's it all working out for you?"

Well, there was a loaded question. "Good? I think?" The semitruck in front of him pulled into the center lane to turn, and he breathed a sigh of relief as he hit the gas and made a wild run at actually approaching the posted speed limit for the first time in he didn't even know how long. "I mean, I like not shaving."

She hummed, and he peeked over to find her frowning.

His stomach did a little dip. "You don't like it."

That was fine. It didn't matter if she didn't find him attractive like this. She'd never found him attractive anyway.

She shook her head. "I didn't say that."

"You didn't have to."

"It's just that—" Letting out a huffing sigh, she raked her hand through her hair. "I didn't want to like it, okay? On principle."

What principle was that?

Before he could ask, she crossed her arms. Begrudgingly, she admitted, "But it's kind of growing on me."

That shouldn't buoy him up so much. So he deflected. "Technically, it's growing on me."

She groaned. "You're going to have to give Tom tips on how to make the worst freaking dad jokes."

"What can I say? It's a gift."

"Did you keep the receipt?"

"Hardy har har," he fake laughed.

And she said his jokes were bad.

A minute passed before she ventured, tentatively, "So what do you think about that? Chloe and Tom expecting?" She shrugged at the questioning look he darted her way. "We haven't had much of a chance to talk about it."

Only because she'd been avoiding him. "I think it's great."

She regarded him for long moment before announcing, "You're envious."

He really needed to concentrate on driving here, but he shot her a confused glance. "I am not."

Okay, fine, maybe he was, but just a little.

"You absolutely are." She sat back in her seat, smug.

"I really don't know where you're getting this from."

"You always wanted kids."

"Yeah. So?" That didn't mean he was pining for a happy accident of his own.

Her knee bobbed up and down, and he could feel the weight of her stare. "Isn't that all a part of Operation New and Improved Graham? First you get the beard, then you get the house."

"Those had literally nothing to do with each other."

"Then you get the wife and then you get the two point five perfect children."

"Ideally, yeah, that'd be great." He was mostly just focused on getting out on his own at the moment.

"So any luck working on meeting Mrs. Right?"

Oh, jeez. They were wading into really dangerous territory now.

In general, he tried not to talk about his love life with Elizabeth. That could get complicated sometimes, considering that they were best friends, but the fact that he didn't have much of a love life to speak of tended to simplify matters.

"I've been busy," he tried, and he really had been. Between his day job, meeting with Duke about taking over as volunteer coordinator for the historical society, helping Elizabeth win support for her festival, and filling out the same fifteen forms over and over and over again for his mortgage processor, he had his hands full.

Elizabeth could smell weakness, though. "Chop, chop," she said dryly. "Those two point five kids aren't going to gestate themselves."

That rubbed him all kinds of the wrong way. "For Pete's sake, E. I'm not looking for a brood mare."

"I'm just saying…"

"Well, stop saying it." Did she really think so poorly of him? Or was this just more of her being salty about him "abandoning" her to move into a home of his own? "Yes, I'd like kids, and before that, I'd like to get married. But I'm looking for more than a walking, talking uterus." His throat tightened. "I'm looking for a partner, you know?"

"I was just kidding," she said, a twist of discomfort to her tone.

And he should have taken the out. Laughed along and moved on.

But he was on a roll now. "I want someone I can share inside jokes with and make a home with." Dad jokes and puns and references to things that happened half a dozen years ago.

A home full of color and art and so many knitted and crocheted blankets that it had might as well be a fort.

A place that he was happy to come home to, because his favorite face in the world was going to be there waiting for him.

"I want someone I can go on road trips with and volunteer on town projects with and…"

Oh no.

He'd finally tipped his hand too far. He'd let on that the person he was looking for was obviously, inevitably, perpetually *her*.

For a minute, the only sound in the car was their breathing and the hum of the motor. He gripped the steering wheel so tightly he was bound to crush it if he wasn't careful, forcing himself to keep his gaze focused on the road ahead.

"Well," she finally said, voice rough. "Good luck finding that on Tinder."

Everything inside him sank. Oh, for crying out loud. He glanced over at her, and she was looking away, and that was fine. He wanted her to remain oblivious.

So why was he so hurt that that was exactly what he was getting?

He forced himself to chuckle, only it wasn't funny. Relaxing his grip on the wheel, he combed a hand through his hair.

"So anyway. That's what I'm looking for. With the right person, kids would just be a bonus."

"Even if Mrs. Right didn't want them at all?"

"It'd be a disappointment." There was no sense lying about it. "But not a deal breaker."

"Hmm."

She was still gazing out the window, making it impossible to gauge her reaction, but there was an openness to that hum.

"What about you?" He resisted the urge to nudge her with his elbow over the console. "What if your Mr. or Mrs. Right was dead set on having kids?"

"Why would that be a problem?"

He jerked his head in her direction, almost swerving

out of his lane, but he caught himself. "I thought you were one hundred percent anti-kids."

"I'm not anti-kids."

"But I thought you didn't want them."

She complained about the gremlins in her art classes all the time. She'd talked at length about how she wasn't cut out for motherhood—or responsibility of any kind, really. He knew it was all nonsense, but he really believed that that was how she felt.

"They're not part of my five-year plan, if that's what you mean," she conceded. "And left to my own devices, I don't think I'd decide to go to a sperm bank or anything and ask to make a withdrawal."

Graham grimaced. "Holy TMI, Batman."

"But if Mr. or Mrs. Right was really into having kids, I guess I could try it."

"Uh, kids aren't like samples at Costco, you realize."

"Of course." She swatted at him. "More, I'd be okay with *a* rug rat. I might not be ready to commit to having a whole baseball team of them, but I know plenty of people who had one and still seem to do other things besides chasing tiny humans around."

"I know plenty of people who had three and still do other things besides tiny-human chasing."

She fluttered a hand in his general direction. "Sure, sure. But what I'm saying is, I'm open to the idea of it, with the right person, in the right situation, so long as they're willing to start small."

Well, consider his mind blown. It didn't change anything, of course. When he'd imagined the alternate universe where they decided to be together romantically, he'd contented himself with the idea that they'd have fur babies. A dog for him and maybe a cat for her. The fact that alternate-reality him could have human babies, too, only made the picture more complete.

"Great. For you and the future Mr. or Mrs. Right." He even managed to sound happy for her hypothetical partner.

Mostly. He may not have been overwhelmed by jealousy when it came to Tom and Chloe, but a little green monster was definitely dancing around in his chest now, and the sharp wistfulness of it crept into his voice. Elizabeth didn't miss it, either. She narrowed her eyes at him pointedly enough that he caught it in his peripheral vision. "What?"

"Nothing, just…" He put his blinker on, checked his mirror, and shifted over to pass another slow-moving truck, using the brief time to try to squash the monster down. As he moved back into his lane, he explained away his reaction—not untruthfully. "…didn't realize that I could still be learning new things about you."

For better or worse, that seemed to content her.

"What can I say?" She shrugged. "I'm full of surprises."

That she most certainly was.

It had been a decade and a half since Elizabeth had dealt with a loose tooth. But an hour later, she couldn't help but be reminded of the weird—yet somehow irresistible—nerve twinge that came with poking at one. Over and over and over.

She looked up from the sock she'd been knitting to cast a glance in Graham's direction.

The instinct to prod at that loose tooth tugged at her again.

Leaving Charlotte's traffic jam in their rearview mirror, they'd left heavier topics of conversation behind, too, but the things he'd said about his Mrs. Right continued playing in her head.

His weird reaction to her saying that she wouldn't necessarily be opposed to having a kid kept playing there, too, but she could mostly ignore that.

His search for a partner was intimately tied to his decision to move out, though—another subject she'd been trying not to poke him about for the past two weeks.

Put the two of them together, and she was a laser-focused tooth-poking machine.

She finished her row of stitches, folded her needles into her knitting, and put them back in her bag. She shifted in her seat to face him more fully and tried not to get distracted by how irritatingly handsome he looked in profile with that stupid beard. As she did, her stomach did a little dip. She'd been noticing his good looks a lot recently, which was weird. It wasn't that she'd ever found him repulsive or anything. He'd always been cute, even when he was a gangly teen. But there was something different about his attractiveness now, and she didn't know how to feel about it. Probably annoyed. Hadn't enough changed between them over the course of the past couple of weeks? She wanted to get them back on even ground, not open up a whole new sinkhole when their dynamic obviously wasn't like that.

"Seriously, though," she said, trying to stay focused, "are you on Tinder?"

The car didn't swerve out of its lane, but it was a close call. "What?"

"I was joking earlier when I said good luck finding your perfect life partner on there, but I'm also really curious. Where are you trying to find your perfect life partner?"

He visibly squirmed, and oh yeah. Poke, poke, poke.

"I don't know."

"Tinder is a place to start, I guess..."

"I am not on Tinder," he finally admitted, a note of exasperation entering his tone.

Which mostly just told her that she was on the right track.

"Why not?"

He stole a glance in her direction, his grip firm on the wheel. "That site's for hookups, isn't it?"

"Mostly." She'd scrolled it a time or two herself and had always been boggled by the number of people on the hookup site who said *NO HOOKUPS* in their bios. "Some folks go there looking for more, though."

"Doesn't sound like my speed."

"Then what apps are you on?" She rattled off a half dozen of them, but his mouth only twisted farther down. "Wait—you are on a few dating apps, right?"

There he went, squirming again. "Yeah."

She reached out and pinched his arm—lightly. He was driving after all.

He still yelped. "Hey!"

"I can tell when you're BS-ing me, you know."

"I'm not BS-ing you."

She fixed him with her worst, most accusing stare, wasted as it was considering his gaze was on the road.

He could clearly feel it, though.

"I have one account." He paused. "From five years ago. But I did reactivate it last week."

"That's it?"

"What more am I supposed to do?"

"Hold on." She blinked rapidly a few times, holding her hands up in front of her chest. "You're making big changes in your life. Beard, contacts, house, perfect life partner who you can laugh with and road trip with and build a home with."

Those were his words exactly, and they made sense. Of course they did.

So why did saying them out loud twinge almost as badly as that stupid loose tooth?

He opened his mouth, but she cut him off. "But you're not actually doing anything to try to find said perfect life partner?"

He grumbled something beneath his breath, but whatever it was, she couldn't make it out.

"Want to speak so the whole class can hear?"

Exhaling, he scrubbed a hand through his hair. "Nothing." When she went to pinch him again, he raised his arm to ward off the attack. "I told you I've been busy," he said, like that was an excuse.

"Well, you don't look very busy to me now."

Indignant, he gestured at the steering wheel. "Excuse me, but—"

"You're excused." Without hesitating, she swiped his phone out of the center console and unlocked it.

"Hey—"

She scrolled through his apps and wrinkled her nose when she found his one dating app. "This thing was even still in business to let you reactivate?"

"It wasn't the most auspicious process," he admitted.

"Did it link you to your My Space account?"

"Maybe."

"This is ridiculous." She went to the app store and typed in the name of an app she'd tried once only to find most of the people on there to be serious, somber professionals looking for serious, somber people. Terrible for her, but for Graham... "Perfect."

She tapped the button to download and install it.

"What are you doing to my phone?"

She opened the app and started following the prompts to make a new profile. "Say cheese."

"What?" He glanced at her but then back to the road.

She couldn't exactly take a head-on shot of him, given the circumstances, but she held the phone out a bit and got a surprisingly decent angle for a three-quarters composition.

"Cheese," she said to herself, and he laughed, and her chest squeezed.

She'd never understand why this upstanding citizen of a guy let her get away with all her antics. Stealing his phone, putting a new app on it, taking pictures of him. Would anybody else indulge her so far—much less laugh along as she did it?

She pulled the phone back, closer to her face.

Her heart did that weird jumping thing as she checked out the photo she had taken. His laughter shone in his eyes, brighter than ever without his old glasses in the way. Tousled by the wind, his hair gleamed with hints of gold. His beard made his whole face look longer, leaner, more dignified without seeming too self-serious. Behind him, the sun was just beginning to set, leaving streaks of gold and pink in the sky.

"I probably look like a dork," he said.

"You look like an album cover circa 2010." That was when all the hipster bands took over the airwaves with their jangling guitars and ukuleles and beards, right?

He scrunched up his face. "Is that a good thing?"

It kind of was, but she just shrugged. She was starting to get used to swallowing back the weird reactions she'd been having to how attractive he looked. She scrolled on to the profile part and began typing things in.

"Passionate about history, public service, volunteer work." Okay, now that did make him sound like a dork. A good-hearted dork, which was what mattered to her, but still a dork.

"Wait, are you making a dating profile for me right now?"

"What else are you passionate about?"

"Mostly stopping my roommate from making a dating profile for me." He reached over to snag the phone back from her, but it was a half-hearted effort at best.

"I'll just skip ahead. Enjoys…" What did he enjoy, besides history, public service, and volunteer work? "A quiet night in, but never turns down a night out at the bar with friends."

"Seriously, E—"

"Ooh, this is a good one—'Choose four words your friends would use to describe you.' See, you're lucky I'm the one doing this for you, because I already know."

"So do I." He counted off on his fingers, " 'Boring,' 'bland,' 'terrible cook,' 'boring.' "

She whipped her head around. "I wouldn't describe you as any of those things."

"Really?" he asked, skeptical.

" 'Really?' " she parroted back. "That's messed up, dude."

"It's the truth."

Something uncomfortable turned over in her gut. "It's the farthest thing from the truth, and if it was anybody else talking about my best friend like that, I'd slap them."

"Are you trying to say I'm a good cook?"

"I'd say your terrible cooking doesn't make the top fifty list of ways I'd describe you."

"There's fifty?"

"The site's only asking for four." She hardly had to even think before she rattled off, " 'Hardworking,' 'loyal,' 'dependable,' 'great sense of humor'..."

"That's four words right there," he grumbled, but he didn't actually sound annoyed about it. If anything, he sounded pleased. "And I thought you didn't like my dad jokes."

A lump formed in her throat. They really were extremely, extremely bad.

And endearing.

"The future Mrs. Lewis is going to love them. And so will your two point five children." She didn't know why she was going and getting emotional about any of this. Probably best to move on. She typed in her descriptions of him and answered the next few softball questions before getting to the real meat of the thing. "Speaking of the future Mrs. Lewis, they want to know what you're looking for."

She breezed through the first few criteria. Ages twenty-five to forty; any race, obviously.

" 'Most prized qualities,' " she read out loud. "I'm thinking punctuality, education, family values."

"*What*?"

This time he did swerve out of his lane. They only grazed the rumble strip, but she still let out a little yelp of surprise, nearly dropping his phone as she flailed around for something to hold on to. "Jeez—"

"What are you talking about, E?" he said, voice gruff in a way she struggled to read. He glanced over at her again, and there was something wild in his eyes. Something she'd never seen in him before.

"I don't know." She threw her hands up. "Are you trying to say that's not what you're looking for in a future wife?"

"First the walking uterus thing, now this," he muttered, his gaze darting back to the road, thank goodness.

A sudden jolt of self-consciousness stole over her. A warm dash of shame followed right on its heels.

She'd thought this would be fun. Sort of. Okay, so she'd mostly been trying to push that darn tooth out of its socket, but she hadn't meant to upset him enough that he would turn into some sort of a reckless driver. Honestly, she hadn't even known that that was a thing Graham Lewis could be.

The tight set to his jaw and the unfamiliar brightness in his gaze had her rethinking all kinds of things she'd imagined her best friend could be.

"Where would you even get an idea like that?" he asked.

"I don't know." She shifted in her seat. She'd overstepped so badly here. She'd thought she was helping, but apparently she was just proving what a crappy friend she was. No wonder he'd decided to move out. She fought to keep the growing defensiveness out of her tone. "Every girl you've ever dated has been nice and quiet and responsible."

"And there's a reason I only went on, like, three dates with any of them!"

"I'm sorry." She blanked the screen of his phone and went to put it back, but he stopped her.

"No—you started this. Let's finish it."

"We don't have to. I shouldn't have."

"What I want is a person who makes me laugh." He sat up straighter, the strange cast to his gaze resolving into a bright focus that she at least could recognize—even if it in no way lulled her into thinking she was in anything like familiar territory right now. "I want someone bold and interesting, who challenges me to try new things and tugs me out of my shell. I want someone who's not afraid of anything. Someone creative and strong and just..." He glanced at her and then, quickly, away. "Someone who makes me happy, you know?"

A fire had lit his voice, but with that last sentence, it flickered, and a string inside her chest pulled at her heart.

She couldn't type that into a text box on a dating app. She couldn't even think it.

Before she could stop herself, she laughed, uncomfortable and wrong and not sure why she felt any of that. "For crying out loud, G. If that's what you want, you could have just stayed at Hemlock House with me."

And it was the wrong, wrong, wrong thing to say. She knew it the instant it was out of her mouth.

Something in his expression crumpled. The spark that had burned so brightly in him for a second there went out.

"No," he said, bitterness coloring the words. "No, I couldn't."

CHAPTER TEN

❧ ❧ ❧ ❧ ❧ ❧ ❧ ❧ ❧ ❧ ❧ ❧ ❧

W hat about this?" Elizabeth called from the other side of the tent.

Graham looked up from his phone, where he was still trying to figure out how to erase the dating profile Elizabeth had put together for him while he'd been driving. Which was a stupid thing to do. Nothing she—or he—had said had been untrue. If he really wanted the future he claimed he was working toward, he had to get serious about putting himself out there again.

So what if it felt like he was putting all of his energy into the contradictory twin goals of helping Elizabeth and getting himself out of Elizabeth's inescapable orbit? He'd be closing on the house in another month. Once he moved and she had her festival approved, he'd have time to start thinking about the next steps of his plan. For now, all he was trying to do was keep putting one foot in front of the other, while struggling in vain to keep from putting either foot right into his own mouth.

Fat lot of good that had been doing him. At least twice today, he'd basically told Elizabeth he was in love with and wanted his perfect life and his perfect family with *her*.

But no matter how many times he all but spat it out, she remained as oblivious as ever.

Maybe more so.

A low, angry pit of resentment burned away at the bottom of his stomach. Of course she was oblivious. The idea of the two of them being more than friends was so impossible that she would never think of it on her own, no matter how many times he practically waved a sign declaring his feelings in her face.

"Yo, Graham." Elizabeth waved her hand, and his vision snapped into focus. "Hello? You in there?"

"Yeah, yeah, sorry." He pocketed his phone and did his best to pay attention, but it was a losing battle.

He'd really been looking forward to this trip, hoping it might be a chance to get things back to normal between the two of them, but that had just been wishful thinking on his part. Nothing was normal. He was tired from driving all day, and his heart was sore.

And now Elizabeth was standing there, trying to get him to look at paintings by some landscape artist.

Coming out to the festival tonight had been a crummy idea. He should have just gone back to the hotel after dinner and decompressed with a book or something, but no. Elizabeth had wanted to come scope out the art, and so off he'd gone.

"What's the matter?" Elizabeth asked for the fifteenth time tonight. "I thought you liked this kind of stuff." She gestured again at the painting she'd been trying to show him. A flicker of hurt darted across her features. "Or am I completely wrong about what you like again?"

His heart twisted harder at the defensiveness in her

tone. The only thing worse than how he kept getting his feelings trampled on was how stung she seemed to be every time he tried to set her straight.

"No," he promised, looking the painting over. "It's great."

It was, too. This artist's work was absolutely his taste, depicting beach scenes with a mix of expressiveness and realism. She'd even zeroed in on his favorite of the bunch, with a big blue sky that rolled over water dotted with brushstrokes that felt to him like the ocean breeze was actually rippling his hair.

In fact...

"Wouldn't this one be perfect in your new living room?" Elizabeth offered, stealing the words right out of his brain, it seemed.

He stroked his beard thoughtfully, a smile tugging at the corners of his lips.

Then Elizabeth had to go and lift her brows. "That is, if you're still planning to move into the place, considering all you want in life is exactly what you already have."

And there they went again. The burn in his gut was approaching a boil.

"Don't."

She was trying to provoke him. He knew that. But she was so good at it, was the thing. She knew exactly where to dig, and he was running out of patience here.

Couldn't she be happy for him?

Did she have to keep making this harder than it already was?

"I'm just saying," she tried again.

He blotted it out, turning away, because it didn't matter how much he liked the art. Scrubbing a hand through his hair, he scanned the crowd out in the street.

The festival was clearly a success, with the entire main strip of Half Moon Cove converted into an informal gallery. They'd already wandered through a half dozen of the tents set up to display the entries to the art fair. The one thing they hadn't wandered by was a place to get something to eat.

His stomach growled, the half a burger he'd half-heartedly munched on at dinner a distant memory.

"Don't they have any food stalls at this thing?" he asked.

Elizabeth laughed. "Come on, cranky. Let's get you fed before you transition into full-on hangry territory."

"I'm not cranky," he groused, and yeah, yeah, he heard exactly how cranky he was in his tone, too.

"Uh-huh." She went to thread her hand through his arm to lead him toward the other end of the strip, and that was normal—that was exactly what she would have done on any other trip.

But he couldn't take it tonight.

He jerked his arm back like he'd been burnt. He couldn't look at her.

"Maybe I should just head back to the hotel."

"Okay," she said slowly. "We can do that."

Oh God no.

Sharing a room had been normal, too. They always shared a room, and he loved it—almost as much as he loved her.

But if they had to spend one more minute cooped up together, with him in this mood and with her so intent on trying to set him off, he was going to lose it.

"No," he said, too forcefully, and this was only going to make the tension between them worse. "You should enjoy the festival." He gestured around, trying to put on a happy face and failing miserably. "Don't let me rain on your parade."

"Too late for that," she muttered, but he could hear it.

Ugh, he was getting this all wrong. "You'll have more fun without me."

"No," she said, more firmly this time. She looked up, and he met her gaze, and it was like looking into the sun. "I won't. I never have as much fun when I'm not with you."

"That's not true."

"It is, you *dork*. Now let's just get some food in you, and—"

"Food isn't going to help," he finally broke, and that was a lie. Food would definitely help, but he didn't care right now. She poked and she poked, and then she downplayed his feelings, and he was sick of it. He sucked in a deep breath, trying to keep it together, but everything he wasn't saying was bubbling to the surface now. "Forget it," he tried, taking a step back. "I can find my way to the hotel on my own."

"Of course you can." She advanced, and hurt crept into her voice again, skewering him through. "Since you're so fond of doing everything on your own all of a sudden."

"That's not fair."

None of this was fair.

"What's not fair is you telling me you want one thing and then going and doing something else." Brightness flashed at the corners of her eyes. "What's not fair is you acting like everything was great with us for the entire summer and then deciding to move out behind my back."

"Like you didn't do it first," he hurled, and oh yeah, the seal had burst now. He was a volcano, struggling desperately not to explode, but the pressure was finally too much.

"What—"

"You're the one who applied to all those residencies this spring. You decided to leave."

She shook her head. "But I didn't—"

"But you were going to. You were going to leave me." And he would have been fine. Heck, it would have broken the cycle he'd stuck himself in. No way he could have kept hopelessly holding this torch for her if she'd been on the other side of the country.

No, she didn't get in.

But it didn't matter. Everything had changed. She'd pretended to just go back to normal, but there was no normal anymore.

He couldn't keep living with her and wishing for more. He needed to face the fact that she was never going to want what he did. She might not have left then, but she would. Someday.

He had to move on. No matter how much it killed him to.

She sucked in a breath, realization dawning. "Is that what this is about? Because I'm done with that. I'm staying. You can stay."

"I can't." It was like pulling a Band-Aid off only to find another flipping Band-Aid lying right there underneath, over and over again.

"Why?" she yelled, and it was too loud. Everyone was looking. They were having this argument here, in a random tent in a random town, surrounded by strangers, but they had to have it.

The only way out was through.

"Because—" he started.

But she wasn't listening. "What are you looking for? What won't you tell me?"

And heaven help him. Her eyes blazed with hurt and anger, and he'd seen that look on her face before. He'd seen her leave her mother's house, indignant and deserving so much better than she'd gotten, seen her claw her way back after rejection upon rejection, seen her build a life full of art and creativity and laughter and...

...and...

Before he knew it, he'd closed the space between them. He stood near enough to feel the warmth of her. Her soft scent of vanilla and jasmine wrapped around him, and her cheeks were flushed, her dark eyes going wide, and she was so beautiful he could scarcely breathe, and he was about to make the biggest mistake of his life.

He wanted to laugh. All this time. All these years.

These two miserable weeks of trying to hide his reasons, but he never could hide much. Not from her.

And honestly. At this point...

What exactly did he have left to lose?

Something electric zipped down his spine. He tingled all over, adrenaline flooding his system, and that was his only excuse.

"You want to know why I'm really leaving? You want to know what I'm not telling you?" He sucked in a breath.

She nodded.

He reached for her, dragging her in. He crushed his mouth to hers, and she gasped, and that wasn't right. None of this was how this was supposed to go, but it was his only chance.

He kissed her, firm and terrible and the most wonderful thing he'd ever felt. She tasted like her cherry lip gloss, and she was warm and so perfect in his arms, and he was going to imprint this in his memory—forever.

For a second—one taunting, brilliant fraction of a second—she kissed him back, gripping his shirt to keep him where he was. He had exactly long enough for his heart to rise and an impossible thrill to shoot through his body.

Then the hand on his shirt went firm. She pushed him back, breaking the kiss, and he let her go as if she'd hit him with a cattle prod.

"E—"

"What the hell, Graham?"

And he was so, so screwed. Her lips shone pink, and he was never going to be able to look at her the same way again.

From the sheer shock in her gaze, she was never going to be able to look at him the same way again, either.

His heart sank into his toes. A fresh wave of misery and mortification washed over him.

Because suddenly he remembered.

What exactly did he have to lose?

Everything.

CHAPTER ELEVEN

✿ ✿ ✿ ✿ ✿ ✿ ✿ ✿ ✿ ✿ ✿ ✿ ✿

What. Just. Happened.

Elizabeth put her hand to her lips, gawking in utter confusion at the guy she was closest with in the entire world. The dude she shared her life and her home with. He'd seen her bras hanging from the curtain rod in their bathroom. He'd seen her with bedhead and the flu, and he'd listened to her rant for fifteen years now about...well, everything. He knew every single one of her screwups.

And he was currently backing away from her slowly. After having *kissed* her.

What a kiss, too. Awkward at first because she hadn't known what the blippety-blip was going on there for a second, but then she'd melted into it. He'd smelled like sandalwood and Funyuns and *home*, and when he'd opened his mouth against hers, she'd lost her mind for half a breath.

Then she'd remembered. This was Graham pressing his lips to hers.

Her mind whirled.

Before she could put it together to say a single functional sentence, he took another step away from her. "I'm so sorry."

"What—" she started. But her brain kept on short-circuiting. "I. Just. How?"

Misery colored his expression, and oh God, she was messing this all up.

But he had kissed her. Worse, he had kissed her by way of answering the questions *Why are you leaving?* and *What are you not telling me?*

Which opened a whole new bucket of worms.

He was leaving because he wanted to kiss her. He wasn't telling her that *he wanted to kiss her*, and—

Her stomach flipped itself inside out, everything she'd known and assumed about their friendship going up in smoke. Her voice cracked as she asked, "How long?"

Because this hadn't been some impulsive thing. Well, okay, clearly it had, but it hadn't been some impulsive thing he hadn't thought about before. This kiss had meant something.

"Does it matter?" he replied. Based on the fact that his face had gone white as a sheet and his ears had flared crimson, she was pretty sure that, yeah, it mattered. It mattered a lot.

Too much.

"Graham..." Her heart squeezed so hard she couldn't breathe.

All this time? No. It wasn't possible.

But apparently it was.

"I know, I know." How did he manage to sound more tortured with every word? "Just." His whole face crumpled. "Forget it."

"How?"

"Please. Pretend it never happened."

"But—"

Before she could say another word, he turned.

"Graham, wait—"

He shook his head. Spine straight, gaze focused ahead, he stalked out of the tent, and she darted forward to follow him.

But then she stopped herself. She stared after him, agape, torn in half by her warring instincts. He was distraught. Going after him was second nature.

His reason for being distraught at the moment, though, was . . .

. . . her.

As he disappeared into the crowd, the rest of the world seeped back in. She glanced around. A handful of old ladies were watching, looking for all the world like they regretted not bringing popcorn to the show. Over by the paintings she'd been admiring, a middle-aged man smiled ruefully. To a buddy standing next to him, he said quietly, "And here I thought they were going to buy a painting."

Elizabeth's cheeks flamed.

"Sorry," she mumbled to him. Then more loudly, she added, "We really do love your work."

The artist smiled, and Elizabeth turned away. She made her way outside, head in a fog, still lost as far as where to go.

Chasing after Graham now would probably be the worst of all worlds. He'd been pretty clear in his message that he wanted to forget this ever happened.

And she'd been pretty clear that there was no way on earth she could imagine doing that.

A little bit of time to cool down and think this through would probably help them both. Nerves rattled around in the pit of her stomach, though. He'd driven them here, so he had the car keys. He wouldn't just get in and start driving, would he?

No. That was much more her style than his. He was responsible, loyal.

And angry. Miserable after letting go of a secret he'd apparently been holding on to now for, what? Fifteen years?

The whole idea still boggled her mind. As she wandered aimlessly through the festival, she replayed their entire friendship in her head, looking for the signs, but if he'd really had feelings for her this entire time, what sorts of signs was she even supposed to be looking for?

When they'd first met in middle school, he'd been a little tongue-tied around her, she guessed. He'd been shy around everyone back then, though, so she'd never imagined it had anything in particular to do with her.

Had he ever said anything that should have tipped her off? He definitely hadn't when they were in high school. She would remember that.

Or would she?

In those days, she'd been an untamed ball of rebellion. Her mom and Ned and her sisters had been so stifling. Her mom had demanded perfection and obedience, while Elizabeth just hadn't been cut out for that sort of thing, so she'd gone as far as she could in the opposite direction. Her dating life had been no exception. The more inappropriate the guy or girl who happened to catch her eye, the better.

Graham, who had slowly but steadily become a part of her inner circle in those years, hadn't even been on her radar, romantically. Even then, he'd been prim and proper. Straight A student. His mom ironed his jeans. It was honestly a testament to how fun and easy he was to hang out with that she'd ended up remaining friends with him at all. He was more June's type than hers.

Bringing him around the inn probably just gave her mom false hope.

After that, though...

Dating people exclusively for their shock value lost a lot of its appeal after she moved out of her mom and stepdad's house. They were already disappointed and betrayed; piling any more drama on top of that seemed like overkill.

By then, she and Graham were well established in their dynamic. Even if the newer, more sedate her of the past half dozen years had considered him as a possible partner, he'd made his preferences clear. He liked women who were responsible and family oriented.

Or at least that was what she'd thought, right up until this afternoon.

She stopped dead in the middle of the street, and the people behind her mumbled a few choice words as they shifted course to go around her.

Of course. This afternoon. When she'd told him what she thought of his taste in women and he'd said that she was wrong.

Worse, he'd told her that he wanted...

...her.

Oh no. That was what he'd been saying, wasn't it? Only she hadn't heard it, because it had always seemed so clear that he liked women who wanted the same things he did out of life.

She'd had good reason to think that, too. He'd never been unclear about his general goals. Chill job, helping people. House a few miles from his parents' place. Wife. Kids.

The handful of women he'd dated over the years had more or less fit the image she had in her head, too.

And okay, maybe in hindsight none of them were quite as Betty Crocker as she'd imagined he would want, but she'd figured, hey, nobody was perfect.

Except he'd kissed *her*. He'd looked her in the eyes, and in that brief, fleeting moment before he'd reeled her in and pressed his mouth to hers, she could have sworn...

...to him, she *was* perfect.

She started walking again, not paying attention to where she was going, utterly in a daze.

She wanted to laugh. Didn't he know better? They'd been best buddies for half their lives. Nobody better understood her flaws.

But he liked her anyway.

If she weren't so horrified and ashamed, she'd probably be flattered.

Graham was the best guy she knew. No one on earth was kinder or more supportive or a better listener or a better friend. Nobody else put up with her crap or seemed to enjoy her company as much. Nobody else brought out the best in her or challenged her the same way. She was at her most comfortable with him.

She couldn't lose him as a friend. It was not an option. She had to handle this just right.

She'd go back to the hotel. She'd tell him in her kindest, most grown-up voice that she didn't see him the same way.

Only...

...she'd never so much as allowed herself to think about him that way. He lived one hundred percent in friendship territory in her mind. She'd always known that he deserved—and wanted—better than her, so she'd never considered looking for anything more from him.

But then she replayed her last few minutes of bewildered rambling to herself. *No one in the world* was a better fit for her. These past couple weeks, when she couldn't read him and thought that she was losing him, both as a roommate and a friend, she'd been a mess.

It wasn't as if a deep bond like theirs had to be romantic. Platonic love was love all the same.

If things really were as platonic between them as she'd convinced herself they were, would she have responded in the same way to his kiss, though?

Would she have spent the past two weeks suppressing these weird, tingly new feelings she was having whenever they touched? Or trying to pretend she didn't think he looked obnoxiously hot with his new beard?

Would she be thinking about what it would be like to try kissing him again? This time with her head on straight and her eyes open?

Somehow, over the course of her little mental breakdown, she'd managed to meander her way back to their hotel. She slowed as she approached it. It was a cute place—not as cute as the Sweetbriar Inn, of course, but still cute.

Inside, Graham had probably twisted himself into a pretzel by now.

She stared at the hotel's front door for a really, really long time.

Finally, her heart pounding, her fingers and toes tingling with nerves, she took a deep breath and headed in.

Graham was going to wear a hole in the carpet. He paced the length of the room again. Every time he completed his circuit, he got stuck in the same loop.

He should go. Pacing outside would be better than

pacing in here. Fresh air always did him good, but he couldn't handle the throngs of people out there. He definitely couldn't look at art, and he didn't know the area beyond this little strip.

He should *go*. Get in the car and drive. He'd leave a note, of course, plus money for a rental and the number for a place to call, and seriously—did he actually think that he could do that? Just run away from this?

There was no getting away from Elizabeth. He laughed, unhinged, and raked a hand through his hair. He'd been trying to shake himself out of her orbit for the past few months, and look where it had gotten him.

For fifteen years, he'd kept his secret.

Now it was out there, and he was so mortified, he wanted to . . . to . . .

He jerked around and raised his fist.

Only to drop it.

Punching walls was stupid. It only hurt the wall and you.

He had to stay. He'd acted rashly, and now it was time to face the music.

But even as he started pacing again, rehearsing how on earth he'd talk his way out of this, the misery swirling around in the pit of his stomach was joined by a faint thread of lightness.

His secret was out. Yes, there was going to be fallout, but he didn't have to lie anymore. After she kindly but awkwardly let him down, he'd probably have to go back to pretending he didn't have feelings for her, but it wouldn't have to be this weight on his chest.

Maybe he could really, actually move on.

He laughed again, but at least it sounded less serial killer–y, so that was progress.

Before he could get too proud of himself, the sound of footsteps in the hallway outside their room shattered his calm. He turned toward the door, half expecting it to be another false alarm—there were a lot of people staying here, what with the festival and all.

The footsteps stopped, though. He held his breath. When the lock made that little whirring noise, his brain went haywire, and then the door opened, revealing none other than Elizabeth...

...beautiful, brilliant, strong, incredible Elizabeth, her long black hair tousled by the wind, her flowing skirt swirling around her ankles, her cheeks flushed. His heart tightened like a vise, and his brain shot off in a rocket to outer space, taking all his carefully worded speeches with it.

All he could manage to say was "We don't have to talk about it."

Stupid. Of course they had to talk about it. He *wanted* to talk about it.

"Just pretend it never happened," he begged.

She regarded him for a long minute. Why hadn't he left? He could have wandered the beach and gotten kidnapped by pirates and drafted into the merchant marines and it would have been *great*.

Whereas this—this was torture.

Silently, projecting a serenity he knew one hundred percent for sure was just for show, she took off her jacket and tossed it on top of her suitcase. She crossed the room toward him.

Foolish, reckless, idiotic hope sparked through his lungs. He fought to douse it with the cold water of his heart. She was going to let him down gently. That was always how this was going to end.

"Look," he tried again, and why couldn't he stop *talking*?

"So it occurs to me," she said quietly, coming to stand barely two feet away from him, "that I may not have reacted completely coherently out there."

He barked out a laugh that was only slightly serial killer–y. "It's not your reaction that needs explaining."

"I think it does, though." Slowly, as if she were approaching a skittish animal—and really, was the comparison all that far off?—she reached out a hand.

Her fingertips tracing down the side of his face burned, even through the beard. Pain flashed along his ribs.

"E…"

"I like the beard. And the contacts. They make you look really handsome."

"Thanks?" What was happening here? His brain began to filter back into his cranium, but it was only in bits and pieces.

She swallowed. "You've always been handsome."

This was the weirdest gentle letdown in the history of the world. "You don't have to—"

"You caught me by surprise." She dropped her hand to rest it against his chest, and pinpricks of electricity zipped along his ribs. "One second you were my weird, dorky best friend Graham, being annoying and inscrutable."

"Um…"

"And the next…" Her gaze flickered down to his mouth and then back up. "The next you were kissing me."

He remembered.

Oh, wow, did he remember. It rushed back to him now. The heat of her lips and the way her body seemed to fit so perfectly against his. The shock of it all. The pleasure— and the hopelessness.

"I'm sorry, E, I should have asked—"

"Shh."

He clamped his mouth shut so hard it hurt his jaw.

"You took me by surprise. But this whole time I've been wandering around the festival, trying to figure out what just happened, I—" She paused to lick her lips, and what was she doing to him? "I couldn't stop thinking about it."

"You couldn't?" His voice *squeaked*—this was pathetic.

She shook her head. "You took me by surprise, and I—I was wondering." She paused again, because she was actually trying to kill him. "Could we try it again?"

There went his brain. Poof. Exploded in a cloud of smoke, while in his chest, despair and elation did a dance on his heart.

"Elizabeth..." Did it all come through in that one little word?

Then she was bridging the sliver of space remaining between them. Her hand on his chest rose to cup the back of his neck. His vision swam.

She tugged gently, rising onto her tiptoes at the same time.

When she pressed her mouth to his, he saw stars. His battered heart broke and reformed all at once. Without his leave, his hands went to her waist.

Her lips parting, she darted forward with her tongue, and that was it.

In a haze of disbelief and wonder, he tugged her in, crushing their mouths together. Her taste seared into him, and he'd wanted this for so long.

He still couldn't trust it.

He pulled away to gasp. "You have to mean it. This can't be a game. Not for me."

"It's not," she promised automatically, and he didn't doubt her for a second.

She could be thoughtless sometimes. Oblivious, clearly. But she was never cruel. She wouldn't play with his heart. At least not on purpose.

She bit her lip, and he braced himself. "But this is all really new for me, you know? I didn't see it coming."

"I got that," he said dryly. This time when he chuckled, it hardly sounded maniacal at all.

Just sad.

"Not because you're not a great guy," she swore.

"Sure—"

"I just never thought about it." She shook her head. "That wasn't how we were."

He forced himself to loosen his hold on her. "It's fine."

"But maybe we could be."

The renewed spark of hope twinkling inside of him was deadly. "E…"

"Not a game," she promised. "More of…an experiment."

He didn't like the sounds of that, either. He went to pull away, even though it killed him.

But she held on tight. "How do we know?" she asked. "How do we know if we fit together that way if we don't…" She gestured vaguely at the space between them. "You know."

He raised a brow.

"Ugh," she groaned, "you know what I mean. If we don't"—she swallowed—"try it out."

Any remnants of his brain poured out his ears.

Try it out.

Was she?

No.

"You want," he breathed.

"Only if you want."

"I want." The words came out too intense. Wow, did he want.

But that still didn't change anything.

And it didn't seem to for her, either. "I can't promise you anything." She took his hand in hers. "Except that we will *always* be best friends. Always. No matter what."

Could he handle that? One night of being with her the way he'd always dreamed of, full with the knowledge that it might be the only one?

"We don't have to," she hedged.

No matter which way he went, he'd be a fool. A fool for missing his chance if he said no. A fool for risking the most important friendship of his life if he said yes.

As if she could sense how torn he was, she leaned in closer. Holding his gaze, she pressed one more achingly soft kiss to his lips.

She started to pull away.

And only one thing was absolutely certain.

He'd be the biggest fool of all if he let her go.

CHAPTER TWELVE

❋ ❋ ❋ ❋ ❋ ❋ ❋ ❋ ❋ ❋ ❋ ❋

About a million emotions flitted across Graham's face as Elizabeth stood there, holding her breath. She'd done a lot of reckless things in her life; heck, she'd gotten herself and Graham arrested that once. But even having Officer Dwight catch them getting a little carried away with the "defacement of public property" part of their senior prank had nothing on the cliff she'd careened them toward this time.

Yes, Graham had been the one to kiss her.

But she'd been the one to ask him to kiss her again.

She was the one who'd offered to go a whole lot further than kissing, and this had to be the wildest risk she'd ever taken.

But suddenly, standing at the edge of the precipice, waiting increasingly impatiently for him to decide whether to pull her back from it or take the leap, it occurred to her that he might very well say no.

One hour ago, she'd never had more than a casual, passing thought about sleeping with her best friend. Now, the idea that they might not was crushing her.

"Graham," she started, a hint of the sudden panic she was feeling creeping into her voice.

Just like that, his gaze snapped back into focus. Determination flashed across his eyes. He reached for her, and she just about fell over, the relief crashed into her so hard.

They both dove into the kiss this time, all the tentativeness and the weirdness finally fading away. His mouth was soft and warm, the onion snack-breath gone, replaced by the mint of his toothpaste and a taste that was just... *him*. A thrill shot through her at the thought of discovering if that was really true or not when she kissed him again tomorrow and the next day and the next, and *wow*, her brain was getting ahead of itself.

So much for an experiment to see if they had any chemistry. Apparently, they had a metric ton.

As they kissed, he walked her backward through the room toward the closest bed—his, thankfully, considering hers was currently occupied by half the contents of her suitcase. His was pristine, though, because of course it was. He parted from her lips just long enough to shove the covers back.

Then, to her absolute shock, he all but tackled her onto it.

"Whoa, tiger," she laughed between hungry, delicious kisses.

"Sorry." He started to pull away, but she dragged him right back down.

"Don't be."

With a groan, he attacked her mouth, and seriously, honestly, she'd never put any thought into this. But three days ago, if anyone had asked her what she thought her best friend would be like in the sack, first she'd have told them that that was a super weird thing to be thinking about. Pressed, she'd have guessed he'd be considerate, gentle, slow, and methodical—and he was all of that.

What she wouldn't have predicted was the fire in his kiss, or the way he'd press her down into the mattress. How he'd use his teeth or how sure his hands would be as they skated up and down her sides.

A moan escaped her as he blanketed her with his body. One of his legs fell between hers, and the weight of him against her center sent a shock of pleasure zipping up her spine. She gasped, and he groaned and ground into her, and her eyes sprang open.

Holy crap.

Her best friend was *hung*.

"You've been holding out on me," she said, panting, reaching a hand into the space between them to curl around his length through his jeans.

His eyes fluttered closed like he was in either ecstasy or pain. "Sorry?"

"Stop apologizing."

"I'd say sorry, but..."

This was ridiculous.

She dipped her hand beneath his waistband, and that sure got him to stop talking already.

It kind of shut her up, too, thank goodness, or she probably would have said something completely inappropriate about the fact that she was touching his dick, and if she ruined the mood right now, she'd hate herself forever.

Instead, she gave him a tentative stroke. The sound he made as he pushed into her touch lit her up inside. It suddenly occurred to her that she could be touching a lot more of him, too. With her other hand, she pushed up his shirt, and *holy abs, Batman*.

She wanted to ask him when he'd gotten so ripped,

but again, no stupid questions right now. Instead, she just enjoyed all that smooth, hot skin that was suddenly available to her.

She probably shouldn't have been surprised when he decided to do precisely the same.

She still was, though, her breath catching as he slipped a hand beneath her top. When he cupped her rear and kissed his way down to the valley of her breasts.

And lower...

Buy a girl dinner first, she thought to herself, delirious, but as she stared up at the ceiling and let him pull down her skirt and underwear, she remembered exactly how many times he'd done that already. Hundreds of dinners over more than a dozen years, and then his mouth was on her, and she could barely think anymore.

Not to wonder how he'd learned to be such an expert at this particular skill, and not to ponder how they could have been doing this after all those dinners over all those years.

All she could think about was how good it felt.

How right.

Just as the pleasure threatened to become too much, though, she reached for him.

He started to shake his head, clearly a man who finished what he started, but she tugged harder at his hair. "I want you inside me when I—"

He scrambled up her body at speed then. It was all a mad rush as she tore off his clothes. Before she knew it, they were both naked, and when had he gotten so hot? He stared down at her with the same wonder in his eyes, and it was almost too intense to be looked at that way. To be seen for more than she had ever really imagined herself to be.

She swallowed hard as second thoughts crowded her mind. What if she really wasn't what he thought she was? What if his interest in her turned to dust once they actually crossed this line?

What if their friendship did? The magnitude of the risk they were taking by sailing into uncharted territory like this was almost too big to contemplate.

Like he could sense her momentary panic, he brushed a fingertip down her cheek. He nudged her chin up until she was gazing right into his eyes again. Just like that, her fears melted away. "You're so beautiful."

He really believed that, didn't he? The absolute certainty in his voice soothed her further. Taking this step with him was risky, sure. But they were *them*. They'd figure it out, no matter what happened next.

"You're not so bad yourself," she teased.

A flicker of a smile curled his lips. He kissed her again, soft and warm.

It didn't stay either warm or soft for long, though. Heat grew everywhere they touched, and she broke away. "Where's my bag?"

He got up to get it, and she absolutely watched his backside as he went. He returned, fast, and she dug in the zippered pocket for a condom. She handed it to him, and his Adam's apple bobbed.

He put it on and settled back into the cradle of her thighs. Butterflies swirled in her stomach, which was absurd. This was just sex. And it was just Graham.

But sex with Graham...

He kissed her again, blanking her mind.

"You sure?" he breathed.

She wasn't sure about anything.

Except that she wanted this.

She nodded, brushing a hand through his hair. "Yeah."

Slowly, he pressed inside.

As he did, her world turned inside out.

After this, nothing between them was ever going to be the same.

But maybe, she thought, as they began to move, that could be a good thing.

Somehow, miraculously, they might be *better*.

A couple of hours later, Graham lay on his back, sweating, gasping, and generally reduced to a euphoric post-orgasm lump. Elizabeth rolled off of him with a groan and flopped down beside him.

"Well," she said, sounding about as dazed as he felt, "I don't know about you, but I'd call that experiment a success."

How she managed to string together so many words in a row escaped him.

He nodded as vigorously as he could after three rounds of mind-blowing sex with the woman he'd been in love with for over a decade.

He turned his neck to look at her, and his heart melted all over again. Postcoital, she was *glowing*, her soft, bare skin gorgeous and golden. Her full pink lips were parted and her tangle of hair was spread out across the pillow like she was a mermaid.

All he could do was pray she wasn't actually a siren.

With a groan, he sat up. He dealt with the condom then returned to the bed. He pulled the covers up, because she was always cold. She smiled gratefully and snuggled into him, slotting her feet between his thighs, and his chest squeezed so hard he could barely breathe. How many nights had they spent sitting on the couch, fully clothed, her cold feet tucked under his calves for warmth?

This was their friendship, right here. Only naked.

He wanted to laugh—not psychotically at all, thank you very much. A very normal, sedate laugh.

All this time, he'd had feelings for her romantically but he'd rarely allowed himself to think about much more than kissing her. But even if he had, he never could have imagined how their partnership would translate to the bedroom. How they could be so eerily in sync. How giving and soft she'd be, or what noises she'd make when he touched her. How it would feel to lose himself inside her.

How it would feel now. When the heat of passion had been quelled, leaving them just... them.

But naked.

It was the stuff of his wildest dreams, honestly.

So why was the elation filling his chest accompanied by a swirling sense of unease? Was it just that this all felt too good to be true?

Or was it the fact that this had been a successful experiment—had it ever—but deep down, at least in Elizabeth's mind, it was still just that?

An experiment. One she could decide to bring to an end whenever she wanted to.

Where would that leave him and his wildest dreams then?

Without warning, Elizabeth peeked beneath the covers, letting in a draft of cold air.

"Hey—"

"Just checking if you're wearing your overthinking socks."

Right. The pair she'd gotten him for Christmas a

couple of years ago. They looked like normal black dress socks from the toe to the ankle, but higher up, where they'd be hidden by his pants, they said in frenetic, neon green letters, "Shh, I'm busy overthinking things."

He relaxed back into the pillow. Leave it to Elizabeth to call him out on that, even now.

Desert dry, he told her, "As you can see, I'm not wearing anything at all."

Neither was she, a fact he was trying to ignore, but with little success.

"Yes, I did notice that." She let the covers fall back over them. Rolling over onto her side, she propped her head up on one hand. With the other, she reached out and poked at his bottom lip. "Now spill."

Catching her hand in his, he gave her fingertips a little kiss, still blown away by the fact that he was allowed to do that and that it wasn't weird at all. He narrowed his eyes at her as he let her go. "Just to be fair, it's not as if I'm the only one here who's been doing some overthinking."

That first time they'd fallen into bed together, she'd gotten this look on her face—like she couldn't decide if he was a wonder or if she was about to freak out and call the whole thing off. He'd practically been able to hear the gears turning in her head. He might have even caught a whiff of smoke.

She'd made up her mind quickly enough, thank goodness. If she hadn't, he'd been about to call things off himself. He had no desire to push things past where she enthusiastically consented for them to go.

The taste of her uncertainty had lingered, though. Even now, it fueled his own.

"That's fair," she allowed.

He searched her gaze for a moment. All he really

wanted to do was bask in the afterglow, but keeping his overthinking socks on, even metaphorically, was going to ruin it anyway.

"I'm just…" Gathering his words, he ran his fingertip along hers. Finally, he settled on "…wondering what comes next."

She covered his hand with her own. "Well"—a sparkle twinkled in her eye—"first, I'm thinking snacks. Then maybe sleep?"

He loved her so freaking much. Her lightness; her ability to take things one step at a time.

But that wasn't helping him with his metaphorical sock situation. Gently, he asked, "And then?"

"I don't know."

That was what he'd been afraid of. He pulled back by a fraction, bracing himself for the worst, but before he could get too far, she caught his hands again. Half sitting up, she squeezed his fingers tight.

"All I know, Graham, is that you are the most important person in the world to me." Sincerity made her voice crack.

"You're the most important person in the world to me, too."

"I like what we just did." Her eyes widened meaningfully. "*Three times*."

His body stirred at the reminder. "Me, too."

She raised a brow. "I want to do it again."

He bit his tongue against the impulse to make a joke. *Just give him a minute.*

But she wasn't talking about a fourth round right now. Neither was he.

He waited for a second, watching the hesitation in her eyes. Quietly, his heart falling, he continued for her. "But?"

She let out a rough breath. "But keeping you as my friend is the most important part."

That didn't sound like bad news.

"Okay," he agreed. "Then let's make sure we do that."

Her forehead crinkled. "You really think it could be that easy?"

Definitely not.

"I think it sounds like we both want the same things."

"Which are..." She held his gaze, like she was trying to pluck the words from his brain, and to be fair, she did a pretty good job. "...to make sure we stay friends, and to be, you know—" She gestured between the two of them. "This, too."

Seriously. The stuff of his wildest dreams.

Doing his best to tamp down his pounding heart, he nodded. "That would be my vote." This was the important part, though. "But only if it's what you want, too."

She thought carefully, and it both killed him and made him feel so much better. She could be happy-go-lucky sometimes, but she was treating this with the seriousness it deserved.

"I think I want to try."

Okay, fine, he gave up. He let go his tight control of his hope, and his heart exploded into fireworks in his chest. A smile so big it hurt spread across his face.

"I'm so happy you said that."

With that, he attacked her again, kissing her senseless, and who knew what would happen next? All she'd said was that she wanted to try. It was an upgrade from an experiment, but it was still provisional at best. This wasn't a marriage proposal.

It was still amazing, and he was going to enjoy it for as long as he could.

She melted into the kiss, and they got lost in it for a while.

Eventually, she came up for air, though. Nudging him back, she asked, serious again, "Do you think we should tell people?"

He wanted to shout it from the rooftops.

But he could also see the other side of things. Their friends were going to give them so much crap about this.

And if it didn't work out...If "trying" didn't end up being enough for her...Or if after a few weeks she remembered that she liked exciting people and that he was still boring, uptight, overthinking him...

...the pain of their experiment failing would be bad enough. Keeping this a secret might at least spare him adding in some public mortification, too. Struggling to keep his voice neutral, he asked, "What do you think?"

"I think I don't want to hide." She ran her fingertips through his hair, one corner of her mouth tilting down. "But I also don't want my mom to give me that *look*."

He knew exactly the one. His mom and dad had their own versions of it that they were going to train on him too. "Me neither," he agreed. He hesitated before asking "So where does that leave us?"

"I guess..." Her teeth worried at her soft bottom lip. "...we just act like us? But with more hand-holding?"

"Only not in front of our mothers."

"For now," she hurried to add. "Just while we're seeing if this all fits."

And okay. Yeah. That made sense. It was so much more than he had ever dared to hope for. She was really truly going to give this a chance.

While also leaving room for the chance that it wouldn't fit.

He swallowed hard. "And if it doesn't?"

She gazed up into his eyes. Firm, she told him, "Then we just go back to being best friends."

Because that was their priority. They'd both agreed as much.

He managed a smile before dipping down to kiss her again.

Because even as he was agreeing with her about their plan to try this out, his heart was twisting in his chest.

Going back to being best friends was a good option. A great one, even. One he'd counted himself lucky to have back a couple of weeks ago, when he'd finally decided to move on.

But now that he'd had this taste of more...now that he knew what it felt like to be able to press his lips to her fingertips and curl his hand around her side...

...could they ever really go back?

CHAPTER THIRTEEN

There she is!" The next morning, Elizabeth spotted her friend Kat standing beside the entrance to the coffee shop where they'd agreed to meet. Kat was a white woman in her thirties with curly red hair, a knitwear wardrobe to rival Elizabeth's own, and the coolest tattoos running all up and down her arms.

Kat looked up from her phone to scan the crowd, and Elizabeth lifted one hand to wave. The other she curled even more tightly around Graham's. A little thrill went through her as he squeezed back.

She glanced up at him. It was wild how much could change in so short a time. Yesterday, they'd been dancing on each other's last nerves. She'd been stuck in this cycle of provoking him and feeling hurt when it turned out that all of her assumptions were wrong.

She could never have guessed the biggest wrong assumption of them all.

He liked her. Like, *liked her* liked her.

And after an enthusiastic night of experimentation, she'd come to the tentative conclusion that she might *like him* like him, too.

It was too soon to say anything for sure. They might have done a one-eighty from their dynamic yesterday, but rewriting fifteen-odd years of history was another matter. She'd told him she wanted to pursue this new connection between the two of them and see where it might lead.

The pressure of getting it right hung over her head, though. Her mom wasn't the only one who was going to give them smug looks when she found out. All of their friends would have opinions, too. Then there was Graham's family. Phew boy, was she ever not looking forward to hearing—from Graham—what Judge Lewis was going to have to say. Heaven knew he would never say it to her directly, but Graham would get an earful. Then he'd act like it didn't bother him, but deep down, it would drive him nuts.

Not that any of that was worth borrowing trouble about right now. Today, they were at an arts festival by the beach. The sun was shining and Graham was gorgeous and all her worries about their new, developing, experimental relationship status could wait until they got back to Blue Cedar Falls.

Quickening her pace, she led Graham over to where Kat was waiting for them.

Kat beamed, holding out her arms. "Look at you! You're early!"

"Wonders never cease." Grinning, Elizabeth dropped Graham's hand to throw her arms around her friend, not mentioning that she was mostly early because she hated irritating Graham with being late.

Kat hugged her back. "It's so good to see you."

"You, too." Elizabeth pulled away, pausing to admire the knit fabric looped around Kat's neck. "Oh, wow, this is gorgeous. Is it a Nightshift?" Elizabeth had been eyeing that shawl pattern for ages.

"Sure is. The yarn is to dye for." Kat smirked. "Get it? To *dye* for? With a 'Y'?"

Letting go of the end of the shawl, Elizabeth groaned.

Beside her, Graham said, "I get it."

"You would," Elizabeth said fondly. She patted his arm. "Graham, this is Kat. Kat, Graham."

"Graham, huh?" Kat shot Elizabeth a saucy look that said she remembered the name.

Elizabeth ignored the implication behind her gaze. Beautiful day, fun festival, no borrowing trouble about what people were going to think about her hooking up with her best friend. Right? Right.

Graham extended his hand like a perfect gentleman, even if his ears were turning red. "Pleased to meet you."

"Hey, there you are." A tall Asian guy with short, spiky black hair, a killer jaw line, and an awesome black leather jacket sidled up to them.

Graham's eyes lit up. "David, hi."

They exchanged a little side hug, and Elizabeth raised her brows. "I thought you said your municipal government buddy was a nerd."

This David guy was anything but.

Graham opened his mouth as if to explain, but David waved them both off. "It's cool, I'm definitely a nerd when it comes to local government."

"Spoken like a true politician," Kat said, a small, wry smile on her face.

"You two know each other?" Elizabeth asked.

"Small town," David explained. "Everybody knows everybody."

Graham laughed. "We might know a thing or two about that."

They headed inside together to grab a table. As they

got settled in, Elizabeth and Kat caught up, and David and Graham did much the same. A server came by to grab their orders, and once they had their coffees in hand, David looked to Elizabeth and Graham expectantly. "So, I hear you guys are trying to piggyback off our glory over on the obviously inferior mountain side of the state."

Graham scoffed. "'Inferior.'"

"I just call 'em like I see 'em." David lifted his hands in front of himself.

"Now, now." Kat rolled her eyes. "Both sides of the state have their perks."

"Like beaches," David said.

"Look—" Graham started, and ooh boy, time to nip this argument in the bud.

"So yeah," Elizabeth interrupted, "I'm trying to get a clothesline arts festival off the ground, and a fuddy duddy gallery owner down the way is trying to stop me, and I need your help."

All gazes turned to her. Graham grinned, while David smirked in amusement.

Kat let go of her coffee to rub her palms together. "Well, why didn't you say so?"

To Elizabeth's delight, Kat was not just a participant in the Four Winds Arts Festival; she was also on the organizing committee—a fact she really could have volunteered when they texted about meeting up a few days ago, but Elizabeth of all people appreciated that late was better than never. Graham pulled a notebook and a pen out of nowhere, while Elizabeth opened up the note-taking app on her phone, and they furiously took down everything Kat had to offer about how the event here in Half Moon Cove had come together, as well as how it had evolved over the years.

"I'll send you our PowerPoint we give to the budgeting committee every year," Kat promised.

"And I'll give you the budgeting committee's analysis of their PowerPoint," David said to Graham. "It's less colorful, but it does have more numbers on it."

Kat swatted at him, mocking indignance. "Hey!"

"Am I wrong?"

"You can be both right and rude." Kat crossed her arms over her chest.

"We'd be grateful for both," Graham said smoothly.

"It's been a great event." David gestured outside. "You can see we bring in quite a crowd."

"It really picked up after we started advertising more widely," Kat added. "It easily pays for itself these days, though, and local businesses are thrilled by all the extra visitors."

That would be a good selling point. Would it be enough to overcome Patty's objections, though?

Elizabeth frowned. "How about your more establishment art scene?"

The Four Winds Festival had that independent artist vibe Elizabeth was particularly hoping she could bring to Blue Cedar Falls with her show.

"It's a delicate balance," Kat conceded. "The vast majority of the artists whose work we feature aren't represented by galleries, but some are. In the end, it was easier to make peace than it was to make war." She shrugged. "The couple of art dealers we have here have become 'partners.' We have a tent showcasing their people's work."

Ugh. That sounded miserable. How could she possibly "partner" with a person who put her work down every chance she got? She could hear Patty's voice in her head, snidely disparaging the other artists she and her committee would end up selecting for the show. They deserved to be celebrated, not dumped on yet again.

Her opinion must have been clear on her face.

"It's not all bad," Kat promised. "Most of the stuff they choose is pretty good, and the selection committee does confer with the dealers about what goes in and how it fits with the theme and the rest of the work."

"And everybody's happy with that compromise?" Graham asked carefully.

"Happy might be a strong word, but it seems to work."

Elizabeth still wasn't convinced. Patty's soulless, corporate taste would stick out like a sore thumb in the kind of festival Elizabeth envisioned. But there wasn't any point belaboring this. "We'll take it under advisement."

"Anything else we should consider?" Graham asked David.

David had a few other tips, but most of it was in government-ese, putting paid to her original idea that a guy who looked that cool couldn't possibly be a nerd; he definitely was one. Elizabeth ended up typing a few lines full of question marks into her notes app. But that was okay. Graham would fill her in on the finer points later.

As David wound down, Kat glanced at her watch and winced. "So sorry to cut this short, but I actually have to run. But I'll be at the abstract art panel tonight if you want to swing by?"

"Wouldn't miss it," Elizabeth agreed. She stood to give Kat a hug before she took off.

David downed the rest of his coffee, too, reiterating his plan to send Graham a bunch more specifics before heading toward the door. Elizabeth watched them go, her mouth pulling to the side.

"Think there's something going on between the two of them?" she asked idly.

"I think we're the last people in the world to speculate." As he said that last bit, Graham pressed his leg to hers beneath the table, and her heart did that smooshing thing it seemed to like to do whenever he was affectionate with her today.

"Fair enough."

"So now what?" Graham closed his notebook and tucked both it and his pen into the pocket of his jacket. "Wanna stroll around some more?"

She glanced outside. On the one hand, yes, that would be great. They'd walked a decent chunk of the festival, but there were more nooks and crannies to explore. Spending a day strolling arm in arm with her best buddy who just happened to be extremely hot and excellent in bed would be fun.

On the other hand...

"Actually." She raised her brows meaningfully, letting her gaze dip to his lips and running her foot up his calf. "I was thinking maybe we should go back to the room and, um, work on the presentation?"

Which was true. They'd just gotten a ton of great information that would help them with making their case.

Graham swallowed hard, getting her meaning immediately. He leaned in, and his warm breath against her ear made her shiver. "And by work on the presentation, you mean work on the presentation naked, am I right?"

She pulsed inside. Pulling back, she met his eyes. "You are one hundred percent, extremely, completely right."

* * *

They totally did work on the presentation. Naked.

Eventually.

Later that night, Graham lingered in the back of the library meeting room where the abstract art panel had been held, waiting while Elizabeth chatted with Kat and a few of the other artists who'd been speaking. It had been a nice event, if a little over Graham's head, but he hadn't minded. Any time the art talk had gotten too conceptual for him, all he'd had to do was turn his head and the most beautiful art in the world had been right there for him to enjoy.

How freeing was it to be able to just sit there and stare at Elizabeth? She'd been so wrapped up in the discussion, she hardly seemed to notice. But even if she had, he was allowed to gaze at her with undisguised affection now. Here, far away from home, no one could judge them or give them crap about the tentative change in their relationship status.

So he looked his fill, mapping the gentle slope of her nose and the sparkle in her dark eyes and the soft pink fullness of her lips.

The little mark he had left on the side of her neck.

Even now, catching a glimpse of it from across the room, his body reacted to the sight. Once they returned to Blue Cedar Falls, he'd have to be more careful, but it wasn't as if he'd sucked a giant, middle-school-level bruise into her skin. It'd fade by tomorrow.

The memory of it wouldn't, though.

Eventually, a couple of maintenance people arrived, quietly signaling that it was time to head out. The discussion up front wound down, with folks exchanging numbers and packing up their things. As Elizabeth parted from the group and headed over toward Graham, he put his hands in his pockets, mentally preparing for her to announce that they were going out for drinks or something—which would be fine. Not quite what he wanted after a long day, but fine.

To his surprise, she tipped her head toward the door without any mention of additional plans she might have made.

"Have fun?" he asked as they wandered through the dimly lit shelves toward the building exit.

"That was fabulous. We definitely have to have some artists' roundtables at our festival." She held up her phone. "A couple of the panelists said they might be interested." Bouncing as she walked, she tucked her phone back away. "This is going to be so awesome."

Graham smiled, warmth filling his chest. He loved seeing her so excited. He really hoped they could get this thing off the ground and bring it to life the way she wanted to.

Outside, the sky was a deep, dark blue, the first stars coming out and a bright yellow moon hovering overhead. The arts festival had turned into a block party, with lots of young people clustered near the tents, libations in hand. Down the street, a band played, while the sounds of a DJ filtered through the air from the other direction.

Blue Cedar Falls would balk at anything quite this lively; half the town had protested Clay trying to open the Junebug, at first. But like Kat and David said, it had taken a while for the Four Winds Festival to work up to this.

Graham waited for Elizabeth to decide which way to

go—his money was on the live band side of the festivities, but you never knew.

Turned out, he would have lost his bet, either way.

She turned to him, her expression open. "So what else do you want to do while we're here?"

He paused, frowning. "Huh?"

It wasn't unusual for her to ask him his opinion. But at an arts festival, he'd assumed that she'd be the one steering the ship.

She didn't seem to have any interest in taking the wheel, though. She spread her arms out from her sides as if to encompass the whole of their surroundings. "We came, we saw, we conquered. Now what?"

"I mean..." He raised his brows meaningfully.

She rolled her eyes. "We live together. We can do *that* anytime." Then she seemed to catch what she'd just said. "You know. At least for the next month or two."

Right. They hadn't discussed his impending status as a new homeowner since they'd fallen into bed together; they hadn't exactly had a whole lot of free time. But considering that her irritation about it had been one of the driving factors that had led them to fight, he supposed they couldn't exactly avoid the topic forever.

Truth be told, he'd given it quite a bit of thought in what few spare moments he'd had. A part of him was tempted to call his Realtor and rip up the contract tomorrow.

A more mature part of him recognized that that was probably the worst thing he could do. Shaking things up in his life had been a good thing. The road had been circuitous and melodramatic, but eventually, it had led him here.

Staying in their apartment together forever would be easy, but it wasn't what he wanted, in the long run. In this new relationship he hoped to build with Elizabeth, he wanted to look forward. Not back.

Subtly deflecting, he reminded her, "You're welcome at the new house anytime." Only the thinnest shred of self-preservation kept him from inviting her to move in right now. "We're already planning a sexy pajama movie night, remember?"

"How could I forget?" Her tone was fond, but there was no mistaking the undercurrent flowing beneath it. She still didn't like the idea of him moving out.

He really didn't want to relitigate it right now.

He nudged her elbow with his, directing her back to the question at hand. "So what do you want to do tonight?"

"Uh, look at art all day," she said, as if it was obvious. "Or make some. But I can do both of those when we get home, too." She tilted her chin up to look at him. "Seriously. This whole trip has been about me. We should do something that's for you."

She wasn't wrong. He was still touched, though.

He cast his gaze about, trying to think about what he'd do with the evening if the world were his oyster. More sex with Elizabeth was apparently being tabled for now. Going back to the room and reading definitely belonged on the list of things they could do at home. Which left...

"It is a shame we never made it to the beach," he mused.

Elizabeth grinned and took his hand. "No time like the present."

She started marching off in the direction of the nearest cross street, but he laughed and held on to her hand, pulling her back. "It's nine o'clock at night."

She wrapped her arm around his neck, and heaven help him, he was never going to get used to that. "So?"

Momentarily struck speechless, he stared at her pretty face, lit by the streetlamps and the moon, and in that moment he would have followed her anywhere.

It just so happened that where she wanted to go was where he wished they'd already gotten, and he was pretty sure there was a metaphor buried in there somewhere.

As it was, who was he to resist?

He swallowed, struggling to make his voice work. "Well, when you put it that way..."

Her smile lit her entire face. She rose onto her tiptoes to kiss him. When she pulled away, it was to take his hand again.

Ten minutes and only one wrong turn later, they found themselves at the entrance to the public beach. The waves crashed and roared, the sounds and lights of the festival receding.

As soon as they made it to the sand, Elizabeth kicked off her shoes. Graham generally wasn't the kind of guy who walked around barefoot—one bad jellyfish sting when he was eight had taught him his lesson—but he couldn't resist the freedom of sand between his toes, the allure of the wind and the girl by his side.

Barefoot, her shoes abandoned by the rocks, Elizabeth danced onto the beach. The breeze took her hair and her dress, leaving her looking like something wild, there in the moonlight. She twirled in a circle, arms outstretched, and she was so beautiful, he could hardly breathe.

She turned to him, one hand extended.

It was probably stupid to leave their shoes there; if somebody snagged them, it was going to be a painful walk back to the hotel, but he couldn't bring himself to worry about that right now. He ran across the sand toward her and picked her up the way he'd always wished he could. Lifting her high, drinking in the sound of her laughter and the light of her smile, he spun her around and around. Dizzy and happy, he set her down and kissed her, soft and wet and warm. Her hands on his chest, she pulled away. They stared into each other's eyes for moments that seemed to drag on and on, and he wanted to say something. He wanted to say much, much too much.

She knew how he felt.

And he knew she was still figuring her own feelings out.

Staying in the present wasn't his strong suit.

But it was hers.

Her gaze drifted over his shoulder. She lifted her arm to point off into the distance. "How far do you think it is to that pier?"

Without letting go of her, he turned. The wooden structure farther up the beach glowed with warm amber lights. It was probably a quarter mile away. Maybe more.

He took her hand in his. "Let's go find out."

Together, they picked their way across the sand. Elizabeth steered them closer to the water. He rolled his pants up to his ankles and let the surf lick at his toes. It was cold, and probably full of jellyfish looking for round two, and he didn't care.

They weren't the only ones out roaming the beach. They passed an older couple walking an enthusiastic and very wet yellow Lab, plus a small group of teenagers drinking out of bottles wrapped in paper bags.

"Ah, youth," Elizabeth remarked as the kids' laughter receded into the distance.

Graham shook his head fondly. "Didn't you and Chloe and Dahlia do basically that last summer?"

"Shh." She patted his arm. "It's different."

He looked down at her. "Is it?"

"They think the whole world is in front of them." A rueful twinge shadowed her tone.

"And it isn't for us anymore?" He felt like the world was more open and full of possibilities now than it ever had been back when he was a teen. Part of that was his new relationship with Elizabeth, and part of it was his new house and his newfound determination to go after his goals. He knew who he was and what he wanted, and for the first time in so long, it felt like he was getting somewhere with it.

But maybe for Elizabeth, that wasn't so true.

"It's just different. I have rent to pay." She nudged him with her elbow. "You'll have a mortgage soon."

"True. But I'll have a home, too." Responsibility came with privileges, and this was one he was excited for.

Elizabeth shrugged, like she didn't want to engage with that particular thought right now, which was fine. He'd been the one to redirect things the last time she'd brought up his decision to buy a house and move out.

"I guess I just look back on those days and feel so...naïve." She kicked at a bit of seaweed in her way, her gaze off toward the faint line of the horizon. "I thought I'd get out of my mom and Ned's house and just have, like, boundless freedom or something. Spend all my time making art and eating Cheetos."

"You do eat a lot of Cheetos."

"Shut up, onion breath," she fired back, but it wasn't mean. She sucked in a breath and sighed it out. "I may still drink with my friends on the beach sometimes, and make art and eat Cheetos. But I know full well that reality's always going to be there waiting for me the next day."

The sudden heaviness of what she was saying caught

him off guard. Elizabeth had been taking on more responsibility of late. Helping manage her family's inn more, trying to launch this festival. Even applying for all those artist residencies last spring—the idea that she might leave had broken his heart, but he'd been proud of her for investing in herself and working toward her goals.

Part of what he loved about her was that she could be in the present and embrace the joy, though. He didn't like the idea of her getting beaten down by life or losing that spark that had always lit her up from within.

"It's all a balance, though, isn't it?" He phrased his reply carefully.

Balance had always been an element of their friendship, after all. She balanced him out, and he helped balance her, and it was great.

But were the scales all really as even as he'd imagined?

"I guess," she conceded.

"You'll figure it out."

"I know."

They walked in silence for a while, but it wasn't the easy, peaceful quiet that had surrounded them a few minutes ago.

He considered what she'd said, both now and after they'd gotten out of that artists' panel. "How are things going with making art?"

Once upon a time, she'd done most of her studio work in their apartment, so he'd always known exactly how it was going because he was literally tripping over it every day. After deciding not to pursue any more residencies, she'd put the money she'd earmarked for that adventure into renting a studio space in a converted in-law apartment at a friend of a friend's parents' house. He didn't get to see the process as much anymore, which was good for his dry-cleaning expenses, but less great for getting to enjoy what she created.

"Fine," she replied, but she didn't seem so sure about it. "It's just hard to find the time to really concentrate on it. I work so much, and the festival is like this twelve-pound breech baby that I'm trying to deliver by cesarean."

Graham laughed. She wasn't wrong.

"Once the town council gives you the thumbs-up, you'll have more time."

"I hope so, but the work doesn't end there. Kat sent me another list of all the stuff their committee does every year to keep the event going. It's *long*."

"You know I'll help. All our friends will, too. Not to mention May and June."

She snickered. "I'm already having to beat June off with a stick, she wants to take over so bad."

"She just wants to help."

"I know. But I feel like I have to do this myself."

Ah. More quietly, suddenly certain he was getting to the root of things here, he said. "You know you don't have anything to prove, right?"

When she laughed this time, it wasn't funny at all. "I spent twenty years earning a reputation as the black sheep of the family. Heck—maybe of the entire town."

"That's not true," he said automatically.

"I think my mom and June might disagree," she countered, dry.

He considered her for a second, pursing his lips. "I know this isn't really how your family works." They had their own dynamic, which he'd never completely understood. So much went unsaid, and Elizabeth always assumed the worst about her mom and sisters' intentions. Some of it was cultural; she'd told him more than once that Chinese

American families were just different, in this unexplainable way that he would never presume to understand. "But is it possible you're being a little too harsh about them? Not *everything* they say is designed to give you a hard time."

She kicked the sand and looked off into the distance. "Maybe." She let out a sigh. "Our history is what it is, though. I *do* have something to prove."

They were within a stone's throw of the pier now. The railings and beams cast deep shadows across the sand. He stopped and turned to face her.

Real doubt darkened her eyes. He reached out to brush the backs of his knuckles down the side of her face.

"Not to me, you don't," he said quietly.

She rolled her eyes and started to argue, but he pressed a gentle kiss to her mouth.

When he pulled back, her bottom lip quivered. "Why are you always so nice to me?"

Wasn't it obvious? But instead of saying it out loud, he pulled her in for a hug. "Why wouldn't I be?"

Her silence spoke volumes; she clearly had a lot of reasons to offer, but he didn't want to listen to any of them.

"Why can't we just stay here forever?" she asked against his chest, her voice pouting. "Look at art, walk on the beach, bang in a hotel room."

Laughing, he drew back. Some of the sparkle had returned to her gaze.

"Okay," he agreed, even though they both knew that wasn't an option—not really.

"Awesome, glad that's settled." Throwing her arms around his neck, she rose onto her toes in the sand and pulled him down into a kiss that deepened fast.

They stood there together like that for a long time. He

luxuriated in the closeness and connection. Falling into bed together had been great—and it wasn't as if he would have minded hiding under that pier and falling into one of those support pylons, either. But they'd had enough sex in the past twenty-four hours that getting their clothes off didn't feel like the goal. Just being together, here in the salty air, beneath the bright moon...

Maybe that was the point of everything.

The sound of a dog barking higher up on the beach broke them out of their trance. They let go, and he marveled again at her kiss-bitten lips and pink cheeks. The chill of the night air hit him, not helped much by their wet feet and the soaked hem of her skirt.

Reluctantly, he tipped his head the way they'd come. "Are you ready to head back?"

He meant to the hotel, but they both heard the other part.

Tomorrow morning, they'd pack up their things and get in their car for the long drive home. Their isolated, carefree bubble couldn't last.

But that didn't mean it had to pop, either. They could hold on to this new, fragile thing they'd found together here. They could figure out a way to keep it alive, even as they slipped back into their everyday routines. The vision he'd had of his future—the one he was going to build to try to move on from her—it could adapt and change. It could include her. If she wanted it to.

Sighing, she followed his gaze up the beach toward the road. "I guess it's time."

With a soft smile, he took her by the hand.

And just hoped that she wouldn't let go.

CHAPTER FOURTEEN

Monday afternoon, trying in vain to scrub paint out of her dress, Elizabeth cursed Graham for saying no to her idea about just staying at the beach forever.

Yes, she'd chosen Blue Cedar Falls as her home. Yes, all her family and friends were here. Her studio and her stuff and her maybe-sort-of boyfriend were here. But still. Playing hooky for the rest of her life with said maybe-sort-of boyfriend wouldn't have been so bad, would it?

"I got you some paper towels, Ms. Elizabeth."

Elizabeth turned away from the sink to find sixteen-year-old Mackenzie Boyd holding a fresh pack of the wildly ineffective rough brown paper towels the community center supplied.

"Thanks." She tugged a few free and took one final swipe at the smear of yellow ocher soaking into the fabric.

Sigh. She knew better than to wear anything she cared about to her teaching job, but she was headed over to the inn next, so she'd worn something not terrible. At least she'd been smart enough to take off her scarf. She could probably hide the worst of the stain with that.

"Want me to go get the mop, too?" Mackenzie offered.

"Nah, I got it. You should get back to your project." Elizabeth put on her best teacher-y smile and marveled all over again at what a decent kid Mackenzie was.

You'd hardly know she was snooty Patty Boyd's younger daughter.

You *certainly* wouldn't know based on appearances. They had the same blond hair, but while Patty's was cut in a short asymmetric bob that she teased within an inch of its life, Mackenzie left hers long and dyed the tips pink. She wore ripped black jeans and band T-shirts and boots, and she had an eyebrow ring, and really, the whole thing gave Elizabeth the most bittersweet, nostalgic vibes.

She knew better than to play favorites among the students in her afterschool teen program. But if she had a bit of a soft spot for the artsy, iconoclastically dressed younger daughter of a lady who always seemed to have herself so put together...

...well, could anybody blame her?

Mackenzie went and got the mop anyway, which proved all over again what a great kid she was. Elizabeth stopped fussing about her own clothes and went over to the boy who'd been messing around and knocked over his palette. His expression was all defiance and guilt, and okay, yeah, Elizabeth was way too familiar with that, too. No need to lecture a kid with that look on his face. He already knew. Instead, she just directed him Mackenzie's way and told him he needed to do the mopping up himself. He acted put upon, but he didn't give her any lip, so she let it go.

She continued around the room, giving the students pointers and feedback. Asking what she hoped were thought-provoking questions to help them continue to explore. Not everybody had a ton of talent, but they made up for it with effort. As far as she was concerned, her job was to nurture whatever love they had for making things, whether they decided to follow her into the boondoggle of trying to actually earn a living in a creative field or just hang on to it as a passion while making better choices with their lives.

When Butterfingers finished mopping up, Mackenzie took him to the back to show him where to put the cleaning supplies away.

Which was of course when Patty decided to show up, huffing, "Can anyone explain to me why my daughter, for whom I'm paying to learn about art, is currently working as a janitor?"

Elizabeth bit her tongue so hard she almost drew blood. With a smile, she indulged a quick daydream in which Butterfingers dropped a palette of paint all over the white pantsuit and pink silk scarf Patty had been cavalier enough to wear into this of all rooms.

Then she forced herself to smile. "Mackenzie," she called, "your mom's here."

"Hi, Mom." Mackenzie returned from the rear of the classroom and waved. "Just need to clean my stuff up."

"Be snappy about it." Patty returned her attention to Elizabeth. She scanned her up and down, and her mouth curled into a frown. "Love your outfit."

Elizabeth didn't miss a beat. "Me, too."

Or at least she did now. Maybe she should paint some more of it to match the splatter. It could look cool.

Patty put on her stern voice. "I wasn't joking earlier. It's the staff's job to clean this place up, isn't it? The students are here to learn."

Seriously, she was going to need stitches in her tongue.

"Learning about community is part of the community center's mission." That went over like a lead balloon. Elizabeth sighed and crossed her arms over her chest. "Mackenzie pitching in wasn't necessary, but I think you should be proud of how helpful she is."

Patty harumphed, her gaze on the other side of the room, and Elizabeth looked around, wishing a student would spill some more paint to get her out of this conversation before Patty brought up—

"So your big presentation to the town council is coming up next week."

Elizabeth internally groaned. "It sure is."

She and Graham had worked on the presentation some more during the drive back home yesterday—which hadn't been as much fun as working on it naked in their hotel room, but it had been a lot more fun than setting up a dating profile for him and poking at his soft spots like she had on their way there, so everything was relative. When she headed over to the inn after class, she was going to throw June a bone and see if maybe she wanted to give it a look over, too.

"You think you're ready?" Patty asked.

Elizabeth side-eyed her. The tilt of her mouth seemed carefully neutral, but there was definitely a sneer in her eyes.

"I will be."

"Well, I suppose we'll see about that."

"Look." Before Elizabeth could think about it too much, she turned to face Patty fully. A big part of her wanted to tell the lady off. The Blue Cedar Falls Clothesline Arts Festival was her idea. Literally the entire point of it had been to give herself, her friends, and all the other artists in the area who had been rejected by the established galleries a venue to showcase their work. She didn't need the town's resident gallery owner giving her a hard time right now.

But then Kat's words floated back to her. Out in Half Moon Cove, the organizers of their indie art festival had decided it wasn't worth making enemies of the art dealer types.

Graham's opinion on the matter floated back to her, too. He'd always been a better diplomat than she had. She summoned his calm now as she unclenched her jaw.

"I'm really not trying to undermine you here, Patty. You know that, right?"

Patty blinked, as if she was as surprised by Elizabeth's attempt to be nice as Elizabeth was herself. Then she laughed and waved Elizabeth off. "Please, you're keeping the one person in town who's made a career in the art world out of your little art fair. Tell me how that's not undermining me and my business."

Okay, that hurt. Elizabeth was trying to make a career for herself. This *little art fair* was a big part of her efforts, in fact.

But she was still channeling her inner Graham and using it to help her keep her cool. "The fact that independent artists are organizing the event doesn't mean you won't benefit. The crowds are still going to be walking past your gallery. Tell me you can't capitalize on that."

Patty scoffed. "Crowds? That seems optimistic."

Calm. Elizabeth was *calm*.

Once again, the extra time she'd been spending with Graham helped her out, feeding her brain the right words to say. "Our projections show we can be a big draw."

"Ha. I'll believe it when I see it." Patty took a step closer, her eyes narrowing. "You and your friends have been screwups since you were in elementary school. This 'festival' is going to be a disaster, and it's going to lose the town money, and the town council knows it."

"That's not true." Okay, fine, Elizabeth had been a screwup, once upon a time, but she'd changed. Her friends were vibrant and creative, and some of them were even successful.

Her determination to show this town what she was worth grew another three sizes. She had meetings coming up with Deandre Harris and Brynn Jones from the town council this week, not to mention the interview with Lou Ellen from the *Chronicle*. All Patty was doing was egging her on to prep harder for them and be more persuasive.

But Patty wasn't done. "Even if by some miracle you do manage to get anybody to come to this *thing*"—the word practically dripped condescension—"don't pretend they're going to be my clientele. They're going to be more bohemian riffraff." She waved a hand dismissively. "Your types look, but they never buy. There's a reason I show only quality work in my gallery."

Elizabeth's gut clenched, and she curled her fingers into her palm tightly enough to hurt. "Your boring taste isn't the only measure of quality."

"You don't know the first thing about the business of art." Patty jabbed a finger toward her chest. "Or this town. You and your friends and your family. Not to mention your sister's new boyfriend." Her mouth twisted further down. "Thinking you know best about what this place needs."

"Wait, what?" Why was she dragging Clay into this?

In the weirdest twist of this entire weird conversation, Patty's frown suddenly quivered. Something flashed across her eyes, and was it—it couldn't be hurt, could it? "Well, some of us have been here our whole lives. And we're not going to let you all keep dragging this place down."

Flinching backward, Elizabeth opened her mouth to reply, but what on earth was she supposed to say to that? For better or worse, she was interrupted when Mackenzie rejoined them, backpack slung over her shoulder. "Okay, Mom. I'm ready."

"It's about time," her mother snapped. She took a breath and tugged on the hem of her blazer. Voice icy again, any emotion gone, she shot at Elizabeth, "See you at the town council meeting next week."

What on earth had all of that been about? Shaking her head, she watched them go for a second, then she turned around.

Only to whirl right into another student carrying an open jar of red-tinged turpentine.

Which splashed onto the other half of her dress.

She exhaled out a deep sigh.

Seriously. Why hadn't she and Graham just stayed at the freaking beach?

Elizabeth was still pondering the question a couple of hours later when she plopped down behind the front desk of the Sweetbriar Inn.

June regarded her levelly from the other side of the lobby, where she was plumping pillows and rearranging magazines. "Trip went that well, huh?"

"Trip was amazing." *So* amazing. Exhaling hard, she wiggled the mouse to bring the computer to life. "And that's the problem."

June smiled. "Ah."

"Don't 'ah' me." Did her older sister always have to be so knowing about everything?

Making her way over to the desk, June rolled her eyes. "I'm just empathizing. It's tough to get back to normal after some time away." The curve of her lips softened. "When Clay took me up to Alaska this summer, I almost didn't want to come home."

"Really?" Elizabeth couldn't hide her shock.

Getting her uptight sister to take a week off had required a full-court press from Elizabeth, May, and their mom. Heck, Ned had practically shoved her onto the plane. Right up until the moment the cockpit doors had closed, she'd been chanting instructions at them about how to run the inn that they'd been managing for literally their entire lives.

It had been a stroke of genius on Clay's part to make sure they spent most of their well-deserved vacation in a remote area without cell reception. June had returned from her week away well-rested in a way Elizabeth wasn't sure she'd ever seen her.

She'd also returned with about three million new ideas for ways to expand and improve the family business. Elizabeth and the rest of the family had needed a vacation themselves after the flurry of activity June threw herself into with all her renewed energy.

To hear that she'd actually enjoyed her time away— much less nursed the same fantasies of just never coming back—was a surprise, to say the least.

June exhaled dramatically as she joined Elizabeth, sitting down primly in the other chair behind the desk. "Believe it or not, I do actually like having time off."

Elizabeth narrowed her eyes at her, then looked away, shaking her head. "Yeah, no."

June kicked her, and Elizabeth just barely managed to suppress her yelp. "I'm not a robot, you know."

"I know." Elizabeth reached down to rub her ankle.

Of course her perfect, overachieving older sister wasn't a robot.

Maybe a cyborg, but definitely not a robot.

"Look." Elizabeth recrossed her legs, subtly scooting her rolling chair a little farther back so as to stay out of range. "All I'm saying is that when I asked if you might have a few minutes to help me look over my presentation, you said, and I quote, 'Yippee!'"

"I don't think I did."

"You might as well have." There had been unfettered glee in her eyes, for sure.

June pretended to get up. "Do you not want my help? Because I can go—"

"No, silly." Elizabeth reached for her hand and pulled her back down. "You and your cyborg eyes are exactly what I need."

"Cyborg?"

"Shh." Elizabeth grabbed her bag from under her desk and pulled out her laptop to show June what she and Graham had put together so far.

Kat and David's information had really helped them flesh their proposal out with specifics, including some projections for the future if they could successfully get their festival off the ground. As a bonus, they'd also put Elizabeth in touch with some other contacts who had provided additional support.

As Elizabeth walked June through the case they'd built so far, her thoughts kept flashing back to the weird confrontation she'd had with Patty at the community center. There was more going on than Patty just wanting to stop a festival that was going to hurt her business. Elizabeth truly believed she had a compelling enough case that she could get people to see past Patty's objections, but what if there was something she was missing here?

June offered some feedback, and Elizabeth made a couple of adjustments, plus a pile of notes about things she wanted to talk over with Graham. When they hit the end of the PowerPoint, Elizabeth closed the window and sat back in her chair, chewing at the inside of her lip.

"How long did it take you and Clay to win Patty over about the Junebug?"

To hear the two of them tell it, Patty had been ready to chain herself to a tree if she had to, she was so opposed to the idea of a rough-and-tumble dude like Clay opening a bar on quaint, idyllic, perfect Main Street.

June sat back, too. "Oh, wow. What are we at now? Sixteen months and counting?"

"Wait—" The Junebug had been open for a solid year.

"We didn't so much win her over as go around her."

Now she had Elizabeth's attention. "How?"

June hummed, tapping her chin. "If I recall correctly, it involved a lot of Clay groveling to Dottie Gallagher."

Right, the other leader of what Clay liked to refer to as the Main Street Busybody Association. Getting her on their side would have been key, in Clay's case, but Elizabeth didn't know how much help she'd be with the Clothesline Arts Festival.

"What else?" Elizabeth pressed.

"I baked a few pies. Oh, and we hired Patty's friend's husband's band to play at the bar a couple of times."

Elizabeth could work with that. "Think they're available for spring of next year?"

June winced. "I'm pretty sure they're always available." In a lower voice, she confided, "They're really not very good."

Elizabeth made another note on her pad to build a second live music stage at the far, far, *far* end of the strip.

"You know . . ." June mused.

Elizabeth cut her off. "I know, I know, I should try to find a way to include her as a part of the festival."

Kat thought so, David thought so. Graham thought so.

"Just an idea," June said.

An idea she hated. She mentally rolled her eyes at herself. It wasn't just her own personal prejudices talking, here. Considering how worked up Patty had gotten when Elizabeth had tried to channel her inner Graham at her today, it was also an idea that had a smaller chance of success than a North Carolina snowball-throwing contest. In August. She really didn't want to talk about it anymore, though, so she closed her laptop and glanced at the time. She fluttered a hand toward the door. "Aren't you supposed to be off canoodling with your boyfriend?"

June checked her own watch and did a double take. "Oh, wow, I didn't realize it had gotten so late." Standing, she grinned. "I guess time flies when you're looking at slide decks."

Elizabeth coughed into her elbow. "Cyborg."

June narrowed her eyes but didn't dignify the comment with a response. She stepped into the office that separated the Wu family residence from the inn and grabbed her purse and jacket. "Tell Mom I'll be back before ten."

"Tell her yourself," their mother called from the other side of the door between the office and the family living room. She emerged from behind it a few seconds later.

"Have a good night," June told her.

"Sure you don't want to stay? Your stepfather and I are starting *Bridgerton*."

Elizabeth choked on nothing, and June coughed, too.

May and Elizabeth loved those kinds of shows. Back when the first season had come out, May had still been living in New York, but they'd binged it together anyway, feverishly texting each other their reactions to every twist, turn, and sex scene. June had still been acting like she was above watching racy period dramas, and Elizabeth had taken not a small amount of glee in scandalizing her with screen caps from the most lurid parts.

So basically, yeah, totally something fun to watch with your mom.

"Uh, thanks," June stammered, "but I have to go meet Clay."

Their mother smiled, her eyes twinkling the way they always did whenever the discussion turned to June's beau. "Tell him hi for me."

Elizabeth shook her head. Would her mom at least try to pretend she didn't have a crush on the dude?

"You have got to put a ring on that man's finger," Elizabeth said, "or Mom is going to divorce Ned and do it herself."

"I can hear you," Ned's voice called from the other room.

Their mom scoffed, waving her stronger hand dismissively. "He's June's soul mate. I already have my own."

"Darn right you do," Ned muttered.

Elizabeth looked to June, ready to laugh at how red she'd probably be turning with all this soul mate talk. But to Elizabeth's surprise, her complexion was basically its normal color—with maybe just a hint of a grin curling her lips.

"Wait." Elizabeth tilted her head to the side. "Are you planning to put a ring on it?"

Ah, there was the bloom of pink creeping up her neck. "I mean..."

Their mother gasped and put a hand to her mouth. "Clay's going to be my son-in-law?"

"Cart." June held out one hand, then the other a good foot or so behind it. "Horse."

"But you're thinking about it."

"We've..." She seemed to choose her words carefully. "...discussed it."

Elizabeth wanted to jump up and down and clap.

Her mother actually did, as well as she could with her cane. "When? How?"

"We haven't committed to anything. But we've been together for over a year now. We've kind of said that come the spring, if we're both still happy, maybe we'll go ring shopping."

Leave it to June to make a plan to plan to get married. "That's awesome."

"There's just a lot to figure out." June glanced uncertainly at their mother and then at the door behind her. "Like living arrangements, for example."

"You wouldn't move into Clay's place above the bar?" Elizabeth asked.

"It's an option." She darted her gaze in their mother's direction again. "But like I said, there are other factors to consider."

"Clay is welcome to move in here," their mom said graciously.

June didn't visibly recoil, but it was close.

And just like that, Elizabeth got what June was trying not to say. Their mom and Ned were getting up there now. Their mom had already had the one health scare. She'd recovered amazingly well, but their future—and the future of the inn—was something to be considered.

June's dedication to both was a big part of why she'd

never moved out. But she deserved a chance to pursue her own future.

A thread of anxiety wove itself around Elizabeth's chest.

It was going to be up to the other Wu sisters to pitch in. Having May back in town would take some of the pressure off Elizabeth, but she'd still have to step up her involvement if she was going to have even a fraction of June's cyborg shoes to fill.

As if she could read Elizabeth's mind, June waved off both her and their mom. "Anyway, no need to borrow trouble."

"Borrowing trouble is literally one of your top five favorite hobbies," Elizabeth pointed out.

"Just something to think about," June said firmly.

"Believe me," their mother chimed in, "I *never* stop thinking about you and Clay getting married." Her eyes took on a glassy sheen, and she pressed a hand to her chest. "Who would have guessed? Two of my girls all settled down with nice young men."

Elizabeth rolled her eyes, but it was mostly to cover for the little twinge she felt at being left out of the "June and May have their lives together club" again. "May's not settled down."

"Please," their mom scoffed. "She's been settled down with Han since she was sixteen. Just took her a decade or so to realize it."

And okay, fine, Elizabeth couldn't argue with that.

Dryly, she said, "Maybe the four of you can have a double wedding."

June held up her hands, even farther apart this time. "Cart. *Horse*."

Elizabeth turned away, that twinge growing behind her

ribs. "Well, the good news is that I can hold down the fort during your double honeymoon."

"Thanks? I think?"

"Someday, maybe you'll settle down, too," their mom said, and forget a twinge. Her chest was full-on squeezing now.

Her mother said that kind of thing all the time, so it really shouldn't get to her anymore. But there was never hope in her voice. Just this weird condescension that Elizabeth still had no idea of how to interpret. All she knew was it didn't feel good.

She'd been trying to prove that she was a semi-responsible adult for ages now. She'd pitched in more here at the inn. She'd organized the fundraiser to help pull the family out of debt after their mother's medical bills had nearly bankrupted them. And now here she was, following in June and May's footsteps, attempting to put together a full-fledged community event.

If none of that was enough, then was there anything that ever would be? "Ha-ha," she said dryly. "As if. You know I'm not the type."

But even as she said it, a tiny spark of lightness appeared in her chest.

She might be talking a big game about not fitting in with her deeply committed, all-but-married-to-nice-men sisters. But her negative self-talk about her own unstable and erratic love life didn't ring quite as true as it normally would.

Not when she was heading home to Graham tonight. The same way she'd been heading home to him for pretty much her entire adult life—and yet different, too.

More.

They were still testing the waters on this new dimension

to their relationship. She was still terrified that she wasn't really what he wanted in life. Or that somehow she'd screw this up and end up losing her best friend.

But this small part of her was wondering if she was more like May than she ever would have guessed.

If she'd settled down when she was sixteen, too.

And it had just taken her a decade or so to realize it.

CHAPTER FIFTEEN

"G raham," Mindy called from the front office the next day. "You got a minute?"

Frowning, Graham glanced at the clock. He still had another ten minutes left on his lunch break, and he'd been hoping to finish the bit of research he was doing on the historical society's options for their upcoming renovation of the old bell tower on Main and Larch. He rolled his eyes at himself in his head. His father would probably say it was another low-profile, thankless job, but to him, it was fascinating. So fascinating he hadn't been able to resist digging right into it, even though he'd been supposed to pass it on to someone else.

Turned out the biggest danger of becoming volunteer coordinator for the group was taking on a couple of the juicier volunteer assignments yourself.

And the biggest danger of staying at your desk for your lunch break was never actually getting to finish your lunch break.

"Graham?" Mindy called again, her tone more pointed. "It's Dottie."

Graham closed his eyes for a long second. Right.

"Coming," he replied. He made a quick note of where he'd left off and wolfed down the last bite of the turkey and brie wrap Elizabeth had made him this morning after his attempt at cooking a pot of chili the night before to divvy up for lunches this week had gone down in literal flames.

Out in the front office, Mindy shot him a grateful look, and he smiled. On the other side of the counter, eighty-something-year-old Dottie Gallagher had made herself comfortable, perching on the seat of her fancy new walker.

"Take your time, take your time," she said, clearly not wanting him to take his time.

As warmly as he could, he asked, "What can I do for you today, Mrs. Gallagher?"

Dottie Gallagher was a lifelong resident of Blue Cedar Falls and a regular here at town hall. In addition to running the flower shop on Main Street, she found time to stick her nose in every single person's business. The question was whose business she'd decided to stick it in today.

"Patty's new sign in front of her gallery is forty-nine inches tall."

Of course it was. As Dottie had reminded him many times, an ordinance stated that displays over forty-eight inches in height needed to be approved.

"I assume you've documented this egregious infraction?"

"I most certainly have." She creakily stood and reached into the basket of her walker to produce a small stack of papers, including an ink-jet printed photograph of the offending sign, detailed measurements, and her own account of her giving Patty notice of the violation.

Graham paged through it all before nodding. "I'll inform the powers that be."

"Well, the powers that be had better be snappy about it."

"I'm sure they will be."

"Not like last time."

"Definitely not like last time." Heaven knew how Dottie had coped when poor Bobbi Moore had taken three days to fix an "unsightly" hole in the awning over her bakery.

Dottie waggled a bony finger at him. "Don't think I won't take a saw to the legs of that monstrosity."

Graham could absolutely picture it. "I would not dare to underestimate, ma'am."

"Patty could learn a thing or two from you." Dottie leaned in, a conspiratorial twinkle in her eyes. "Word on the street is that she's trying to tank that little art festival you and your girlfriend are trying to put on."

Graham swallowed. Elizabeth had filled him in on her latest run-in with Patty Boyd the night before. They'd both been trying not to let the woman get in their heads, but it was tough.

"Well, don't you worry." Dottie winked at him. "I've still got a trick or two up my sleeve, you know."

"I don't doubt it," Graham said delicately.

Only a fool would get in the middle of Dottie and Patty's long-standing feud, but if they'd decided to make Elizabeth's proposal for a clothesline arts festival the latest ring for their ongoing wrestling match, there wasn't much he could do except get out of the way.

Apparently satisfied, Dottie steered her walker toward the door, only to narrowly avoid a collision with Mayor Horton.

"Well, aren't you a vision today, Mrs. Gallagher?"

"Save it, Johnny." Dottie waved him off. "You had your chance in ninety-three."

Mayor Horton snapped his mouth shut, and Graham did his best to keep his from falling agape. He'd only barely recovered by the time Dottie had made it to the exit and the mayor had made it to the desk. Mayor Horton shot Graham one look, and Graham did his best to convey with his eyes that they need never, ever discuss it.

Huffing out a breath, Mayor Horton straightened his tie. "Lewis," he said by way of greeting.

Graham nodded. "Mr. Mayor."

"I was just swinging by for—"

"Here you go, sir." Mindy reappeared at Graham's side now that Dottie was gone and passed the mayor a small stack of papers.

"Thank you kindly." Mayor Horton gave the pages a quick once-over before rolling them up. He looked about ready to be on his way, but even as he pointed himself toward the hall, he paused. "You ready for next Tuesday?"

Ten minutes ago, Graham would have said that yes, he and Elizabeth were as ready as they could be for the big presentation to the town council—even with Patty stirring up trouble. Dottie deciding to enter the fray on their behalf was a positive development, but it still made him nervous.

"Think we're in good shape," he said, hedging.

"I'll be rooting for you." The mayor saluted him before continuing back to his office.

Mindy had retreated to her desk, where she tugged her purse out of the bottom drawer of her filing cabinet and slung it over her shoulder. "Well, I'm off to lunch. You got the desk?"

It wasn't as if he could go back in time and reclaim

the last, lost ten minutes of his lunch break, so he just nodded. The rest of his work on that historical society bell tower project could wait until he hit a slow patch later in the day. For now, the people of Gotham needed him.

Naturally, about ten times more Gotham residents ended up needing him than he'd been expecting, and those precious ten minutes of time to work on his passion project never materialized. As he signed out of his computer at the end of the day, regretfully waving the minimized research windows he'd never gotten a chance to pull back up goodbye, he shook his head. He really did like his job managing the front office here at town hall. But the day-to-day grind of it could get to be a little much sometimes.

He wasn't quite Elizabeth, yearning to just stay at the beach forever—as tempting as that might have been. But would a longer-term vacation from people needing pet licenses and park pavilion reservations or help mediating squabbles with their neighbors really be so much to ask? One he could focus on serving the town in a different way?

Apparently yes, considering he ended up having to put out two more small fires on his way out the door. At least they were metaphorical, so that was something.

By the time he made it outside, he was wound up and more than ready to head home. Elizabeth had given him a ride that morning since she was working at the inn most of the day. Her shift would be ending soon, so he walked on over to meet her there.

The autumn air on Main Street was cool and crisp. He exchanged hellos with a half dozen people bustling out and about. He gave a bit of side-eye to the outrageous, forty-nine-inch sign standing outside Patty Boyd's gallery to advertise her upcoming artist's reception.

"Hey there, Graham," a voice called as he crossed the street toward the inn.

He spotted Bobbi Moore waving to him from in front of her bakery. She, her wife, Caitlin, and her dad, Duke, were loading what was probably a mouthwatering pile of pastry boxes into the back of Duke's truck.

"Hey, there." He slowed.

A broad smile spread under Duke's big, bushy mustache. "How's it going?"

"Great. Making some good progress on that bell tower project." Sort of.

"Glad to hear it." Duke raised a brow. "How about on getting ready for next Tuesday? Dottie Gallagher swung by this afternoon and told me it's going to be a full house for the town council meeting."

Graham's stomach did a little dip. "Did she now?"

"Sure did."

Well, that didn't add any pressure to the situation. He projected as much confidence as he could as he assured Duke, "It's coming along great."

"Maybe think about sliding that PowerPoint into my DMs."

"That is *not* what that means, Dad," Bobbi told him, pinching the bridge of her nose.

Duke ignored her. "I'd be happy to take a look, is all I'm saying."

The handful of times Graham had met with Duke about historical society business, he'd tried to talk up the festival idea. Duke had seemed politely interested, but this was a more generous offer. "That'd be great, sir."

He stayed to chat for another couple of minutes while

Bobbi and Caitlin grabbed the last few boxes from inside. Once they were all loaded up, Duke jangled the keys. "If you'll excuse me, my daughter's delivery van is broken down, so apparently, I'm her ride."

"No problem."

As Graham turned, he checked his watch. Time had gotten away from him; his own ride was going to be eager to head out.

His heart swelled inside his chest. He and Elizabeth didn't have anything special planned for tonight, and he couldn't be happier. Things between them were still new and tentative, but they were also still old and boring, and he didn't know how he could have gotten so lucky.

Or how long it could last.

He might be delighted with the status quo, but it seemed hopelessly optimistic to imagine she'd be happy with it forever. Elizabeth never dated anyone for long, and he wasn't exactly her usual type. It seemed pre-determined that eventually she'd move on. Hopefully, she'd stand by her promise that they'd stay best friends, no matter what. He didn't know how he'd handle losing both the new intimacy they'd discovered *and* the most important friendship of his life.

He shoved his hand in his pocket and gripped his keys tightly. Despite his fears, he wasn't going to resign himself to losing either. He was trying to show her that they were great together as a couple. That they could take the best parts of their friendship and add in the awesomeness of being able to make out on their couch, and that they didn't need anything more.

Take tonight, for example. She'd cook, he'd try to help, and she'd shoo him away, because they hadn't had a chance to replace the fire extinguisher yet. Then they'd take their plates to the couch and argue over whether to watch more of the Viking show he was into or the rom-com she was loving, and probably settle on the murder show they both liked. They'd eat their dinners in front of the TV, only instead of hanging out in the recliner, he'd sit right next to her. He'd put his arm around her and miss every bit of the gruesome plot because he'd be too busy marveling over the fact that this was his life now. The same and different. Best friends and more.

He couldn't wait.

So naturally, just as he got to the top of the inn's blue painted steps, his phone went off. He considered ignoring it but couldn't help glancing at his watch.

The sight of his Realtor's name popping up on its face gave him pause.

He pulled out his phone and hovered with his thumb over the screen. Through the lobby's windows, he could see Elizabeth sitting at the front desk, her hair up in two little buns on the top of her head and looking so cool it still made him do a mental double take to think that she was choosing to be with him—even if was still weird and tentative.

He shifted his thumb to float over the button to decline the call.

But then he remembered not to be self-sabotaging twit. This was a major deal. Purchasing his first home. He didn't want to muck it up.

He answered the call and brought the phone to his ear.

"Hey, Crystal."

"Graham, I'm so glad I caught you. Everything's fine," she rushed to tell him, "but the home inspector we were hoping to hire is booked out into next month."

"Oh." That was disappointing. Or so Crystal had told him.

"Except he had a last-minute cancellation for tonight, and the owners are amenable."

Wow. That was fast. "Great."

"I hoped you'd think so. I'll call him back and tell him to come right on over. How soon do you think you can be here?"

Right, she'd told him that attending the inspection would be a good idea. He'd just assumed it wouldn't happen for another few weeks.

He opened his mouth to say he was on his way. But then his gaze caught on the interior of the inn again. His dreams of snuggling with Elizabeth on the couch went up in smoke.

Then again...

Maybe he had an idea for some even better plans.

The nature of his and Elizabeth's relationship had changed dramatically over the past few days. What hadn't changed was the sour twist to her lips every time he mentioned the new house. He hadn't really brought it up since they'd returned home, but it was in the back of his mind to revisit it with her. Make sure she understood that he still intended to go through with both the purchase and the move.

Try to help her see that this was a *good* thing. For him and his future.

And hopefully for her and for their future, too.

Well. No better time than the present.

His gaze still on her through the window, he told his Realtor, "We'll meet you there in ten."

"All right, then. I'll get a copy of the full inspection report to Crystal sometime tomorrow."

As Graham, his real estate agent, and the man who was apparently the most sought-after home inspector in the entire western half of the state—who would have even guessed that *that* was a thing?—finished up business, Elizabeth drifted away from them.

She ran her fingertip along the edge of one of the built-in bookshelves in the living room, where they were standing.

It was a nice bookshelf. Graham's collection of biographies and glorified textbooks would look great on it. Heck, there was enough room that he could probably go to one of those estate sales he and his mom enjoyed hitting up on weekends and grab a whole caseload more. She let one corner of her lips curl upward, thinking about how excited he'd be to arrange them here once the house was his.

Then her gaze caught on one of the framed photos the current owners had on display, and her smile shifted. The Carroways were an older couple of empty nesters. Their kids were about June and May's ages, both of them with children of their own. The big eight-by-ten glossy framed on the shelf was a shot of the whole family from the previous Christmas, she was pretty sure, all gathered around a tree covered in heirloom glass ornaments and looking like something out of a Norman Rockwell painting.

She dropped her hand.

The same squirmy, uncomfortably hot feeling that had been plaguing her all evening started wriggling around in the pit of her stomach again. Ever since Graham had burst into the inn's lobby—ten minutes late, she'd been ready to go send out a search party—and asked her if she'd come with him to a last-minute home inspection appointment, she'd been working to keep her unsettled, self-conscious feeling to herself.

It was a struggle, though. The entire time the inspector had been doing his thing, looking for anything that might be wrong with the house, Graham had kept glancing over at her, this hopeful smile on his face. He was like a puppy, so excited to show her around, constantly looking to her for her reaction. And she was excited for him. She really was. The house was great.

So why did she feel so out of place here?

She still hadn't figured it out a couple of minutes later. The inspector took his leave. Graham's real estate agent gave him her thoughts on how things had gone, and then she motioned toward the door. "Shall we?"

Elizabeth turned, more than ready to go.

The relief must have shown on her face, though, and not in a good way, considering how Graham's own expression drooped.

"Actually." His Adam's apple bobbed. To Crystal, he asked, "Could we have a couple of minutes?"

Crystal glanced between the two of them before shooting Graham a fake, professional smile. "Of course."

Only once the door was closed behind her did Graham cross the space to Elizabeth.

"So?" He stopped a foot or so away. "What do you think?"

And there was that hopeful face again, only with this tinge of wariness just underneath it.

Ugh, it felt like kicking a puppy to let on how she was really thinking, though she was pretty sure he knew.

She thought the place was okay, but it didn't *fit* the way their apartment back at Hemlock House did. She didn't understand why he wanted to move when they were so happy where they were.

Finally, she settled on "I think it's nice."

Yup. Kicked puppy.

"That's all?"

She bit the inside of her lip, but that flash of a crestfallen expression on his face fell away, replaced by a determined smile.

He took her by the hand and dragged her down the hall. "Just look at it."

He took her on the same tour the inspector had, except instead of pointing out any possible faults, he started rattling off features like he was competing with Crystal for her job.

"Look at this kitchen! It's bigger than our whole apartment. The cabinets are real cherry, too, and once I swap out the countertops and the appliances, you're going to be blown away."

"You don't even cook," she told him, laughing.

"I'll learn," he promised, already hauling her along, and okay, even she had to admit the place was more fun when they were racing through it like this, his hand wrapped around hers and his voice bright with genuine excitement.

"You better get good fire insurance."

"I will."

He led her out the back of the kitchen to what they'd been referring to as a "bonus room"—how that was different from a real room, she didn't know.

"Check out the skylights," he urged her. "You can't tell now, but the sun streams in them in the morning, and it's gorgeous."

"You're hardly around in the morning."

He was always at work. On the weekends he was running around restoring bell towers and trying in vain to impress his father or hitting up rummage sales with his mom.

But he was already off to the next thing. They shot back through the kitchen and the dining room.

"So much room for entertaining," he told her.

"Entertaining who?"

But he didn't answer. He took her up the stairs.

"Three bedrooms and an office."

"More places to put your history textbooks?"

"More places to do whatever I want," he told her firmly.

And how could she resist that smile? That optimistic, domestic, happy smile that made her genuinely believe that all this ridiculous, lovely man wanted in the entire world was this two-story raised ranch.

Just for a second, she let his joy eclipse her skepticism. She let it push away that tiny bit of hurt still making her chest feel tender when she pushed at it.

She tugged on his arm when he went to take her into the main bedroom. He came back to her willingly, and she reached up to clasp her hands together behind his neck.

The same strange and yet wonderful thrill of being so casually intimate with him zipped through her, made even more intense when he curled his arms gently around her waist. This should be weird; since moment one, she'd kept thinking it should be weird. But it wasn't, even now.

Looking up into his eyes, she twirled a finger through that soft bit of scruff at his nape. "I think the house is nice, Graham." She really, honestly did. She swallowed, trying to speak past the lump in her throat. "I think you're going to be really happy here."

"I think *we* will."

And he sounded so sure of himself. So why was she this giant mess of doubts?

It wasn't just that she'd never pictured herself as a homeowner. Buying a house seemed like the kind of thing that stable, normal people did. Despite the new leaf she'd been working to turn over these past few years, that still didn't feel like her. She loved the idea of Graham including her in his grand, domestic fantasy, but did she really fit?

She pulled back a few inches. Her voice cracked. "I thought you bought this place specifically to move on from me."

He considered her for a second, but the smile didn't fall from his face. Warmth shone in his eyes as he brushed a stray lock of hair back from her face. "And you see how well that worked out?"

She couldn't quite decide whether to swoon or be really annoyed about that.

As if he could sense her conflict, he shook his head. "E. I bought this place because I didn't think we were an option, and I needed to look to my future." His throat bobbed. "I don't want to put too much pressure on anything. I know we've only been together for less than a week."

"Yes," she said, her tone dry, because joking when your maybe-sort-of boyfriend was trying to say something big and emotional definitely showed that you were stable and mature. "I clearly barely know you."

He rolled his eyes and continued on. "But I'm not going to beat around the bush here. I want my future to include you." He squeezed her hand gently. "Here."

She sank her teeth into her lip, trying to imagine it. On the one hand, it sounded incredible. This place was stuffy and decorated in the height of eighties fashion, but she could see the potential in it. They could move a bunch of their stuff on in, and she could pick out some new pictures for the walls. A few big plants and a fresh coat of paint, and this place could feel like theirs.

On the other hand, the very idea of it all made her chest feel tight. She'd said repeatedly that she was here in Blue Cedar Falls to stay. But this was *permanent* permanent. It was grown-up and responsible, and those were both things she wanted to be. But was she?

How long until she screwed something up? Graham had always tolerated her idiosyncrasies in the past, but there was this part of her that still felt on edge, waiting for the day he woke up and realized he couldn't handle her lack of punctuality or her inability to find her sunglasses on top of her head. That kind of stuff might be fine in a friend, but in a significant other? That was different.

And maybe that was just her insecurity talking. Ever since she was a kid, she'd felt like she was never good enough. Being with Graham made her feel like she was the most special person in the world, but old ways of thinking died hard.

"Graham . . ." And this killed her to say, but she had to do it. "You don't know if you're really going to feel that way in a year, much less however long your mortgage is."

"Thirty-year fixed," he replied automatically, and she tried not to swallow her tongue.

Thirty *years*. She didn't know what she was going to have for breakfast tomorrow, and he was thinking about his life three decades from now.

As if he could hear her spiraling thoughts, he shook his head, taking her hand and placing it over his heart. "Look. We've done everything backward here."

She huffed out a watery laugh and swiped at a treacherous bit of stinging at the corner of her eye. "You think?"

One corner of his mouth curled up. "I mean, we did sleep together about ten years before our first kiss."

She rolled her eyes so hard she almost sprained

something. "In *sleeping bags*. Literally sleeping. Not anything else."

On the floor of the gym at the afterparty for their junior prom. He'd gone with some girl from the debate club with braces, and she'd gone with a twenty-year-old dropout who had a neck tattoo and a band. They'd both ditched their dates before the night was done.

She'd thought it was a tragedy.

But in the end...

Lying there beside the bleachers. Talking quietly through half the night, giggling about anything and everything.

It hadn't been such a tragedy after all.

And neither was this. Standing here in this big, expensive house that he was so in love with, her hand in his after all this time.

His grin softened, and he stroked his thumb against hers. "We're doing this all backward, too. But I almost missed out on my chance to be with you because I was too scared to tell you how I really felt. I'm not going to do that again. Whatever we're doing here together... it could be forever for me." He rushed forward, cutting her off before she could protest any further. "And I don't expect you to be thinking that far ahead."

Seriously, would it be a smoothie tomorrow morning or overnight oats? She had no idea.

But that wasn't the point, and this wasn't the time for kidding around.

"Not because I'm not serious about this," she clarified.

"I know." His smile was both genuine and just this little, tiny bit sad. "You know how I feel. What I want."

She nodded, her throat tight as she swallowed. She did. More or less.

"But for now, we take stuff one step at a time. And we'll see how it all works out. Okay?"

How the tables had turned. Usually, she was the fly-by-the-seat-of-her-pants type. It hadn't always gone great for her. She relied on his careful planning, in fact, to help balance out her more reckless instincts.

But now here he was, trying to get her out of her own head. Trying to convince her to live in the moment.

It was a good look on him, truth be told.

"When did you get so confident?" she asked, a smile tugging at her cheeks.

He smirked. "Two weeks ago, apparently."

She laughed, but inside, her heart constricted. It was true, what he'd said. If he'd never told her how he felt, they might never have ended up here.

"I'm glad," she told him. Then she tipped up onto her toes. When their lips met, it was soft and warm, and it felt exactly like home.

Unlike this house, which still felt like a boulder of responsibility wrapped in a dingy rose and teal valance swag. But she could work on that.

Closing her eyes, she deepened the kiss.

She might not have a lot of confidence in her ability to be the partner he deserved, but his earnestness had disarmed her. The least she could do was try.

CHAPTER SIXTEEN

✳ ✳ ✳ ✳ ✳ ✳ ✳ ✳ ✳ ✳ ✳

The following Tuesday, with less than an hour to go before the town council meeting, locked in a conference room with Elizabeth while she rehearsed, Graham was so nervous he thought he might be sick.

Which didn't even make sense. He wasn't the one who had to stand up there and convince seven prominent members of local government that an independent artists' festival would be a great thing for the town. This wasn't like that time he got stuck presenting his group's civics project to the entire student body back in junior year. He actually *had* been sick psyching himself up for that.

Today, he was safely behind the scenes, exactly where he liked to be.

Unlike Elizabeth, who was about to undergo trial by fire.

He let his gaze drift away from the figures she had projected on the screen to look at her, and his heart skipped a beat.

That didn't make any sense, either. He'd been sneaking peeks at her face for fifteen years. Granted—he'd only been free to do it without being terrified of her catching him and realizing exactly how gone he was for her for a week and a half. But this wasn't anything new. For ages now, he'd been encouraging her and supporting her. She'd encouraged him and supported him just the same; heck, he never would have made it onto that stage to give that stupid civics report without her basically shoving him onto it.

Everything felt different now, though.

He was so proud of her.

And, wow, did he ever hope that all their hard work paid off today.

He hoped she got to hear the whole town tell her she was as amazing as he thought she was.

She glanced his way, and he smiled, nodding. Only when she looked away did he let his mouth go flat again.

He honestly didn't know how the vote would go. They'd poured so much energy into getting the presentation perfect. They'd lobbied all seven council members, meeting with them and laying out their case and listening to their specific concerns. Both their families had gone to bat for them, and the good—or at least begrudgingly supportive—opinion of Judge Lewis went a long way. Lucille Lewis and June Wu's opinions went nearly as far, but even with all of them on their side, this wasn't a slam dunk.

The town of Blue Cedar Falls could be fickle. Public sentiment turned on a dime, and Patty Boyd wasn't to be underestimated. Graham still had a sinking feeling that the woman had something up her sleeve, and Elizabeth seemed convinced that her opposition was personal. Dottie Gallagher talked a good game about showing her up, but their feud had been a stalemate for decades. Who would come out on top was anybody's guess, and Graham couldn't help picturing himself, Elizabeth, and their arts festival as grass being trampled under their elephant feet.

Not that he would ever compare either of them to elephants. *Ever.*

"Okay," Elizabeth mumbled, "Yada yada yada." She skipped through a few of the meatier slides. Graham would have protested if she hadn't nailed them in the last run-through back at their apartment.

She picked up again in the closing arguments section, which was one of the strongest. Her natural passion overcame her uncertainty.

Now all she had to do was show the folks in charge a fraction of the brilliance he knew she was capable of.

Clicking over to the final slide, she turned to him. "So? What do you think?"

"I think you're going to knock their socks off." He rose from his seat as she rolled her eyes.

"Please," she demurred, waving him off.

"I mean it."

She looked away to grab her laptop and stuff it in her bag, which was one of the more sedate options from her closet—a black vegan leather tote with only a single Notorious RBG pin for flair. As she packed up her things, he closed the distance between them.

He put his hands on her upper arms and tugged her around. She let him wrap her up in an embrace, hugging him in return and sagging into him.

"I should have gotten June to do this part."

"You definitely should not have."

"At least I know she wouldn't mess it up."

And he hated how down she could get on herself. The casual way she dismissed her own abilities always ramped up when she was stressed, but it drove him nuts, especially now.

"You're not going to mess it up," he promised, continuing on when she tried to interrupt, "and even if you do, the important thing is that you worked so hard. No one could be more prepared than you are right now."

"Imagine that," she said dryly, "me, doing my homework."

"So much homework." He closed his arms around her more tightly, resting his cheek against the top of her head. "No matter what happens out there, don't you forget that."

She hesitated for a second. When she spoke again, her voice was smaller. "Do think they're going to go for it?"

"Yeah," he said, as confident as he could be. "I do. But if they don't, just remember it has nothing to do with you and everything to do with small-town politics."

"Ugh, you suck at pep talks."

"Sorry."

She pulled away, but he didn't let her get far. He ducked down to look her in the eye. "You're amazing."

He kissed her then, warm and soft.

All too soon, she stepped back for real. Grabbing her bag, she tucked a lock of hair behind her ear.

"All right." She sucked in a deep breath. "Let's do this."

The instant they went out the door, she put a careful distance between them, and he swallowed hard.

They'd said back in Half Moon Cove that they didn't want to hide what was going on between them. In the end, they hadn't had much of anyone to hide it from. They'd both been so busy, they'd hardly spent any time together outside the safety of their own apartment. Alone together, they'd gotten up to all sorts of shenanigans, but out in public, they'd played it safe.

And that was fine. Good. Smart, even.

Elizabeth had been the one to bring up the *I told you so* look her mother would give them, but his mom would be even worse—and that was to say nothing of his father. Or their friends.

Besides. His throat tightened. Things were still so new between them. What was the point of telling everybody that they were together now when it might not even last? He knew he wanted a future together, and he'd told her as much. While she clearly cared about him, she wasn't ready to think that far ahead. Until she made up her mind, he'd keep his adoration to himself.

Even if it was killing him to.

And it had never killed him more than it did as they rounded the corner toward the council chambers.

And found the entire town of Blue Cedar Falls waiting for them there.

"What are all these people doing here?" Elizabeth hissed out of the side of her mouth, standing there frozen in place outside the chambers.

Seriously, they had to be violating the fire code. The room was supposed to fit only fifty, but there had to be more crammed in around the edges. Apparently, it wasn't a problem, though, considering Officer Dwight and Fire Marshall Owens were seated together near the front of the peanut gallery.

Her chest tightened, but before she could start freaking out completely, Graham gave her arm a gentle squeeze.

He gestured ahead of them. "I think they're here to support you."

And okay, yeah, there was definitely a contingent of friendly faces. Her mom, her sisters, their boyfriends. Graham's parents—though Judge Lewis looked as annoyed and above it all as ever. Chloe, Tom, Dahlia, Archer, Stefano. The whole crew from the community center. Heck, her high school art teacher, Mrs. Freeman, had shown up. When Elizabeth's gaze connected with hers, she flashed a smile and a double thumbs-up, and Elizabeth's breathing eased.

Right until she caught sight of Patty and her gaggle of middle-aged women in blazers and fresh-from-the-salon hair. A few of their husbands sat among them, looking just as excited about the proceedings as Judge Lewis.

Then there was the row dominated by Dottie Gallagher and the bright green rolling walker she'd parked right in the middle of the aisle. Fire Marshall Owens should *really* have some thoughts about that, but far be it from Elizabeth to tell a guy how to do his job—especially when it came to bossing Dottie Gallagher around. The woman did what she wanted, and all Elizabeth could do was cross her fingers that Graham's intel about her having it in for Patty again might play to her advantage today.

"You gonna be okay?" Graham asked.

No. She was going to have a panic attack.

But instead of telling him that, she nodded stiffly.

Through sheer force of will, she managed to unglue her feet from the carpet. Her whole body flashed hot and then cold and then hot again as she made her way to the front of the room. Most of the actual members of the town council were already there. Duke Moore she knew well enough, considering he was June's best friend Bobbi's dad, and Graham said he was on their side. She felt pretty good about Brynn Jones, too. Naya Holmes, an older Black woman, worked with the community center, and she'd been openly, vocally supportive of her idea. Natalie Jenkins, Richard Brown, and Jerry Stein were all Patty's friends. Natalie and Richard had at least agreed to meet with her, though neither of them had seemed particularly swayed by her arguments. They'd mostly brought up Patty's same BS about Elizabeth not having enough experience to take on such a big project. They thought it would lose the town money and damage its "sterling reputation." Elizabeth was pretty sure they were just mad they hadn't come up with the idea themselves. June had practically taken over tourism development in this town. Seeing her feckless baby sister start showing them all up too must burn.

Jerry hadn't even been willing to hear her out, but then he always had been a jerk.

That left Deandre Harris as the lone swing voter. He was a young Black man who had earned his seat the previous year by championing local business. He seemed to get along with Patty in her role as Main Street Business Association president, but he also was a big proponent of all of June's big initiatives to increase tourism in the area. He'd listened attentively when Elizabeth and Graham had spoken with him, but if he'd made up his mind, he was keeping his cards close to his chest.

"Here." Graham held out the cable to connect her laptop to the projector. She took it from him, their fingertips grazing, and she didn't think it was by accident. He held her gaze, and she remembered the feeling of being safe in his arms back in that conference room. The support and care he'd poured into her. That was what she needed to summon now.

Then she got so lost in his pretty eyes that she dropped the stupid cord.

Muttering a curse word under her breath, she bent to pick it up. Her hands kept shaking as she set her computer up, but eventually she managed to get the first slide of her presentation showing on the screen. Graham hovered, and she wanted both to tell him to go sit down and to beg him to stay and hold her hand.

Finally, it was time. Mayor Horton arrived, and the entire room went quiet.

Well, except for Dottie, who was in the middle of telling a salacious story about her neighbor's pool boy, but even she cut off after she noticed everybody else had stopped talking and it was just her babbling about some twenty-something-year-old guy's butt when he wore his Speedos.

"What are you all looking at?" Dottie griped.

"Ahem." Mayor Horton took his spot at the podium. He smiled to the assembled crowd. "Good evening, folks, it's nice to see so many of you come out tonight." He rambled through some opening remarks. Hopefully none of it was too important, because Elizabeth missed about ninety percent of it.

She didn't catch any more of the rest of the business proceedings, which included something about regulations on sign heights on Main Street—why anyone would care about that, she had no idea—and reviewing bids to renovate the dog park on the other side of town.

"And finally," he said. Graham elbowed her, and she looked up to find Mayor Horton smiling in her direction. "Our main agenda item for tonight, a proposal from someone you know from her mug shot."

"One time," Elizabeth groaned, but people were too busy laughing to hear her protest.

"Ms. Elizabeth Wu." He raised a brow at her. "Ms. Wu?"

Well, with an introduction like that...

Red-faced and sure she was going to trip over her own skirt, she headed over to the podium. Somehow or other, she managed to make it there without incident.

"Thank you, Mr. Mayor." She reached up to grasp the microphone and tilted it down. She narrowed her eyes at him. "I think."

That got even more laughs than his crack about that one time she got picked up by Officer Dwight, which put her on slightly more even footing.

She made the mistake of looking out at all the people waiting to watch her fall flat on her face. Patty Boyd's sneer spoke volumes about what she thought of Elizabeth and her chances, and a part of Elizabeth wanted to pack it in right now.

But then she forced herself to keep scanning. She repeated all of Graham's words of encouragement in her head. She'd worked her rear end off for this moment. If she could get this festival approved, she could prove that she was a responsible adult. She'd create her own venue for getting her artwork out there, and she'd support the work of so many others who hadn't been able to find an audience through the traditional paths. This was important. She was capable. She could do this.

As that last thought zoomed through her head, she turned her head to catch Graham's eye. He stared back at her with an intensity that still managed to take her breath away.

You got this, he mouthed.

Damn right she did.

With that, she took hold of the remote for the slideshow and launched into her speech. It went great at first. She did all the crap June had told her to. Made eye contact. Spoke up. Most folks seemed interested, and she gathered steam. As she hit the data and figures section, a few people in the audience sat up straighter. Officer Dwight looked kind of confused, and she slowly realized that he wasn't the only one.

A slow smile slid over June's face. She glanced to the side to find her mom with a similarly smug expression—one she'd seen plenty of times before, but always directed at May or June. Ned had this knowing tilt to his mouth, and her chest squeezed. He always had believed in her, back in the day, before she'd mucked everything up. Maybe he still did.

Maybe *she* did.

That said, as she reached the conclusion section, her nerves threatened to steal over her again. Graham himself had said it—no matter how well she did, town politics were still going to be an issue. She may have managed to impress a few people, or least not trip over the floor-height bar they had set out for her, but that didn't mean the members of the town council would decide that her proposal was a good choice for Blue Cedar Falls.

All of this hard work could have been for nothing.

Only that wasn't completely true, was it?

Even if she didn't have the votes, no one could say she hadn't tried. She'd put her all into something, and she'd done awesome at it. She'd researched and hobnobbed and figured out how on earth to make an animated gif play inside of a PowerPoint presentation.

She'd opened herself up to her sisters, asking for help when she freaking hated having to do that.

She'd opened herself up to Graham.

Mostly by poking at him until he cracked, but still. That was just more evidence that she could be persistent when she wanted to be. No matter how this festival went—or how their evolving relationship turned out—she'd reached for something new in so many dimensions of her life.

That had to count for something, right?

Finally, she hit the end of her presentation. She set down the clicker and inhaled deeply. She turned to the members of the town council. "Any questions?"

Before they could answer, applause burst out. She blushed and gave a smile to the crowd. May, June, her mom, and Ned beamed back at her. Graham's mom did likewise, and even Judge Lewis seemed vaguely impressed, which was nice for a change.

It wasn't their opinions she was trying to sway, though. She looked back over at the people who would actually be voting tonight.

As expected, Duke, Naya, and Brynn seemed happy with her work. Natalie and Richard kept their reactions more guarded, while Jerry—the jerk—outright scowled. She glanced at Deandre, but she still couldn't seem to read him.

"Thank you, Ms. Wu," Mayor Horton said, bringing things back to order. "Counselors, do any of you have any questions?"

From the other side of the room, a sharp voice called out, "I do."

Patty Boyd rose from her seat.

Elizabeth sucked in a rough breath. Just standing up here and talking in front of everybody, asking them to entrust her with something this big, felt like going ten rounds with a prize fighter. All she wanted to do was sit down and have someone put a water bottle—or better yet, a martini glass—in her face.

But from the hostility in Patty's gaze, Elizabeth mentally put back on her gloves.

She still had another ten rounds to go.

CHAPTER SEVENTEEN

❋ ❋ ❋ ❋ ❋ ❋ ❋ ❋ ❋ ❋ ❋

Graham couldn't be the only one holding his breath as Patty made her way to the mic set up in the center aisle. Dottie shoved an orthotic sneaker-clad foot in her way, but Patty nimbly stepped over it and around the old woman's walker, her head held high.

"Well," Mayor Horton said dryly, "I suppose if none of the counselors have any immediate questions, we can start in with the public comment period."

Patty didn't miss a beat. "Ms. Wu, would you like to explain to the counselors why it is specifically that you're shutting out local businesses with years of expertise in this area?"

"I wouldn't say—" Elizabeth started.

"Actually, I'd like to hear an answer to that, too," Jerry piped up.

"No one is being shut out of the festival. It's for everyone in Blue Cedar Falls." Elizabeth stood up straight, her shoulders square.

"But you and your friends will be doing all of the selecting," Patty pointed out.

"As I explained, the show will cast a wide net, with an open call and a mission statement that will keep the festival as inclusive as possible."

"But it will be a juried show, in which you and your friends will be the jury."

Graham winced. They'd discussed this at length. While Elizabeth would have loved to just let everyone in the world come and hang up their stuff, creating a show with a flow to it and a vision, one that would draw the kinds of crowds needed to make an event like this successful for the community as a whole, would require at least some level of curation.

"A group of *independent* artists from the local community will be serving as the selection panel."

"While professionals with real experience in the art world will be excluded."

Elizabeth's mouth flattened into a line, her color rising, and oh boy, Patty was getting under her collar now. "With all due respect—"

"Where are your qualifications?" Patty demanded. "Your degree? Your experience running events of this magnitude?"

A loud, rough cackle rang out through the room.

All eyes turned to Dottie Gallagher, who stood, gripping the handles of her walker to take her down the aisle to stand beside Patty.

"Excuse me, I am speaking."

"Good luck with that," Dottie told her. "What I want to know is what qualifications you had when you took over the Pumpkin Festival back in '05 and then ran it into the ground for a decade."

"I did not—"

"You kind of did," Naya interjected, leaning forward

to talk into the microphone located in front of her counselor's chair.

"I have qualifications," Elizabeth said, trying to get things back under control. "I've been working as an independent artist and teacher since I was eighteen."

Darn right she had.

"June's the one who brought the Pumpkin Festival back," Clay said, and how this was turning into a referendum on the Pumpkin Festival, Graham had no idea, but apparently it was.

June patted his hand. "Thanks, babe."

"What do you say, June?" Deandre asked.

Graham's nerves crackled. He still couldn't get a read on which way Deandre was leaning.

June looked around, as if surprised to be called on. "I think the arts festival is a great idea. It's exactly the kind of new, innovative project that's helped Blue Cedar Falls rebuild over the past year."

"But what do you think about trusting it to your sister?" Jerry prodded. "You have to admit her track record is..." He wiggled his hand back and forth.

Graham's face flashed hot with anger. Before he could think to stop himself, he stepped forward. "Her track record amounts to a dozen teenage indiscretions."

"One of which got her arrested," Patty reminded them all.

"And me right along with it. We spray-painted a wall—not robbed a bank." Oh God, Graham was going to be sick after all. Those public speaking nerves flared, and his stomach churned, but he could do this.

He glanced at Elizabeth, who stared back at him with terror and pride. Then he shot his gaze toward his parents. His mom's expression was pretty similar to Elizabeth's, but his father's was stoic, and not in a good way.

Whatever. This wasn't about them; it wasn't even about him.

"You trust me to run half of town hall," Graham reminded them.

"And Elizabeth has done nothing but support her family and this community these past few years," May offered. "Right, Officer Dwight?"

Officer Dwight sighed. "She hasn't ended up in my squad car again, if that's what you mean."

"Hardly a high bar," Patty tried.

"Oh, please—*you've* ended up in the squad car," Dottie reminded her.

Patty threw her hands up in the air. "Because you accused me—falsely, I might add—of possession."

"I planted my medical MJ stash on her," Dottie said, sotto voce.

Mayor Horton scrubbed a hand over his face. "Dottie, please stop confessing to crimes during town council meetings."

"Let's get back to the point," Deandre urged.

Patty seized on that. "The point being that there is no reason for established galleries to be cut out of this festival."

"It's not like she's shutting you down, Patty," Chloe spoke up. "Your doors will be open, just like any other day."

"But," Dahlia added from beside her, "with about ten times more foot traffic from art lovers from all over the state."

"Maybe the country," May added.

"She's got a point," Deandre said.

Patty glared. "Crowds of penniless hippies won't help my gallery." She glanced around pointedly. "Or any of the other local businesses you claim will benefit. Or our town's reputation. Established professionals with connections to the art world could bring in established artists and collectors of means."

"But think about the little guy." May's boyfriend, Han, rose to his feet.

More than a couple of curious whispers went up. Han ran the Jade Garden with his mother, as well as the Jade Garden Annex, which was his own—wildly successful—pet project where he did upscale Asian fusion. He was well-known around the community, but he didn't make a big stir, in general. His mom was the one who went to Main Street Business Association meetings and advocated for their restaurants.

She was nowhere to be seen today, though. Whereas Han certainly was.

He cleared his throat. "June—who is not a professional festival organizer, by the way—"

"It's true," June agreed.

Nodding at her, Han continued. "—and the whole Taste of Blue Cedar Falls selection committee gave my pop-up a shot when I had no experience outside of a secret menu at my mom's restaurant. That opportunity opened up all kinds of doors to me."

One of Patty's friends said, snidely, "So did your girlfriend writing a review about you in *Passage* magazine."

Han held his hands up in front of himself. "I'm just saying. Lots of folks who haven't found their audience could benefit from a local, independent venue giving them a chance."

Duke steepled his hands in front of his mustache. "It

sounds like just about everyone thinks an arts festival is a good idea."

"I'm not so sure about everyone," Jerry said, but Nancy and Richard didn't raise any objections.

"Is there a compromise to be found?" Deandre asked, looking to Elizabeth and then Patty. He raised a brow. "Mrs. Boyd, if this festival were approved, would you be willing to lend some of your valuable expertise to our organizing committee?"

Graham sucked in a rough breath. That actually wasn't a terrible idea—for all that it would be difficult to manage. Up by the podium, Elizabeth visibly bristled, and for a second he worried she was going to tell everyone exactly what she thought of Patty. The woman had been rude and dismissive, and he didn't blame Elizabeth at all for not wanting her to be involved.

But Elizabeth held her tongue. Pride bloomed in Graham's chest. She'd hate every second of working with Patty, but if it meant getting this festival off the ground, she'd do it.

Patty wasn't nearly so mature. "Absolutely not." She turned up her nose. "I'm not going to be scapegoated when this 'committee' runs this so-called arts festival into the ground."

"Patty," Duke warned.

"Well, I'm not," she huffed, crossing her arms over her chest. "Now, if the town council wants to hand over the reins completely..."

"Wait a minute—" Elizabeth started.

"One motion at a time," Mayor Horton interrupted, shutting Patty down, and Graham could at least be grateful for small favors.

"The current motion," Deandre said, "being the matter

of Ms. Wu's proposal for an *independent* arts festival. It is a risk, handing it over to relative outsiders, to both the art world and to this magnitude of project…"

Graham could almost see the moment teetering on the edge of a knife. A sudden determination filled him. His stomach churned, but he swallowed past it to step forward. To stand beside Elizabeth. "Counselors, if I may be so bold, this event—which you all—"

"Most all," Jerry muttered.

"—which most all of you believe to be a good idea, was proposed, researched, and organized by an outsider to the art world." A stone lodged in Graham's throat again. "But an insider to the heart of Blue Cedar Falls. Elizabeth Wu knows this town. She knows what it needs. She's the one to bring this thing to life." He glanced down at her, and his ribs squeezed inward as she stared back at him, wide-eyed. "Give her a chance," he begged them, "and you won't regret it."

He couldn't quite tell if she wanted to kiss him or kill him. He was overstepping here, rising to defend her when she was perfectly capable of defending herself. But he'd worked in local government his entire adult life. He wasn't going to let the question get reframed.

Not without speaking up for what he believed.

This girl—this woman. She was worth taking a chance on.

He wished he had earlier.

But he was so unbelievably grateful that he had now.

"Well." Mayor Horton cleared his throat. "At this point, I think we've heard from just about everybody."

"And their grandmother," Duke agreed.

"I think we need a few minutes to discuss this privately?" Naya suggested.

Mayor Horton nodded. "We'll hold the vote in fifteen minutes."

With that, the counselors fled the scene, while Graham and Elizabeth were swarmed. Graham snuck a peek over toward the other side of the chambers, where Patty had a gaggle of her own surrounding her.

"Oh, Graham, sweetie." Graham's mom threw an arm around him. "Look at you, talking in front of people without throwing up."

"It was a near thing," he assured her, though he hardly felt it now.

Funny, how sticking up for something you really believed in made it easier to swallow your nerves.

"See?" His father gave him a rough clap on the back. "Not so bad." He gestured at the vacated chairs where the members of the town council had sat. "Could be you up there in another couple of years."

Oh, wow, no.

Fortunately, his attention was pulled away by Tom coming over to shake his hand. Everyone seemed to have something to say about how the presentation had gone, some prediction to make about what would come next, though at this point it was all speculation.

Elizabeth broke away from her family to come over to him. "What you said back there..."

Her dark eyes sparkled, and he breathed a sigh of relief. There was no sign of her wanting to hit him after all.

He longed to pull her into his arms. As it was, he shoved his hands in his pockets and tried to put the full depth of his feeling into his gaze. "I meant every word of it."

"I know." She licked her lips. "Graham..."

But before she could say whatever she was going to tell him, Mayor Horton tapped on the microphone to call everyone back to attention. Graham looked up, surprised to find the members of the town council retaking their seats.

A warm touch grazed the back of his hand. Graham held out his palm, and Elizabeth slipped hers into it. It was something they might have done before they'd become a couple, but it felt different now.

He held on for all he was worth.

It didn't matter what they said. That was what Elizabeth chanted to herself over and over in her head. Small-town politics. Dumb Officer Dwight poisoning people against her for the past fifteen years. No big deal.

But as Graham gripped her hand, she knew it was a lie. What they said mattered. It mattered to her self-esteem and it mattered to her ambitions. On a practical level—it *mattered*. If this festival failed to launch—or worse yet, if Patty sank her claws into it—she'd be back to square one, looking for a way to get her work in front of people.

Heck, maybe she'd have to open her own gallery.

Ha. Like that would ever happen. She'd need a small fortune, and Patty would probably just end up protesting the zoning board meeting instead of the town council one.

Pulling her out of her doom spiral, Mayor Horton addressed the reseated members of the town council. "Counselors, we're ready to vote on Ms. Wu's proposal for an independent clothesline arts festival, to be held in downtown Blue Cedar Falls next spring, organized by Ms. Wu and a committee of her choosing. Let's just go down the line, shall we? Duke?"

The mustache twitched with his smile as he looked to her and Graham. "I'm in."

"Naya?"

"Heck yes."

Hope dared to rise inside of her, but Jerry was up next.

"Jerry? Do I have to ask?"

"A big fat no from me, John."

"We knew that," Graham whispered, squeezing her hand.

Elizabeth nodded but couldn't speak.

"Natalie?"

"It's a no from me, too—though I would be happy to reconsider if we had a more experienced committee leading the project."

Ouch. Elizabeth refused to flinch, but it was a close thing.

"Richard?"

"Same."

Double ow.

"Brynn?"

Brynn shot her a warm smile. "Ms. Wu has convinced me. I vote yes."

Which brought it down to the wire, exactly the way they'd expected.

Mayor Horton could be an announcer on a reality show, he leaned into the drama so hard. "That leaves you, Deandre. The fate of the festival is in your hands."

Deandre gazed at her across the space, and she struggled not to squirm.

Then one corner of his lips curled upward. "I say we listen to Mr. Lewis and we give this young lady a chance."

Instantly, chaos broke out. June jumped up and cheered, and Clay and May and Han and Ned were right there with her. Her mom stayed in her seat, one hand on her cane, but her smile was broad. Graham's mom and Tom and Chloe and Dahlia and the whole crew whooped and hollered, and Elizabeth felt faint.

Was this really happening?

"Pinch me," she challenged Graham.

He laughed and pulled her into a hug, and it felt so good. Her entire nervous system was on overload. She half expected to wake up in a hospital and be told the last couple of weeks had all been a coma-induced hallucination, but no. She pinched her own wrist where it was looped around the back of Graham's neck. She didn't snap out of it. There was no beeping of hospital machines or a friendly nurse to tell her she'd been unconscious for years.

This was real.

All of it.

She pulled back, but she kept her hands on Graham's shoulders.

"Congratulations, E," he told her, but his gaze was too intense. "You did it."

Only that wasn't quite right, was it?

"We did. Graham—" Her throat tightened. She could hardly speak, could hardly breathe. Adrenaline flooded her veins, and wow, was she ever going to crash later, but in this moment, she was flying high.

Everyone she cared about had come out for her tonight. Her friends, her family. The town had entrusted her with a responsibility even she didn't know if she was up for.

And through it all, there had been Graham. Amazing, incredible Graham, who'd supported her for years. He'd been by her side, driven out with her for her research project, made spreadsheets and PowerPoints and crunched numbers and listened to her rehearse *so many times*. He'd lobbied the town for her.

He'd stood up in front of all these people. His face had turned green, but he had done it.

He'd told them to take a chance on her.

And it was high freaking time she took a chance on him, too.

Without giving herself a moment to think it through, she looped her hands behind his neck again. Hauling him down, she looked him right in the eyes, silently asking for permission even as she was rising up onto her toes.

Understanding flashed across his gaze, followed immediately by a smile that blinded her.

Then he was the one crashing his mouth to hers. It was an awful kiss, their teeth bumping, and they were both grinning like idiots, and it didn't matter. She opened to him, and he opened to her, and then it was great, it was amazing, it was reckless and perfect, and everybody they knew was going to give them *so much grief.*

He pulled away, still smiling as hard as she was, and for just a second, time stood still. They were doing this. For real. No hiding and no hedging their bets.

"Well, dang," a voice said, breaking through the haze.

A full body flush eclipsed Elizabeth's body. She buried her face in Graham's chest, and he wrapped his arms around her tightly. She twisted her neck to peek out from the warm safety of his chest to find her sister May grinning like she had just won a one-hundred-dollar bet. Which, considering the way Han was reaching into his wallet, might actually be true.

"Did you know about this?" their mom interrogated June and Ned.

"No," June insisted.

"You know everything I know," Ned told her.

Her mother turned her gaze to her, and yup, there was the *I knew it* look Elizabeth had been waiting for.

"Is it too late to run back to the beach?" Elizabeth asked Graham, hiding her face in his shirt again.

Laughing, he rubbed his warm hands up and down her arms, soothing her the way that only he could. "Pretty sure." He kissed the top of her head. "You have an arts festival to plan, after all."

"Darn right you do." She looked up to find Chloe standing there, arm in arm with Tom. "You also have some explaining to do."

"Congrats, man," Tom told Graham, ignoring them both. The two men shared a look that made Elizabeth's stomach do a little flip-flop, but Graham seemed happy, so she chose not to examine it too closely. He shifted his gaze to Elizabeth. "And congrats on the festival, too, by the way."

Dahlia broke in. "We have so much work to do." She turned her head to the side. "Hey Clay, you better get down to the Junebug, because you have a lot of customers heading your way."

"I'll warn Zoe," Clay grumbled, heading toward the exit.

"Save the corner booth for us," Graham told him.

Clay held up a hand in acknowledgment.

Dahlia rubbed her hands together. "Festival planning strategy session plus two-for-one pitcher night. What could go wrong?"

"So much," Elizabeth groaned, but there was a warmth in her chest.

"Festival planning *and* dirt dishing," Chloe insisted. "I need to know how *this*"—she gestured between the two of them—"happened."

"I don't care how it happened," a new voice broke in.

Elizabeth and Graham turned as one to find his parents

standing to the other side of their friends. Elizabeth swallowed. Judge Lewis, with his clenched jaw, didn't look happy.

Mrs. Lewis, on the other hand, beamed. "All I care is that it finally did."

"Mom." Graham's eye roll was audible. "Please."

Elizabeth glanced up at him, empathy tugging at her chest. His cheeks were as red as hers felt, only there was more than just the general embarrassment of letting everybody you know find out you're now on making-out terms with your longtime best friend.

People like Tom and Graham's mom—clearly they'd known about Graham's interest in her. Was this the reaction he'd been dreading when they'd agreed not to shout their new status in anybody's face at first?

Graham's mother shifted her gaze to Elizabeth, tilting her head and raising her brows. "And you, young lady, now have no excuse not to come to Judge Lewis's sixtieth birthday bash."

"Lucille," Judge Lewis warned.

"Oh, shush." Mrs. Lewis batted a hand at him. "Our son has a date to a family event. This is exciting!"

Yeah, the hard line of Judge Lewis's mouth was definitely a picture of excitement.

Elizabeth glanced away, desperate for a reason to get out of this conversation. As Graham and his parents continued talking, her gaze caught on Patty, standing on the other side of the chambers with Jerry, Natalie, Richard, and a few other of their friends.

A new wave of uneasiness roiled in her gut.

She might have gotten her festival tonight, but Patty wasn't going anywhere anytime soon. She'd have to deal with her at some point.

But not tonight. Tonight, she had her festival and she had her Graham, and everybody knew it. Nothing could bring her down.

It was after midnight by the time they made it home. Graham's vision was all fuzzy around the edges, his fingers clumsy as he dropped his keys for the third time.

Stupid, amazing, wonderful two-for-one pitchers.

"What are you *doing*?" Elizabeth laughed, sagging into him so hard she nearly tipped him off balance.

He returned the favor, ducking down to pick his keys up off the ground and sending her stumbling. He reached out an arm to catch her, and she giggled as she folded herself into him, and his heart was so big it scarcely fit inside his chest.

The fourth time was the charm. He fit his key to the lock, turned the knob, and the door to their apartment swung open.

"Ta-da!" he announced, flinging his keys heaven knew where. He'd figure it out in the morning.

Elizabeth stumbled in after him, lowering her voice to imitate a sportscaster. "Door three, Graham one."

"Hush." He kicked the door closed and reeled her into his arms.

She came so willingly.

All night, out at the Junebug, celebrating their victory with their friends, he'd stopped himself from touching her a dozen times—only to remember, over and over, that he was allowed to. She *wanted* him to.

And sure, their buddies had given them some crap about it. Dahlia and Chloe had insisted on knowing every detail, and Tom had been insufferably smug.

But it had all been loving. Their friends were happy for them.

He was so happy he could hardly even help himself.

Heart soaring with the sheer, incredible, brilliant impossibility of it all, he crushed his mouth to hers. She tasted like vodka and cranberry and victory and everything he'd ever wanted in his life, and words he shouldn't say threatened to pour out of him. He deepened the kiss and closed his eyes.

"Well, hello there, handsy," she mumbled, even as she was pulling at his jacket.

He belatedly realized he was groping her, and okay, maybe he'd had a beer too many, but could anybody blame him? Poor sober Chloe had promised to drive everybody home before the first order had been placed. He and Elizabeth had been the honorees of the best party he'd been to in years.

And now here he was. Tugging off her clothes in their living room.

Which was stupid. There were beds right down the hall.

He couldn't seem to stop himself long enough to get to either of them, though. In the week or so that they'd been doing this, they'd taken turns more or less, ending up in his room more often than hers, just because it was neater, but it didn't matter. He'd sleep with her on the couch if he needed to.

Actually, that was a pretty good idea.

Tossing her jacket aside, kissing her deeper, he steered her in the general direction.

"Watch the—" she warned.

The TV tray where he'd left a bunch of his notes for the bell tower renovation went tumbling as they banged into it. She pulled away.

He shook his head. "Leave it."

"Who are you?" She clung to him, laughing harder, and the way she tilted her chin up left her neck exposed, so he sealed his lips to that tender skin. She let out a gasp that went right to the very center of him.

"I have no idea," he answered, lowering her down to the couch.

Impulsively speaking in public, revealing information about his personal life to other people. It was all new for him.

He liked it. He liked it so, so much—almost as much as he liked—

"Elizabeth," he groaned, tugging off her top.

She unbuttoned his shirt and slid it off his shoulders, and all this skin was destroying what few brain cells he had left.

Lying there together on the couch, they got lost in kissing for what felt like forever. Urgency built inside him, but just as he started to slide his hand down toward her skirt, she ran her fingertips down his face.

He drew back to look her in the eye through the dimness.

Wonder filled her gaze. "I can't believe they gave approval for my festival."

"What can I say? Hard work and dedication pay off."

"Says the hardest worker I know." She combed her fingers through his hair. "Couldn't have done it without you."

He had put in a lot of extra hours helping her out. If it had been anybody else asking, he might have had flashbacks to junior high and the jocks who used to pretend to be his friend so he'd give them a hand with their homework. But it was Elizabeth, who liked him for who he was.

"Of course you could have." He went to close the space between them again, but she laughed.

"You keep saying things like that. Like you were so sure it was going to happen."

He hadn't been. Not at all. What he had been sure about was...

"What can I say?" He shrugged. "I—" He caught those too-soon words again, pushing them back inside. He swallowed. "I believe in you."

She paused, a moment of silence holding between them. His heart pounded against the insides of his chest.

She knew what he wasn't saying. She *knew*.

Slowly, carefully, she nodded. "I believe in you, too."

And he wasn't disappointed. For heaven's sake, there was no reason to be. He had everything he wanted in this entire world.

He shook off the slight twinge in his chest and smiled before hiding his expression with another kiss. Making his tone light, he prodded, "You better. All our friends know we're shacking up now."

She groaned, but not in a sexy way. She covered her face with her hands. "My *mom* knows we're shacking up now."

He kissed the backs of her knuckles and every bit of her face available to him until she moved her hands away, revealing mortified and yet still joyful eyes.

"If it helps," he told her, "my dad does, too."

She buried her face in his shoulder this time. "Ugh, your dad's *party*..."

"It's going to be great." He hugged her tight, imagining it now.

Social functions with his family—especially ones that included his brother and his father's friends—were awkward at best. He'd sort of been dreading the entire thing.

Not anymore. Everything was more fun with Elizabeth. Sure, there'd be some intrusive questions, especially from Pete, but he didn't care. They could steal expensive appetizers and sit at a table in the back and gossip about everyone and then go make out in the coat closet. It would be awesome.

She shook her head. "I don't own a pearl necklace."

"You don't have to."

"I won't fit in."

And he got it. He really did. She'd always been sort of intimidated by his family; his father's stone-faced routine ever since the senior prank incident hadn't helped. Her concerns were valid and real.

All he could offer her was... "You always fit in with me."

Hallmark card levels of cheese surrounded them, but it didn't matter. It was the truth.

Finally, she lifted her face from his shoulder.

His heart swelled, and he cupped her cheek to brush his thumb beneath her eye. "Always," he repeated.

The way she was looking at him was too intense—like maybe she believed him and maybe she didn't, but all he could give her was what he had.

So that's exactly what he did.

CHAPTER EIGHTEEN

❀ ❀ ❀ ❀ ❀ ❀ ❀ ❀ ❀ ❀ ❀ ❀ ❀ ❀

W hatcha doin'?"

Elizabeth just about jumped out of her skin as she whipped around to find her sister June standing behind her at the front desk of the inn. "Good grief, you're as bad as the cat."

Said cat gave her a sneering look from where she was perched on the counter, her tail threatening the vase of flowers carefully arranged there. Elizabeth narrowed her eyes at the beast. "Don't give me that look. You made me drop a tray of pancakes yesterday morning when you leaped off of that bookshelf."

The cat preened, which was basically an admission of guilt.

"Sorry," June said. She pointed at the door that led to the office separating the lobby from the family's living area. "I thought you would've heard me coming in." She looked to the computer screen. "You must've been pretty absorbed."

Elizabeth had been, actually.

Two weeks had passed since the town council had voted to let her proceed with her arts festival idea, and it had been a whirlwind. Between her other jobs, she'd been busting her rear end, trying to get things in motion. Calls for submission had to go out, sponsors had to get lined up. Right now, she was putting her awesome graphic design skills to work trying to cobble together some print ads. It turned out that travel magazines had ridiculous lead times—a fact she probably would have known if she were more experienced, a voice in the back of her head kept reminding her. She hadn't been able to place all the ads she might have liked to, but she'd gotten a few, including one May had managed to secure for her at *Passage*. The deadline was tonight, though, so she needed to hustle.

"It's just something for the festival." Elizabeth minimized the window and held up a hand. "Before you ask, yes, I checked all the inboxes and turned over the three rooms that were on the list."

June pulled a face. "I wasn't going to ask."

"Right," Elizabeth scoffed.

"I wasn't." Something like hurt flashed across her sister's face. "Why do you always do that?"

Elizabeth paused, scrunching up her brow. "What?"

June gestured in her general direction. "I don't know. Act like I'm accusing you of something."

"Uh." Elizabeth chuckled, but it wasn't funny. "Probably because you usually are?"

That had always been the dynamic between them. Growing up, June was their mother's good little soldier. She took it upon herself to help keep Elizabeth in line. Even after Elizabeth got fed up and moved out—when she really could have used a friend instead of another disappointed mom—June lorded her decision over her. Reminded her over and over again that she had been the one to leave the family.

As if she weren't right here, day in and day out.

Elizabeth braced herself, ready for this to turn into yet another fight.

To her surprise, though, June sighed. She pulled out the other chair behind the counter and sank into it. "I thought we were past this."

Elizabeth had no idea what was going on. "Past what?"

"Do you not remember the time last year when you rescued me after I totally botched handling Mom's medical debt and nearly lost the inn?"

"Uh..." Yeah, that was pretty hard to forget.

"Believe me, ever since then, I have stopped judging anything you do." Pink crept up June's cheeks, and Elizabeth wanted to pinch herself. Was her perfect, holier-than-thou sister actually embarrassed about her previous attitude?

Truth was, now that Elizabeth stopped to think about it, June had been a lot more chill of late, in all aspects of life. Maybe Graham had been right the night they talked about this on the beach. Elizabeth kept reading all this recrimination into everything her sister said. But maybe she'd just been acting out this old role she was so used to playing. When really, deep down, both of them had grown. "Oh."

June shot her a conciliatory smile, then pitched her voice lower. "Plus, we all know that whenever Mom's behind the desk, she's either reading mystery novels or playing mahjong online."

"True..."

When she put it that way, Elizabeth getting so defensive seemed kind of ridiculous. There was a lot to do to keep this place running, but all of them goofed off in their own way when the desk was slow.

She glanced at June, and a pang of guilt echoed behind her ribs. She really had been unfair with her.

That said, June had been kind of unfair to her for about twenty years. But if she could stop, then maybe Elizabeth could, too.

"So seriously," June said, tipping her head toward the screen. "What were you working on?"

Instinctively, Elizabeth wanted to deflect. But she was looking at her sister in a new light. She often accused June of taking over everything or acting like Elizabeth wasn't competent enough to do things herself. Genuine interest lit June's eyes, though, and she swallowed. "You really want to know?"

"Absolutely."

She was so earnest, Elizabeth shook her head. It seemed impossible that anyone could actually be this excited about a project that technically didn't even involve them.

Then again, she thought about Graham and his bell tower renovation and how invested he was in that. If there was anything she'd learned from becoming even closer with him these past few weeks, it was that there was no end to his enthusiasm for his nerdy, nerdy little hobbies. She loved his unguarded, unironic glee.

Maybe June's nerdy little hobby just happened to be planning town events.

"Well, it's this ad I'm trying to get finalized." She twisted around enough to pull up the graphics program she'd been using. As it appeared on the screen, she glanced over her shoulder at June, still subconsciously expecting a criticism.

None came, though. June gazed past her at the image and nodded in approval. "Looks good—I like the font."

"Thanks." Just like that, a tension she hadn't even realized she'd been holding melted away from her shoulders. "Here." She clicked to another window. "Let me show you some of the other stuff I've been working on…"

Five hours later, Elizabeth was feeling unexpectedly buoyant about her relationship with her previously least favorite sister.

And absolutely lead-balloon levels of down in the dumps about her progress on getting those ad materials ready to send off to *Passage* before the deadline.

She and June had just gotten so carried away looking at spreadsheets and to-do lists—seriously, Elizabeth didn't even know who she was anymore—that she'd lost track of time. She'd barely made it to her kids' ceramics class. After that, she'd run right home and planted herself in front of her laptop to get the placeholder text for the ad replaced with the real thing and the final tweaks made.

She was just getting it all set to send when a knock sounded on her bedroom door.

"Mmm-hmm?" She had a pencil in her mouth, but she got the idea across.

The door tipped open. "You almost ready?"

The pencil fell out of her mouth as she swung her gaze toward Graham, who stood there in her entryway in a freaking suit and tie, and *Hello, nurse.* He always dressed neatly, but the dark suit and the crisp white shirt and the ever-so-slightly-whimsical emerald-green tie she'd picked out for him that brought out the hint of red in his neatly trimmed beard… Well, he looked good, was what she was saying.

Then it registered in her fried brain. He looked good because they were supposed to be heading to his father's big sixtieth birthday bash.

"I am so sorry," she scrambled. How had she lost track of time *again* today? "I'm like this close—"

Then the sparkle to his dark eyes hit her.

He was messing with her. "You have an hour."

"Oh, thank *God*." She still had clay in her hair.

"Just wanted to make sure you hadn't forgotten."

Thank God he couldn't read her thoughts to know how close that was to the truth. "Who, me?"

He was kind enough not to answer. "Do you have a second?"

"Uh…" She glanced back at the screen of her computer. The ad sat there, all ready to go, and it was time to stop futzing around with it. She scanned it over one last time, then held her breath and hit send. All the air felt like it went out of her.

Nodding, she pushed her chair back from her desk and rose. "What's up?"

The twinkle in Graham's eye softened. "I have a little something for you."

She tilted her head to the side, her interest piqued. "Oh?"

In so many ways, her and Graham's relationship had morphed seamlessly from best friends to more. They still hung out, still goofed around and watched obscure films and ate takeout and met up with their friends on Friday nights at the bar. They just also made out a lot and slept in each other's beds.

There were a few other small differences.

For example, he'd never pulled an oblong satin box from behind his back before.

Her heart fluttered, because despite claiming to be hardcore, she was a mushy pile of mush.

"Graham..."

"It's not a big deal," he promised.

And it wasn't like he'd never given her a gift before. They each had spotted a little something the other might like from time to time and brought it home, beaming.

He'd never looked at her like this while giving it to her before.

"You shouldn't have." That was what you were supposed to say, right? "People are going to think I'm just sleeping with you for your fancy small-town bureaucrat salary."

"They wouldn't dare."

She flicked her gaze upward. "Your dad would."

She reached forward and took the present anyway. She flipped open the lid.

Inside lay a copper pendant. It was an abstract shape—just a bunch of swirls, really, but it was cool. Definitely handmade. Inset within one of the swirls was a milky white pearl.

She darted her gaze to his.

His smile was tentative. "You said you didn't have a pearl necklace."

She laughed, open-mouthed. "This isn't what I meant, you dork."

"I know." He took her by the hand and pulled her in. "You never have to change who you are to fit in with my family, you hear me?"

Her heart gave a little thump. She wasn't so sure about that. What she was sure about was that he believed it.

"Do you like it?" he asked.

She nodded. "I love it."

It was exactly her taste, the pendant strung on a black leather cord. It would look awesome with the little black dress she'd borrowed from June.

It'd make her feel like herself, even in a fancy, respectable dress.

She looked up at Graham, her heart thumping harder now.

He'd known that. He'd known she was psyching herself out, and that she'd planned to get dolled up in a costume meant for someone else. And he'd gotten her something she'd love, because he didn't want her to change.

And if he believed in her that hard...If he cared that much...

Who knew? Maybe she actually did belong.

Or maybe she didn't.

Walking into the ballroom at the old Morrison mansion on the far southern end of town, Elizabeth wanted nothing more than to walk right back out the way she'd come. There was a reason why she didn't attend family events with Graham, despite fifteen years of friendship.

On the surface, the Lewises were super normal, but Graham's dad's dad's dad had been some sort of minor oil baron or something. The money hadn't stayed in the family—there were stories of a spendthrift uncle twice removed who blew most of it the better part of a century ago. But that hadn't mattered. Even fleeting money bred power, and the Lewises had been fixtures in government and politics in the Carolinas forever. When Graham had been a kid, his dad had even tried to run for Congress a couple of times, only it hadn't worked out. Being a county judge was pretty good in Elizabeth's book, but to hear Graham tell it, it left Judge Lewis as more or less the slacker of the family.

Not that you could tell, looking around. The Morrison mansion was the fanciest place in the area. Usually it hosted big weddings and corporate retreats, but apparently it was open for milestone birthday parties, too. The whole place was done up in gold and black, with bunches of balloons floating in various corners of the giant room. Elegantly set tables were scattered around, leaving space for a very empty dance floor in the middle. Elizabeth suppressed a snicker at the big speakers set up to either side of it. The last time she'd been here, it'd been for a wedding with a killer DJ who'd kept the party hopping and the bass thumping. Tonight, the only action those speakers were likely to see was the quiet hum of mellow jazz—maybe a Tony Bennett crooner if things got really out of hand.

"Relax," Graham murmured in her ear. He ran a hand down her arm, sending goosebumps in his wake.

Realizing exactly how tensely she'd been holding herself, she let out a deep breath and unclenched her jaw.

"You're gonna owe me for this."

Graham laughed. "Just wait until you have me over for family dinner at the Wu house. I'm sure that'll be payback enough."

"Not even close." Besides, it wasn't as if she really needed to subject him to that particular indignity. Whenever she started dating anyone, someone in her family usually insisted on her bringing them round, but they already knew Graham.

Just then, Graham's mom spotted them. "There you are!" She came on over, and Elizabeth's body tightened again. Graham's mom was great. She'd always been really nice to Elizabeth, and her smile even now was utterly genuine.

Following behind her, though, was Judge Lewis, who'd been wearing the same scowl for the past dozen years, as far as Elizabeth could tell.

"Hey, Mom." Graham gave his mother a hug. "You look beautiful."

She did, too, her gray hair up in an elegant twist. Her black and gold dress fit the color story of the evening without looking too severe.

"You clean up good yourself," she told Graham, straightening his tie. She turned to Elizabeth with a wink. "And who is this lovely lady on your arm?"

"Hi, Mrs. Lewis," Elizabeth said.

"Oh, my goodness, Elizabeth! I hardly recognized you." She grinned and leaned in for a hug, which was super weird, but okay.

Elizabeth glanced up at Graham, who seemed much too pleased by his mother's acceptance of her.

"She does look different when she's not behind bars," Judge Lewis harumphed.

Graham's mom pulled away to glare at him. Elizabeth's face warmed, but Graham put his arm around her. "One time," he reminded his father.

"One time too many."

Elizabeth did her best to ignore him and looked around. "Is there anything we can do to help?"

Thanks to Graham's careful herding, they'd actually arrived a few minutes early.

His mom shook her head. "Everything's taken care of. Just enjoy yourselves."

Right. Sure, simple.

At least it got a little bit easier as a squeal broke through the suffocating air. "Uncle Graham!"

Graham lit up as his five-year-old nephew, Harrison, tackled his legs. "Hey there, buddy."

Elizabeth turned to find Graham's brother, Peter, approaching, looking handsome as always—there was an undeniable family resemblance. Peter was clean-shaven, though, and his suit had a different crispness to it. As a hotshot DC lawyer, he probably had a whole closet full of fancy bespoke ones. Beside him was his wife, Priya, a stunning woman of Indian descent with brown skin and gorgeous black curls who didn't look any less elegant for the three-year-old girl in a frilly pink tutu she was carrying on her hip. Bringing up the rear was the kids' nanny, an older white woman with orange hair named Jolene.

Greetings were exchanged all around. The little girl, Anya, clung to Priya, despite Jolene's quiet offer to take her, which Priya politely brushed off.

"Sorry we're late," Pete told his parents. "Got caught up at work."

"That's my boy." Judge Lewis broke into a smile for what seemed like the first time.

"Well, I'm just glad you're here," their mom said. She directed her attention to her granddaughter. "And I'm especially glad *you're* here."

"You want to say hi to Grandma?" Priya prompted.

"Hi." Anya waved before burying her face in her mom's hair again.

"She's shy," Pete explained. "We're working on it."

Elizabeth mentally rolled her eyes. "Totally normal."

Half the kids in the pre-K class she taught stuck to their parents like glue for at least the first three lessons.

Priya shot her a glance of appreciation before directing

a playfully annoyed one at Pete. "That's what I keep telling him."

Pete rubbed Anya's back. "Gotta buck up sometime if she wants to be president."

"Astronaut," the little girl mumbled.

"Oh, right, I forgot, president was what you wanted to be *last* week. I'm so behind."

"I want to be a T. rex!" Harrison roared.

"Good ambition, little dude," Graham told him, ruffling his hair.

For a fleeting fraction of a second, Elizabeth pictured him doing the same thing with a different little boy. One with straighter hair and a complexion closer to her own, but with the same bright eyes and smile, and oh, wow. Just a few weeks ago, she'd been talking about how *maybe* she might be open to having a kid, if whatever partner she ended up with really wanted one. Now here she was, her ovaries taking over her brain after never speaking to her before in her life.

She shook it off, clasping her hands together in front of herself.

Which was when she realized that said hands were empty. "Crap," she muttered. "I forgot my clutch in the car."

"I'll get it," Graham volunteered. "You wanna come with me?" he asked Harrison. "We can race?"

"T. rex race!" Harrison barreled ahead, his arms curled to look like claws, and heaven help her if her ovaries didn't give a weird little flutter again when Graham didn't miss a beat, doing his best dinosaur impersonation too.

"These boys," his mom sighed, like maybe her ovaries still had a few feelings about matters, too.

Priya shook her head and smiled, finally passing Anya

off to Jolene. "I don't know how you raised two of them," she said to Mrs. Lewis.

"Patience and coffee."

"The secrets to life," Elizabeth agreed, and everybody laughed.

Well, everyone except Judge Lewis, who'd gone stone-faced again at the sound of her voice. His gaze was on Graham as he disappeared through the lobby, and a twinge of discomfort pulled at Elizabeth. Should she have insisted on going and grabbing her own bag? Graham had been Johnny-on-the-spot with the whole helpfulness thing, though.

She was relieved when he returned, and not just because his father stopped—or at least paused—giving her the stink eye. He handed her her bag, and she looped her arm through his, grateful she didn't have to make small talk with his family without him anymore.

So of course Pete chose that moment to reach into his jacket pocket and tug out three cigars. "Gentlemen, would any of you like to get some fresh air?"

Judge Lewis clapped him on the back and started making for the door. "I thought you'd never ask."

"Graham?" Pete asked.

Graham cast a glance back at Elizabeth, and she wanted so badly to tell him to stay. But she smiled. "Have fun."

He scrunched up his brow, like he could tell that she didn't love this, but his dad and brother were waiting.

Priya rolled her eyes as they headed off. "Disgusting."

"I can't stand the smell of those things," Mrs. Lewis echoed.

"So gross," Elizabeth agreed. "Graham doesn't even like them."

"He humors his father." Mrs. Lewis patted her on the back. "Come on. I think the bar is open. They can have their stinky cigars—we have chardonnay."

And, well, nervous as she was about hanging out with Graham's family without him, given their new relationship, it wasn't as if Elizabeth could really argue with that.

Graham held his cigar gingerly as Pete lit up his own. Pete took a couple of puffs and let out a low hum of approval. He caught Graham's eye and raised a brow. "Want me to?"

Graham glanced his father's way before nodding. "Sure."

He passed Pete his cigar and let him light the thing for him. It was kind of Pete to offer. Graham had smoked a grand total of twelve of these in his life and always under pressure. He'd never gotten the hang of lighting them, and every time he tried he failed.

His dad didn't look any more impressed at his decision to hand the task off to his brother than he would have been at his fumbling efforts, but at least it was a little less embarrassing.

Pete passed the lit cigar back with a smile. Graham took a puff and tried not to hurl or cough up a lung.

His father accepted the lighter and made quick work of holding the flame to the end of his own. He made the same grunt of appreciation Pete had as he blew out a couple of smoke rings.

It was cool and quiet out in the garden behind the mansion. Classy strings of bare bulbs had been strung up, giving the area a warm glow without interrupting the darkness too much.

Holding his cigar between his lips, his father set

down the stack of tumblers he'd brought out with him and poured a couple of fingers of scotch into each. Now this part of the celebration Graham could get behind. He accepted his glass and held it up.

"To Judge Lewis on making it another time around the sun," Pete toasted.

"Happy birthday, Dad," Graham echoed.

"Thanks, boys." They each took a sip before his father held his glass up higher. "And to Peter Lewis, Esquire, the newest junior partner at Mayhew, Mayhew, and Tenaka."

Graham smiled at his brother. "Hear, hear."

Pete waved it off. "Old news."

Their dad scoffed. "When we only see you twice a year, even old news is new news."

"You're welcome up in DC any time," Pete said smoothly. Only the thinnest hint of an edge underscored the words.

Those couple of times a year that they saw Pete always involved him and Priya packing up the kids and coming down. Graham made it up to DC now and then, and their mom trekked up there regularly to see the grandkids, but Judge Lewis remained firmly in place, expecting everyone to come to him.

Their dad tapped his cigar in an ash tray. "Only a few more years until retirement."

Pete laughed. "Like you're not planning to die on that bench."

Their dad smirked and shrugged, which wasn't a confirmation, but it wasn't a denial, either. "You know what it's like. Jobs like ours pull you in."

"That they do," Pete agreed, and Graham did his best to keep his smile firmly in place.

Maybe someday he'd let his dad talk him into climbing the ladder, using the town hall gig to leverage himself into something higher profile. But that wasn't his goal. He certainly wasn't going to work until he died. When he retired on his sixty-fifth birthday, he'd go fishing and visit his niece and nephew and take on all the projects at the historical society that he didn't have time for right now. Maybe he'd travel.

One corner of his mouth flickered up. Maybe he'd travel with Elizabeth. If the sky was the limit, maybe he'd travel with Elizabeth and their kid.

It might not be what his dad or brother wanted from their lives, but that was fine. Most of the time.

He cleared his throat, feeling the weight of his dad's quiet exclusion of him from the careers-that-pull-you-in club. Best to just go along with it and focus on Pete.

"Seriously, though, man," he said, tipping his glass toward his brother again. "Congratulations on the promotion."

"Thanks." Pete's smile softened, some of the bravado he always put on in front of their old man fading. "I think this might really be the break I was looking for."

"Well, you deserve it."

Nobody worked harder than Pete.

But Pete disagreed. Shaking his head, he gestured with his cigar to the ballroom on the other side of the glass doors. "Priya's the one who deserves it."

Their father let out a little huff, but Graham asked, "Yeah?"

"I've been working ninety-hour weeks trying to get here. Two small kids? Someone has to take up the slack."

"What about Jolene?"

Their nanny was practically a part of the family.

"Jolene's great, and we're lucky to have her, but Priya's still the one holding down the fort." Pete's smile faltered. "She's given up a lot for this."

The two of them had met in law school. Priya had been on a high-flying trajectory of her own, but after Harrison had come along, she'd reduced her hours. Her choice, as she'd tell anyone, but it had come at a cost.

"Worth it," their father told them.

Pete nodded. "I hope it will be. The new salary..." He whistled and took a puff at his cigar. "Let's just say she's going to be a happy woman this Christmas."

"She should be a happy woman any day of the week," their father said.

"We can finally take that trip to Fiji she's always wanted to go on. Put that third story addition on the house." Pete smirked. "Pretty sure she's had her eye on one of those new all-electric trucks, too. Now that'd look pretty good with a bow on it, huh?"

"Wow." Graham tried to take another puff of his own cigar, but it was still terrible. At least coughing from the smoke was better than coughing at Pete's ideas for how he might treat his wife now that he'd made partner.

None of that was within Graham's reach. He was excited about a cozy little two-story house on a cozy side street a couple of blocks off Main Street in Blue Cedar Falls. His idea of a vacation was the Outer Banks, and his car was a pre-owned Kia.

And Elizabeth...

Elizabeth's car was held together with duct tape. She cursed the thing, but she loved it, too. She was happy in their two-bedroom at Poison Place, and she liked the Outer Banks, too.

Right?

They'd talked about their hopes and dreams enough times over the years. He wanted his picket fence and his family—and her, now that he was allowed to say so. She wanted time to make art and a place to show it, and maybe the money to go out for sushi more than once every couple of months. Some nicer yarn and maybe a spinning wheel someday, if she ever had the space for one. She didn't expect anything more from life, or from him.

Or at least that was what she'd always said.

So many of their assumptions about each other had been proven false over the past few weeks, though. For the most part, that had worked out in his favor. She was open to having a family, and despite every single biker and rock star and international soccer player she'd brought home over the past ten years, she was apparently one hundred percent okay with dating a boring dork with a boring life and a boring job.

And he wanted to trust that. He really did. He wanted to trust her.

But how could he? When their history told a completely different story? How long would his allure last?

How long until she wanted something different? Not necessarily a biker—or even a hotshot lawyer who could take her to Fiji.

Just something, someone more exciting than him.

CHAPTER NINETEEN

W ell, ladies." Mrs. Lewis held up her empty wine glass. "I suppose it's time we mingle."

"Ugh." Priya slumped in her chair. "Do we have to?"

"Duty calls," Mrs. Lewis reminded her.

"Ha," Elizabeth laughed. "Serves y'all right for being respectable members of society."

Mrs. Lewis stood, a sly smile on her lips. "Just you wait, Ms. Chairman of the First Annual Clothesline Arts Festival Committee. Respectability looms large in your future."

"Never," Elizabeth groaned, but she rose all the same.

For the past hour or so, Elizabeth, Mrs. Lewis, and Priya had been hanging out in the comfy chairs by the fireplace in the back of the room, and it had been...nice. Most of Elizabeth's fears about coming to a stuffy Lewis family party had not come to pass. Sure, there were bigwigs from the whole western half of the state milling around, eating fancy appetizers and talking about "the economy." Even stupid Jerry was here, and she was pretty sure she'd caught him giving her the stink eye the one time he'd looked over at her.

But after the way the town council meeting had gone, she just couldn't be bothered to pay any attention to him. For the most part, she'd just hung out with these two women. To her delight, they'd all confessed to enjoying the same trashy TV she binged with May. They'd been dishing about period dramas and rom-coms and romance novels ever since.

And sure, Priya had grilled her a little about her new relationship status, but even that had been sort of weirdly, unexpectedly fun. Priya might look like a princess, but she was smart as a whip, with a sense of humor that was drier than their chardonnay.

More importantly, she clearly cared about Graham and wanted the best for him. Her unassuming acceptance of the fact that he and Elizabeth were trying out being a romantic couple made Elizabeth's chest feel all warm inside.

Even if it also made her squirm a little. She still wasn't completely sure if this new arrangement was going to be permanent or not.

As Priya and Mrs. Lewis wandered off in different directions, she glanced around the room again, unsure where to go. The party really was full of respectable members of society, and festival committee chairwoman or no, she hesitated at the idea of trying to insert herself into any of their normal-person conversations.

Naturally, her gaze flitted toward Graham.

She mentally rolled her eyes at herself. Ever since he'd come back in after presumably pretending to smoke a gross cigar with his brother and dad, she'd been sneaking looks at him across the room, subtly checking him out. He looked so handsome in his suit, his hair combed back and his beard neatly trimmed. All over again, it boggled her mind that she'd never realized—or maybe, more honestly, never permitted herself to notice—how hot he was, but now that she knew, it was like she couldn't keep her eyes off him. He'd met her gaze at least half the times she'd peeked over at him, clearly ready to come to her rescue if she gave the faintest hint that she might need one. Each time, she'd smiled at him to convey that she was fine.

And she was. Really. Just because he'd brought her as his date didn't mean he shouldn't get to hobnob with his extended family and his buddies from the history nerd society and work. She didn't need babysitting.

But there definitely were some folks who did.

The sound of screeching floated her way from the hall. Frowning, she followed the noise to find poor Jolene trying to wrangle her own charges as well as a half dozen other kids who had apparently decided that the party was boring and they should all make mayhem out here. They ranged in age from Graham's three-year-old niece, Anya, all the way up to Mayor Horton's seven-year-old grandson, Branden, and they seemed to have decided to make a game out of jumping off every available piece of furniture in the hallway.

"No, no, sweetheart," Jolene chastised Anya, who'd escaped her and had managed to climb onto a side table. The vase perched on the other side of the table tottered.

A couple members of the waitstaff skirted past Elizabeth.

"These rich kids and their brats," one of them muttered.

"I'll go get Christine."

Christine being the manager of the place; Elizabeth had dealt with her a handful of times when wedding parties had booked their receptions here and their blocks of rooms at the Sweetbriar Inn. She was awesome, but she also always had her hands full, especially on event nights like this. She didn't need to add rescuing kids from chandeliers or finding their parents to her list.

And this wasn't Elizabeth's problem. It really wasn't.

But before she could stop herself, she stepped forward. "Hey! Who wants to do an art project?"

"Ms. Elizabeth, Ms. Elizabeth, see what I made?"

Elizabeth looked up from helping little Anya skewer a marshmallow with a pretzel to find Harrison holding up his own dessert creation.

She gave him and his angel food cake dragon a big thumbs-up. "Nice job, buddy."

After her impromptu decision to volunteer as tribute to the pack of wild children terrorizing the hallway, she'd had to think fast. Fortunately, she had a decade of experience to draw on, and she'd landed on the newly set-up chocolate fountain as a perfect solution.

Together with the kids, she'd stolen a whole tray of dippers, as well as a few bowls of liquid chocolate, then commandeered a table in the far back of the room to turn it into a workstation. The kids had dug in with gusto, building graham cracker houses and marshmallow snowmen. Branden had painted a shockingly good chocolate landscape on a plate and was now meticulously decorating it with maraschino cherries and banana slices.

"Art is everywhere and everything," she'd told them.

Who knew if the message had actually hit home or not, but throw a bunch of kids at a messy art project *and* a chance to eat as much candy as they wanted, and you were bound to have a hit on your hands.

"Oh, wow." Priya pulled up a seat beside Elizabeth's, a wry smile on her face. "All y'all sure have been busy."

"Look, Mom!" Harrison launched into an explanation of his masterpiece, while Anya abandoned her project to attack her mother. Elizabeth gave herself a serious pat on the back for keeping that particular little one away from the bowls of chocolate.

Without missing a beat, Priya wiped Anya's sticky fingers and pulled her into her lap, all while asking questions at exactly the right points in Harrison's monologue. Talk about mad skills.

"Do you want to make another one?" Priya asked Harrison.

"Uh-huh, but this time it's going to be a fire-breathing dragon."

"No actual fire," Elizabeth warned. Priya simultaneously nudged the lit candle in the middle of the table farther away from her son.

As Harrison got to work on another masterpiece and Anya settled into munching on a piece of graham cracker, Priya shot Elizabeth a knowing smile. She gestured vaguely at the organized chaos happening at the table. "I trust that this was your doing?"

"Uh..." For the first time, a hint of doubt snuck into Elizabeth's thoughts. After all her time teaching kids' art classes—and without much better to do—it had felt natural to step up and try to find a bored bunch of kids something productive to do. These weren't her students, though. Okay, fine, about half of them had been, at one point or another. But still. Had she overstepped?

Before she could second-guess herself too much, Priya grinned and rolled her eyes. "Not a responsible member of society, my A-S-S," she spelled out.

"Mom," Harrison chided. "I can spell, you know."

"Well, your sister can't." She winked at Elizabeth. "Yet."

"Enjoy it while it lasts."

"Oh, believe me, I will." Not to be distracted, Priya looked to the kids' projects again. "This really is great. You're a natural."

Unexpected warmth bloomed in Elizabeth's chest. So naturally, she deflected. "Eh, it was nothing."

Priya harumphed. Anya finished her graham cracker and tried to snag a chunk of her brother's sculpture, only to be efficiently intercepted by Priya sticking a marsh-mallow in her hand instead.

"Great as this is," she mused, "I will admit I'm not looking forward to the sugar crash. Not your fault," she rushed to add. "They would have found their way to the chocolate fountain eventually, and at least this way they stayed occupied for a while."

"True..." Elizabeth glanced around, considering.

Despite entering its third hour, the party was as lively as ever—which was to say, not at all lively, at least by the standards of an elementary school classroom. Well-dressed people mingled and sipped sophisticated cocktails and ignored their children, and that was basically that. The music was good, but it was light jazz, which didn't exactly pep anybody up.

Her gaze fell on the empty dance floor, and a flash of inspiration lit up her brain.

"Unless..." she said.

Priya scrunched up her brows before following her gaze.

Then she smiled. "Oh, Elizabeth, you are going to be the best addition to the family ever."

"So what's next for you?" Pete asked, nudging Graham with his elbow.

They were standing near the bar, along with their dad

and a couple of his friends. They'd been discussing Pete's promotion and his dad's upcoming docket. Graham probably should have known that his life would become the topic of conversation eventually, but he was still caught off guard.

Graham shot a glance at his dad before looking away with a shrug. "I've got my hands pretty full, between work and historical society stuff. Plus there's the arts festival coming up in the spring."

Their father made a huffing sound in the back of his throat, which Graham did his best to ignore.

Pete laughed openly, but was that better or worse? "You really know how to live on the wild side, huh?"

"I am who I am," Graham told him.

"Never doubted it." Pete gave him a light slap on the back before clasping his shoulder. "You're really happy with the small-town life, though? Managing the mayor's office? I know it's a decent stepping-stone job and all, but you've been standing still on it for a pretty long time."

The incredulity in Pete's tone grated almost as much as all those not particularly subtle huffs and eye rolls his father kept throwing him. The insecurity he'd felt earlier, trying to avoid taking any puffs on that awful cigar and ruminating on whether or not his boring life could possibly be enough for Elizabeth, threatened to resurface.

His dad and brother would never get that he didn't care about climbing up the ranks. If anything, he wished he could step down a rung on the ladder and make more time for the people and projects he really cared about.

He gulped down the last of his admittedly excellent scotch and set the glass on the bar.

Across the room, he caught sight of Elizabeth. Followed closely by Priya and what appeared to be a parade of small children, she was making her way toward the speakers flanking the empty dance floor.

Well, that wasn't suspicious at all.

He patted Pete's hand before ducking out of his hold. "The big-city life's not for everyone," he reminded him. He tilted his head toward the other side of the room. "If you'll excuse me..."

He crossed the ballroom, curious as all get out about what Elizabeth was doing. He'd seen her collecting children like the Pied Piper earlier in the evening, but this was clearly an escalation. She grabbed the attention of the manager of the place, Christine, to whom she made some vague gestures. Christine nodded, clearly distracted, and Elizabeth led her merry band onward. Over by the speakers, she tugged out her phone, and oh no.

No, this was a terrible idea.

The light background music that had been playing all night cut off abruptly. People blinked in surprise, and Graham dashed the rest of the way over.

"What are you—"

Before he could get the rest of his question out, Elizabeth grabbed a microphone and handed it to Harrison.

Feedback split the air. "Grandpa? Where's Grandpa?"

Graham's dad turned away from the door, confusion on his face.

Harrison's face lit up. "Happy birthday, Grandpa!" He turned to Elizabeth. "Hit it!"

With that, the sound of raucous guitars filled the space as the Beatles' "They Say It's Your Birthday" played. Graham's eyebrows hit his hairline as the kids launched into a performance they must have rehearsed. It mostly involved jumping up and down and screaming the song, but there was some coordination involved. Elizabeth and

Priya played sheepdogs, herding them and dancing and singing along. Graham looked over at his dad, who had been joined by Pete. Dismay and amusement warred on his face.

Graham had his own swirling mix of emotions.

He was embarrassed. How could he not be? This was *not* the kind of performance you did at a Judge Lewis birthday party.

And at the same time...

His heart swelled as he looked over at Elizabeth dancing and playing with this gaggle of kids who weren't even hers. She didn't care about the conventions of this kind of party, and it was...perfect. Warmth and happiness filled the void of stuffy party conversation and perfect manners, and this was why he...

Well.

It was why he felt the way he did.

She glanced up, and their eyes connected across the space. She shot him a wincing smile and mouthed, "Surprise?"

It sure was. The best kind of surprise. He almost didn't even care that his dad was going to be grumbling about this for the next ten years.

A hand settled on his arm from behind. He glanced back to find his mom standing there. She gave his biceps a squeeze.

"Well, that certainly livened things up," she said.

He looked back toward the dancing, his ribs tight. "You think Dad's going to lose his mind?"

"Probably. But maybe that's a good thing..."

"Yeah?"

"Lewis men need shaking out of their comfort zones every now and again."

She let go, only to grab his hand and lead him toward the dance floor, where she joined in. He lingered at the edge of the space, one foot on the carpet and the other on the hardwood. To his surprise, his mom wasn't the only one who'd found her way out there. At least a dozen other adults had become part of the fun, including Mayor Horton, who'd taken his grandson Branden's hand and seemed to be trying to show him how to do the twist. Graham touched his phone in his pocket, wondering if he should call 911 now or wait until after the mayor fell and broke a hip.

The song ended, and Anya screamed, "More!"

Kids started shouting suggestions. Elizabeth looked up. Graham followed her gaze to find his dad still standing there with that expression that was halfway between a scowl and a smile.

"Oh, for heaven's sake, Ward," his mother called out, "let the kids have some fun."

His dad narrowed his eyes, but sighed and made a motion with his hand that they should go on.

With a grin, Elizabeth hit a button on her phone.

The kids screeched with delight as "Baby Shark" started playing. Graham groaned dramatically and covered his face with his hands.

Which was about when Priya sashayed her way over to him, acting out the song without a bit of inhibition.

Harrison bashed into him, he was bouncing so hard. "Come on, Uncle Graham!"

And who could possibly say no to that?

Half the room was out on the dance floor by then. The other half seemed vaguely horrified, but forget them. Graham fell into step with Harrison, mimicking his motions. As he clapped his hands together like a mommy shark's jaws, he caught Elizabeth's eye again and smiled. She grinned back, but there was still a self-consciousness to her gaze, and he wanted to kiss it off her face. He wanted to yell at every person in the room—including his father—who dared to act as if she hadn't performed a miracle here.

He couldn't do that, of course. But the kissing part?

Yeah. That he could do.

He nudged Harrison off in his mother's direction, and the kid went happily. Sidestepping Mayor Horton and Branden, he shimmied his way over to Elizabeth and pulled her into his arms.

"Your dad is trying to murder me with his eyes," she hissed.

"He is not."

He probably was.

"I'm sorry—"

"Don't be." He shook his head, pulling back and clasping her upper arms. "You saved this party."

"By ruining it."

"By transforming it."

Because that was what she did. She found the joy and the life where it seemed like there was none. She'd been bringing out the best in him for over a decade, urging him out of his comfort zone, and he needed that.

Everyone here did.

"Thank you," he said earnestly, probably too emotionally, but he couldn't help himself.

She slowed, coming to a halt in his arms. "You really think it's okay?"

"I think it's amazing. I think—" There were so many things he thought. But what he settled on was "I think *you're* amazing."

With that, he kissed her, full and deep and trying to explain to her everything he couldn't find a way to put into words.

Of course, the kids around them whooped and screeched. Someone tugged at the back of his jacket, and he pulled away to find Harrison making a face like he was going to puke, and okay, fine. There was a time and a place.

Elizabeth's whole posture was lighter, though, so he couldn't regret the bit of PDA, gross as the kids might think it was.

The time and the place for more was later, at their apartment, behind closed doors.

The music changed, and he laughed out loud.

Right now, right here?

It was the time and the place for the chicken dance.

CHAPTER TWENTY

Two weeks later, Graham's dad still hadn't said anything about Elizabeth hijacking the audio cable at his sixtieth birthday bash—at least not directly. His pointed glances her way every time they ran into each other spoke volumes, though.

That didn't stop the rest of the town from continuing to be aflutter about it, much to Graham's amusement.

"Is it really true that Mayor Horton did the tootsie slide?" Graham's Realtor, Crystal, asked as she passed him the next in what seemed like a never-ending stack of papers to sign.

"Poorly, but yes," Graham agreed, scanning the document before scribbling his name.

"I'd pay a pretty penny for a video of that," Mrs. Carroway commented.

Crystal laughed. "You and me both."

Graham smiled, waiting as patiently as he could for her to slide the next page over.

It wasn't that he didn't enjoy gossiping about the most dignified people in town letting their hair down for a couple of hours on a Saturday night. But they were here to close on his house.

He shot a glance toward Mr. Carroway. Both he and his wife were in their seventies, with plenty of smile lines to show they'd had their share of joys. He clutched the keys to the house in his age-spotted hands, glancing at them regularly between signature lines, like he wasn't quite sure he was ready to let go of them.

"What about your old man?" Mrs. Carroway asked, pulling Graham's attention back to the discussion. "Judge Lewis bust any moves? It was his party after all."

Graham smiled ruefully. "I'm afraid not."

"Pity," Crystal said.

"He had fun in his own way," Graham assured her.

Crystal hummed like she knew exactly how diplomatic he was being.

By and by, conversation drifted to other subjects— Dottie Gallagher had apparently had a few too many vodka gimlets at the Junebug the other night and let some interesting revelations fly. As they chatted, the stack of papers left to sign shrank until finally there was just one left.

Crystal handed it to Graham with a flourish. He took a deep breath, skimming over the fine print. Then he cracked his knuckles and scrawled his name on the bottom line.

Beaming, Crystal pushed back her chair and stood. "Mr. Lewis, congratulations. You are now officially a homeowner."

"Technically, I'm pretty sure the bank is…"

Crystal laughed the comment off and held out her hand. Graham stood and shook it. He turned to the Carroways and their Realtor and shook hands with them, too.

Mr. Carroway gripped his palm tightly. "We had a lot of good memories in that house, you know."

Graham's chest squeezed. "I know."

"You take good care of it." Mr. Carroway pressed the key into his palm. "Make some good memories of your own, you hear?"

"I will," Graham promised, earnest.

That was why he'd bought the place, after all. To forward his dreams. To build a life and a home and hopefully a family. He couldn't wait.

At the same time, as they wrapped everything up and started drifting toward the door, a thread of uncertainty tied itself into knots inside of him.

When he'd decided it was time to finally move on with his life and start looking for a house of his own, he'd set a whole chain of events into motion. The fact that his decision to separate himself from Elizabeth had been what eventually led to the two of them getting together still boggled his mind, but he couldn't regret a single step they'd taken along the way.

They'd been testing the waters as a couple now for more than a month, and it had been one of the happiest months of his life. He'd thought he knew everything there was to know about her, but it turned out that there was still more to discover—from the soft curl of her body beside his as they slept to the new, even less guarded tirades she went on when something at the inn or the community center or with the festival planning committee tried her patience. He drank it all in, loving the chance to see even more sides to her. He was pretty sure she was happy, too.

He wanted to build this new home, this new life, this new family with her.

He just wished he knew that was what she wanted, too.

Whenever he brought up their future together, she danced around the subject, though.

Well.

He gripped his brand-new set of keys in his hand. The future started now.

That night, Elizabeth arrived at the Junebug before any of her friends.

Clay raised a brow at her as she bustled in the door. "You okay?"

"Fine, just running a little early." And yeah, all right, she could see how that might be a sign that something in the universe was wrong. "What's the special tonight?"

"Han worked up a new yuzu margarita recipe we're trying out."

Elizabeth laughed. "Weren't you the one swearing your bar was going to be a no-frills, old-fashioned watering hole?"

"Yeah, yeah, yeah." He waved a hand, glowering, but he mostly just looked like a grumpy teddy bear. "Then I had to go and end up being friends with a freaking foodie."

"And your life is all the better for it," Han said, emerging from the back room with a case of liquor bottles that he set down behind the bar. He dusted off his hands. "I'm taking over the kitchen for the night, too."

"Ooh." That was a rare treat. "Well, I'll grab a pitcher of the yuzu margaritas, and two of whatever appetizer you're cooking up."

As she was talking, the bell over the door chimed, and Dahlia, Archer, and Stefano spilled in.

"Make it three," Archer corrected. "I'm starving."

"Are you okay?" Dahlia asked, shooting Elizabeth the same mock-concerned look Clay had. "You're early."

Elizabeth threw her hands up in the air. "Is everybody really so shocked by this?"

"Yes," said literally everybody, including May, who had just walked in the door.

"Hey, babe," May said to Han, who shot her a sexy grin as he came around the bar to greet her.

They embraced, and okay, that was Elizabeth's cue to find a table.

They snagged their usual one in the back corner. Chloe and Tom joined them not long after. Elizabeth positioned herself with a good view of the door. As she and her friends caught up on the events of the week, she munched on some awesome barbecue egg-roll things Han had invented. Every time the front door swung open, she glanced up.

Until finally, a familiar face appeared.

Shoving her chair back, she hopped to her feet.

Graham lit up the moment he spotted her. She dashed across the bar, narrowly avoiding a collision with Zoe, who was delivering a tray full of beers to a bunch of guys by the pool table. She threw herself at Graham.

"Oof." He caught her in his arms and planted a kiss on her that went straight to her toes.

"How did it go?"

He'd asked her to go to the closing with him, but she hadn't been able to find a sub for her class. Graham had sent her a selfie of himself standing in front of the new house, the keys dangling from his fingertips, so she'd known things had gone okay, but he was so invested in this home-buying thing. She'd been anxious on his behalf all day.

"Great." He rolled his eyes as he curled an arm around her side and led her back toward their group's table. "I mean, slow as molasses, but all's well that ends well."

"There's the responsible homeowner," Tom greeted him.

"Congrats!" Archer poured him a yuzu margarita—they were on their second pitcher at this point; they really were delicious.

Graham accepted the drink and the applause from the gang.

He took the seat beside Elizabeth and launched into the story of how everything had gone. It was ... really boring, honestly, but Elizabeth was riveted anyway. She squeezed his hand the entire time, trying to remind herself that this was what he wanted in life. She could be happy for him as both his best friend and his girlfriend.

And if she felt a little threatened by his forward progress toward a stable life with a mortgage, well, that was her problem. A part of her wanted the future he said he hoped to build with her, while another part still just didn't see how she fit into it, quirks and shaky credit history and all. But she didn't need to obsess about any of that right now. One crisis at a time, right?

"So when are you planning to be in?" Tom asked Graham. "Still thinking another few months?"

"Depends how long it takes to get the place fixed up." Graham gave Elizabeth's hand a gentle squeeze. "It's not like I'm in a rush or anything."

"Right," Dahlia agreed.

She, Chloe, and May all shot Elizabeth glances that held varying degrees of sympathy and concern. They all knew how torn she felt about the whole thing; they also knew she was putting on a brave face and trying to be mature.

She cast her gaze upward, lifting his hand to her lips to give it a quick kiss to show that she was teasing—even though she wasn't quite sure she was. "Well, you may not be in a rush, but I'm not wasting any time looking for a new roommate. Any applicants?"

"Does Poison Place accept dogs?" Dahlia asked.

"Hemlock House," Elizabeth corrected her.

"And no," Graham told her. "Or I would have adopted one of those dachshund puppies the shelter found last winter."

"Nothing stopping you now." Tom raised a glass.

Graham lifted his own and clinked it against Tom's. "True…"

"Too bad about Poison Place not taking them, though," Dahlia said, pouting. "You know I'd love to move out of my sister's basement, but no way I'm leaving Angel behind."

Angel being her pit bull mix. Elizabeth knew from personal experience that the dog lived up to her name— she was an absolute sweetheart. But the chances of getting Hemlock House to bend the rules for even the most well-tempered of pitties would be a stretch.

"It's not like I have to stay at Hemlock." Elizabeth loved it there, but without Graham, it would never be the same.

"You're leaving Poison Place?"

Elizabeth looked up to find June pulling out an empty seat next to May. She automatically sat up straighter.

"I mean, it's on the table."

"I don't know if it makes any sense for us to find a new place together," Dahlia said, "much as I would love to. I mean, with you and Graham…" She glanced between the two of them.

Elizabeth internally cringed.

It may have been less internal than she'd intended.

"What?" Dahlia asked. "It seems like only a matter of time before you'll be moving in with him."

Graham pressed his ankle to hers beneath the table, and she leaned into him, feeling his support. He was honestly being so nice about not pressuring her that it was almost frustrating. Why was she so torn about this? She adored him. They had so much fun together; they always had. Since they'd made the transition from friends to more, things had only gotten better. She wanted to be with him. Maybe forever, in a house they'd work together to turn into a home.

It was just never how she'd imagined her life, was the thing. She was the irresponsible, flighty artist who'd fled the pressures of home to go be a penniless bohemian. Yes, she'd been working to improve her image and show the world that she could be a disciplined, upstanding member of society. But deep down, she still saw herself as someone who was going to die penniless and alone in a gutter somewhere. Accepting the future Graham was offering her in his perfect raised ranch grated on these old beliefs inside of her.

And Graham. Amazing, incredible, patient Graham actually seemed to understand that, when even she continued to struggle with it.

"It's only been a month, folks," Graham said. "We don't want to rush things."

"Well, if you're just looking for something temporary," June said carefully, "there's always room at our place."

May snorted. "You mean behind Mom's sewing machine? Or between the treadmill and the elliptical?"

Elizabeth laughed. Her room had been converted into her mother's craft space years ago. May's had become home to the exercise equipment more recently, but the point still stood, and June knew it.

June huffed. "I said it'd be temporary." Then she raised her brows. "Or less temporary, if you needed it to be. I'm always happy to stay with Clay, if you want my room."

Elizabeth had the sudden distinct sensation of stepping onto a booby-trapped tile in a video game and plummeting into a pit full of fire and snakes below.

June had already mentioned the fact that she and Clay were contemplating getting engaged. Elizabeth had been braced for the fact that the Wu girls would have to figure out how to take care of their mom and Ned and the inn once June moved out, but no way was she prepared to fall on her own sword—or into a pit of fire and snakes—now.

"Uh, thanks but no thanks." She'd moved out at eighteen for a reason.

Lots of reasons, actually. Some of them had gotten better over time. She felt less of a need to rebel because she gave fewer hoots about the fact that she was never going to measure up to her sisters' shining examples.

But some of her reasons had stayed the same. She was still stubborn, and last she'd checked, her mother was, too. She loved her family deeply, and she wished things could be easier between them; she wished she hadn't left in the heat of an argument, and that her mother hadn't seen it as the worst possible kind of betrayal. But moving back in now? Having to constantly avoid her mom's conversational landmines and the implications that all of her worst fears about herself were true?

Maybe she was getting better about not assuming everything her family said was a passive-aggressive indictment against her. But she still had limits.

June shrugged. "Well, just keep it in mind."

"Will do." She definitely would not. Time to change the subject. "What has you gracing us with your presence tonight anyway?"

"Can't a girl say hi to her sisters?"

May and Elizabeth both narrowed their eyes at her.

She sighed. "Clay's busy making some weird cocktail Han dreamed up. Apparently, it's really popular."

"Because it's amazing." May passed her her glass, and June took a sip.

Her eyes widened. "Oh, dang."

"Right?"

June passed the drink back, only to grab an extra glass from the middle of the table and fill it up. "I'll get the next round," she promised. She took a sip and turned back to Elizabeth. "So how's stuff with the festival shaping up?"

May laughed. "You really can't go three seconds without talking about work, can you?"

From anyone else, it would have been a pointed barb, but May didn't put any heat in the remark, and June brushed it off. "What? I'm genuinely curious."

Time was, Elizabeth would have doubted that, but as they'd worked on the festival together these past few weeks, she'd come to realize that June honestly did think organizing big public events was fun.

"Good," Elizabeth replied. She crossed her fingers under the table for luck. It felt like almost too much hubris to say as much out loud. "Artists' submissions are starting to come in."

"And they're awesome," Dahlia interjected. "We're going to have no problem filling the festival with quality entries."

Elizabeth's chest warmed. It was true—and a huge relief. Among her worst nightmares had been the possibility that she could have shut Patty Boyd out of the selection process only to have a bunch of duds for submissions.

"Well, that's no surprise." June smiled. "Your connections with the art world were never in doubt."

Unexpected warmth rose in Elizabeth's chest and on her cheeks. It wasn't easy to accept such a matter-of-fact compliment from June.

So she turned the spotlight around. "Marketing and publicity is going well, too—thanks in no small part to May."

May tipped an imaginary hat. "Glad I could help."

Graham nudged her elbow with his. "Thanks in no small part to you being awesome, too."

"There is that," she agreed, as flippant as she could be. "But I'm pretty sure it's mostly me having an awesome team."

To her other side, Chloe crossed her arms and let out a sigh. "I'm still so bummed that I can't be a more awesome part of the team."

Ack, right. "It's not your fault you're going to be pushing out a small human more or less as the festival is happening."

"I know," Chloe pouted. "Doesn't make the timing any less crappy." She put a hand on her still barely visible belly. "No offense, little dude or dudette. It's not your fault."

"Definitely not." Tom rubbed her shoulder. "And it's not yours, either."

Chloe let out a little laugh. "I mean, even if it were, it'd technically be half yours."

"How're things going, anyway?" Graham asked.

Tom looked to Chloe, who tipped her head back and forth. "Okay? I guess?"

"Are you feeling any better?" Elizabeth asked.

Chloe made a sour face. "Does barfing only a couple of times a day instead of feeling like I'm going to twenty-four seven count as better?"

"Technically yes?" Archer offered, wincing.

Chloe threw up her hands. "It's not even the physical stuff that's driving me bonkers right now. I was an idiot and started looking at all the birth plan stuff, and the parenting stuff." Her eyes widened comically. She dragged her fingers down her face. "There's *so much*."

Elizabeth cringed in sympathy. "Yikes."

"I just feel like I can barely take care of myself some days, you know?" Chloe dropped her hands to her lap and fiddled with her rings. "How am I ever supposed to do all this stuff?"

Elizabeth's heart and stomach clenched as one. Wow, did she ever know that feeling.

"The good news is you only have to do half of it," Tom reminded her.

"Not even that much," Elizabeth rushed to add. "You've got an awesome team."

Chloe narrowed her eyes. "An awesome team that's also organizing a town-wide event."

"We can do both." Elizabeth projected as much confidence as she could, even though deep down she was nearly as flustered as Chloe seemed.

Why was it easier to believe that she could rally the troops and be there for her friend if she needed them than it was to believe that she could rally herself and take care of the things she needed to do? For the festival, for herself, for Graham and their future.

She'd probably never understand it.

"We'll do whatever it takes," Graham chimed in. A soft grin spread across his lips. "I have full faith."

She didn't doubt *that* in the least.

She just wished she—and Chloe—could summon a little more of that faith themselves.

CHAPTER TWENTY-ONE

❋ ❋ ❋ ❋ ❋ ❋ ❋ ❋ ❋ ❋ ❋ ❋ ❋ ❋

Ａll righty." Graham's dad mopped his brow before crouching down to grip the bottom edge of the sofa. "On three. One, two—"

Together, the two of them lifted the thing over the threshold of the house. Once it was through the doorway, Graham said, "Okay, we're good."

"Getting too old for this," his father grumbled as he shut the door behind him.

Graham bit his tongue as he began sneaking furniture sliders under the two legs of the couch on his end. Originally, his plan had been to get Tom or Archer and Stefano to help him with bringing over the load of furniture from the attic, but his father had decided that today was the day it had to go, and that the two of them could handle it on their own.

"Take a breather," he urged his dad, coming around to the other side.

"I'm fine. Just need a glass of water."

"Paper cups are by the fridge."

A month and a half had passed since he'd closed on the house, and things were finally starting to come together.

The refrigerator itself had arrived just a week ago now, and he'd gotten the water hooked up to the in-door dispenser the other day with only a half dozen mishaps and one change of clothes.

Getting actual dishes in here was another matter. It wasn't as if he spent enough time here to eat real meals. He basically got in, got a project done, and got out. A stack of paper plates and cups had been more than sufficient.

It wasn't exactly environmentally friendly, though. He should probably go out and pick up some real plates, glasses, and mugs, but it was one of those tasks he kept putting off.

At least it was a clear-cut task.

His stomach did a little dip as he hefted the last corner of the couch up an inch to get the slider underneath.

Things between him and Elizabeth had been going so great of late. Their transition from best friends to romantic life partners felt seamless in every way.

Except when it came to this house.

She didn't get cranky every time he mentioned it anymore. But for the moment, the plan was still the same. He'd move out; she'd stay at Poison Place with a new roommate or get a new apartment that allowed dogs with Dahlia. They'd keep dating and someday, when they both decided they were ready, they'd move in together. He hoped that this would be their forever home, but there was a lot of distance between here and there, and he didn't want to go making assumptions. Their being together at all still felt like a miracle. Making plans for what they'd do a year from now or even two seemed like tempting fate.

If things worked out long term, they'd figure out the next steps.

In the meantime, the matter of how they'd divide up their stuff when he moved out was a roadblock he could see looming in the distance. Things like dishes and cutlery were easy; she picked out all of those, so of course she'd keep them for her place. He'd find something cheap or secondhand. Eventually.

His dad returned from the kitchen, cup of water in hand. He gestured at the couch. "You know where you're going with that?"

"More or less."

Graham got in place on the far end of the sofa and gave it a push forward. The furniture movers did their job, helping it glide across the hardwood without much effort. He paused after about a foot to make sure they weren't scratching the floor, but it all seemed to be good.

Ripping out the Carroways's ancient brown-and-gold carpet had been the biggest project of them all, followed only by putting in the new flooring. He'd known that buying a dated fixer upper of a house would be a lot of work, and for the most part, he enjoyed the process of renovating it.

That didn't mean he wanted to fix the hardwood again.

"You're off-center," his dad commented, watching from the other side of the room.

Graham shoved the couch another six inches forward before dusting off his hands. "Won't really know until I get everything else set up."

"So in about five years or so?"

Graham bit the inside of his cheek this time. "I'm not in a rush," he said carefully.

"Clearly."

"Any time you want to come over and tackle a DIY project or two, you're welcome to."

His father huffed out a grunt. "Your brother just hired a contractor for all this stuff when they moved into their new place, you know."

Graham flexed his hands at his sides and turned away. "Well, I'm not Pete."

He sure didn't have Pete's salary, for one thing. Which was fine—he made more than enough for what he needed, plus a healthy bit of savings.

He also didn't have Pete's schedule, thank goodness.

Though it was hard to tell sometimes.

Work had been hectic as hell of late, thanks to Mindy's kid getting sick and spreading the flu to everybody in the family, not to mention half of town hall. As if that weren't enough, Mayor Horton had decided that he should try to get Graham to give the next budget presentation. It was exactly the kind of project his dad would have coached him to take on to "increase his visibility," but he had neither the interest nor the time.

Outside of work, he was booked to the gills, too. There was all the reno work he was doing on the house, of course. His bell tower restoration project for the historical society was moving forward, and he'd had to rustle up a dozen volunteers to staff the group's booth at the upcoming holiday craft fair. Prep work for Elizabeth's art festival was in full swing, and he'd found himself getting happily dragged into all kinds of odd jobs to help. What little time he had left he spent hanging out with the gang at the bar or just relaxing with Elizabeth, and it was great. He was busy and happy, and he'd get around to the moldings when he did, okay?

He was saved from his own temptation to tell his dad precisely that by his phone ringing in his pocket. He tugged it out and glanced at the screen, then winced.

"Sorry," he told his father, "it's the mayor."

His father motioned him to go on. Graham stepped into the hallway while his father pulled out his own phone and plopped on the more or less centered sofa.

Answering the call, he lifted the phone to his ear. "Mr. Mayor."

"Sorry to bother you after hours, but I can't seem to put my hand on those budget numbers we were going over this morning."

Graham had emailed them over before he'd left, but John Horton was not a master of the electronic arts. "There should be a printout in the green folder on top of my desk."

"Appreciate it. Let's see here…"

The mayor must have already trundled his way on over to Graham's office before calling, which was a bit presumptuous, but Graham was going to choose to believe it was just a sign of the man's confidence in his organization. There was the sound of shuffling papers.

"Got it," Mayor Horton said. "You know, I wouldn't have to go rifling through your desk at six o'clock at night if you'd just agree to do the presentation yourself."

Oh, boy, here they went again. "I really think it's best it comes from someone higher up the chain of command."

"Only way to climb the chain is to put yourself out there, you know."

"I appreciate the advice, sir," Graham said, firm but polite, "and the opportunity, but I'm happy where I am right now."

"Suit yourself. But keep the date open, will you? I'm going to keep working at you."

For heaven's sake.

"I'm really quite committed already." Even if public speaking didn't make him sick to his stomach, he'd just been running through his obligations in his head. "Between volunteering for the historical society and renovating the house and helping with the arts festival..."

"You're a busy man, I get it, I get it. How is the festival going anyway? That Wu girl keeping her head on straight?"

"Elizabeth has everything under control," he assured the mayor, wishing it were the first time he'd been asked.

"All right, well, you let me know if things start going off the rails will you?"

"Will do, but I promise, she's doing great, and she's got me as her right-hand man."

"So I hear." Mayor Horton chuckled.

They said their goodbyes after that. Shaking his head, Graham tucked his phone back in his pocket and stepped back around the corner, ready to ask his dad if he wanted to grab some dinner.

Only to find his father on his feet, his face red and his eyes hard.

"Dad—?"

"Don't 'Dad' me." His father took a step forward. "You know, I always knew you were soft, boy, but I never did take you for a fool."

Graham flinched. "Excuse you?"

"Did I or did I not just hear you declining an opportunity from the mayor because of that deadweight girlfriend of yours?"

In his head, Graham replayed his side of the conversation and mentally cursed. He knew he should have taken it outside.

He shook his head. "It's not what you think."

"It's *exactly* what I think."

The harshness of his father's tone took him by surprise. The man never raised his voice. The red tinge to his cheeks was approaching purple, and Graham had to stop himself from taking a step backward.

"That Elizabeth girl. She's got you doing this whole birdbrain festival for her, hasn't she?"

"What? No." Not even close. She was working her tail off.

His father laughed. "How many hours have you spent on it in the past month?"

He hid his wince. There had been an awful lot. He shrugged. "It's not like I keep track."

"Well, you should. Maybe then you'd finally get that she's using you."

That stung. More than it should. Hadn't he thought to himself, that night she got her festival approved, that if it had been anybody else asking so much of him, he would have questioned their motives? But she wasn't like those bullies who pretended to like him so they could copy his homework in eighth grade. She was Elizabeth, his best friend.

Besides. Look at the source. Graham's dad had always had it out for Elizabeth. The man had never liked her, but his antagonism toward her had only grown since they'd started dating. Her awesome hijacking of the DJ booth at his party had been the final straw.

His father had kept his opinion mostly to himself, and Graham hadn't had any desire to go provoking him. Apparently, he hadn't needed to.

"That's not how it is," he promised.

"That's how it's always been." His father jabbed a finger accusingly in his direction. "You've just never seen it because you've been a doormat for her since the day you met."

Crap—what could he say to that?

He turned and headed for the kitchen. "I'm not discussing this."

"I'm not asking for a discussion, I'm telling you what you're too blind to see. She's been riding on your coattails, freeloading off you every step of the way."

"Not listening." But how could he shut off his ears?

He fumbled a cup out of the stack of them and filled it from the dispenser.

His father followed him. "I've held my silence on this for too long. Your mother told me to keep my nose out of it."

"So glad you listened to her."

"But this is too much. You've been holding yourself back on her account, and maybe I could overlook it in the past."

Graham turned back around. "This has been you overlooking things?"

All these snide comments and derisive looks?

His father shook his head, disappointment dripping off of him, and wow. Graham thought he was used to his father not approving of his choices, but apparently he'd had no idea.

"You could be as big of a success as your brother, you know," his father spat at him.

He might as well have punched him.

Graham's whole body tensed. It felt like his shoulders were around his ears. "Right."

"Good grades, good boy, perfect record—until she came along. The minute Officer Dwight called the house—"

Graham almost crushed the paper cup in his hand.

"That was a decade ago, Dad. There weren't even any charges."

"I knew it was her. Talking you into all these hare-brained schemes."

"Because she's fun," Graham finally exploded. "She doesn't have harebrained schemes. She has fun, and I have fun when I'm with her."

"There's more to life than fun. Your career, your education, your prospects. You could be so much more than some mid-level bureaucrat in this backwater town."

"This backwater town?" Graham blinked, shaking his head. "This town where you raised me?"

"You think that was the plan?"

And right. Of course. No, that had never been the plan. The plan had been to win that House seat and then take that to the Senate. Maybe the governor's mansion someday. Only none of that had ever worked out, and he'd had to settle for a long and illustrious career as a respected judge.

"This place was fine to raise you boys," his father said, "but you were supposed to fly the nest and go *do* something with your life. Instead, you stay here, because of her, wasting your life."

"I'm not wasting it." Was this really what his father thought of him? He'd known his dad wanted different things for him, but he'd never realized how deep the shame went. "I'm spending it. I'm good, Dad. I'm happy."

His voice caught.

Because all of that was true. He loved his life, this town—maybe not always his job, but his work wasn't the be-all and end-all. He was involved in the community, and he had the girl of his dreams by his side. He'd bought the house he hoped to raise a family in, picket fence and all.

But that would never be enough, would it?

His father's scowl deepened to the point where it looked like a part of his face. "You're a fool. An unambitious fool, with an unambitious girl with no prospects and no plans. Whatever life you think you're building with her, it's got no damn foundation."

"That's not true." Graham swallowed, and his throat was coated in sandpaper.

"I give it a month. Six, tops."

"We've been friends for decades, Dad." That was worth something. Their foundation was solid bedrock. "I really think we have a future together."

"Well, I think she's getting something out of you." His father jabbed a finger toward his chest. "And once she's gotten it, she's going to move on."

She wouldn't. Not in a million years. They meant something to each other.

And at the same time, doubts began swirling in the back of his mind. They'd gotten together so suddenly. Everything had flipped, and he'd told himself it was because he'd finally made the decision to move forward with his life. He'd been brave and told her how he felt.

But was there something else going on? He'd tried not to, but deep down, he'd been nursing this uncertainty about what she saw in him. He was so different from the men and women she usually went out with.

He told himself that that was *why* they would last, while the rest of her significant others had faded into the background.

The fact that she didn't want to discuss a future together...her squirrelliness about the house...none of that had anything to do with him. She just had to get her head around the idea.

"Well." He crossed his arms over his chest. "I guess we'll just have to prove you wrong."

"Fine. You think that's how it's going to be?" His father had run out of any patience he might have started this conversation with. He swung an arm out in disgust. "Go ahead and be a fool for her. You want to spend the rest of your life running around after her, letting her dictate everything, letting chances to advance your career pass you by? Rotting away in this place, fixing all of her mistakes for her? Be my guest."

"So gracious," Graham rumbled, and he tasted bile in the back of his throat.

His father narrowed his eyes. "Just don't say I didn't warn you."

With that, his father turned to go. Graham didn't stop him. He just curled his hands into fists.

He shouted after him, "Believe me. I won't."

The door slammed shut behind his dad. Graham stared at it for a long minute.

His father had been wrong about literally everything. There was no point even thinking about all the crap he'd said. She hadn't used him. She'd never changed his ambitions or his plans. She liked him for him.

So why couldn't he stop his father's words from echoing in his head?

CHAPTER TWENTY-TWO

❋ ❋ ❋ ❋ ❋ ❋ ❋ ❋ ❋ ❋ ❋ ❋ ❋

Wow." Elizabeth zoomed in on one of the images in Mackenzie Boyd's digital portfolio. "This is amazing. What is it—acrylic?"

"Mixed media. Mostly gouache."

"I *love* gouache." The opaque watercolors had been a game changer for Elizabeth when she'd first stumbled on them a few years ago.

"Me, too." Mackenzie gushed. She pointed out a few other details in the piece.

Elizabeth listened intently while still keeping an eye on the rest of her students.

Mackenzie paused for a second. "You really think it turned out okay?"

"More than okay," Elizabeth said firmly. Mackenzie had really bloomed this year, and Elizabeth had encouraged her to assemble the portfolio to get a head start on applying for summer art programs and maybe even scholarships. "I'd love to see you explore more of this kind of stuff."

"I have a whole series in mind."

Elizabeth grinned. Man, teaching could be a drag

sometimes, but getting to work with kids like Mackenzie who were truly finding themselves, creatively speaking, was one of the best parts of the job.

They finished reviewing the other pieces in the portfolio. As she clicked to end the slideshow, Elizabeth raised a brow. "Have you thought about entering some of these in any contests or shows?"

"A couple, but just ones my mom told me I might have a shot at." Mackenzie rolled her eyes. "She thinks I need more 'refinement.'"

"Well, that's a bunch of malarkey."

Mackenzie laughed, but her smile didn't reach her eyes, and there was real hurt buried in her tone. Her mom's criticism clearly meant a lot to her.

Elizabeth patted her shoulder. "You'll keep honing *your* style as you keep working, whether that's 'refined' or totally wild. In any case, I think you're on the right track."

"Thanks, Ms. Elizabeth."

"And hey—if you want to get a little more exposure, I'll have you know I have an in with the selection committee for the Blue Cedar Falls Clothesline Arts Festival."

"Thanks," Mackenzie said, but her expression soured. "No way my mom will let me enter that, though."

"Oh." Elizabeth probably should have seen that coming, but it still felt like a sucker punch. One of her many, many pet projects was the junior artists showcase, which she couldn't wait to see dotted with work by her very own students.

Mackenzie bit her lip. "I might enter it anyway."

Elizabeth grinned. "Atta girl." Then she forced herself to be stern. "But also listen to your mother."

Smirking, Mackenzie narrowed her eyes. "Like you always did?"

Why, again, did Elizabeth ever relate any personal anecdotes to her classes?

"And see how I turned out?" Elizabeth meant it flippantly, but Mackenzie shrugged.

"Pretty decently, if you ask me."

Elizabeth laughed out loud. Then she registered that Mackenzie wasn't joking. In fact, her face fell a little, and Elizabeth had to mentally pinch herself to stop from laughing even harder.

Wait. This kid seriously thought Elizabeth was a success story?

The whole idea boggled her mind, but she kept it together just enough to put on an assuring smile. "I appreciate the vote of confidence."

That seemed to help a little bit. Mackenzie returned to her seat and started to clean up her materials, but Elizabeth's brain kept spinning. When Elizabeth was Mackenzie's age, the idea that anyone might ever see her as a role model really would have been laughable.

But now? Maybe not so much. She was a more or less functional adult, currently in an adult relationship. Holding down several jobs, paying her rent, and, as Graham kept reminding her, serving as chairwoman for a town board committee. She was making a life in a creative field, which was hard as hell.

It might not be the life anyone in her family, or at Blue Cedar Falls High School, or in the Blue Cedar Falls police department might have wanted for her. But it was a life.

That counted for something, right?

With a hint of a spring in her step, she made her rounds of the room, engaging kids with compliments and feedback.

Of course, Patty Boyd chose that moment to arrive. "Mackenzie—"

Mackenzie waved her off. "Get my stuff, I know, I know."

But instead of scowling at Elizabeth from a distance, Patty crossed the space toward her. Instinctively, Elizabeth braced herself.

"Elizabeth," Patty said, her voice almost simpering, and wow, okay, either she wanted something or this was going to be really, really bad.

"Patty."

"*Loved* the ad you placed in *Passage* magazine. That's the one your sister got for you, right?"

Elizabeth grit her teeth. "May did help me set it up, yes."

"Well, it looks just great, though I was so surprised." She rummaged around in her bag and pulled out a copy.

"Oh?"

Excitement danced in Elizabeth's chest, even as she remained wary about what Patty might be up to.

She hadn't seen the issue yet, and she instinctively shifted closer to get a better look.

Passage really was a gorgeous publication. The cover for this month was perfect, too, with a shot of the Smokies and a feature story on day trips in and around Nashville. May's big article last year highlighting the small towns of the western Carolinas had been a hit; she had bragged that ever since, the magazine had been running more stories about off-the-beaten-path destinations in middle America. Getting the ad for the festival in this issue had been a big win.

Patty flipped through to a bookmarked page in the middle of the magazine. She laid it open on one of the student tables, then stepped back. Elizabeth grinned. The ad looked awesome. She couldn't wait to show Graham and June and May.

Then Patty pointed at the text. "It's just so strange that you wouldn't tell us all that you had changed the date."

Elizabeth's gaze darted to where she was pointing.

Just like that, her grin disappeared. Her stomach did, too, dropping so far down, past her feet and maybe a yard or two into the floor.

That was the wrong date, all right. One full week before the festival. And maybe that wouldn't be so bad, except that she knew for a fact that the last batch of ads she'd placed had been for the correct date. She'd officially publicized her three-day-long festival for two different sets of dates in two different sets of publications.

"I—"

"You did change the date, yes? I know you wouldn't have managed to place an expensive ad in a national publication with the wrong information on it."

And it was such an obvious ploy, but Elizabeth fell for it all the same, darting her gaze up, stricken. She might as well have lit a sign over her head flashing the word guilty in giant red letters.

She'd screwed up. Oh, *wow*, had she ever screwed up. Like, worse-than-anybody-could-have-expected kinds of screwed up.

And Patty knew it, too.

She grinned, so smug it hurt. "I'm sure Mayor Horton and everyone on the town council will be so excited to see how great this turned out."

"Patty…"

"Fabulous job, really." She picked up the magazine

and tapped Elizabeth on the arm with it. "Always knew you had it in you."

Rage burned like fire in Elizabeth's veins, but the anger couldn't hold a candle to the guilt churning in her gut, the heat of the shame that had her cheeks ablaze. She was frozen in place, though.

How could this have happened?

A part of her wanted to blame Patty. Could the witch have gotten the text for the ad changed? It didn't seem possible, logistically speaking, and even Elizabeth knew, deep down inside, that the woman wasn't *that* malicious. She wouldn't throw the town under the bus.

Elizabeth, though? Patty would laugh in glee with every bump Elizabeth's corpse made under the tires.

"Mackenzie?" Patty snapped her fingers.

"Coming, Mom."

"Ta-ta," Patty said to Elizabeth, shooting her a cutesy wave. "I'm sure I'll see you again soon."

In her head, Elizabeth imagined the woman backing up the bus to have another go at her lifeless form.

"You okay, Ms. Elizabeth?" Mackenzie asked.

The world had been narrowing down to the worst sort of tunnel vision, but Elizabeth blinked. The classroom around her snapped back into focus. A wrinkle of concern marred Mackenzie's brow.

Elizabeth had to keep it together. "Fine," she managed, waving the girl off. "Have a nice night."

"Okay..."

Patty didn't look back as she led her daughter out.

Somehow, Elizabeth went through the motions of finishing up the rest of the cleanup. She even had an intelligent conversation or two with students and other parents.

It was all a show, though.

Deep down, she was spiraling. She kept patting her pocket, expecting a call from the mayor—or worse, from June. She could hear it all now. The recrimination, the blame.

The disappointment.

She'd gotten everyone to put their trust in her. So many people had put their necks on the line.

Finally, the last student headed out. She stood there, numb, for about a minute.

Then she dashed for her bag.

She hauled out her laptop and opened it up. The community center Wi-Fi was crap, but it was good enough to get into her old emails. She dug around until she found the message she'd sent with the final creative for the ad, holding her breath as she waited for it to load, some impossible shred of hope in her chest praying that this was all some dream or a trick Patty was playing on her. She'd checked that file a thousand times, and—

It popped up on the screen.

The date was wrong.

Her stomach made another crater in the floor. Fresh waves of shame, guilt, and anger washed over her. She wanted to blame Patty, the advertising guy who'd finalized this all with her—even May.

But deep down, she knew. This was her fault. She'd sent this the night of Graham's father's party, and she'd sworn she'd triple-checked every detail, but she'd been in a rush. She'd sent it off too fast, and now it was out there. There was no pulling it back.

What was she going to do?

A thousand thoughts flitted through her head, but they were a jumble. Most of them were about faking her own death and moving to France—tempting as that was, it wasn't an option.

So what was?

It came to her in a flash.

Standing, she shut her laptop and stuffed it in her bag. She slung the strap over her shoulder and grabbed her coat.

As she flicked off the lights and fumbled for her keys, she still had absolutely no idea how she was going to fix this disaster.

But there was exactly one person she wanted to turn to.

The person she always wanted to turn to.

Graham.

Graham jerked around so fast, he dumped half the thing of cayenne pepper into the stock pot. He cursed, trying to scoop some of it out.

There went his latest attempt at Tex-Mex—and with it his hopes for a quiet, relaxing night in with his girlfriend.

Giving up on the pot, he tossed the spoon aside and wiped his hands on a towel.

To Elizabeth, he asked, "You did *what* now?"

"It was a mistake," she swore.

She'd stormed into the apartment a few minutes ago already worked up, flinging her coat and bag aside and launching right into this story about Patty Boyd ambushing her at the end of the class. Graham had been happy to see her, but he had to admit, he'd only been half listening, what with trying not to mess up another recipe and all.

She had his full attention now.

"I checked the ad a thousand times, but then it was time

to go to your father's party, and we were in a rush, and I sent it, and somehow I missed that the dates were off by a week." She pulled at her hair dramatically. "And now she's going to tell the mayor, and he's going to fire me, and I don't know what to do." She dropped her hands, but her voice only rose. "I don't want to move to France."

He pinched the bridge of his nose. "France?"

"Where else would I go after faking my own death? It has museums, coffee, wine...What's not to love?" She shook her head. "But that's not the point."

"Clearly."

She crossed the space toward him, and he held out his arms by instinct. She buried her face in his chest, then thunked her forehead against his collarbone a few times. "What am I going to do, Graham?"

He rubbed her back.

Before he could offer any actual advice, she pulled back. "Please. Help me, Graham Kenobi. You're my only hope."

He opened his mouth, ready to spout some platitude about how they'd handle it. This really was pretty terrible, but they were a good team, and they were great at fixing things when they inevitably went wrong.

But then his father's words from the other day rang through his head.

You want to spend the rest of your life running around after her?

Rotting away in this place, fixing all of her mistakes for her?

He'd dismissed his father's concerns out of hand. But for some reason, he hadn't been able to stop mulling over the conversation. His father had dug up all the old stuff Graham had been dismissing for ages now. The way

Elizabeth had roped him into that senior prank graffiti incident because she needed him to give her a ride. The way she'd convinced him to spend untold hours preparing her proposal with her. The way other people had used him in the past.

His father's words had been crafted to hurt. They'd been designed to worm their way into his brain, and now there they were.

And here Elizabeth was. Asking him to fix a mistake she'd made.

A single crack opened up in his foundation.

He was going to keep it together, though. This wasn't evidence his dad was right. It was just a thing. Things happened.

He couldn't seem to keep the weird note out of his voice, though, as he tried to sound calm. "What have you tried so far?"

She scrunched up her brows, pulling away by a fraction, and he dropped his hands. "Uh, besides the whole fake death and France thing?"

"Ways to actually fix this."

Taking a step back, she threw her hands up. "I don't know. I mostly freaked out and tried not to wreck my car and came over here. You know I'm no good at this stuff, and you're Mr. Cool in a crisis, so I figured..."

His throat tightened. It sounded to his own ears like his voice was coming from a long, long way away. "You figured I'd be able to take care of all of your mistakes for you."

Flinching, she drew back further. "Um, harsh, dude."

But was it untrue?

"*Is* that the only reason you came to me?"

"I mean..."

And they were talking past each other. He knew that. He knew he was being unfair and asking her to answer questions his father had put forth—questions he hadn't told her about and that she had no reason to understand.

But her flippancy was hitting another nerve.

His heart was pounding so hard, his vision went a little fuzzy around the edges. "Do you ever come to me for anything but to fix your problems?"

"Well, I certainly don't come to you for the cooking..."

The smell of burning chili pulled him out of his haze. He followed her gaze to the stove behind him. He flicked off the heat, still blazing away under the pot. Not that it mattered. The chili had been ruined the minute he dumped in all that extra cayenne.

When he turned back to her, the cheeky smile had dropped from her face.

"Graham," she said carefully. "What's this really about?"

Instinct told him to deflect, but the openness in her expression now pulled at his insides. He was all twisted around, though. He didn't know how to put any of this into words.

He shook his head. "Just something my dad said."

"About me?"

He nodded, miserable.

She pulled in a deep breath before letting it out slowly. "What?"

"Nothing, just the usual crap."

"The usual crap being that I'm a delinquent with bad taste in music who's been a bad influence on you for your entire life."

"More or less." He winced. "Plus..."

His throat tightened, his pulse racing even faster now, but she was patient. Standing there, staring at him levelly, she just raised a brow.

It was like a balloon popping inside his chest. "Plus he blames you for me being unambitious and disappointing."

"Graham..."

"He thinks you use me."

That one made her pause. "Oh."

Oh? That was all she had to say to that?

Was she *confirming* it?

It took her a second, but she recovered. "That's ridiculous."

He gulped in air, but the iron bands around his ribs refused to ease. "That's what I told him."

Only...

She picked up on his hesitation. Her posture stiffened. . For the first time in this entire conversation, she seemed to be as uncomfortable as he felt, and that wasn't what he wanted, but what was he supposed to do?

"You don't seem that convinced," she said, crossing her arms over her chest.

"You did just come in here and tell me you needed me to fix things with the festival."

She huffed out a breath. "Because we're friends. Friends help each other."

"Is that all we are?"

The instant he'd asked it, he wanted to pull it back. Never ask a question you aren't prepared to hear the answer to.

They'd been more than friends for months now, but as easy as it was to be physically affectionate, he never felt sure about the change. Part of that was a decade plus of practice thinking it was impossible. The rest was the way she dodged discussions about their future.

The uncertainty she still seemed to have about where they were going fueled his.

She swallowed hard, her throat bobbing. "It's what we were at first," she said. "But Graham, you can't honestly think..."

"I'm not sure what to think." The tightness in his chest paired with a new, sinking feeling that was trying to drag him under.

"I came to you because I care about you."

And he couldn't stop himself. "As a friend."

"As my *best friend*." Her own frustration started to boil over. "My best friend, who happens to be super hot and shockingly good with his tongue."

Why did it make him feel even worse to hear that that was a shock?

"And," she barreled on, "who I like spending naked time with and who happens to be awesome at fixing municipal-level governmental issues."

She was both serious and not, and it was killing him. She always did this. Always mixed the heavy with the breezy, always found a way to make heartfelt declarations feel silly, and it was a way to hide. It always had been.

But he couldn't shy away from this. This entire time, slowly but steadily, his doubts about their relationship had been eating him alive. They were out there now, though. This was the time to confront them, but he was tongue-tied.

For better or worse, she could still read him like a book. She squirmed. "Okay, that was the wrong thing to say."

"You think?"

"I'm upset and I'm messing this up."

She wasn't the only one, for all that she'd had a head start. Even the idea that his father could have been right about her had him turned around, though.

"What if I said no?" he asked.

"What?"

"What if I just said no, you screwed up the whole ad thing, and it's your problem? Deal with it?" His heart pounded. "What would you do?"

"Probably check that you weren't a body snatcher or a Skrull or something."

"Stop messing around," he snapped, too loudly and too harshly, but he was losing his patience here.

"I'm not," she hurled back, just as hard. "My Graham wouldn't do that."

Great, so his doormat tendencies were encoded in his DNA.

"What if I didn't occasionally float you your half of the rent?" It had been years since he'd had to, but back in the day, it had happened a time or two. Just often enough for him to wonder, sometimes, in the back of his mind, if it had anything to do with why she chose him as a roommate. "What if I didn't offer to drive, and didn't go along with all of your plans? What if I weren't willing to watch weird, boring documentaries?"

"Graham..."

"What would you see in me?" His voice cracked.

Because that was the heart of this, wasn't it? A few months ago, he'd never considered that she might like him as more than a friend. Then they'd gotten together, and he'd had his doubts, but her affection for him hadn't been one of them. Now, it sounded like she thought they were more of friends with benefits than lifelong partners, and he got it. She liked people who were exciting and rebellious and interesting.

What did he have going for him besides the fact that he was cool in a crisis? Competent, solvent, steady Graham.

Even as he thought it, bile crept up the back of his throat.

Her mouth hardened. Fire lit in her eyes. Behind it, though, was hurt.

"Do you honestly believe that I'm only with you because of what you can do for me?"

"I don't want to—"

"Because I'm what? The screwup who leeches off my best freaking friend? My—my . . ."

The way she stumbled over her words opened up another crack beneath his feet. Despair pooled in to fill it.

"You can't even say it, can you?"

"What am I supposed to say?" She put on a mocking tone. "My *boyfriend*?"

"It would be a start."

"It makes it sound like we're in seventh grade."

He shook his head. "It makes it sound like we're a couple."

"And kissing you in front of the entire town didn't give you that impression?"

It had, at the time. But since then, nothing had changed. They were already living like a couple, so he hadn't read too much into that, but the fact still stood. She hadn't had him over to her family's place for dinner like she had the other people she'd dated in the past. She hadn't referred to him as her boyfriend. When he'd brought up wanting a future together, she'd squirmed, and when their friends had presumed that they'd move in together soon, she'd looked like she wanted to crawl under the table and die. Bitterness coated his tongue. "You refusing to make any kind of commitment, or act even the tiniest bit like you might want to be with me long term, doesn't give me that impression."

"You're the one who's moving out!"

That was out of left freaking field, but it rolled right in with the rest of this mess just fine.

He tapped his own chest. "Because I'm focused on the future."

"Well, I'm focused on the right here and the right now." Something in her expression crumpled. "I was happy here with you. Then you started changing everything, and it's been good. Like, so good. I'm happy exploring what more we can be."

He heard the doubt. "But?"

"But I'm not a planning-for-the-future kind of person. I'm not the girl who buys a house with a picket fence."

"You can be."

"Well, I'm not sure I want to be." She dragged her palms down her face, and he didn't miss the hint of a sniffle in her breath.

He wanted to go to her. He wanted to wrap her up in his arms and tell her he was sorry for even bringing it up.

"You were the one to kiss me," she finally said. "You chose me. You could have had someone stable and dependable, but you wanted to be with me. And now I feel like you're holding who I am against me."

His whole chest squeezed, and oh God. This wasn't how he wanted to be saying it. But it fell out of him all the same. "I love who you are."

"And I love who you are, too," she said.

It should have been exactly what he wanted to hear—exactly what he'd been longing to hear for so long.

Yet somehow it felt like exactly the opposite.

"You can't have it all these fifteen different ways, Graham," she told him. "You can't tell me you're moving out and accuse me of not wanting a future together. You can't be this helpful, awesome, amazing person who always offers to pitch in, and then get resentful when the first instinct I have is to come to you when I'm upset. You can't give me the chance to be with you and then tear it away the second I express the tiniest uncertainty about whether I can really give you the life you want."

"The life I want is with you." It always had been.

She swabbed at her eyes. When she dropped her hand, her gaze was sad but clear. "Is it, though?"

A knife tore clear through his chest. "What are you saying?"

Her voice wobbled. "What if neither of us knows what we want? What if we care about each other but we aren't *right* for each other?"

He refused to believe it.

"E…"

"What if this was a mistake?"

The knife twisted, leaving him bleeding.

"Maybe we should…" Her throat bobbed. "Maybe we should take a break."

He didn't want that. Not even the teeniest, tiniest bit.

But what could he say to refute it?

He suddenly couldn't look at her. What if she was right? What if they didn't fit? What if he'd lost not just the love of his life? But also his very best friend?

His heart and his jaw both went hard. He took a step back. It killed him to do it, but he forced himself to choke out the words.

"You're right. Maybe we should."

CHAPTER TWENTY-THREE

❀ ❀ ❀ ❀ ❀ ❀ ❀ ❀ ❀ ❀ ❀ ❀ ❀

Two hours later, Elizabeth slammed the door of her studio shut behind her. She stormed across the space to the stack of canvases piled in the corner and rummaged through them until she found a crappy old painting she could paint over.

She tugged the piece she'd been working on last time off her easel and leaned it up against the wall, replacing it with tonight's victim. As she gathered brushes and paints, she slammed cabinets and drawers, and she kept hoping the violence she was unleashing on her poor art supplies would steady the shaking in her hands, but she just kept trembling.

Her vision blurred over. One sob escaped.

With a growl, she swabbed the back of her wrist across her eyes, then firmly told herself, "No."

The single word rang out in the empty space. She pressed her fingers into her eyes hard enough to see flashes of color, but it couldn't stop her from seeing Graham stone-faced and tight jawed as he tossed a few days' worth of stuff in a bag.

As he turned his back on her and walked right out the door.

She'd cried herself out hard enough then. She wasn't doing it now.

What was there even to cry about anyway? They'd had a fight. They'd decided to take a break. She'd messed up not just the arts festival the town had entrusted her with but also the closest thing she'd had to an adult relationship in her life, and it was fine. She'd figure it all out. Graham was going to go stay in his dumb, empty house for a few days. He'd be back.

Probably. At least for a while.

Her heart squeezed so hard, she could scarcely breathe, and she opened a cabinet just to slam it shut again.

He'd be back. Maybe they'd patch things up, and maybe they wouldn't, and either way, he'd be packing his stuff again soon enough. Eventually, with him or without him, as his friend or as his ill-defined something more, she'd end up alone.

She stopped and turned.

She should put on some music. Angry, thrashy music.

But when she pulled out her phone to do precisely that, there was her lock screen, with its stupid, sappy picture of her and Graham canoodling at the bar. It was a selfie she'd taken, her arm wrapped around his neck from behind, her face smooshed against his and his beard scraping against her cheek. He was half yelling at her to get off and half grinning like a fool, his hand on her arm, and they looked so happy.

It was all she could do not to throw the thing across the room.

She put in her code and tapped on her music app. A minute later, the opening riff to a classic woman-done-wrong wailer poured through the speakers, and she put her phone in her pocket.

As best she could, she shoved all thoughts of Graham and his awful face out of her head, focusing instead on getting her palette set up. She swirled a brush through a pile of inky black pigment and summoned her muse.

How many angry nights had she spent shut away in her room listening to music and trying to exorcise her feelings on a canvas? This was old hat to her.

So why wasn't it *working*?

She made a few broad brushstrokes, covering the previous image and trying to decide how it would become a part of the new piece. Instead of unleashing her rage, it just built up a new brand of frustration.

And along with it came a trickle of self-blame that only made the fire inside her burn more painfully.

She hadn't spent enough time in the studio of late. She was rusty. That was the problem.

But what was she supposed to do? She'd been busy working her jobs and planning the arts festival and supporting Chloe and hanging out with Graham and kissing Graham and...

She slashed her brush across the canvas hard enough that the metal holding the bristles together scraped the surface, and she could scream.

All that time she'd been dealing with the festival, she'd been waiting for something to go wrong. No way she could pull the entire thing off, but she'd tried. She'd tried really, really hard. People had believed in her, and she'd wanted so badly to be worthy of that trust.

In the end, she'd just been herself, and the guy she'd thought appreciated and accepted and—hell—maybe even loved her for exactly that... had decided she'd been using him all along.

Tossing her brush aside, she sank into her stool. She

drew in a ragged breath and dropped her head into her hands.

Art wasn't doing her a single bit of good tonight. How could it? She shouldn't be here, alone with a canvas. She should be with Graham.

Graham was her *best friend*. When she was heart-broken or depressed, he was the one she ate ice cream and watched overwrought movies with; he was the one who let her be all gross and snot sob into his shirt and never complained and never judged her.

And now she'd gone and ruined it.

It was almost cruel, the way he'd tried to make her believe that she could have it all. Dangling tantalizing, terrifying futures in front of her face where they were happy together forever. She'd never quite believed them, but she'd stepped out of her comfort zone. She'd dared to see herself as more than the screwup, doomed to failure and rejection. She'd let herself imagine that she deserved the good things coming her way, and that she and Graham could figure out a way to make a life together despite their differences. She still *wanted* to believe that.

But in this moment?

It felt an awful lot like shooting for the stars had left her with nothing at all.

The first time Elizabeth's mom wandered past the front desk and shoved a cookie in her face, she didn't think much of it. She was busy, after all, sorting out reservations for an upcoming wedding.

Inn business wasn't all she had on her plate. Graham had been AWOL for almost forty-eight hours, which might have been the longest she'd gone without talking to him in years. And then there was the festival. Patty hadn't shown up again to rub her screwup in her face, and the mayor's office had been suspiciously silent, but she'd felt the fire under her rear end anyway. In the back of her mind, she was racking her brain, trying to come up with a solution for the festival advertisement misprint debacle that didn't involve her having to admit to everyone that she'd let them all down.

The second time her mom did it—and with a different kind of cookie, no less—she thought it was weird. But weird was pretty much par for the course for her family.

The third time, she caught a whiff of lasagna baking in the family residence, and she wondered, idly, if this was how mice felt when they stumbled upon a block of cheese sitting on top of a pile of wires.

She didn't say no to the cookie, mind you, but she did it with full knowledge that the electric shock would have to be coming soon.

When June strode in half an hour before the family— or whichever portion of it happened to be around on any given night—usually sat down to eat, Elizabeth grabbed her and hauled her behind the desk.

"Well, hello to you, too—"

Elizabeth pinched her arm like they were eight. "What's Mom up to?"

"Ow." June tugged her arm in close and rubbed the place where Elizabeth had gotten her. "I have no idea what you're—"

The bells over the door chimed, and May came in. She spotted them and smiled. "Oh, hey, everybody's here."

Glancing between the two of them, Elizabeth narrowed her eyes. "What. Is. Going. On."

May slowed. "Uh..."

"What?" June complained. "She doesn't get attacked, but I do?"

Elizabeth pointed at June. "You're definitely in on it." She redirected her finger at May. "You I'm reserving judgment about."

"Everybody's in on it," their mom's voice interrupted, her accent thick and her tone clipped.

They turned as one to find her standing there, Ned beside her. Sunny the cat stood at her feet, and all three of them wore the same unimpressed expression.

"Lasagna just came out. Eating in fifteen minutes. Wash your hands and set the table."

Sudden anxiety clamped Elizabeth's windpipe. She gestured vaguely at the computer. "Sure, I'll just—"

"Wash hands," her mother repeated, her firm tone entirely too familiar. "Set table."

Ned backed her up, because of course he did. "You heard her."

Resigned, Elizabeth locked the computer and put up the sign indicating that guests should ring the bell for service. Ned, Sunny, June, and May went on ahead. Her mother waited, probably wanting to make sure Elizabeth didn't make a break for it, which was admittedly tempting.

"I'm coming, I'm coming."

"I know."

In the family's apartment, everybody fell into their roles. May had been back in Blue Cedar Falls for only six months, but you'd never know it. She got plates, June got silverware. Elizabeth put out napkins and tried to pretend she wasn't deeply, deeply suspicious of everyone.

This was definitely a trap, but at least she got to eat cheese.

And wow, was the cheese ever good. Ned set the big nine-by-thirteen of homemade lasagna in the center of the table. There was crusty bread, too, and a salad with those little spicy peppers that Elizabeth loved and nobody else in the family liked. Her mom *never* bought them.

She took one look at it all and gave up. "Okay, fine, what's going on?"

Her mother raised one brow. "That's what I was going to ask you."

"Uh, nothing?" She squirmed inside even as she said it, but putting on her usual bravado was easy enough. "Cool, good talk, pass the ranch?"

June grabbed the bottle of dressing and held it out of reach. "Yeah, not buying it."

"You're siding with her that quickly?" Elizabeth asked.

May rolled her eyes. "She always sides with her."

"Life usually goes better when everyone does," Ned drawled.

Her mother tilted up her chin and fixed her with the stare that had been getting her dander up for almost thirty years. "You spent all day yesterday and today grumping around, not talking to anyone." She gestured at her own visage with her stronger hand. "Your whole face was so sad, you looked like the wobbly smile emoji."

Elizabeth's cheeks flashed hot, even as ice prickled down the back of her spine. So was that what this was? Her family buttering her up for an interrogation?

Did that piss her off or . . . kind of touch her?

Unwilling to examine either possibility too closely, she deflected. "How do you even know about emojis?"

"Probably from her million subscribers," June said.

"They're Sunny's subscribers," their mom corrected,

pointing at the cat, who was watching the proceedings while tearing a stuffed mouse limb from limb, "but that's not the point."

"You did seem a little cranky yesterday," May chimed in.

"I'm always cranky," Elizabeth protested.

"No you're not," Ned said.

June ignored him. "Like, crankier than usual."

"See?" Their mom raised her brows meaningfully. "Everyone is on my side."

That flash of heat on her face zipped down to her gut, and she crossed her arms over her chest. "Well, that's nothing new."

"Lizzie..." Ned warned.

"What? It's not. Everyone here is always against me." Which was childish and stupid, and yet in the pit of her stomach, it rang true.

May rolled her eyes. "Oh yeah, I'm definitely against you when I invite you over and you drink my wine and we watch Mr. Darcy getting out of that swimming hole on repeat."

"You like MacFayden Darcy," Elizabeth reminded her. "Totally against me."

June ignored both of them. A ripple of hurt dashed across her face. "Elizabeth, I thought we were past this."

"Maybe you were," she spat out instinctively, and wow, yeah, okay, she was cranky. She put her hand over her mouth. "I'm sorry. I didn't mean that."

She and June had made so much progress over the past few months. They'd been working together as a team, here at the inn and on the festival projects where June was gleefully—not passive-aggressively—lending a hand. Elizabeth had been working hard to give her perfect sister the benefit of the doubt. In their best moments, she'd honestly believed that June was supportive and on her side, and it had been amazing.

But old habits died hard. There were still the literal decades when June and May had been a unit and Elizabeth had been the weirdo who could never live up to them. She'd thought she'd moved past that, but here she was. Still screwing everything up, even now.

Unbidden tears flooded her eyes. She blinked hard, unwilling to let them fall—not here.

Quietly, May said, "Elizabeth, whatever's going on..."

Elizabeth laughed. Her throat scraped. "It's nothing."

"It's pretty clearly not," June said.

"*Niū*," their mother said, putting her hand over Elizabeth's, and oh no. No, no, no, Elizabeth could not handle her mother calling her *baby girl* like that, the way she used to when she really was a baby.

Back when Elizabeth was still theirs, before she messed up everything and disappointed her mother and her stepdad over and over, before those awful fights and that awful night when she couldn't take it for another second.

She'd walked out that door, and even though she'd been back the next week—even though she'd been back five days a week every week...

...she'd stopped being anybody's little girl.

The tears finally brimmed over.

"I screwed up," she confessed, and she was talking about the present, sure. God knew she had enough disasters currently sitting like rubble all around her. But she was talking about the last decade, too.

She was talking about her entire life.

"I screwed up the festival, and I screwed things up with Graham, and I just..." Her throat closed. She couldn't get anything else out.

A tissue appeared in her hand. She looked to the side to find June standing there, pressing it into her palm, and she took it gratefully and swabbed at her own gross face. But it didn't help. She hiccupped on another sob, and this was pathetic. No one in this family showed emotion. She was screwing up *again*.

Carefully, holding the box of tissues so Elizabeth could help herself, June asked, "Is this about the thing with the ads?"

Elizabeth jerked her face up. "You know?"

June winced and nodded. "Patty stopped me on the street the other day and went on some tirade about it."

"God." Elizabeth laughed and hiccupped at the same time. "That woman is the worst."

"The *worst*," their mom echoed.

"She's really mad that Mayor Horton hasn't made a bigger deal about it," June said, and her voice had that diplomatic edge to it, so clearly she was self-censoring a bit, and for once, Elizabeth was grateful for that.

"Yeah." Elizabeth swiped at her face with a fresh tissue, then tapped her phone in her pocket. "I've been just waiting for his call to fire me."

"I heard through the grapevine that a certain young man had convinced him to lay off for the moment," Ned chimed in, lifting his brows.

Elizabeth's stomach did a little swoop. "You mean..."

"I don't know what happened between you and Graham, but that man would move heaven and earth for you," May said, picking up her fork and digging into her lasagna. When everyone gawked at her, she cast her gaze toward the ceiling. "What? It's getting cold, and it's my favorite."

"Oh my God, eat," Elizabeth told them all.

May and Ned dug in, but June and her mom weren't going to be distracted by a little thing like dinner.

"Do you want to talk it through?" June asked. "I might be able to help brainstorm some ideas."

Elizabeth shook her head. "You shouldn't have to bail me out."

"Funny, that sounds familiar," June said dryly. "Weren't you the one giving me crap about not letting anyone help me last year?"

"That's different."

"How?"

"Because you're..." Ugh, how could Elizabeth say this? Finally, she settled on "*You.*" Both June and her mom stared at her blankly. "You never need help, so you can ask every now and then. Whereas me..."

Their mother barked out a laugh. "You?"

Ouch. "Yes, me." She waved a hand at herself. "Me, who messes everything up and gets arrested—"

"One time," May interjected.

"—and who half the town lobbied against because they thought I was too irresponsible to be trusted with organizing my own idea for an event." The pit of her stomach burned. "Which, I mean, okay, clearly they were right about."

"You made one mistake," June said.

"A really, really big one. And not just one." She swallowed and rubbed her eye. "I've been making mistakes forever. This is just the biggest one of late. I'm not you." She looked from June to May. "I'm not either of you." All her feelings of never belonging in this family suddenly threatened to swamp her. "I never have been and I never will be, and I always thought that was okay."

"Elizabeth..." Her mom frowned.

"Exactly!" Elizabeth seized on the simple matter of her mom saying her name. "*Elizabeth*." She pointed at each of her sisters in turn. "May. June." She touched her finger to her own chest. "*Elizabeth*. See? Since birth I haven't fit in. I'm a screwup and a mess, and—"

"Elizabeth Xiaosheng Wu," their mother said, thunderous.

Everyone shut up. May's fork clattered to her plate. Ned alone kept eating, but with a curious eye to his wife.

Elizabeth swallowed hard. She opened her mouth to protest, but one look from her mom, and she clammed right back up.

"June?" Their mom said. "Born in June. May? Born in May. You? Born in February."

"Okay, so I picked a bad month, I get it."

Their mom shook her head, her speech a quick staccato and her grammar shifting the way it always did when she was on a tear. "Nobody name their baby after February, unless they want it to be weird, goth kid."

To be fair, she wasn't wrong. "Still..."

"You were born two months early. You were supposed to be April."

Yet more self-deprecating comments about how she couldn't even manage to be born right rose to her lips, but she kept them in.

"Elizabeth," her mother continued, "was the name of the nurse who took care of you."

"Oh." Elizabeth sat back. She'd never heard that before.

Her mom's voice softened. "So tiny. The doctors said we should prepare ourselves. You might have problems, might take a long time to catch up, might never be strong. But the nurse told me you were a fighter." A sheen covered her eyes. "And she was right."

"Mom—"

"Your name is *not* about you not fitting in. Your name is about you fighting hard for what matters to you. Even when you are fighting against me."

"Or me," Ned agreed.

Elizabeth looked to him, and his expression was so soft and fond, it just about broke her heart. The weight of the mean things she'd said to him a decade ago lightened. For the first time in so long, it felt like he was looking at her like she was his little girl—even though she'd never been little to him. They'd met when she was a preteen, and she'd given him such a hard time. But he'd always been there, even when she'd been awful to him.

"Or me," June agreed quietly.

Instinctively, Elizabeth looked to May, who chewed and swallowed.

"We're cool." She gave Elizabeth a thumbs-up, and Elizabeth laughed. The two of them never really had fought all that much.

Their mom put her hand over Elizabeth's again and rubbed her thumb across the back. "You do things your own way. Sometimes, I agree, and sometimes I think you have your head in your rear end. But you always belong here."

Yet more treacherous tears threatened Elizabeth's eyes. "Even though—"

"Always," her mom said, cutting her off.

Was that possible? "All the terrible things I said, though." She looked to Ned, apologies she didn't know how to put into words bubbling up in her throat.

"Don't look at me." He held his hands up in front of his chest. "If I held a grudge for a decade, your mother would've been done with me a long time ago."

"When I left…" Elizabeth couldn't get the words out.

"You proved your independence," her mother said. "And I heard you, loud and clear."

"But all this time...I thought..."

She'd thought the worst of herself and of them. She'd been picking at this unhealed wound, never giving it a chance to scab over.

Her mother made a *tsk*ing sound. "What?" She put on a deeper voice, like she was imitating a character from one of her soaps. "'You walk out that door, you never come back?'" She waved her stronger hand dismissively, but her tone was fierce. "You're here every day."

"Five days a week," Elizabeth corrected, scrubbing at her eyes again.

"See?" her mom said, like that was all the evidence she needed that it was all water under the bridge.

And that wasn't true. Elizabeth's rebellious phase— the way she'd acted out to try to get some attention when she felt like she never measured up...the way she'd left—it had informed every bit of her relationship with her family.

But maybe not quite in the way she'd imagined. Her moving out had hurt her mother, but she hadn't "abandoned the family," or whatever she had built this whole thing up to be in her head. Her mom, her stepdad, and her sisters were all here for her.

As if to prove it, her mother squeezed her hand again. "You'll figure out your festival. I believe in you."

"And I'm here to help," June promised, "if you want."

"Thanks."

"And as for Graham..." May started, because of course she wouldn't let that part go unaddressed.

The warmth that had gathered behind Elizabeth's ribs flickered. "We don't need to talk about Graham."

"Pretty sure we do." June took her seat again.

Their mother gave Elizabeth's hand a gentle squeeze before pulling away and picking up her own fork. "I didn't buy the peppers you like to let you get out of talking about *all* your problems."

And okay, there was the warmth again.

Along with it came a flutter of self-consciousness.

It had both angered her and flattered her that her family had buttered her up for this conversation. What exactly did it say about their relationship that they had felt they needed to? How defensive did she really get around them?

Pretty darn, a voice answered in her head.

Sighing, she grabbed the dressing from June and poured a generous drizzle over her salad. She stabbed one of the delicious pepperoncini with a bit of lettuce and a chickpea and popped it all in her mouth. It was so good, it was almost worth the interrogation.

She chewed and swallowed and sighed. "Graham and I had a fight."

"No, really?" May said, faux shocked.

Elizabeth glared at her with an equal pretense of annoyance. "His dad put a bunch of crap in his head about how I'm a screwup and a mooch." She grimaced. "And then I asked him to help me with the festival disaster."

"Bad timing," June sympathized.

"Seriously." She rummaged around in her salad for another pepper. June found one in her own salad and deposited it in Elizabeth's bowl, and Elizabeth nodded her thanks. "Anyway, we both said some stuff."

Understatement of the century. He basically accused her of only being with him because she was using him. He'd somehow managed to insult the both of them up, down, and sideways in the process, and just thinking about it hurt her heart.

Her anger wasn't just because he'd accused her of leeching off of him, or basically sleeping with him because he paid for stuff and helped her out.

He'd also implied that he was so unattractive and unlovable that the only reason she would want to be with him was because of what he could do for her, and that was just... It was messed up in a way she didn't even know how to start to address.

"And..." Her salad blurred before her eyes, and ugh, she really didn't need to start crying again. She blinked hard. "I don't know. The whole more-than-friends thing might not work out."

"That sucks," June said.

May shook her head. "That's BS."

Elizabeth sniffed and looked up, raising a brow.

Shrugging, May dabbed at her lips with her napkin. "You guys are, like, soul mates."

"I don't know if I'd go that far."

"Really?" May scrunched up her forehead. "Because it's always looked that way to me."

That made Elizabeth pause. "Always?"

"Always," May, June, their mother, and Ned all echoed.

Elizabeth blinked. She'd known people liked to read more into her and Graham's friendship than existed, but she hadn't realized how deep her family's views ran. "Huh."

"You two will work it out," her mother said with confidence.

"I don't know..."

"I do." Her mom winked. "You're a fighter."

Ned pointed a forkful of lasagna in her direction. "And

if that boy ever tries to imply that you're freeloading off him again, you let me know, and I'll fight him, you hear?"

Elizabeth laughed. "He wouldn't dare."

She wasn't so sure about that; she wasn't so sure Ned could take him, either. Graham might look like—and be—a nerd, but he had some muscles under those neatly pressed shirts. Still, just the fact that her stepdad would threaten him on her behalf had her broken heart swelling all over again.

Her family's insistence aside, she wasn't sure she and Graham could mend things. Even if he didn't see her as a parasite and maybe worse, they wanted different things from life. She'd thought they could get past their different visions for their futures, but could they?

As dinner table conversation finally started to move on, Elizabeth stuck another pepper in her mouth.

She still didn't have any answers.

But a few days ago she'd worried she'd lost Graham, and in so doing, that she'd lost everything.

It helped to know that at least she hadn't lost this. Her family might be ridiculous and judgmental and emotionally stunted at times.

But they had her back.

So maybe she could have her own back, too.

CHAPTER TWENTY-FOUR

❊ ❊ ❊ ❊ ❊ ❊ ❊ ❊ ❊ ❊

There you are." Graham hunched over to snag the book he'd been looking for. It hadn't exactly been an exhaustive search; there were only three rooms of this big house he was using.

The kitchen, where he reheated selections from the stash of frozen dinners he'd picked up—or if he was feeling nuts, maybe made himself a ham sandwich. The living room, where he sat on the couch his parents had given him.

And here. The bedroom, where he slept in a sleeping bag on the floor, because it was apparently impossible to get a decent mattress delivered in less than a week around here.

He stood, a hand on the sore spot at the small of his back.

Sure, he could have gotten Tom or Archer or someone to help him move his bed out of his and Elizabeth's apartment. The idea of going that far hurt more than his lumbar, though, so he was dealing with the whole sleeping bag situation. For now.

Book in hand, he returned to the living room. His footsteps echoed on the hardwood, and not for the first time in the past three days, he had to wonder what on earth he had been thinking. What was he going to do with all this space? He'd been planning for his future and the family he wanted to have someday, but at the moment, his future...

...well, it looked as empty and lonely as this old creaky house.

Annoyed with his own moping, he plopped on the sofa and cracked open the book to where he'd left off last night.

Only he couldn't focus on the words on the page.

His gaze drifted to his phone, sitting on the arm of the sofa, and he scowled.

Elizabeth hadn't called him these past few days, and he hadn't called her. They hadn't run into each other—though he wasn't exactly sure how they would have, considering he'd been hiding in his office and here. He still hadn't decided how he'd handle Friday night. Missing out on hanging with their friends would officially cross a line he wasn't sure he could come back from, but he couldn't imagine sitting there, either, not being able to touch her when he'd finally gotten it through his head that he was allowed.

Of course, he could always try talking to her like a damn grown-up, but that seemed pretty impossible, too.

He was saved from descending any further into his own morose navel-gazing by the sound of the doorbell. His stomach flipped. What if Elizabeth had driven over to hash things out?

But when he peeked through the glass panel in the door, his heart fell. It was just his mom—probably here to double-check he was still alive. He'd sent her a curt text letting her know he'd be staying here for a few days, but he'd avoided any further explanation as to why. Normally, his mom would be one of the first people he'd turn to in a crummy situation like this, but she'd tell his dad, and then his dad would gloat, and he just couldn't handle that.

So he plastered on a smile and opened the door, ready to welcome his mother in and struggling to come up with some pretext for being here.

Only it wasn't just his mother standing on his porch.

His father stood right behind her.

"Oh." He couldn't hide his surprise.

His mother stepped forward without missing a beat. She put a box in his hands and told him, "Don't worry, he's going to behave."

His dad glowered but kept his mouth shut.

"Um, okay. Come on in," he said as his mother was sweeping past him and inside.

She led the way to the kitchen and started unpacking a tote bag into his fridge. "I brought you a few casseroles and a pot of soup, plus some greens for a salad. Heaven knows you're probably living off of frozen dinners and ham sandwiches here."

"I'm an adult, Mom." An adult living off of frozen dinners and ham sandwiches, yes, but an adult all the same.

She closed the fridge and looked him square in the eye.

He dropped his gaze. "Thank you, ma'am."

Satisfied, she tipped her head toward the box he was holding. "There's more in there."

So there was. He unpacked the extra couple of casseroles. "How long do you think I'm going to be here?"

"Hopefully about five minutes, but heaven knows you Lewis men are stubborn."

He met his father's gaze for the first time since he'd stonily followed them in.

"Speaking of which, your father has something he'd like to say to you. Don't you, Ward?"

With what looked like real effort, Graham's father coughed into his wrist, then said, "Your mother tells me I owe you an apology."

Graham blinked. "Um…"

"Ward." His mother wagged a finger in his direction.

His father sighed and scrubbed a hand over his face. "The things I said to you about Elizabeth were out of line."

"And more importantly, they were none of your business," his mother added.

"May I continue?"

"You may," she allowed.

"I should have kept my nose out of things. I'll never understand your friendship—or relationship, but it works for you, and that's what matters."

Graham had to stop himself from laughing. Now? His father wanted to come to him and say these things now?

Somehow, he managed to maintain his composure. Addressing both of them, he said, "I appreciate the apology." His stiff upper lip threatened to crack. "But I'm pretty sure the damage has been done."

"Oh, sweetie," his mom said, reaching for his hand.

He let her give his palm a squeeze before pulling away. "It's fine."

"It doesn't seem fine to me."

"I don't know what it is. Or what will happen." This was the closest he'd come to talking about any of this.

His stomach tied itself into knots as he stood there, and his voice wobbled. "But it's probably all for the best."

"Have you tried to patch things up?"

And how did his mother know? He'd given her the scantest possible amount of information, and somehow, by sheer intuition—and what seemed like it might have been a fairly intense grilling of his father—she'd put all the pieces together.

"Not really, but…"

"But what?"

But he was too scared to try? But he was sure he'd already ruined the best, most important relationship of his life, romantic, platonic, or otherwise?

But if he tried to patch things up with her and failed, then where would that leave them?

Maybe more importantly, but if he tried to patch things up and succeeded, what would happen then? Did it change anything?

Or would she always believe she didn't fit in her vision of his life? Would he always question whether or not she really loved him as he was?

His mother pulled him out of his spiral with another gentle nudge of her hand against his.

He looked up. "I just think we might want different things."

And there were a lot of ways he might have expected his mother to react. What he didn't see coming was her laughing in his face.

Shocked, he pulled his hand away, but she grabbed him right back. In desperation, he looked to his dad, but Judge Lewis looked exactly as confused as he felt.

"Mom?"

"Oh, Graham, sweetheart." His mom dabbed at her

eyes with the hand that wasn't clasped around his wrist. "Seriously?"

"What?" His bewilderment faded to be replaced by a prickle of irritation.

As if sensing his new tone, she swallowed the rest of her laughter. Standing up straighter, she shook her head and gestured around. "Graham. Have you looked at this house?"

For days, he felt like he'd seen nothing beyond these walls. "Repeatedly."

"And yet you don't see a bit of what I see, do you?"

"Lucille," his father tried.

She waved him off, all her attention on Graham. "You said you were buying this place to make a clean break from Elizabeth, and I held my peace. But every inch of this house is meant for the life you *want* to build with her."

He shook his head instinctively. "No, it's—"

"Gorgeous kitchen," she insisted.

"Yeah, I mean—"

"You don't cook. Or when you do, it ends in literal flames. You know who cooks wonderfully?"

He clamped his mouth shut, because the answer was obviously Elizabeth. Some dawning realization hovered just above his head, but he wasn't willing to look at it just yet.

His mother tried a different tack. She pointed down the hall. "And that room with the great natural light? That's her studio."

"No," he tried, but the truth of it shone brighter.

"The quirky architectural details, the color of the tile in the bathroom, even."

"The gray is nice."

His mom narrowed her eyes. "The gray is flecked with purple, and it is unique, and it is one hundred percent for her, Graham."

And what was he supposed to say to any of that?

"But…"

But what?

His mother's voice softened. "Graham, I don't know what differences the two of you have had, or if maybe you know something I don't and she really does want a life that's different from the one you do. But from day one, even as you've been trying to get some space from her, you have been planning a life that is all about the future you want with her." She tightened her grip on his hand. "You'll find a way to make this work."

And could that possibly be true?

His heart cracked wide open. "I don't know if she wants any of that, Mom."

"She lights up around you," she told him, a suspicious glint to her eyes. "The same way you do around her."

"It's not that easy."

"It can be. If you want it to."

And he did. So badly.

They'd lived out of each other's pockets for years now. He knew her better than he knew himself, and she knew him. She brightened every corner of his life, and yes, whatever future he had, he wanted it with her bringing art and magic and joy to his days and nights.

He wanted it here, with her.

And he'd do anything he had to to bring that dream to life.

But before he could do a single thing, his phone rang in his pocket.

He swiped his eyes and fished it out. Tom's number

flashed across the screen, and he frowned. Tom never called. He looked to his mom, who raised her brows.

Taking a step back, he answered the call.

"Hey, Tom—"

"Graham." Tom's voice shook. "It's Chloe." He audibly swallowed. "We need a ride to the hospital—now."

CHAPTER TWENTY-FIVE

❀ ❀ ❀ ❀ ❀ ❀ ❀ ❀ ❀ ❀ ❀ ❀

Elizabeth barreled through the doors of Pine View Medical Center's ER half an hour later. She was pretty sure she had paint in her hair and probably a few streaks on her dress, too, and she didn't care. She'd had to leave her class halfway through; fortunately, one of the other teachers had been able to cover for her.

As she charged the nurses' station, flashbacks assaulted her. A year and a half ago, she'd rushed in here just the same. Her mom had had a stroke, and June had brought her here, and no one would tell them anything. Ned had been calm but stone faced, reciting that bit about *one crisis at a time* and urging them not to jump to conclusions. June had been a wreck, and there'd been nothing Elizabeth could do except try to distract them both.

Nothing had ever been the same again. Her mom had recovered, but it had been dicey for days, and she still suffered the aftereffects. Ned was more grizzled, old in a way he'd never been. June had buried herself in work. She'd always been touchy and judgmental, but there'd been a new brittleness to her that hadn't receded for months. May had swooped into town and then right back out, and Elizabeth had never felt more alone. She didn't know how she would have gotten through it if it weren't for Graham.

Graham—who stepped forward right then, looking like a freaking knight in shining armor as he held out his arms, and she couldn't help herself. Nothing was right between them, but she crashed into him all the same. He hugged her tightly, and she let him, soaking in his heat and strength.

She could have stayed like that forever.

Only they were standing in front of the nurses' station in a crowded ER waiting room. They had basically thirty seconds before someone bumped into them and brought them back to reality.

"Sorry," she said as an orderly strode past her. Pulling away from Graham, she scrubbed a hand over her eyes and nose.

"Come on." Sure and confident, Graham touched the small of her back and guided her over to the corner of the room. "They just took her back. Tom's with her, but we have to wait out here."

Elizabeth sat down. "Is she okay? What happened?"

"I don't know. Tom called. Something was wrong; she was bleeding and dizzy and nothing felt right, and..." Graham rubbed his eyes.

The gleam to that shining armor dulled. Elizabeth's heart squeezed inside her chest.

Dark circles hung beneath Graham's eyes. He was paler than usual, his hair unkempt, and he hadn't trimmed the edges of that sexy beard in days—which made sense. He'd packed like three things before he'd left. His shaver hadn't been one of them. It had been sitting on his shelf in the bathroom for two days, taunting her every time she brushed her teeth.

And this wasn't how they were supposed to be reuniting. This wasn't supposed to be happening at all, but they definitely weren't supposed to be thrown together again like this.

But she couldn't regret it.

"Graham…." She swallowed, and her throat hurt. "I know we need to talk about stuff, but—"

"Not now," he agreed, firm.

She let out a breath of relief.

Then she put her head on his shoulder, exactly the way she would have if this had happened before they'd gotten together. He curled an arm around her, and it was so normal, and yet completely different.

And for now, at least, it was enough.

Dahlia, Archer, and Stefano all arrived together another forty-five minutes later, and they went through the same rounds and rounds of questions with no answers. May and her boyfriend, Han, showed up not too long after, and Elizabeth teared up all over again as she wrapped her arms around her sister.

"You didn't have to come."

May just hugged her tighter and scoffed. "As if."

They borrowed more chairs and ended up with a section of the waiting room that looked more or less exactly like their usual section at the bar.

Elizabeth laughed, too high and nervous, but what else could you do? "I don't suppose they'd let Clay deliver us a pitcher of margaritas."

"I can go to the cafeteria and try to put together some apps," Han offered.

Awkward silence eclipsed them all. Graham chewed on his nail, while with his other hand he drummed out a rhythm on the back of her chair. Outwardly, he was calm, but he had his tells. Elizabeth glanced around.

Then she pulled out her bag and found the deck of playing cards in the bottom. It had worked well enough when her mom was here for days.

"Anybody wanna play spit?"

"Ha-ha!" Elizabeth called in triumph, raking up her pot of chewing gum and pennies from the center of the table Archer had stolen for them from the other side of the room. Spit had been too raucous to carry on for more than a few rounds, but poker was a game you could play anywhere and for anything.

But instead of anybody trash-talking her, everybody had gone silent. Elizabeth frowned and followed Graham's gaze to the door.

Tom stood there, a smile of pure relief stretching his face.

Elizabeth let out a breath she hadn't even known she'd been holding.

He approached, and they assaulted him as one.

"What happened?" Graham asked.

"Is she okay?" Elizabeth demanded.

"How're you?"

"Can we see her?"

Elizabeth's stomach did a little flip. She was almost afraid to ask. "The baby?"

Tom held up his hands and breathed out deeply. "Chloe and Squirt are both going to be fine."

He explained in shaky detail that her placenta was in the wrong place or something. She'd lost a ton of blood, and the doctors had been worried, but they'd been able to get everything sorted.

"She's going to have to rest—a lot," Tom stressed, "and there might be more issues to worry about down the line, but for now, they're both all right."

"Thank God." Graham put a hand on Tom's neck, and Tom leaned right in and gave him a hug.

"Don't leave us out," Dahlia protested, and from there it turned into one giant pile of the whole half dozen of them trading hugs.

When Elizabeth got her turn with Tom, she caught his eye. "Can we see her?"

He nodded. "Just a couple at a time, though."

Elizabeth looked to Graham instinctively. Everybody else sat down, like they assumed the two of them would be the ones to head in first, and it wasn't as if Elizabeth was going to argue with that.

As Tom led them back, Elizabeth braced herself. The first time she'd seen her mom in the hospital, it had been a shock. Her mother was a force of nature, and the sight of her laid out and sheet white and connected to a million machines, barely able to talk—it had broken something in Elizabeth's brain.

It was the best sight in the world then to see Chloe half sitting up in bed, pale but smiling as she sucked on a straw.

"Hey," she croaked, holding out the drink, which Tom immediately swooped in and took.

"Hey." Elizabeth glanced at Tom for approval before taking the chair beside the bed. Graham stood at its foot, a fragile smile on his face.

"Y'all really didn't have to come," Chloe told her.

Elizabeth waved it off. "You know me, I love this place."

Chloe's voice cracked, and her eyes shone. "You really don't."

And yeah, Chloe knew that well enough.

"I'm just really, really glad to see you and Squirt doing okay." She gestured vaguely at Chloe's midsection.

The wobble in Choe's voice grew as she put a hand on her tummy. "I was so scared, Elizabeth."

"I know." Elizabeth leaned forward to pull her friend into a gentle hug, but there was nothing gentle about the way Chloe gripped her back. She shook with a rattling sob, and Elizabeth's whole heart trembled right along with her. "Shh, you're okay," she mumbled.

But Chloe wasn't having any of it. "I'm not. I'm not okay at all."

Elizabeth glanced up at Tom while still letting Chloe cling to her. "The doctors said—"

"I know, but that's not—I'm—" Chloe pulled away, leaning back into the bed. Tears ran down her face. She reached for Elizabeth's hand, and Elizabeth held on tight. "*I'm* not okay."

"Chloe…" Tom said.

Chloe shook her head. "I can't stop thinking that this was my fault."

Tom sucked in a rough breath, and Graham made a disapproving sound in the back of his throat.

Elizabeth shook her head fiercely. "That's not true."

"But what if it is? You know me." Chloe gripped her hand even harder. "You know how we are."

And yeah, that Elizabeth did.

"I forgot to take my vitamins two times last week," Chloe barreled on. "Tom has to set alarms on his phone to remind me."

"It's fine," Tom tried.

"I ate a goat-cheese ravioli at a client meeting before I remembered I'm not supposed to eat soft cheeses. I got stuffy and took a Benadryl. And me and Tom did"—Chloe's eyes widened meaningfully—"you know, *stuff*."

Elizabeth shook her head. "I'm sure—"

"What if I can't do this?" Chloe teared up all over again. "I could barely take care of myself, and now I have to make choices that affect this poor, defenseless little person, and what if I'm just not capable?"

"No," Elizabeth finally interrupted, and even she was taken aback by the firmness in her tone.

Chloe must have been, too, because her anxiety avalanche finally paused.

Elizabeth squeezed her hand and said it again. "No. You are one hundred percent, completely, totally capable."

"But…"

"So what if you forgot to take a vitamin? So what if you leaned on your better half to remind you?" Elizabeth glanced at Tom, who had gratitude written all over his face.

She wanted to glance at Graham, too, but it felt too raw to do so.

So she focused on Chloe. "That's what he's there for, right? That's why he's your other half."

"But—"

"If both halves were the same, then what would be the point? Just two of the same person walking around with all the same strengths? But also all of the same weaknesses?"

Elizabeth's heart pounded harder, but Chloe let out a terrified little laugh, so maybe she was getting through.

"None of the things you're blaming yourself for could

have caused your body to build a little clump of cells a few inches too far over to one side, you hear me?"

"I know, I just—"

"And if the ravioli was cooked, it was *not* a problem." Elizabeth had read enough pregnancy pamphlets over Chloe's shoulder to know the score.

"Still…"

Elizabeth raised her brows meaningfully. "And as for the *you know*—"

"Which the doctor also specifically said was fine," Tom chimed in, his cheeks the color of a beet.

"I know, I know." Chloe hid her face in her other hand.

But Elizabeth wasn't going to let her run away from this.

"Then why are you blaming yourself?" she pressed.

Chloe glanced upward, blinking hard. "I just." Her voice shook. "I've always been this screwup, and now I have to be responsible, and I don't know…I'm afraid, I…"

Elizabeth swallowed hard. "You're afraid you're not enough."

A ringing started in Elizabeth's ears as Chloe snapped her gaze to hers. "Exactly."

"You're afraid you can't be the person you think other people need you to be," Elizabeth said.

Chloe nodded furiously, and hot shame rose on Elizabeth's face, because she knew that feeling all too well.

Or maybe the uncomfortable warmth was Graham's gaze searing into her.

She kept her focus on Chloe, though. "But that's not who you need to be."

"But—" Chloe shook her head.

"No buts at all." And there was that conviction bleeding into Elizabeth's tone again. "Who cares if you forget things sometimes or occasionally prioritize your comfort or aren't always perfect every moment of every day?"

"Um, the American Academy of Pediatrics?" Chloe swabbed at her eyes.

"All you need to do is love that nugget you're cooking in there, okay?" Elizabeth rubbed her thumb into Chloe's palm.

"I do." Chloe rubbed her belly. "Heaven help me—it's just this blob in there, but I love her already."

"Then you'll do right by her. I know you will."

"What about—"

And it was like talking to a stone wall or...

...well, it was like talking to herself, truth be told.

But that just meant she knew exactly what to say.

"You are enough, Chloe. I know you think of yourself as irresponsible." And wow, were Elizabeth's word echoing in her ears right now, but she couldn't think about the other meanings behind what she was saying. "I know you think you have to do things a certain way, but you don't. There's no right way to be a mom or a—" She swallowed, finally daring a glance at Graham, but his gaze was so soft and full of love that she had to look away again immediately. "Or a partner. You just be you, and it's so, so much more than enough."

More tears leaked down Chloe's cheeks, and there might have been a few pooling at the corners of Elizabeth's eyes as well.

"I didn't know you did pep talks," Chloe said, laughing and crying.

Neither did Elizabeth, but she was happy to own it. "Well, I do now. It's part of this new leaf I'm turning over. It's all about self-acceptance and..." She glanced up at Graham again, and their gazes really connected this time. "And about deciding I don't need to be defined by anybody's expectations—not even my own. I don't need to be defined by my past."

Not by her screwups or her rebellious streak or Graham's dad's wrong ideas about who she was.

She squeezed Chloe's hand. "You don't need to be, either."

"Okay. I like that idea."

"We'll mom and wife and girlfriend however we want to."

"None of those are verbs," Tom lamented, but he was smiling, so Elizabeth didn't take the correction too hard.

"Shh." Chloe waved him off. "We're having a moment here."

"Darn right we are," Elizabeth agreed. "You're going to be okay. You and the nugget."

"And you, too," Chloe told her. It was her turn to glance up at Graham.

Elizabeth followed her gaze. Graham nodded. "We're all going to be okay."

"Oh, phew." Chloe dropped her head back into the pillow dramatically. "You two fighting these past couple of days was stressing me out so hard."

Elizabeth laughed. "I didn't even know you knew about it."

"Everybody knows about it," Tom said.

Ugh, this town.

"Well, we're all going to be okay." Elizabeth patted Chloe's hand one last time before releasing it.

For the first time in what felt like a really long time, she actually believed it.

CHAPTER TWENTY-SIX

"Go home," Tom ordered them all a few hours later.

Home.

Graham glanced at Elizabeth, who mock scowled at Tom as she kept shuffling the deck of cards.

This entire time, she'd been a rock, helping talk Chloe through her fears, supporting Tom, and keeping morale up here among the troops in the waiting room. If she wanted to stay all night, he would back her up.

He couldn't say it would be without reservation, though.

Ever since their gazes had met across Chloe's hospital bed, he'd been dying to get her home. They'd agreed that whatever they had to say to each other could wait while they dealt with this crisis. But their decision to be patient didn't stop his heart from racing.

Hearing her talk about who she was and who she wasn't—and on whose terms she was now determined to live her life…He hadn't known he could adore her any more, but the fire in her eyes had lit a flame behind his ribs.

He'd made a mistake, allowing himself to doubt her for a second. He'd made yet another one by letting her doubt how he felt.

Never again.

He'd stay here as long as he needed to in order to support his friends, but he couldn't wait to get her alone. To find out if she meant what he thought she said; to make sure it wasn't too late for them to work this out.

So when Tom raised his brows and made his tone more firm, he had to admit that he was already reaching for his coat.

"Seriously," Tom told them. "Go home. Visiting hours are over. Chloe's fine, and it isn't going to do anybody a bit of good for you all to sleep on the floor tonight."

Graham looked around and found the whole squad wavering. One glance at Tom showed that he definitely meant business. Graham might have his own selfish reasons for wanting to head out, but he had good, selfless ones, too. Backing Tom up, he said, "He's right."

Apparently, that was enough to turn the tide.

Elizabeth exhaled dramatically. "Fine, fine."

The others started gathering their things.

"I'll swing by again in the morning before work," Graham offered. "I can grab some stuff from your place if you need."

"Thanks." Tom held out his hand, and Graham took it, then used it to reel Tom in. He clapped him on the back, and Tom hugged him tightly for a second in return. Graham let go and smiled in reassurance.

He was still a little floored that of all the people in the world, Tom and Chloe had called *him* when they needed help. For so long, he'd imagined he was on the periphery of their friend group, accepted only because he was attached to Elizabeth. But somehow, at some point, the connection had deepened.

And apparently Elizabeth wasn't the only one who

occasionally underestimated herself—or the way they were regarded by the people who cared about them.

Tom waved goodbye to them at the door, and they spilled out into the parking lot. The cool night air smelled like heaven, and above them floated a clear sky of stars that seemed to go on and on and on.

As Dahlia, Archer, and Stefano headed to Stefano's truck, May and Han veered in the opposite direction. May cast a glance back at Elizabeth, one brow raised as she less than subtly looked from her to Graham and back again. Elizabeth, who'd been matching Graham's intentionally slow pace, waved her sister off, her cheeks flushing pink.

Was it bad that that gave Graham even more hope?

May and Han kept walking. By the time Graham and Elizabeth reached the end of the path, where they would have to separate to head to their cars, Graham's chest was full of butterflies, his throat brimming with all the things he wanted to say. Things he'd wanted to say to Elizabeth for days and maybe years and definitely hours.

But all he could manage to summon to his tongue was her name.

"Elizabeth..."

She turned to him, resolve in her eyes, her chin tilted up. "Tom told us to go home, Graham."

Darn right he had. "I know." His throat grated as he swallowed. "And that's exactly where I want to go."

"Not house," she clarified. "*Home.*"

"I didn't miss that part."

"Good, because if you had..." She lifted her brows in a pretense of menace. She raised a curled fist as well.

He caught her hand, feeling light in way he hadn't in days. "I'm going home," he promised. He shifted his grip on her hand, cradling it in his own—and not just to stop her from decking him, which if she had, he would have deserved. He rubbed the inside of her palm with his thumb. "It's the only place I want to be."

Her gaze softened. "I missed you, you idiot."

"I missed you more."

He pulled her in, and something inside him was soothed back into place when she came easily. He held her for a long minute, just soaking her in.

But they'd waited long enough, holding their tongues.

"I'm so sorry," he breathed into her hair.

"You should be," she agreed.

"I never should have said any of the stuff I did. All the crap my dad was spouting…"

"It doesn't matter."

"But it does." Of that much, he was certain. He let her go, but only far enough that he could look into her eyes as he spoke. "He doesn't *get* us. He never has. I shouldn't have let him get in my head, much less repeated any of his BS at you."

She rolled her eyes, but the hurt in her gaze was impossible to hide. "I mean, I told you as much at the time."

"And I should have listened," he said, earnest and firm. He curled his hand around her waist, half expecting it to feel weird or uncomfortable, but it wasn't. The gentle intimacy of the touch felt *right* in a way he could scarcely explain. "We're a team, okay?"

"Yeah." She nodded, sniffing and smiling so hard it felt like it pulled at his own lips. "Absolutely."

"I don't care how anybody else thinks it looks or how it works."

"Me neither."

His heart swelled, pressing against the inside of his

chest. It still felt impossible to believe she liked him exactly the way he was, but he wasn't going to let it eat at him anymore. He trusted her. No one—himself included—had the right to question her loyalty. She deserved better than that.

She deserved the world.

"All that stuff you said back in Chloe's room..." he started.

"I meant it," she said, not a bit of hesitation to her tone. "I'm tired of thinking I'm a screwup—even if I do mess up a lot."

He shook his head, hard. "You *don't*, though."

"Don't sugarcoat it."

"You made one mistake. It could have happened to anybody."

Because that's what he should have said the night she brought this to him. That was the truth.

"But—" she started.

"But nothing."

He wanted to shake her.

He wanted to hold her close and protect her from all the mean things anyone had ever said to her—especially the mean things she said about herself.

"Elizabeth..." He brushed a hand down the side of her face, trying with all his heart to will her into feeling what he felt. "You're incredible. You've done so much to launch this thing, worked so hard, all while taking care of your family and your friends, of me, of my family—"

"Ha, ha," she said dryly.

"It's true. At my dad's birthday, you were the life of the party." She'd breathed life into spaces that were cold and dull.

She breathed life into *him*.

But she still didn't believe it. "Your dad hated it."

"So what? I loved it. I love—" He caught himself. He felt the word, and he held it on his tongue.

And then finally, finally, he let it go.

"I love you," he confessed, and it felt like a weight lifting off of his chest.

Her eyes gleamed. "You *idiot*." She threw his arms around him. And then, against his ear, she told him, "I love you, too."

Forget a weight being lifted. Light and warmth flooded his insides, and he clutched her so tightly he could scarcely breathe.

He drew back and leaned down, and she leaned up, and then they were meeting in the middle. He crushed his lips to hers, and it was like coming home.

"I want to spend my whole damn life with you, Elizabeth Wu. Every day and every night. I want to build a home with you."

"I want that, too—"

"And it doesn't have to look like anyone else's idea of it." He drew on her own words from earlier. "We define what our home and our life look like. Paint a rainbow on that picket fence if you want to."

"I just might," she said, laughing and maybe crying a little, and heaven help him, he might be doing both, too.

"I don't want just any wife. I want you, in all your chaos and glory."

"You have no idea what you're getting yourself into."

But wasn't that just the thing? "I've lived with you for years. I know *exactly* what I'm getting myself into."

And yet, that also wasn't true. He'd spent so much time with her, but as they'd deepened their relationship, he'd realized just how much deeper there was to go. She'd let him in in a whole new way, showing him the parts of her that were hurt and the parts of him that were healed. He loved her more now than he'd even known he could.

"I know you'll always surprise me," he told her, and that was one of the very best parts of being with her.

"And I know you'll always be there for me." She put her hand over his chest. "Steady as a rock."

A tickle of insecurity tugged at him. "And that's okay with you?"

"That's *perfect* for me." She cupped his face, stroking her thumb against his cheek through his beard. "I'm not the only one who has to get past some weird ideas about what the other one wants. I want to be with you for you."

"Even when I'm old and boring?"

"Graham." She eased up onto her tiptoes again and planted a gentle kiss on his lips. "You could never be boring."

And he still didn't know how to believe that.

But he wanted to.

Laughing, he held her closer. He kissed her again, and the heat of being with her like this after spending days not touching her threatened to overwhelm him. Their tongues tangled, and tingles shot down his spine.

Like she felt the same sparkle of attraction and connection, she grazed his lip with her teeth.

But the conversation wasn't quite done. "So that's it then?" she asked. "We take over a decade of history and roll with it, and just toss out everything we thought we knew about ourselves and what the other person wants?"

"Seems pretty straightforward to me." It didn't, of course, and yet somehow, it did. He brushed her hair back from her face, still marveling at the miracle of being able to hold her like this. "You are so much more than you ever give yourself credit for, E."

She smiled, soft and so gorgeous. "So do you."

"So forget all the expectations. Forget all the ideas of who and what we're supposed to be. We just..." And oh, wow, he really was losing his mind here, but in the best possible way. "...wing it."

Laughing, she kissed him again. "Never in a million years did I imagine you suggesting that as a serious strategy."

"It's always worked for you."

She blinked, a strange look passing across her eyes.

He opened his mouth to ask what, but she put her finger across his lips.

Her eyes flew even wider. "Graham."

"Yes?" he asked against her finger.

She dropped her hand from his lips, and a grin broke across her face. "I know how to save the festival."

"I have to say." Dottie Gallagher shook her head. "This is pretty ballsy, even for you."

Across the conference room table, Mayor Horton laughed and held up his hands. "I had nothing to do with it, Ms. Gallagher. I promise, this is all Mr. Lewis and Ms. Wu."

Approximately thirty-six hours had passed since Elizabeth had had her flash of inspiration in the hospital parking lot. She pressed her knee against Graham's beneath the table, letting his warmth, support and—yes, love—pour into her.

No one defined them but them. Either them as individuals, or together as a couple. They were more than anyone imagined, especially themselves.

And so was her festival.

She smiled at Dottie. "So? Can we count on you to help?"

Dottie let out a quiet cackle. "Sure, why not? I want to see how this all plays out."

"Glad to have your support, Ms. Gallagher," Graham said diplomatically. He was as calm, cool, and collected as ever, but the way he squeezed Elizabeth's knee showed he was just as nervous and excited as she was.

This particular part of their scheme had been his idea, after all.

Mayor Horton shifted forward in his chair. "Well, no time like the present." He pressed the button for the intercom. "Mindy?"

The receptionist's voice came over the speaker. "Yes, sir?"

"Could you send her in, please?"

"Yes, sir."

Dottie swiveled her chair around and grabbed the handles of her walker. She'd just about gotten herself up to standing by the time the door burst open.

Dottie didn't miss a beat. She shot a wink at Elizabeth before shouting at Mayor Horton, "Don't you try to sweet talk me, John. I'm going to tell everyone what a mess this has all turned out to be."

"Please, Ms. Gallagher. Be reasonable." Mayor Horton's poker face wasn't quite as good as Dottie's, but alas, whose was?

"Ha!" Harumphing, Dottie turned theatrically. She somehow managed to make her glare even sharper.

Elizabeth had been resisting the temptation to look to the door, but now that Dottie had directed her attention that way, she felt allowed to peek.

Patty stood there, her brows pinched in confusion.

"Who would've imagined?" Dottie shook her head. "You and me on the same side again, Boyd?"

Patty's eyes widened.

"I'm telling you, John," Dottie shot over her shoulder. "I'm taking this whole operation down." She glared at Elizabeth and Graham, and wow, Elizabeth was glad she was in on this, or she'd be shaking in her fashionable mid-calf combat boots.

"What—" Patty tried.

"Swing by the florist shop when you're done with these knuckleheads, and we can talk strategy," Dottie told her. "You and me are going to be best friends for the next four months."

Elizabeth managed not to wince. Overselling it a little much, Dottie?

But the act was having its intended effect. "I hardly can believe that," Patty grumbled.

"Ms. Gallagher," Mayor Horton said.

"I can show myself out."

Dottie only grazed Patty's foot with the front wheel of her walker, so she really was trying to act like they were a team now; normally, she'd have gone right over it. Patty stepped out of the way. The conference room door slammed shut behind Dottie.

Mayor Horton scrubbed a hand over his face. "I'm sorry, Patty—"

"What on earth is going on here?"

And okay, it was Elizabeth's turn now. She blinked rapidly, trying to summon a tear or two. "The festival," she managed, a quiver in her voice.

"Dottie Gallagher got wind of Ms. Wu's…ahem, difficulties with her advertisements."

"You can't let her shut it down," Elizabeth pled.

Graham's hand on her knee said that maybe she was overselling it a bit, too, but her heart wouldn't stop thumping in her chest.

The corners of Patty's mouth curled upward, only to fall again, her conflict clear on her face, and yeah, Graham's idea to use her and Dottie's rivalry to their advantage had been a stroke of genius. The woman was all turned around.

But that was the heart of the plan, wasn't it? Subvert everyone's expectations.

Then show them all exactly what Elizabeth was worth.

"Now, Ms. Wu—"

Addressing the mayor, doing her best to block out Patty's presence entirely, even though she was the one she needed to convince, Elizabeth plowed ahead. "Please, sir, I know I made a mistake." Everyone made mistakes. This one was a doozy, but it didn't negate the rest of what she'd managed to accomplish. "But we've done so much to make this festival a huge success. The Sweetbriar Inn is one hundred percent booked for the weekend, and more than half of them cited the arts festival as their reason for coming to town. We have almost as many food vendors coming in as Taste of Blue Cedar Falls. Local restaurants are already filling up on reservations."

"That's all well and good, Ms. Wu—"

Elizabeth raised her brows at him for cutting her off so soon. They'd rehearsed this. "Submissions for the show itself have been pouring in. We have stellar entries, including all the hidden, undiscovered gems I promised and some higher-profile artists." She rattled off their names. "Ina Ortiz, Xi Chen, Jackson Howell—"

"Did you say Jackson Howell?" Patty interrupted.

Elizabeth's pulse kicked up another notch as she nodded.

Ina Ortiz and Xi Chen had already been on the docket; Elizabeth had secured the attendance of both after meeting them at the artists' roundtable at the Four Winds Arts Festival. Jackson Howell, one of the most successful unrepresented artists in the region, was a more recent addition.

As in yesterday. She'd secured him yesterday, in a mad dash of phone calls to Kat and everybody else she knew in the art world.

Not all of her talking points were last-minute, though. "Critics and journalists are coming, too." She listed the half dozen publications that had committed to covering the festival.

Patty took a step forward at the couple of more prestigious titles.

Mayor Horton paused a little longer this time before shaking his head. "I know you've done a lot to bring attention to the arts community in our area and help our local businesses, Ms. Wu, but your mismanagement of the event has Ms. Gallagher talking to the town council about canceling it completely."

"Meddling busybody," Patty groused. She pulled out a chair on the other side of the table. "Don't you think that's a bit of an overreaction, John?"

"I don't know..." Mayor Horton trailed off.

And this was it. The moment of truth.

When asked point-blank if she might be willing to compromise on this festival and help Elizabeth organize it, Patty had laughed and flat out refused, declining to share any of the blame for what she purported was going to be a total disaster. But the festival wasn't a disaster.

It had met one little hiccup, but other than that, it was shaping up better than anybody could have imagined.

Sucking in a rough breath, Elizabeth put her hand over Graham's. She snuck a glance at him out of the corner of her eye, and caught the warmth in his smile. The easy confidence and the memory of him telling her he believed in her.

They helped her believe in herself.

"Patty, I know we've had our differences in the past." Understatement of the year. But she could hold in her pride. She could be humble and respectful, and she could fight for this event that she'd poured her heart and soul into. "But I don't know who else to turn to. If they cancel the festival, then all of the artists who are coming in for it and all that press…it goes down the toilet. Would you— Can you—?" She swallowed hard. "Would you please help me?"

Sharp lines appeared above Patty's brows, like she was as surprised to hear those words coming out of Elizabeth's mouth as Elizabeth was to be saying them. Elizabeth held her breath, waiting for what felt like eons as those lines disappeared.

And then slowly, miraculously, a rueful smile curled Patty's lips.

Graham intertwined their fingers beneath the desk. Elizabeth's heart stopped beating, but that was all right. She didn't need it to.

"Ridiculous girl." Patty shook her head. "Don't you know? That's all you had to say in the first place."

CHAPTER TWENTY-SEVEN

❊ ❊ ❊ ❊ ❊ ❊ ❊ ❊ ❊ ❊ ❊ ❊ ❊

Four months later…

From the other side of the gazebo in the middle of Pine Hollow Park, Mackenzie Boyd cupped her hands around her mouth. "Ten minutes to curtain."

A twin burst of nerves and excitement raced up Elizabeth's spine.

There weren't any literal curtains to speak of, but she peeked out from behind them all the same. The entire park was filled with tents and awnings displaying the best, most innovative art the region had to offer. After months and months of preparation, the First Annual Blue Cedar Falls Clothesline Arts Festival was ready to open. It was bigger, better, more colorful, and more inclusive than she could have hoped.

It was also beginning a full week earlier than she had planned. But that was neither here nor there.

After she and Graham had pulled off their gambit to win Patty over to their side by making her think Dottie was against her, followed by Elizabeth wantonly demonstrating her own competency, Patty had thrown herself into coordinating gallery sponsorship and spotlights for the festival. In addition to pledging support on behalf of her own business, she had roped in a dozen others from all four corners of the state. They now had booths sprinkled throughout the festival, as well as big, glossy pages in the event program.

Elizabeth had gotten to keep her indie vibe and her focus on unrepresented artists. Patty had gotten her chance to be in charge of something, as well as an opportunity to promote her gallery. Probably most importantly of all, she'd gotten to feel included in the proceedings.

Blue Cedar Falls was changing. New residents were bringing in new kinds of visitors, and some folks from the old guard sometimes got their dander up about it all. But when everyone worked together, they could pull off miracles.

They could also shepherd in an even newer generation. Once Patty had removed her objection to Mackenzie participating, the younger Boyd had not only submitted her work for inclusion in the show, but also volunteered to head up the teen spotlight. She might still look like a rebel, but she was officially a rebel with a cause—not to mention a community.

Before Elizabeth could go getting too emotional about it, a horn honked. Startled, she glanced in the direction of the sound to find Dottie Gallagher shooing slow-moving pedestrians out of her way as she rolled through on her motorized scooter. To Elizabeth and her team, Dottie called, "You all planning on starting sometime this century?"

"Says the woman who held up a Main Street Business Association meeting for an hour last week because we didn't have hot water for tea," Patty yelled back, craning her neck from where she stood at the top of a ladder she'd insisted on climbing to straighten a banner that had clearly already been straight. "You old bat," she muttered, but the retort was almost good-natured for once.

The two women would probably never actually be friends, but after Dottie had completed her role in Graham and Elizabeth's little production to win Patty over, they'd ended up working together on organizing the raffle. There had been no attempted murders during the proceedings, so it had basically been a rousing success.

"I hate to admit it, but I'm with Dottie," Chloe said, wandering past. She gestured to the three-week-old baby strapped to her chest in a rainbow-colored sling. "This little one is going to wake up cranky any minute now, and I'd prefer not to have to whip out a boob in the middle of the opening remarks."

"I told you I'd take her," Tom hollered from where he was running AV wires to the podium set up on the steps.

"Nah." This look of absolute beatific bliss passed over Chloe's face as she smoothed back a tuft of blond hair on their daughter's head. "We're good."

Were they ever. Even Elizabeth's historically skeptical ovaries gave a little pang.

Despite Chloe's many, many worries about motherhood and how she was bound to muck it all up, she'd taken to it like a duck to water. After her brief stay in the hospital, she'd weathered the bed rest and the anxiety of frequent doctor visits. She'd been careful to a fault, and she'd leaned on Tom and Elizabeth and Graham and all their friends. Ultimately, baby Margaret had been born strong and healthy; her mom had proven herself to be stronger than she'd ever been willing to admit.

Elizabeth was achingly proud, so happy for them all that it hurt.

Over by the podium, Tom tapped the mic. The sound

carried through the big speakers set up to either side of the gazebo, and a bunch of folks in the crowd turned in interest. Elizabeth checked the time. With less than a minute until they were supposed to begin, she glanced around.

Banner securely hung, Patty had returned to the ground, a self-satisfied smile on her face. Dahlia, Archer, and Stefano all stood back.

A warm presence inserted himself at her side.

Elizabeth looked up to find Graham standing there, looking gorgeous as ever, the sun reflecting off the red-gold highlights in his hair and beard. She leaned into him instinctively, a wave of calm washing over her just because he was near.

Smiling softly, he took her hand in his. "You ready?"

Elizabeth looked out across the crowd. The members of the town council were scattered around, glad-handing and enjoying the day; even Jerry didn't look like he was having a bad time. Mayor Horton stood over by the pop-up stand Han had set up for the Jade Garden Annex, a cardboard tray of Han's famous hoisin tacos in his hand. He caught her eye and gave her a thumbs-up.

Nodding, she sucked in a breath. But she kept scanning until she found the rest of her crew. Her biggest supporters.

Her family.

She found them all right. Front and center and ready to cheer for her—exactly where they'd always been, and exactly where she should have always known they would be.

Her mother noticed her looking and tapped her watch. Elizabeth chuckled as Ned put a hand on her shoulder. He looked to Elizabeth and gave her an assured smile, like she had all the time in the world. Looking at him, she felt like she did. *One crisis at a time*, as he always liked to say.

Next to him stood June, who beamed at her and waved. The gold band around her finger glinted in the sun. Her new fiancé Clay stood beside her in silent, solid support. Rounding out the group was May, who looked weird without Han attached to her hip, but she had a notebook in hand and a freelance assignment from *Passage* magazine to cover the festival, so she wouldn't miss him too much while he worked.

Surrounding them all was this tiny town that had taken them in as kids. It had nurtured them through the years, each in their own unique ways. Elizabeth wouldn't romanticize it. Sometimes, this place had educated her at the school of hard knocks. But she'd learned her lessons all the same.

A lump formed at the back of her throat.

A year and a half ago, this place had been on the verge of dying. The Wu sisters had been scattered.

Now here they all were. June had brought the town back to life, and May had shown it to the world. Now Elizabeth was leading it onward into a future that was blindingly bright.

Graham squeezed her palm. She looked away from her family and back to him.

Her heart swelled. His gaze was patient and kind and everything it had ever been—but also so much more.

These past few months hadn't been completely smooth sailing, but what ever had been? They were still best friends, at their roots, but the love that had grown between them ran deeper than she ever could have imagined. He was her biggest cheerleader, her rock, and her support. The yang to her yin. Her perfect complement. Her partner—in festival planning, house renovation, and life.

"I'm ready," she promised him.

Ready for absolutely anything.

At the end of the evening, Graham smiled at a group of tourists wandering by before double-checking the lock on the last display. As he did, he hummed to himself, exhausted and proud.

The first day of the festival had been a smashing success. The entire community had come out, and enough out-of-town visitors had shown up to patronize local businesses that the festival's future was secured for years to come. New, unrepresented artists had sold pieces and found a venue for their work.

It was everything Elizabeth had dreamed and more. Instead of dividing the community, it had united it. She might never think of herself as a leader, but he knew the score. Everyone else around here did, too.

As if to prove it, a voice came from behind him. "Not a bad day, huh, Lewis?"

Graham turned around to find Duke Moore standing there, his wife, Tracey, beside him, as well as his daughter, Bobbi, and her wife, Caitlin. "Not bad at all," he agreed.

"Congratulations," Bobbi told him.

He shook his head. "Save the congratulations for Elizabeth."

"Oh, she'll get plenty," Duke said. "But don't act like you had nothing to do with it. Anyone with eyes can see what a great job you did here."

One corner of Graham's mouth curled up. He still preferred working behind the scenes, supporting people with big ambitions, but he couldn't pretend he didn't enjoy having his efforts recognized.

And since Duke had brought it up...

This whole adventure between him and Elizabeth had started with him learning to assert what he wanted. And now, half a year later, he'd seen enough results to understand that that was something he needed to keep doing, over and over again.

His pulse quickened, and he put his hand in his pocket, feeling the metal teeth of the key he had stashed in there. It sent a whole different set of nerves firing off inside him, and yet somehow, it grounded him, too.

"Speaking of great jobs." Graham glanced at Duke's family. This might not be the best time to bring this up, but based on his previous interactions with the Moores, they weren't unaccustomed to talking shop. "The response on the historical society's bell tower grant came in."

"Oh?"

Graham paused for dramatic effect for a solid fraction of a second. "We got it."

"Well, damn, son."

"It'll fund construction, and"—he swallowed, summoning his nerve—"a salaried position."

Duke's bushy mustache twitched. "Is that so?"

It sure was. He'd written it into the proposal himself, his nerves rattling the entire time.

Funny, how his father had been badgering him his entire life to be more ambitious. Climb the ladder, reach for the stars. Graham had finally taken his advice, but in exactly the opposite way his old man intended it. He'd gotten ambitious, all right. Ambitious enough to ditch the job his father had always hoped would be a stepping-stone to higher office, and instead sidestep his way into a job with an even lower profile, less room for advancement, and less stability. But if it worked out, it would have him following his passion and doing something he loved.

Swallowing down his anxiety, he nodded. "I'd like you to know I'll be putting my hat in the ring. I hope I'll have your support."

"My support?" Duke laughed. "You just saved me a month of HR BS. I'll have to talk it over with the board, but I'd hire you on the spot."

Just like that, Graham's heart rate smoothed out. He wanted to fist pump or whoop out loud, but somehow he restrained himself. "I appreciate it, sir."

There was that mustache twitch again. "How many times do I have to tell you? Stop calling me 'sir.'"

Yes, sir, Graham thought, but instead, he just said, "Right."

The Moores said their farewells and moved on. With a spring in his step, Graham did the same, heading for the gazebo that served as the festival committee's base of operations.

He spotted Elizabeth ahead and quickened his pace—until he recognized that she was talking to a woman he didn't know. He slowed a few feet away.

"Give me a call next week," the stranger said, holding out a card.

Elizabeth's voice came out high, and she nodded like a bobblehead. "I will."

They shook hands, and the woman walked away.

Graham tilted his head to the side as he approached. "E?"

She turned to him, her eyes wide. She grabbed his hands, the card still grasped tightly between her fingers. "That was a gallery owner from DC."

"Wait—seriously?"

"Seriously." Elizabeth vibrated. Only a backward glance over her shoulder at the gallery owner seemed to keep her from shouting. "She liked my work and wants to see more."

A broad grin took over Graham's face. "That's amazing."

"I know. I just." She blinked rapidly. "This whole festival—it wasn't about me, but..."

"But your work deserved a showcase just as much as any of the other unrepresented artists here."

She shook her head. "I can't believe it."

"I can." He pulled her into a hug, squeezing her tightly. Drawing away, he kissed her hard and deep, and she curled her arms around him in return.

"Did you talk to Duke?" she asked when they both came up for air.

"I did."

"And?"

"And he tried to offer me the job on the spot."

She grinned, bright and wide. Lifting a hand, she waggled a finger in his face. "I told you so."

"That you did." He caught her finger and pulled it to his lips, smiling as he kissed her soft skin.

"We need to celebrate." She sagged. "Or nap. Maybe a nap and then a celebration?"

Laughing, he let her go. "Pace yourself. This is just day one."

She groaned and butted her head into his shoulder dramatically, but she was smiling as she did. "How are we going to manage nine more days of this?"

"The same way we always do."

"Coffee and the magic of friendship?"

"Exactly." Tucking her in against his side, he tilted

his head toward the path that led to where they'd parked. "And maybe a good night's sleep."

"Overrated," she told him, but with the way she was drooping, he had no doubt she was due for one anyway.

She was so tired that as he got behind the wheel of his car, he wavered for a minute. Maybe the surprise he'd had in mind could wait until another time. It had been a stressful, exciting whirlwind of a day. They'd both had wins. Why put that in jeopardy?

He looked over at her, though, and she was so beautiful, there in the seat beside him, her soft features lit in the golden light of the sun setting over the mountains.

His throat dry, he asked, "Do you mind if we stop by the house before we head home?"

"As long as you don't expect me to wield any power tools."

He laughed. She'd pitched in with renovations over the past few months, continuing to fix up the house to fit both their tastes, and they'd made a ton of progress. But that wasn't why he wanted her to come with him to visit the place tonight. "No power tools," he promised.

"Okay," she agreed with a shrug.

His heart rose into his throat as he drove the familiar streets, eventually turning onto Mulberry Street. He parked in the driveway and glanced up at the darkened windows.

"Come on." They got out, and he took her hand.

She furrowed her brows at him. She always had been able to read him. "You're acting weird. Why are you acting weird?"

"I'm not." He definitely was.

But he wasn't going to admit that as he unlocked the door and opened it wide. Palming the key, holding it so tightly that it bit into his palm, he flicked on the lights.

Elizabeth blinked as she looked around. "Whoa."

Whoa was right.

For months now, they'd been working and working to turn this house he'd bought into a home. He'd continued living with her at Hemlock House, but as time had passed, he'd grown more eager to stop living life in transition. He'd started down this path toward his future, and now he wanted to jump into it with both feet. He wanted it to be *their* future. He wanted them to leap with hands entwined.

And so, today of all days, even though it had been a logistical nightmare, what with the festival and all of their responsibilities, he'd coordinated everything to have the finishing touches put on the place. Appliances had been delivered and installed. He and Tom and Archer and Stefano had snuck over here mid-morning. They'd hung curtains and artwork and strung lights.

He'd also made one other, important stop.

As if on cue, barking sounded from the next room.

Elizabeth's eyes flew wide. "Was that—?"

Nodding, he gripped her hand and led her to the mudroom. There at the baby gate Tom had expertly helped him install yapped a twenty-pound, fifteen-inch-tall black-and-tan rescue dachshund named Dragon, whom Graham had officially taken in as a foster dog that afternoon. Graham had spent a couple of hours helping the little dude get comfortable before leaving him with a pile full of toys to destroy while he finished up his duties at the festival.

Dropping into a crouch, he opened the gate, and the

dog bounded out and into his arms, licking at his face like he was covered in bacon. "Hey," he said, running a hand down the dog's side, "glad to see you, too, buddy. "

Laughing, he turned to Elizabeth, who grinned.

There was a wariness to her eyes, too, though.

"You're finally ready to move in," she said, and it wasn't a question.

There was no reason it would be. Their apartment didn't allow dogs, and this guy was going to need a lot of attention as he got acclimated to his new home.

Picking up the dog, Graham nodded. "I am."

"Oh." She was trying to keep a neutral face but failing.

Graham's heart hammered in his chest. "Elizabeth..."

Before he could continue, Dragon lunged for her, tongue first. Elizabeth cracked a smile as Graham struggled to contain the beast. Dragon licked her face, and she gave him a laughing scratch behind the ear.

"Dragon, meet Elizabeth. Elizabeth, Dragon."

"Nice to meet you," she told the dog in all seriousness. Her gaze returned to Graham's. "But Graham..."

"Come with me." He leaned over to set Dragon on the ground and took Elizabeth by the hand. He shook his head when she opened her mouth to protest.

Followed closely by what he hoped would be their new dog, he led the way down the hall. His pulse hammered harder.

She stopped at the doorway.

He did, too, his gaze intent on her face as he tried to gauge her reaction. Ten different emotions flitted across her face. Doubt entered his heart.

"I should have asked," he blurted.

She held up a hand, fumbling to place a finger over his mouth.

He shut up on cue. But his patience lasted only a matter of seconds. "E..."

"You brought my studio here."

"Only part of it." As much of it as was easy to transport, just in case he had to schlep it all the way back across town tomorrow.

Beneath the skylights, he'd set up her easel and a fresh canvas. Her palette and paints and chair, and wow, he really hoped he didn't have to pack it all up again tomorrow.

"Graham." She turned to him, dropping her hand. Her eyes were soft in a way that gave him hope.

"I'll never regret buying this house," he told her. "Because as much as you hated it, it was part of what brought us together. Before that, I'd resigned myself. You'd never see me the way I saw you..."

"I'm sorry."

"Don't be." He caught her hand in both of his. "We never would have worked as more if we'd started that way. We began as friends, and that's what we'll always be. You're my *best* friend, Elizabeth. And the love of my life." He swallowed, his throat impossibly dry. "I'll never regret buying this house," he repeated, "but I will always regret you not having a chance to help me pick it out. Deep down, though, you were always there with me. This place was always meant to be ours—whether I realized it or not."

Her eyes sparkled, and the corners of her mouth curled upward. "Are you saying...?"

"I'm ready to move in. But I don't want to." He let go to reach into his pocket. He pulled out the key and held it out in his palm. "Not unless you're ready to, too."

Their lease was up next month. She had vague plans to

extend it, but she'd never finalized anything. He'd hoped that was because she knew.

"Elizabeth Wu. Will you move in with me?"

She laughed, throwing her head back. But at the same time, she was placing her hand over his, accepting the key and his heart all at once. "You dork, we already live together."

But he wasn't going to let her deflect. "Move in with me here. Make a life with me. Here."

Make a forever.

Her laughter faded away. With all seriousness, she stepped into him. Key held firmly in her hand, she curled her arms around him. As always, the press of her body so close thrilled him, but not as much as the openness to her expression. "Graham," she said quietly. "My life has always been with you."

With that, she leaned up onto her toes. He dipped down to press his mouth to hers. He sank into the kiss, but inside, he was floating.

And just like that, he was home.

DON'T MISS JUNE AND
CLAY'S STORY,
*THE INN ON
SWEETBRIAR LANE*

AVAILABLE NOW!

ABOUT THE AUTHOR

Jeannie Chin writes contemporary small-town romances. She draws on her experiences as a biracial Asian and white American to craft heartfelt stories that speak to a uniquely American experience.

She is a former high school science teacher, wife to a geeky engineer, and mom to an extremely talkative kindergartener. Her hobbies include crafting, reading, and hiking.

You can learn more at:
JeannieChin.com
Twitter: @JeannieCWrites
Facebook.com/JeannieCWrites
Instagram: @JeannieCWrites

Looking for more second chances and small towns? Check out Forever's heartwarming contemporary romances!

THE TRUE LOVE BOOKSHOP
by Annie Rains

For Tess Lane, owning Lakeside Books is a dream come true, but it's the weekly book club she hosts for the women in town that Tess enjoys the most. The gatherings have been her lifeline over the past three years, since she became a widow. But when secrets surrounding her husband's death are revealed, can Tess find it in her heart to forgive the mistakes of the past...and maybe even open herself up to love again?

THE MAGNOLIA SISTERS
by Alys Murray

Harper Anderson has one priority: caring for her family's farm. So when an arrogant tech mogul insists the farm host his sister's wedding, she turns him *and* his money down flat—an event like that would wreck their crops! But then Luke makes an offer she can't refuse: He'll work *for free* if Harper just considers his deal. Neither is prepared for chemistry to bloom between them as they labor side by side...but can Harper trust this city boy to put down country roots?

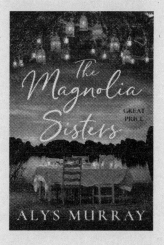

HER AMISH PATCHWORK FAMILY
by Winnie Griggs

Martha Eicher, formerly a schoolteacher in Hope's Haven, has always put her family first. But now everyone's happily married, and Martha isn't sure where she fits in...until she hears that Asher Lantz needs a nanny. As a single father to his niece and nephews, Asher struggles to be enough for his new family. Although a misunderstanding ended their childhood friendship, he's grateful for Martha's help. Slowly both begin to realize Martha is exactly what his family needs. Could together be where they belong?

FALLING IN LOVE ON SWEETWATER LANE
by Belle Calhoune

Nick Keegan knows all about unexpected, life-altering detours. He lost his wife in the blink of an eye, and he's spent the years since being the best single dad he can be. He's also learned to not take anything for granted, so when sparks start to fly with Harlow, the new veterinarian, Nick is all in. He senses Harlow feels it too, but she insists romance isn't on her agenda. He'll have to pull out all the stops to show her that love is worth changing the best-laid plans.

RETURN TO HUMMINGBIRD WAY
by Reese Ryan

Ambitious real estate agent Sinclair Buchanan is thrilled her childhood best friend is marrying her first love. But the former beauty queen and party planner extraordinaire hadn't anticipated being asked to work with her high-school hate crush, Garrett Davenport, to plan the wedding. Five years ago, they spent one *incredible* night together—a mistake she won't make again. But when her plans for partnership in her firm require her to work with Rett to renovate his grandmother's seaside cottage, it becomes much harder to ignore their complicated history.

THE HOUSE ON MULBERRY STREET
by Jeannie Chin

Between helping at her family's inn and teaching painting, Elizabeth Wu has put her dream of being an artist on the back burner. But her plan to launch an arts festival will boost the local Blue Cedar Falls arts scene and give her a showcase for her own work. If only she can get the town council on board. At least she can rely on her dependable best friend, Graham, to support her. Except lately, he hasn't been acting like his old self, and she has no idea why…

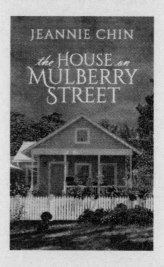

STARTING OVER ON SUNSHINE CORNER
by Phoebe Mills

Single mom Rebecca Hayes isn't getting her hopes up after she has one unforgettable night with Jackson, a very close—and very attractive—friend. She knows Jackson's unattached bachelor lifestyle too well. But in his heart, Jackson Lowe longs to build a family with Rebecca—his secret crush and the real reason he never settled down. So when Rebecca discovers she's pregnant with his baby, he knows he's got a lot of work to do before he can prove he's ready to be the man she needs.

A TABLE FOR TWO
(MM reissue) by Sheryl Lister

Serenity Wheeler's Supper Club is all about great friends, incredible food, and a whole lot of dishing—not hooking up. So when Serenity invites her friend's brother to one of her dinners, it's just good manners. But the ultra-fine, hazel-eyed Gabriel Cunningham has a gift for saying all the wrong things, causing heated exchanges and even hotter chemistry between them. But Serenity can't let herself fall for Gabriel. Cooking with love is one thing, but trusting it is quite another...